KILL or be KILLED

D1430273

IMAGE COMICS, INC.

Robert Kirkman — Chief Operating Officer
Erik Larsen — Chief Financial Officer
Todd McFarlane — President
Marc Silvestri — Chief Executive Officer
Jim Valentino — Vice-President
Eric Stephenson — Publisher
Corey Murphy — Director of Sales
Jeff Boison — Director of Publishing Planning & Book Trade Sales
Chris Ross — Director of Digital Sales
Jeff Stang — Director of Specialty Sales
Kat Salazar — Director of PR & Marketing
Branwyn Bigglestone — Controller
Sue Korpela — Accounts Manager
Drew Gill — Art Director
Brett Warnock — Production Manager
Leigh Thomas — Print Manager
Tricia Ramos — Traffic Manager
Briah Skelly — Publicist
Aly Hoffman — Events & Conventions Coordinator
Sasha Head — Sales & Marketing Production Designer
David Brothers — Branding Manager
Melissa Gifford — Content Manager
Drew Fitzgerald — Publicity Assistant
Vincent Kukua — Production Artist
Erika Schnatz — Production Artist
Ryan Brewer — Production Artist
Shanna Matuszak — Production Artist
Carey Hall — Production Artist
Esther Kim — Direct Market Sales Representative
Emilio Bautista — Digital Sales Representative
Leanna Caunter — Accounting Assistant
Chloe Ramos-Peterson — Library Market Sales Representative
Marla Eizik — Administrative Assistant

IMAGECOMICS.COM

Standard Cover, ISBN: 978-1-5343-0228-0
DCBS Variant, ISBN: 978-1-5343-0558-8
Forbidden Planet/Big Bang Comics Variant, ISBN: 978-1-5343-0560-1
Newbury Comics Variant, ISBN: 978-1-5343-0559-5

KILL OR BE KILLED Volume Two, August 2017. First printing.
Contains material originally published in magazine form as KILL OR BE KILLED #5-10.
Published by Image Comics, Inc. Office of publication: 2701 NW Vaughn St., Suite 780, Portland, OR 97210.
Copyright © 2017 Basement Gang, Inc. All rights reserved. KILL OR BE KILLED™ (including all prominent characters featured
herein), their logos and all character likenesses are trademarks of Basement Gang, Inc. unless otherwise noted. Image Comics®
is a trademark of Image Comics, Inc. All rights reserved. No part of this publication may be reproduced or transmitted, in any form
or by any means (except for short excerpts for review purposes) without the express written permission of Basement Gang, Inc.,
or Image Comics, Inc. All names, characters, events, and locales in this publication are entirely fictional. Any resemblance to actual
persons (living or dead), events, or places, without satiric intent, is coincidental. Printed in the USA.
For information regarding the CPSIA on this printed material call: 203-595-3636 and provide reference #RICH–748968.

 Publication design by Sean Phillips

Volume Two

KILL or be KILLED

Ed Brubaker
Sean Phillips
Elizabeth Breitweiser

Clifton Park- Halfmoon Public Library
475 Moe Road
Clifton Park, NY 12065

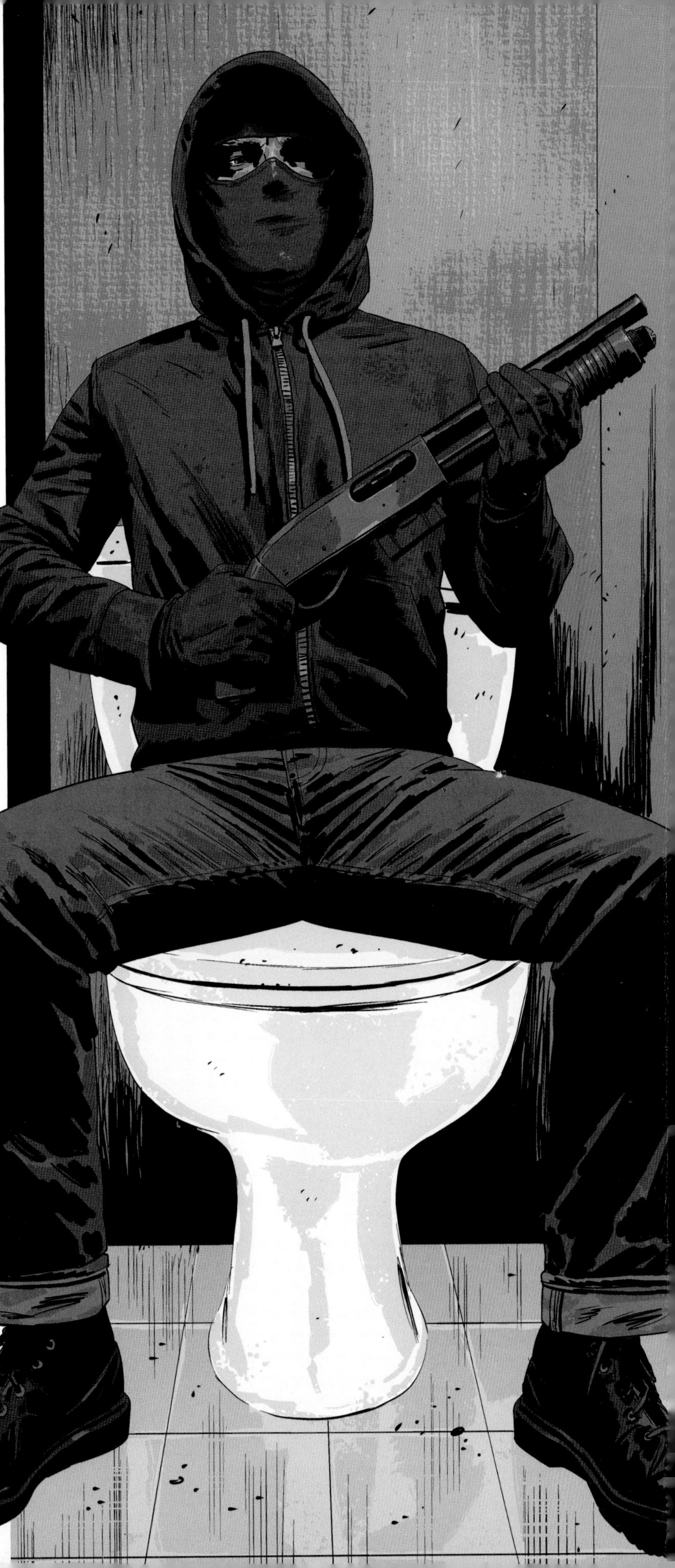
I don't believe in fate, but you can't deny that things in life sometimes fall together like there actually is some big cosmic plan at work.
Which would suck for about 95 percent of us, right?
Because that means that everything in your life is exactly how it's "meant" to be.
All your striving to change things... The entire idea of self-determination... It's all a joke.
If you have a shitty, sad-sack life, that's because it was preordained. Maybe by God, if you believe in God.
That's why, unless you're born a billionaire or something, we reject fate.
We have to believe we're not trapped in whatever place the world decided to spit us out into...
We have to believe we make our own destiny.

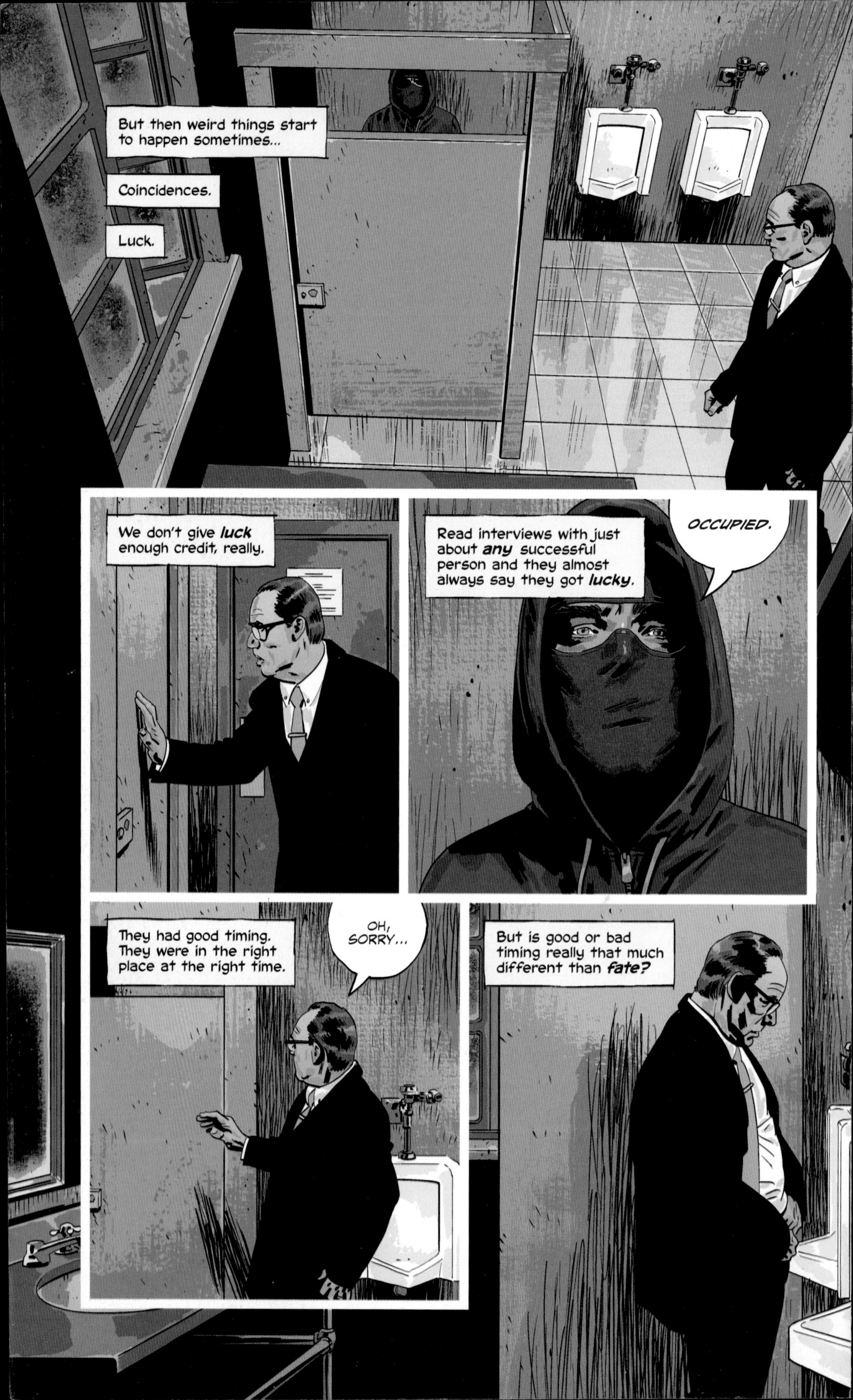
But then weird things start to happen sometimes...
Coincidences.
Luck.
We don't give *luck* enough credit, really.
Read interviews with just about ***any*** successful person and they almost always say they got ***lucky***.
OCCUPIED.
They had good timing. They were in the right place at the right time.
OH, SORRY...
But is good or bad timing really that much different than ***fate?***

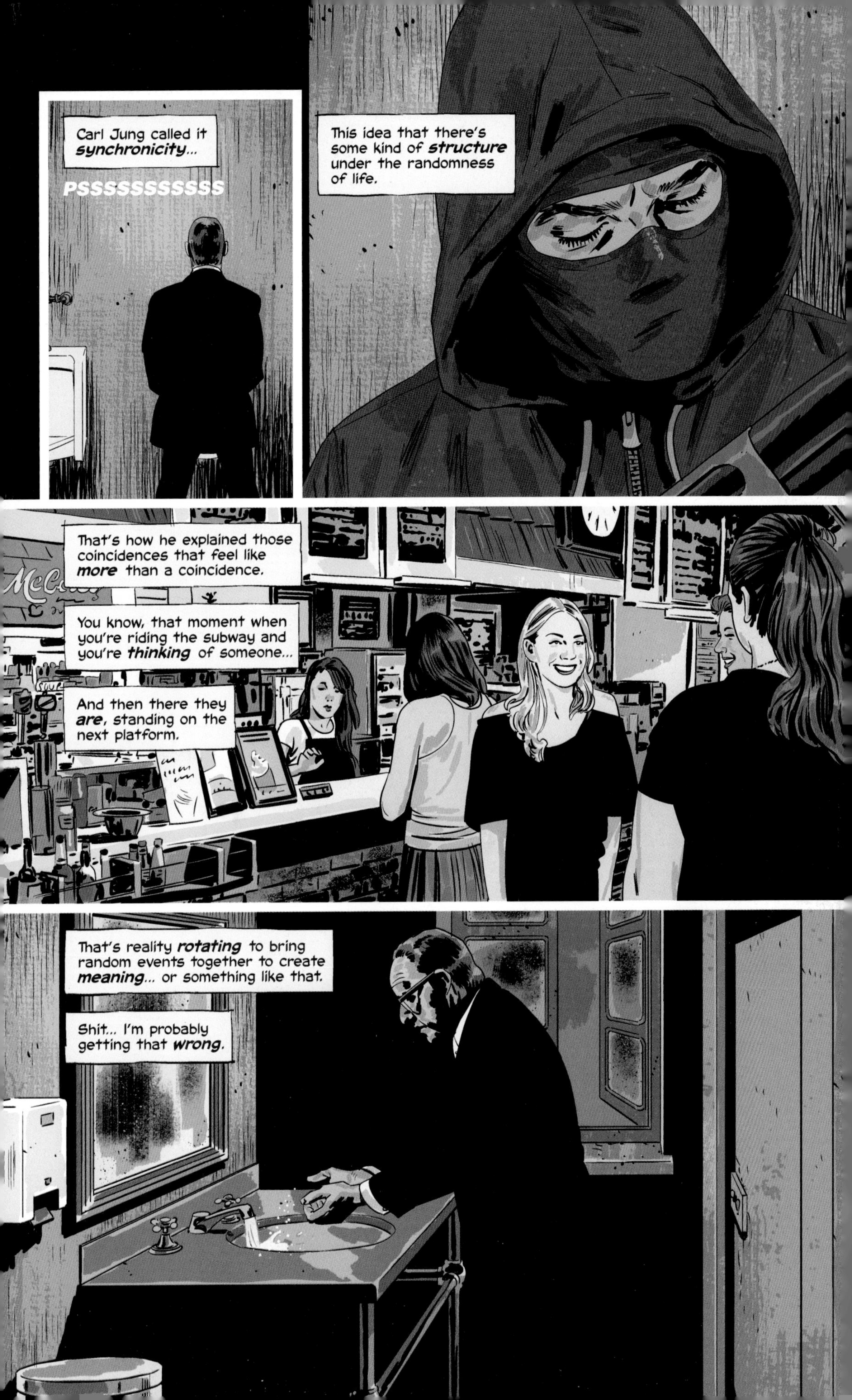
Carl Jung called it *synchronicity*...
PSSSSSSSSSS
This idea that there's some kind of *structure* under the randomness of life.
That's how he explained those coincidences that feel like *more* than a coincidence.
You know, that moment when you're riding the subway and you're *thinking* of someone...
And then there they *are*, standing on the next platform.
That's reality *rotating* to bring random events together to create *meaning*... or something like that.
Shit... I'm probably getting that *wrong*.

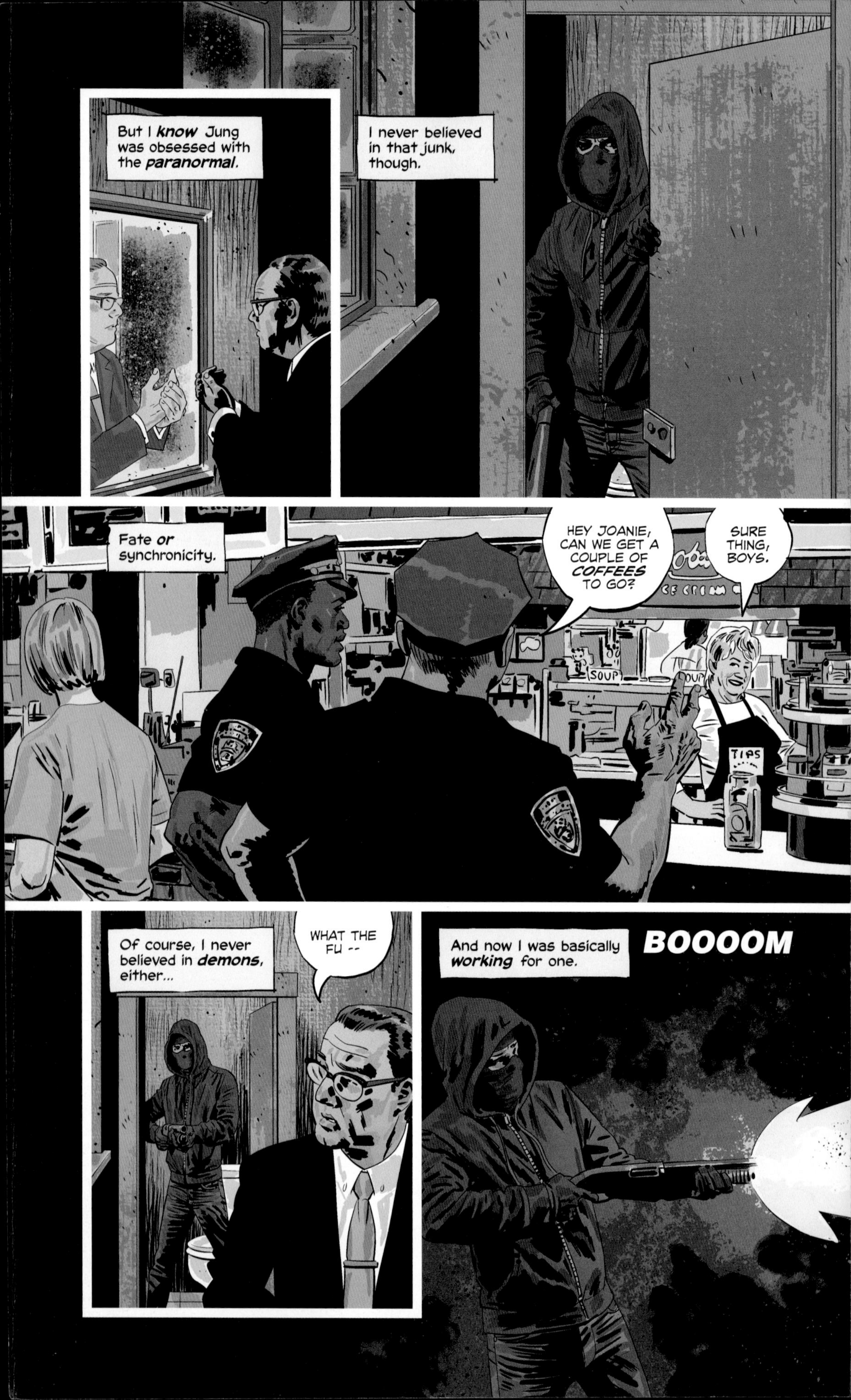

But I *know* Jung was obsessed with the *paranormal*.
I never believed in that junk, though.
Fate *or* synchronicity.
HEY JOANIE, CAN WE GET A COUPLE OF *COFFEES* TO GO?
SURE THING, BOYS.
SOUP
TIPS
Of course, I never believed in *demons*, either...
WHAT THE FU --
And now I was basically *working* for one.
BOOOOM

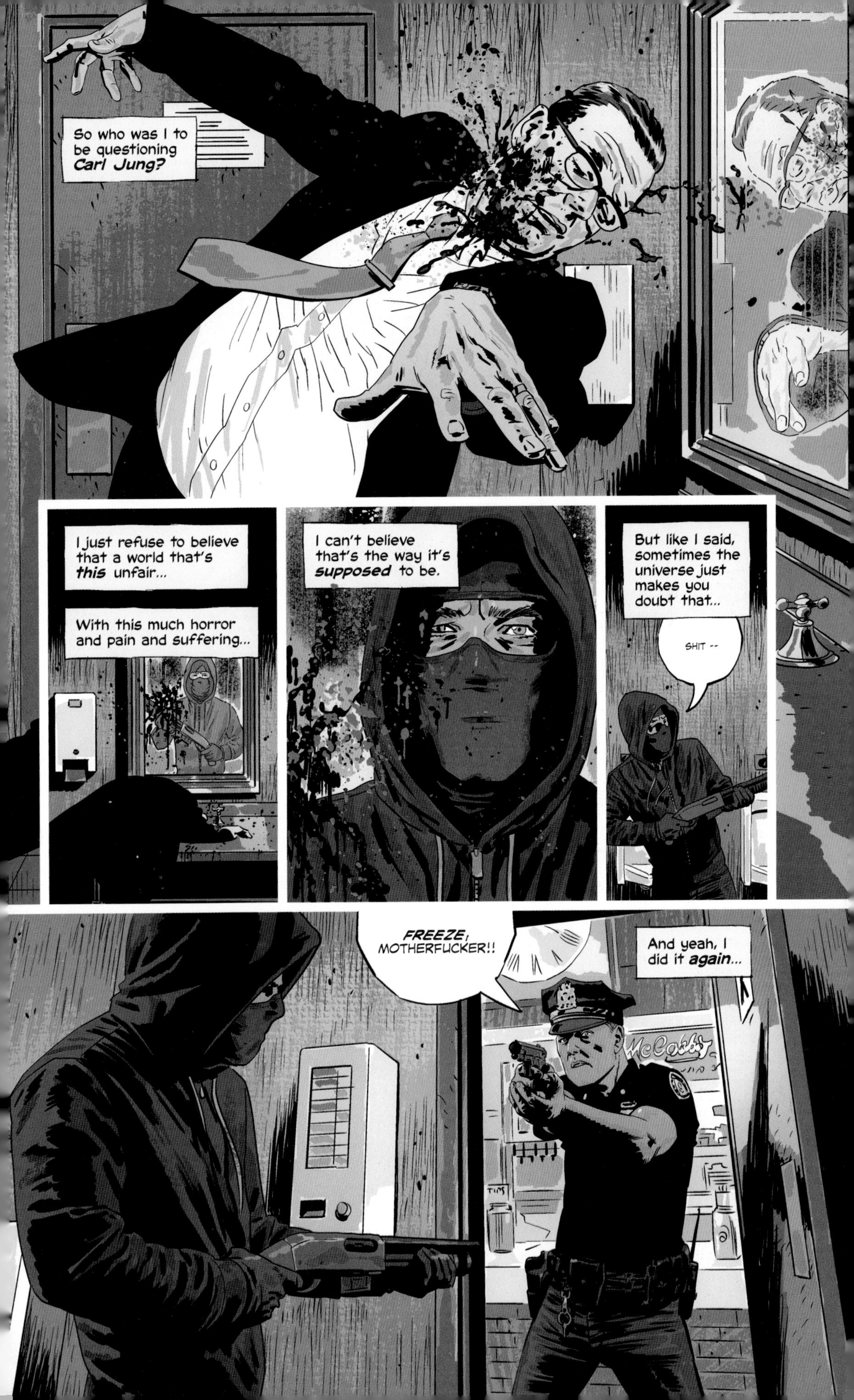
So who was I to be questioning *Carl Jung?*
I just refuse to believe that a world that's *this* unfair...
With this much horror and pain and suffering...
I can't believe that's the way it's *supposed* to be.
But like I said, sometimes the universe just makes you doubt that...
SHIT --
FREEZE, MOTHERFUCKER!!
And yeah, I did it *again*...

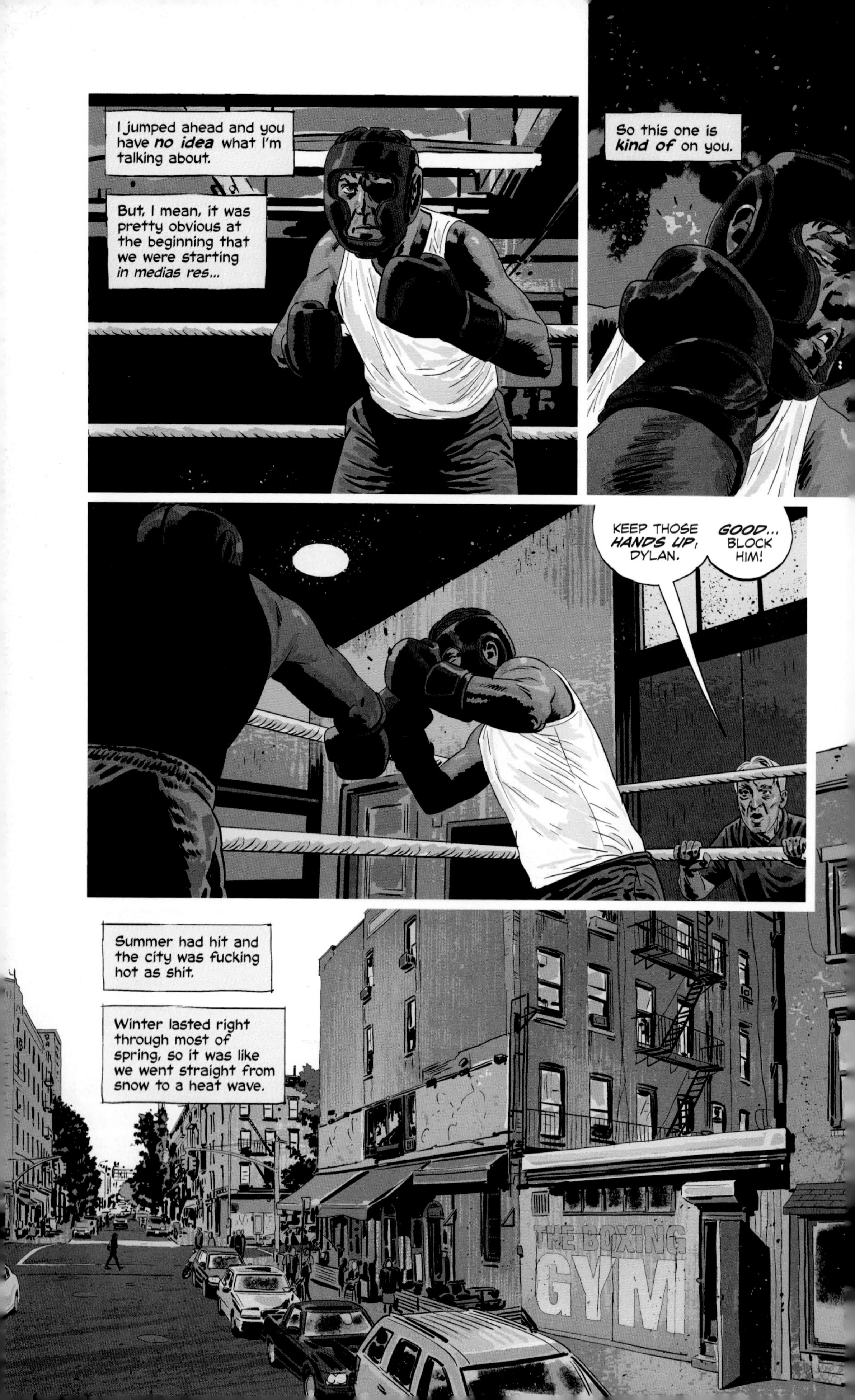

I jumped ahead and you have **no idea** what I'm talking about.
But, I mean, it was pretty obvious at the beginning that we were starting *in medias res*...
So this one is **kind of** on you.
KEEP THOSE **HANDS UP**, DYLAN.
GOOD... BLOCK HIM!
Summer had hit and the city was fucking hot as shit.
Winter lasted right through most of spring, so it was like we went straight from snow to a heat wave.
THE BOXING GYM

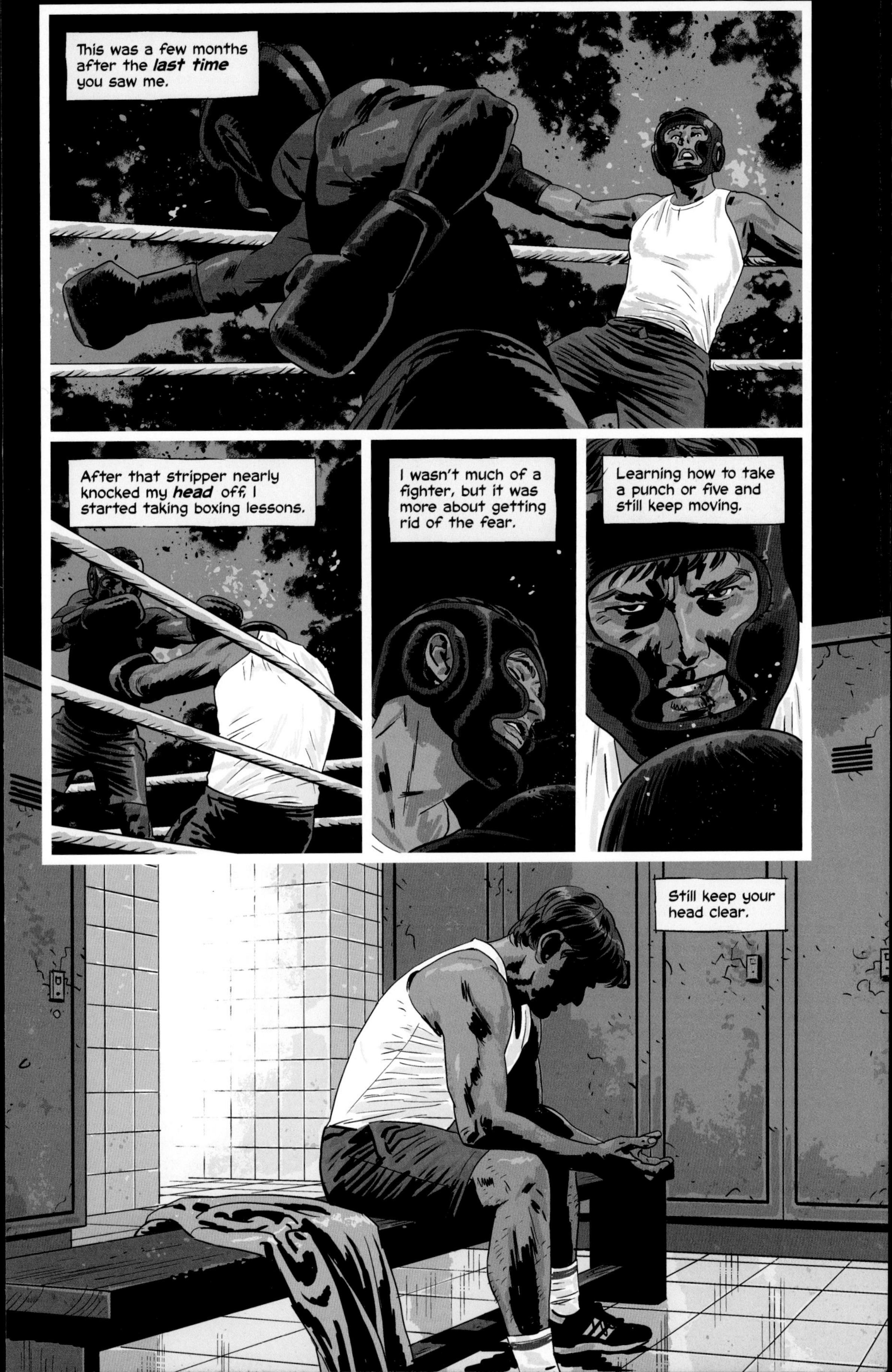
This was a few months after the *last time* you saw me.
After that stripper nearly knocked my *head* off, I started taking boxing lessons.
I wasn't much of a fighter, but it was more about getting rid of the fear.
Learning how to take a punch or five and still keep moving.
Still keep your head clear.

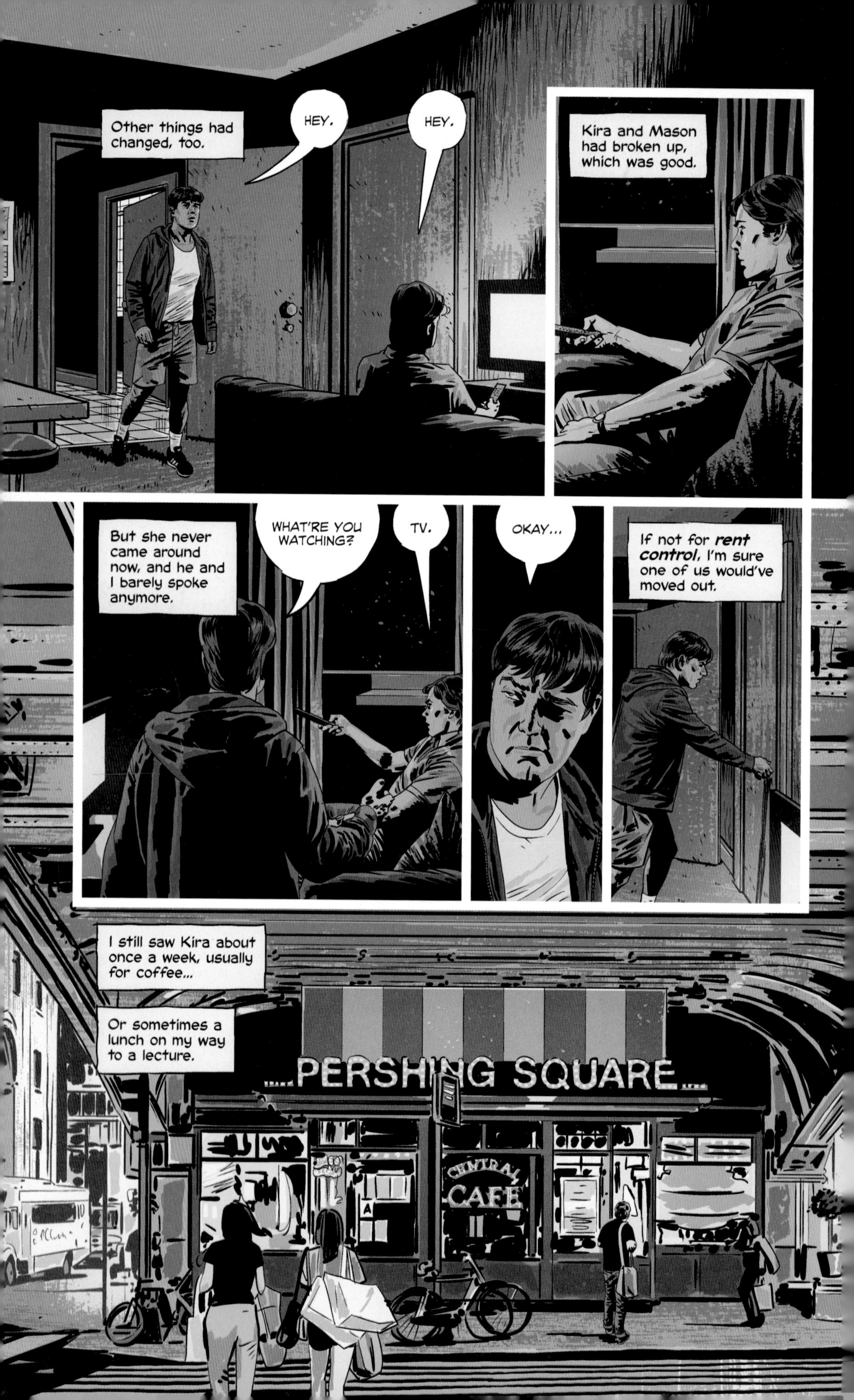
Other things had changed, too.
HEY.
HEY.
Kira and Mason had broken up, which was good.
But she never came around now, and he and I barely spoke anymore.
WHAT'RE YOU WATCHING?
TV.
OKAY...
If not for **rent control**, I'm sure one of us would've moved out.
I still saw Kira about once a week, usually for coffee...
Or sometimes a lunch on my way to a lecture.
PERSHING SQUARE
CENTRAL CAFE

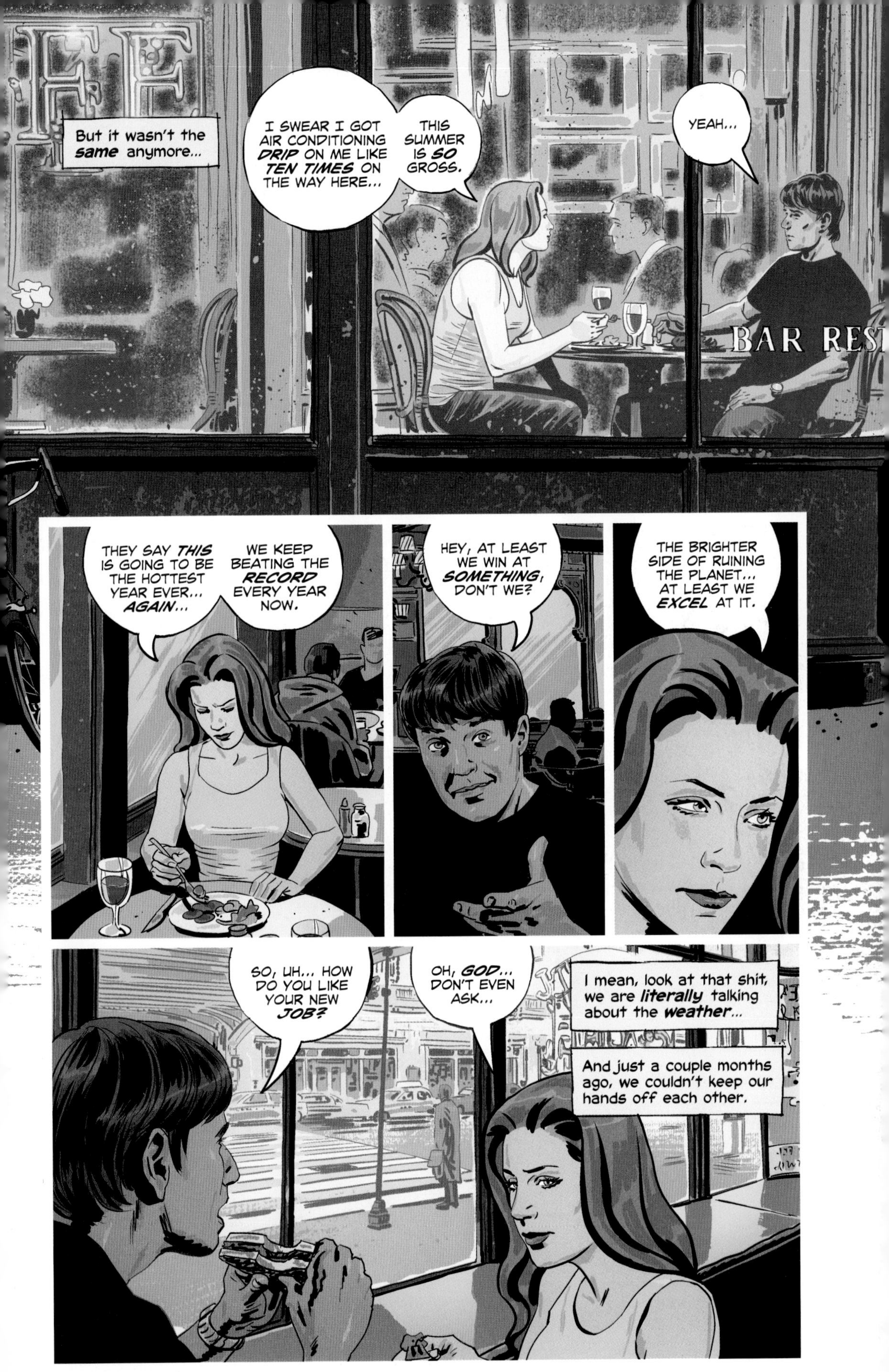

But it wasn't the *same* anymore...
I SWEAR I GOT AIR CONDITIONING *DRIP* ON ME LIKE *TEN TIMES* ON THE WAY HERE...
THIS SUMMER IS *SO* GROSS.
YEAH...
BAR REST
THEY SAY *THIS* IS GOING TO BE THE HOTTEST YEAR EVER... *AGAIN*...
WE KEEP BEATING THE *RECORD* EVERY YEAR NOW.
HEY, AT LEAST WE WIN AT *SOMETHING*, DON'T WE?
THE BRIGHTER SIDE OF RUINING THE PLANET... AT LEAST WE *EXCEL* AT IT.
SO, UH... HOW DO YOU LIKE YOUR NEW *JOB?*
OH, *GOD*... DON'T EVEN ASK...
I mean, look at that shit, we are *literally* talking about the *weather*...
And just a couple months ago, we couldn't keep our hands off each other.

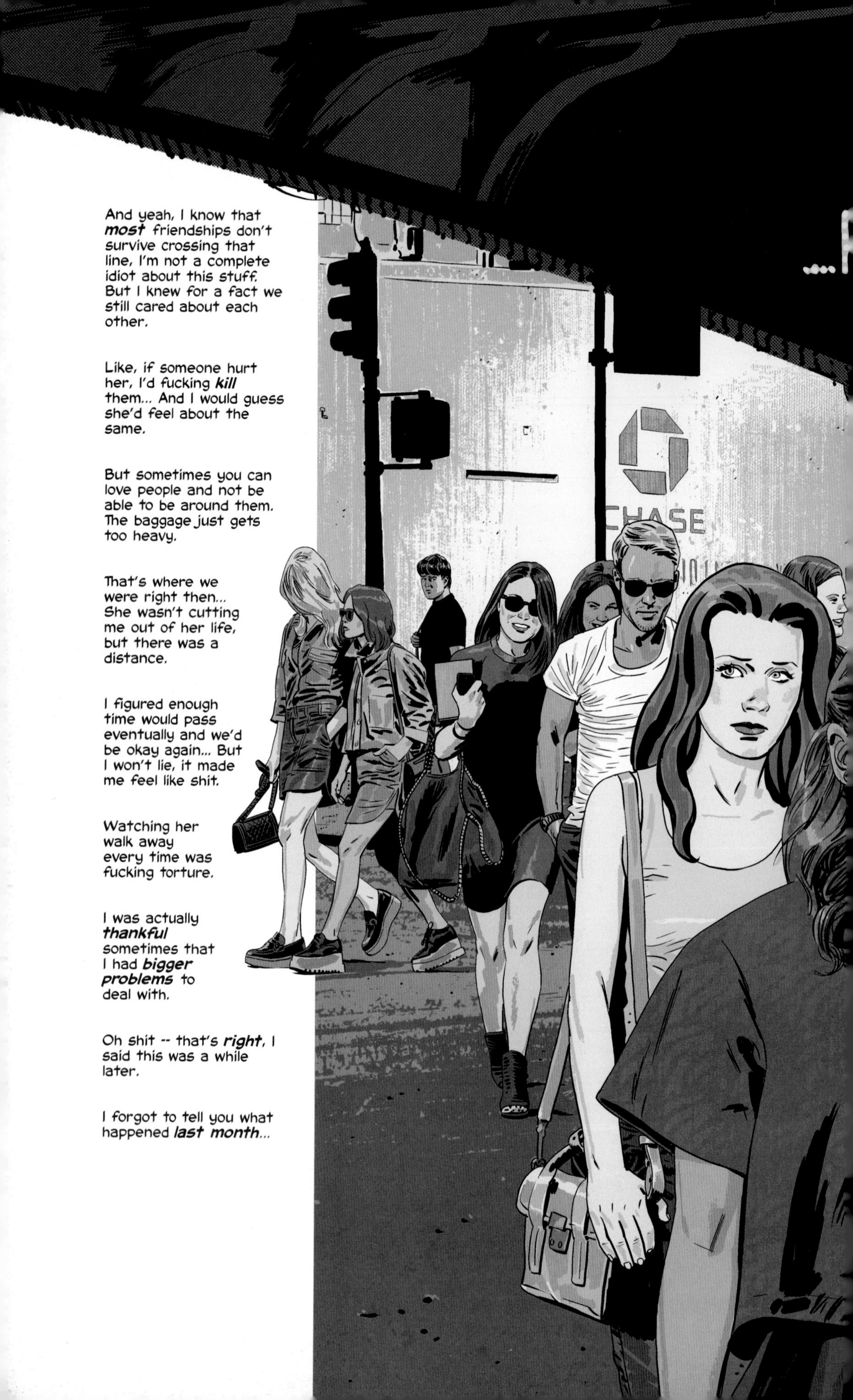
And yeah, I know that ***most*** friendships don't survive crossing that line, I'm not a complete idiot about this stuff. But I knew for a fact we still cared about each other.
Like, if someone hurt her, I'd fucking ***kill*** them... And I would guess she'd feel about the same.
But sometimes you can love people and not be able to be around them. The baggage just gets too heavy.
That's where we were right then... She wasn't cutting me out of her life, but there was a distance.
I figured enough time would pass eventually and we'd be okay again... But I won't lie, it made me feel like shit.
Watching her walk away every time was fucking torture.
I was actually ***thankful*** sometimes that I had ***bigger problems*** to deal with.
Oh shit -- that's ***right***, I said this was a while later.
I forgot to tell you what happened ***last month***...
CHASE

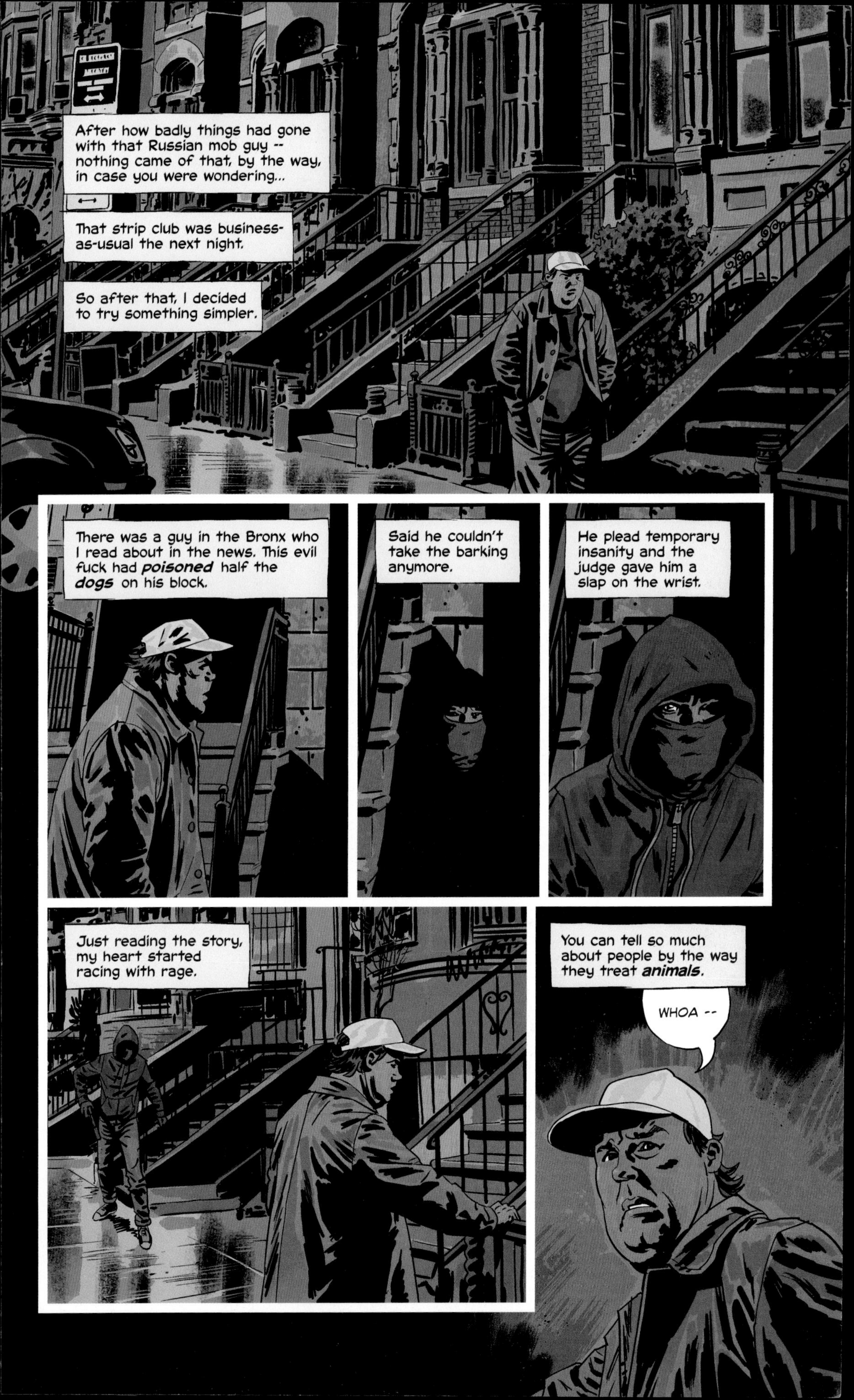
After how badly things had gone with that Russian mob guy -- nothing came of that, by the way, in case you were wondering...
That strip club was business-as-usual the next night.
So after that, I decided to try something simpler.
There was a guy in the Bronx who I read about in the news. This evil fuck had *poisoned* half the *dogs* on his block.
Said he couldn't take the barking anymore.
He plead temporary insanity and the judge gave him a slap on the wrist.
Just reading the story, my heart started racing with rage.
You can tell so much about people by the way they treat *animals*.
WHOA --

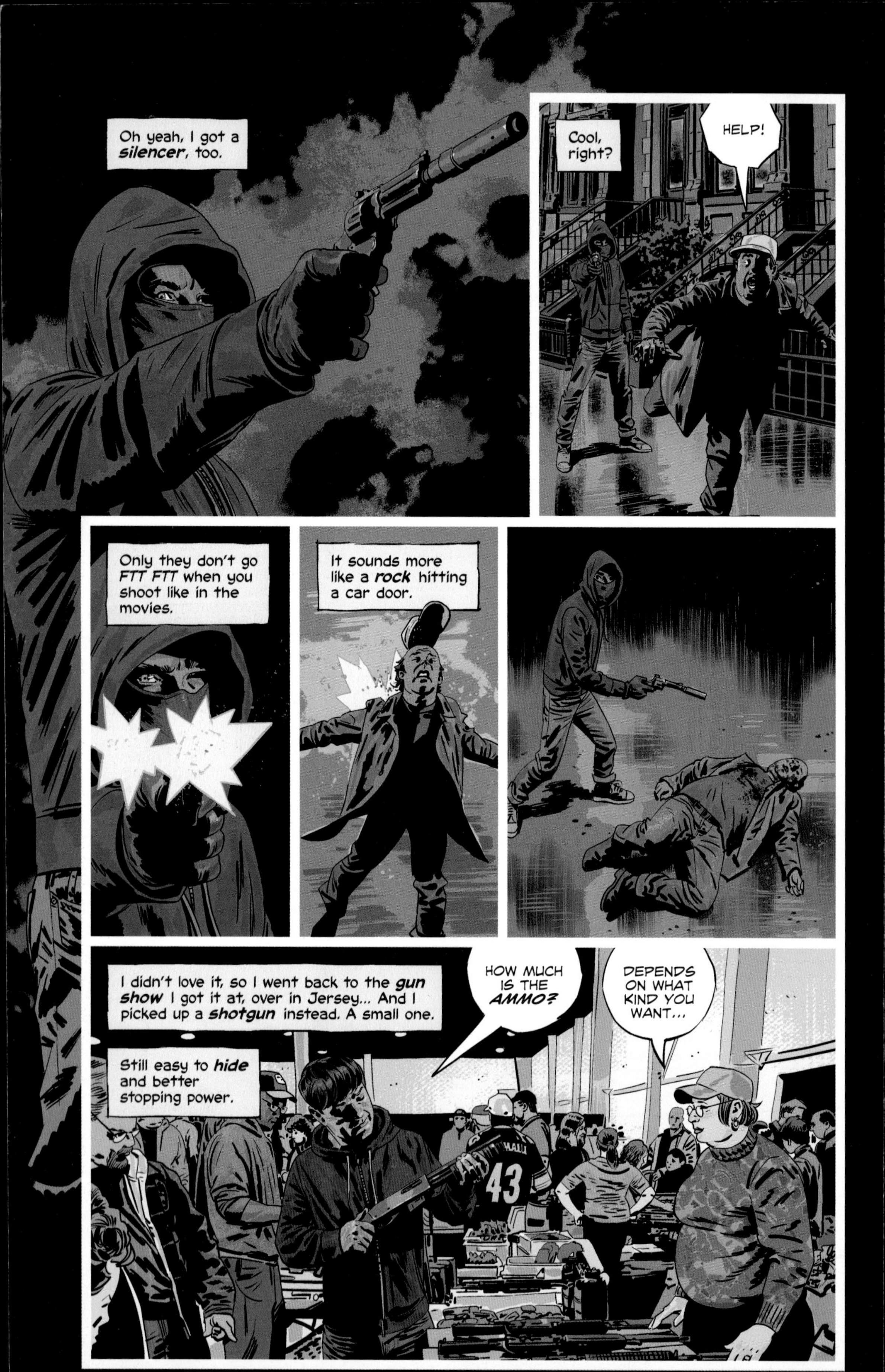
Oh yeah, I got a *silencer*, too.
Cool, right?
HELP!
Only they don't go *FTT FTT* when you shoot like in the movies.
It sounds more like a *rock* hitting a car door.
I didn't love it, so I went back to the *gun show* I got it at, over in Jersey... And I picked up a *shotgun* instead. A small one.
Still easy to *hide* and better stopping power.
HOW MUCH IS THE *AMMO?*
DEPENDS ON WHAT KIND YOU WANT...
43

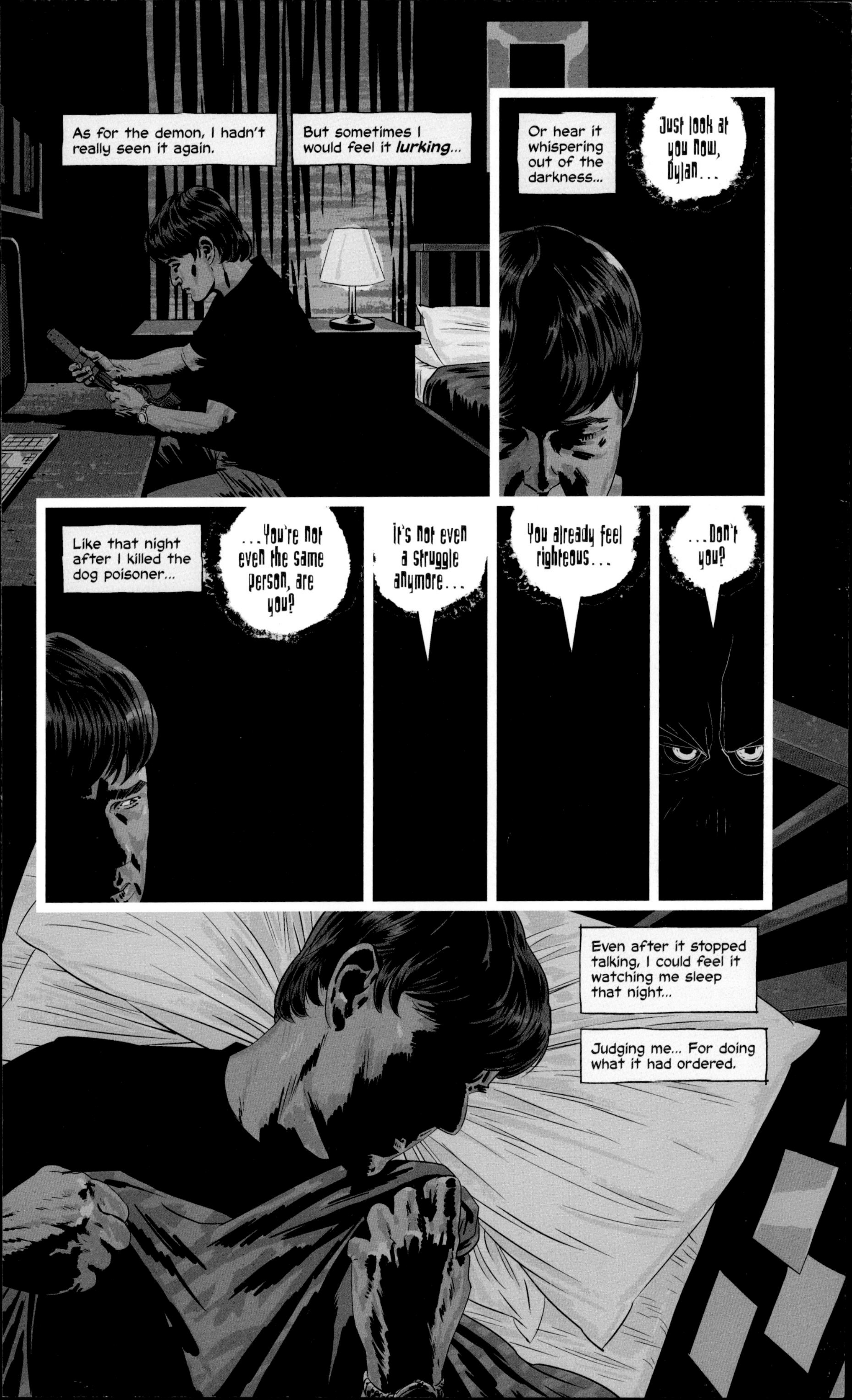
As for the demon, I hadn't really seen it again.
But sometimes I would feel it *lurking*...
Or hear it whispering out of the darkness...
Just look at you now, Dylan...
Like that night after I killed the dog poisoner...
...You're not even the same person, are you?
It's not even a struggle anymore...
You already feel righteous...
...Don't you?
Even after it stopped talking, I could feel it watching me sleep that night...
Judging me... For doing what it had ordered.

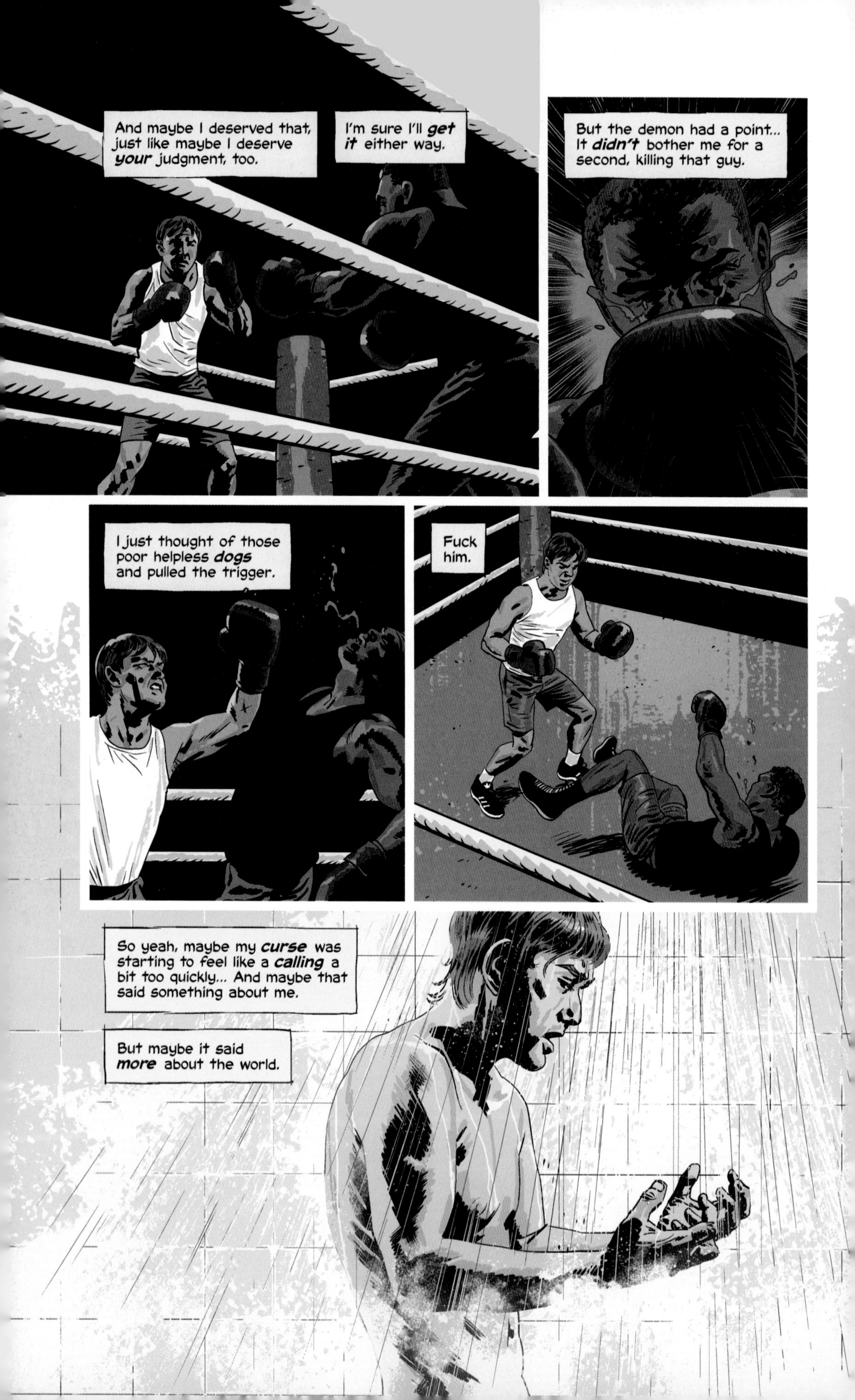
And maybe I deserved that, just like maybe I deserve *your* judgment, too.
I'm sure I'll *get it* either way.
But the demon had a point... It *didn't* bother me for a second, killing that guy.
I just thought of those poor helpless *dogs* and pulled the trigger.
Fuck him.
So yeah, maybe my *curse* was starting to feel like a *calling* a bit too quickly... And maybe that said something about me.
But maybe it said *more* about the world.

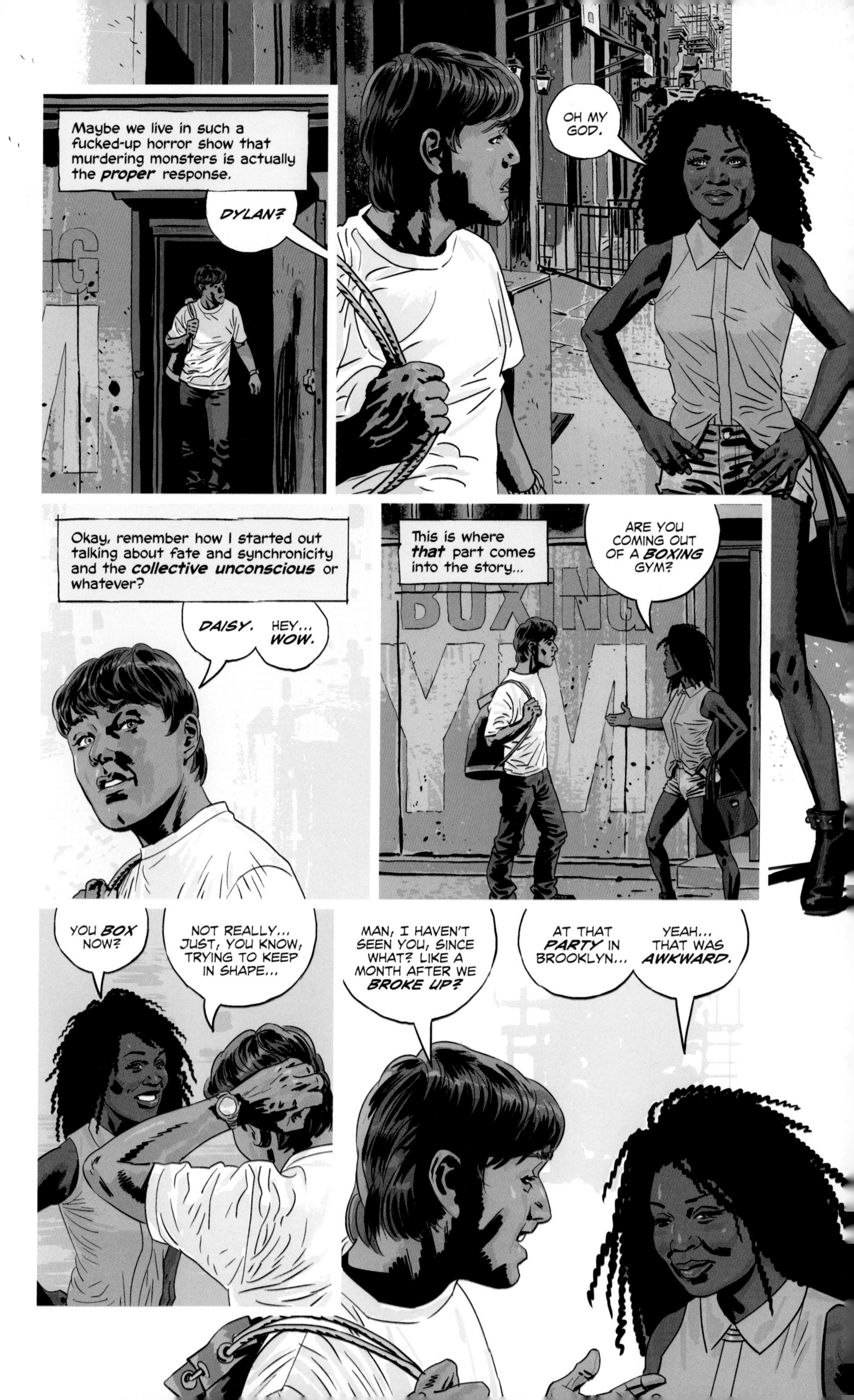
Maybe we live in such a fucked-up horror show that murdering monsters is actually the *proper* response.
DYLAN?
OH MY GOD.
Okay, remember how I started out talking about fate and synchronicity and the *collective unconscious* or whatever?
DAISY.
HEY... *WOW.*
This is where *that* part comes into the story...
ARE YOU COMING OUT OF A *BOXING* GYM?
BOXING
YOU *BOX* NOW?
NOT REALLY... JUST, YOU KNOW, TRYING TO KEEP IN SHAPE...
MAN, I HAVEN'T SEEN YOU, SINCE WHAT? LIKE A MONTH AFTER WE *BROKE UP?*
AT THAT *PARTY* IN BROOKLYN...
YEAH... THAT WAS *AWKWARD.*

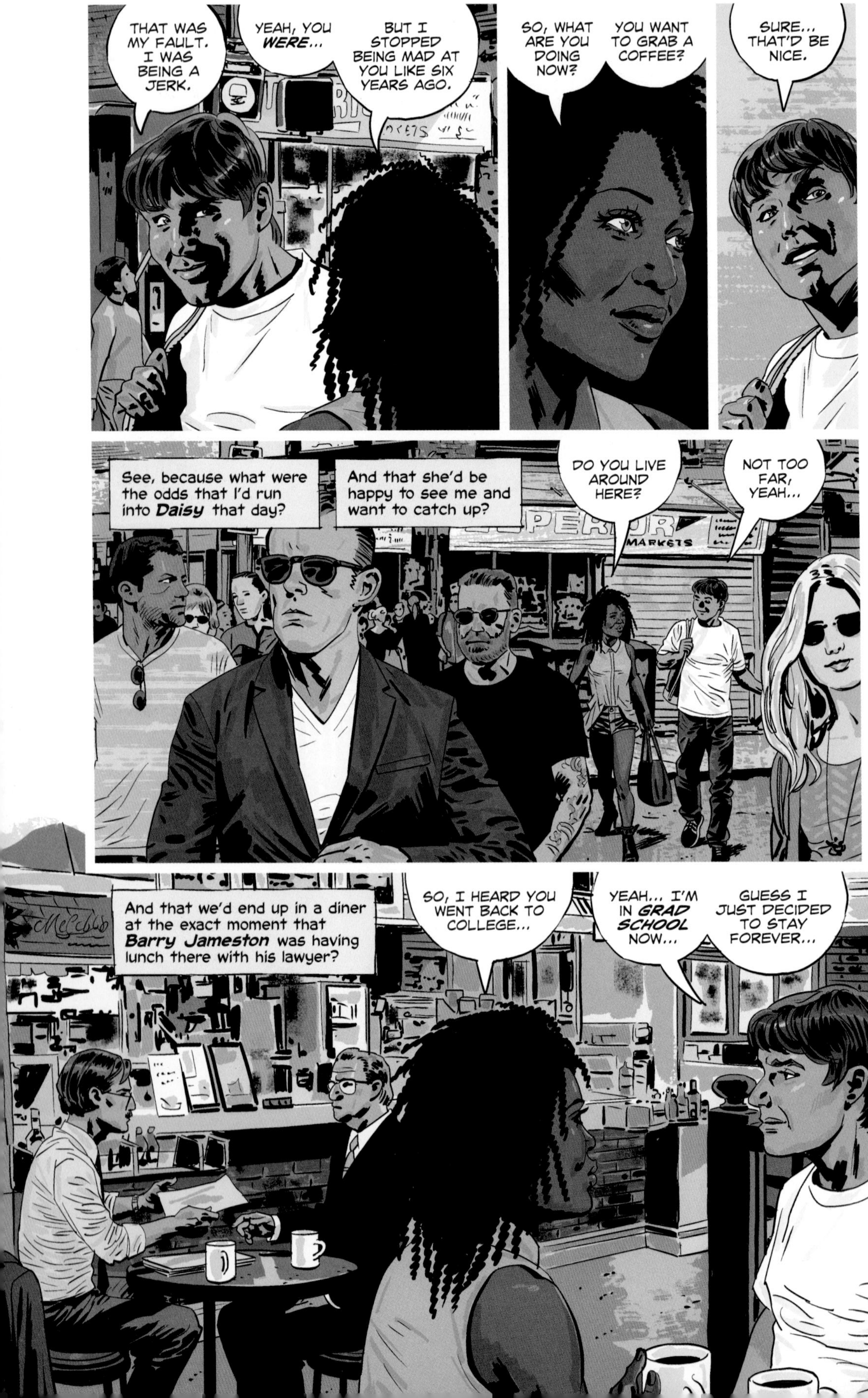
THAT WAS MY FAULT. I WAS BEING A JERK.
YEAH, YOU *WERE*...
BUT I STOPPED BEING MAD AT YOU LIKE SIX YEARS AGO.
SO, WHAT ARE YOU DOING NOW?
YOU WANT TO GRAB A COFFEE?
SURE... THAT'D BE NICE.
See, because what were the odds that I'd run into *Daisy* that day?
And that she'd be happy to see me and want to catch up?
DO YOU LIVE AROUND HERE?
NOT TOO FAR, YEAH...
MARKETS
And that we'd end up in a diner at the exact moment that *Barry Jameston* was having lunch there with his lawyer?
SO, I HEARD YOU WENT BACK TO COLLEGE...
YEAH... I'M IN *GRAD SCHOOL* NOW...
GUESS I JUST DECIDED TO STAY FOREVER...

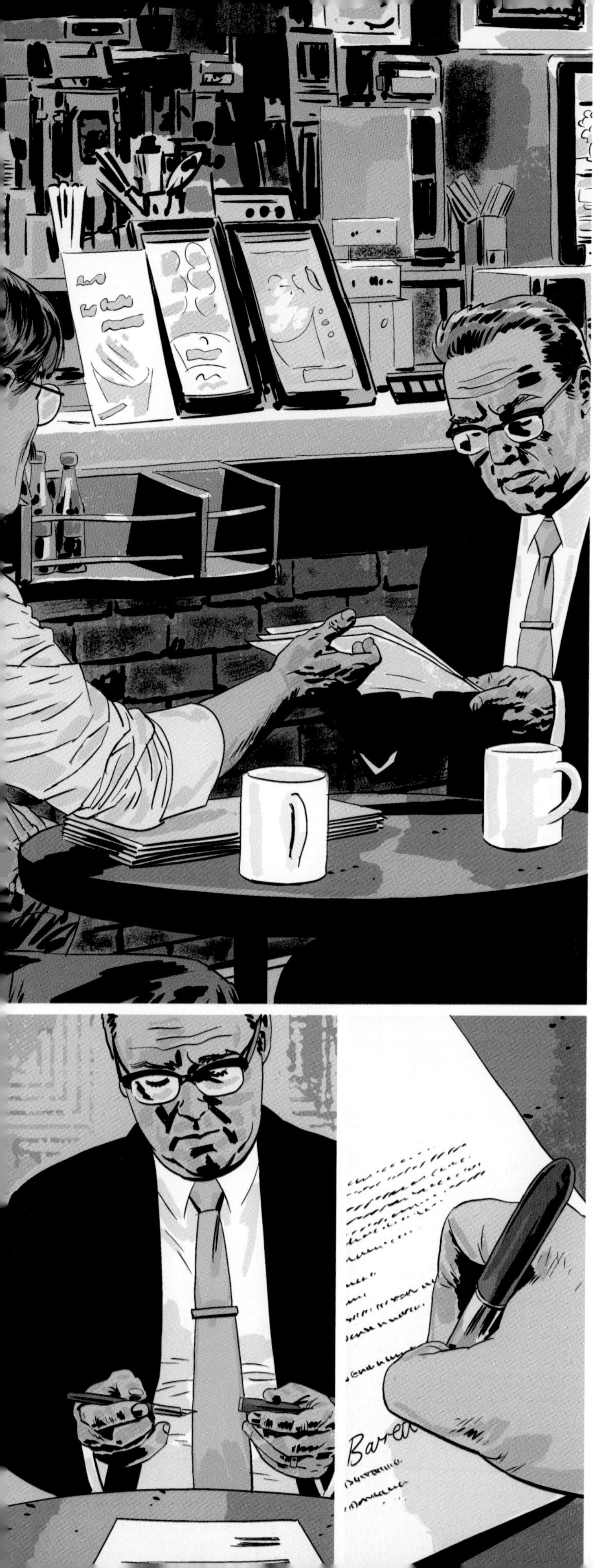

You remember ***Barry Jameston***, right?

Just kidding, of course you don't.

We have a collective memory of five minutes these days, and since Jameston was in the news, we've had an economic meltdown and three Presidential elections.

No one remembers Enron or Bear Stearns or ***Barry Jameston*** anymore.

Jameston ran an ***investment fund*** that was actually a pyramid scheme. When it all came out, thousands of people lost their savings.

People killed themselves, like they always do when some financial scam blows up, but that doesn't get as much coverage.

You mostly hear about which ***movie stars*** it affects, or how some singer lost ten million dollars, and now they only have forty million left.

Which is part of ***why*** we have a collective memory of five minutes.

But I remembered. I read an article back then, about Jameston's ***sentencing***...

The judge listed all the people who were dead because of his actions and said he wished he could give him a harsher sentence.

He did ***four years*** in minimum security. The ***white-collar crime*** country club.

I remember seeing a picture of him playing tennis there once.

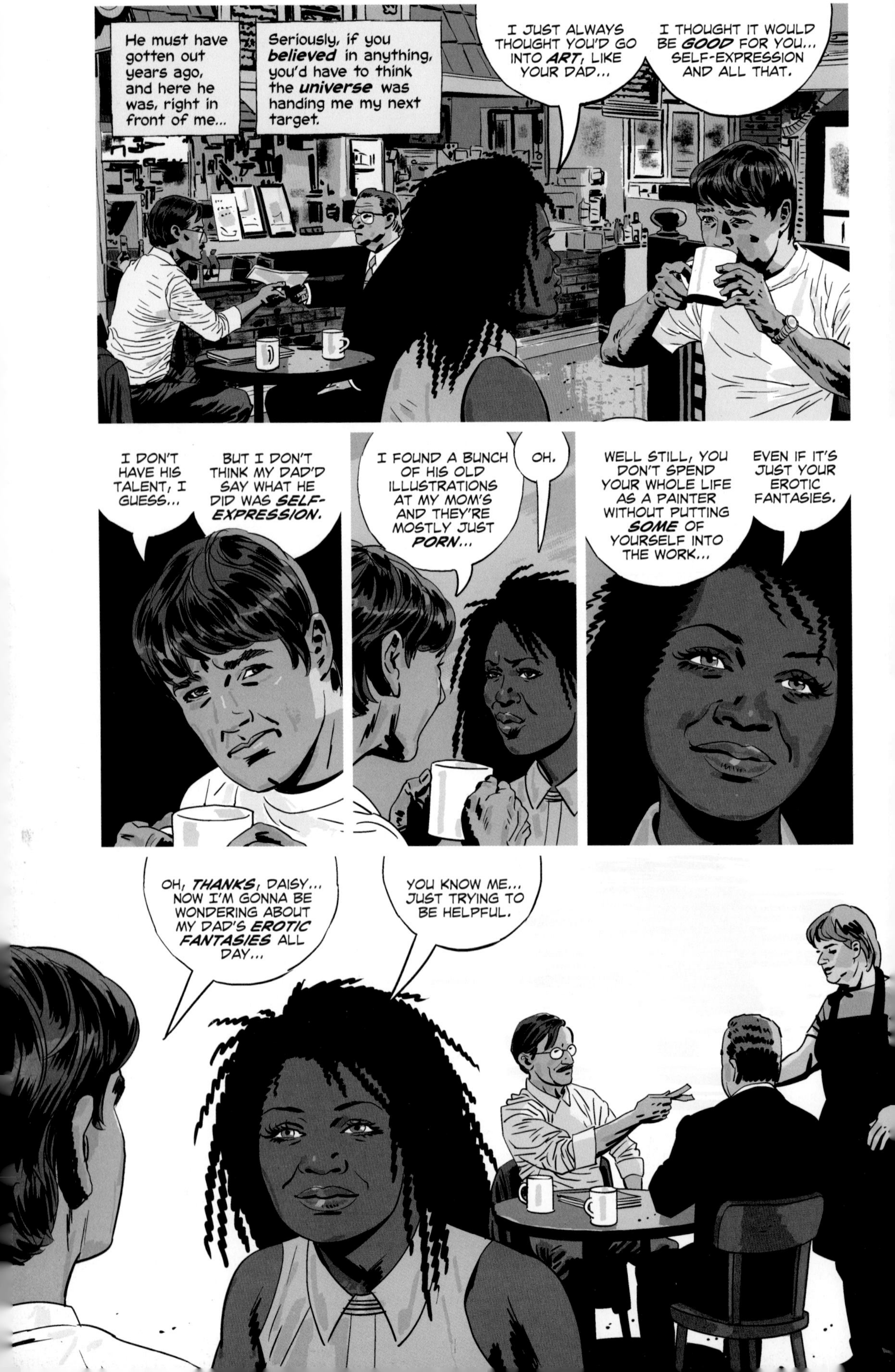
He must have gotten out years ago, and here he was, right in front of me...
Seriously, if you *believed* in anything, you'd have to think the *universe* was handing me my next target.
I JUST ALWAYS THOUGHT YOU'D GO INTO *ART*, LIKE YOUR DAD...
I THOUGHT IT WOULD BE *GOOD* FOR YOU... SELF-EXPRESSION AND ALL THAT.
I DON'T HAVE HIS TALENT, I GUESS...
BUT I DON'T THINK MY DAD'D SAY WHAT HE DID WAS *SELF-EXPRESSION.*
I FOUND A BUNCH OF HIS OLD ILLUSTRATIONS AT MY MOM'S AND THEY'RE MOSTLY JUST *PORN*...
OH.
WELL STILL, YOU DON'T SPEND YOUR WHOLE LIFE AS A PAINTER WITHOUT PUTTING *SOME* OF YOURSELF INTO THE WORK...
EVEN IF IT'S JUST YOUR EROTIC FANTASIES.
OH, *THANKS*, DAISY... NOW I'M GONNA BE WONDERING ABOUT MY DAD'S *EROTIC FANTASIES* ALL DAY...
YOU KNOW ME... JUST TRYING TO BE HELPFUL.

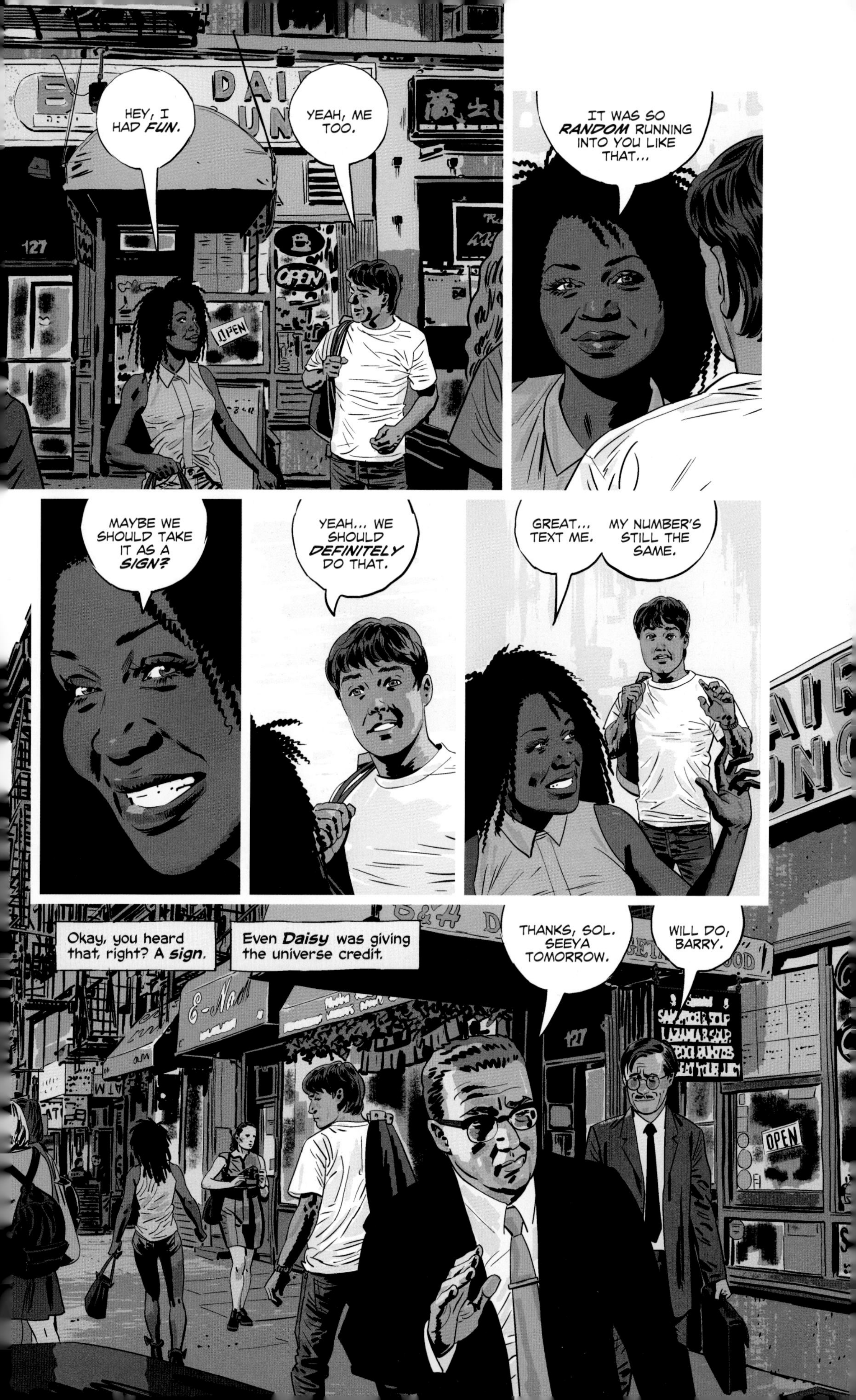
HEY, I HAD FUN.
YEAH, ME TOO.
IT WAS SO RANDOM RUNNING INTO YOU LIKE THAT...
MAYBE WE SHOULD TAKE IT AS A SIGN?
YEAH... WE SHOULD DEFINITELY DO THAT.
GREAT... TEXT ME.
MY NUMBER'S STILL THE SAME.
Okay, you heard that, right? A sign.
Even Daisy was giving the universe credit.
THANKS, SOL. SEEYA TOMORROW.
WILL DO, BARRY.

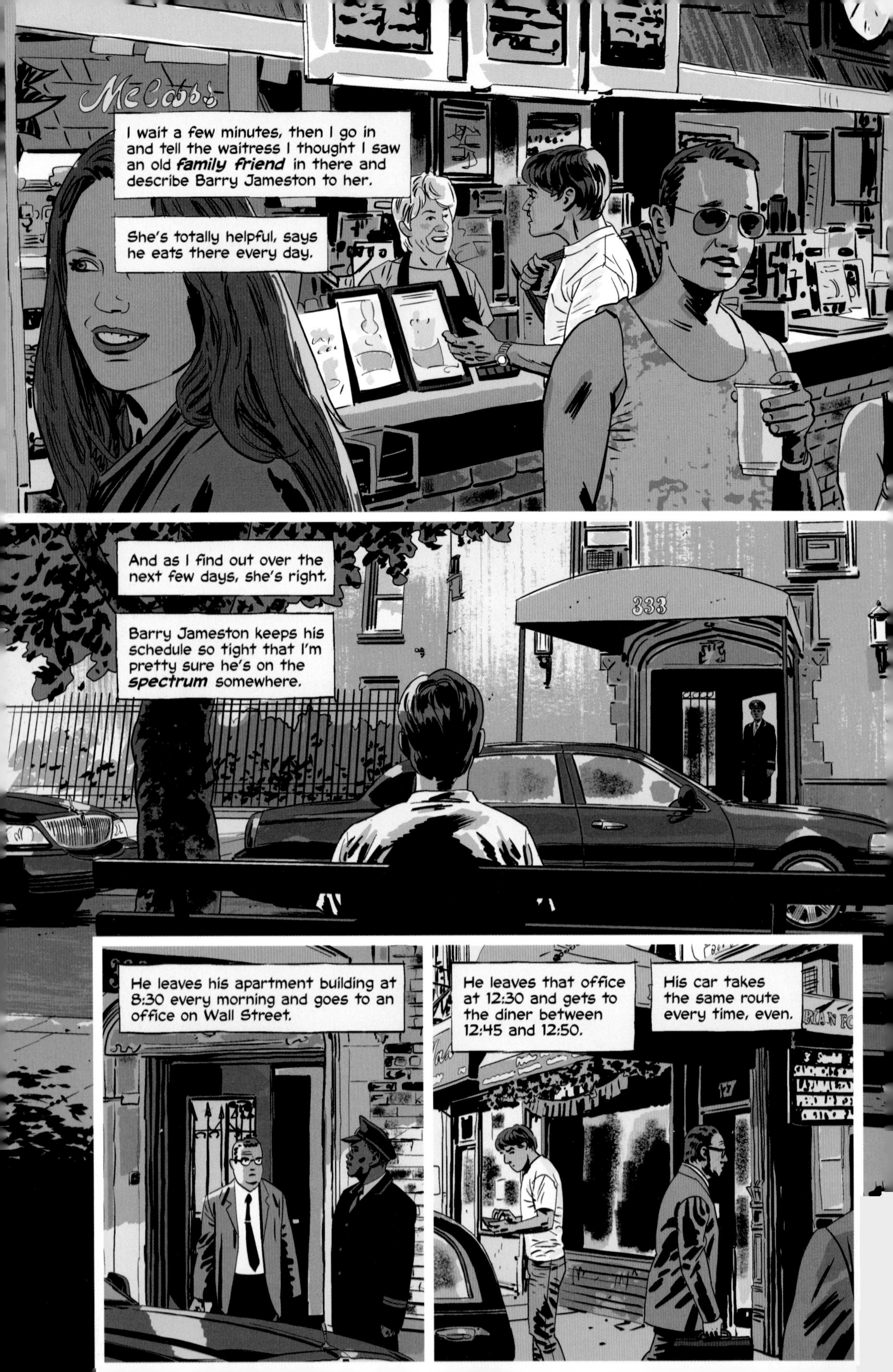
I wait a few minutes, then I go in and tell the waitress I thought I saw an old *family friend* in there and describe Barry Jameston to her.
She's totally helpful, says he eats there every day.
And as I find out over the next few days, she's right.
Barry Jameston keeps his schedule so tight that I'm pretty sure he's on the *spectrum* somewhere.
333
He leaves his apartment building at 8:30 every morning and goes to an office on Wall Street.
He leaves that office at 12:30 and gets to the diner between 12:45 and 12:50.
His car takes the same route every time, even.

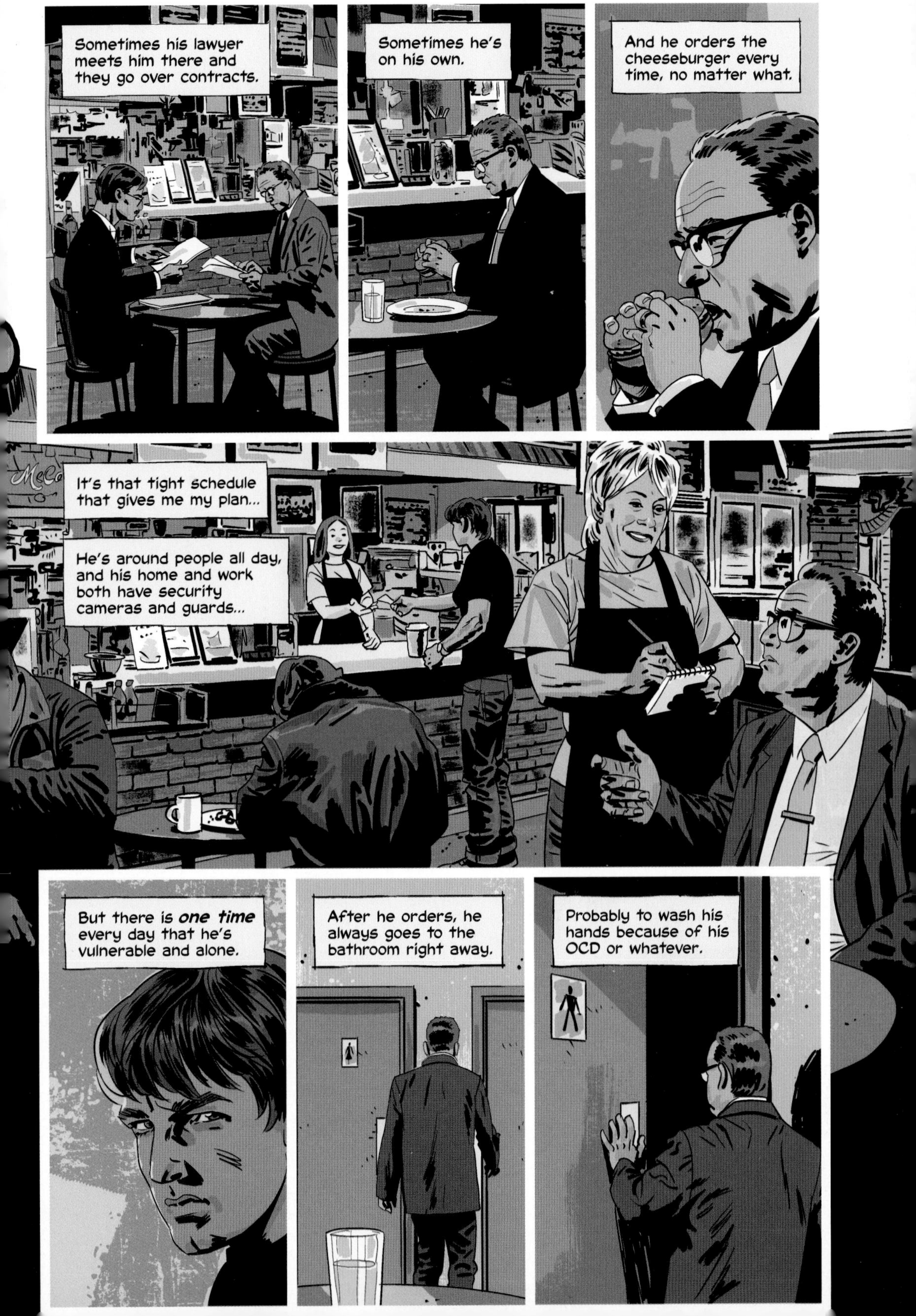
Sometimes his lawyer meets him there and they go over contracts.
Sometimes he's on his own.
And he orders the cheeseburger every time, no matter what.
It's that tight schedule that gives me my plan...
He's around people all day, and his home and work both have security cameras and guards...
But there is *one time* every day that he's vulnerable and alone.
After he orders, he always goes to the bathroom right away.
Probably to wash his hands because of his OCD or whatever.

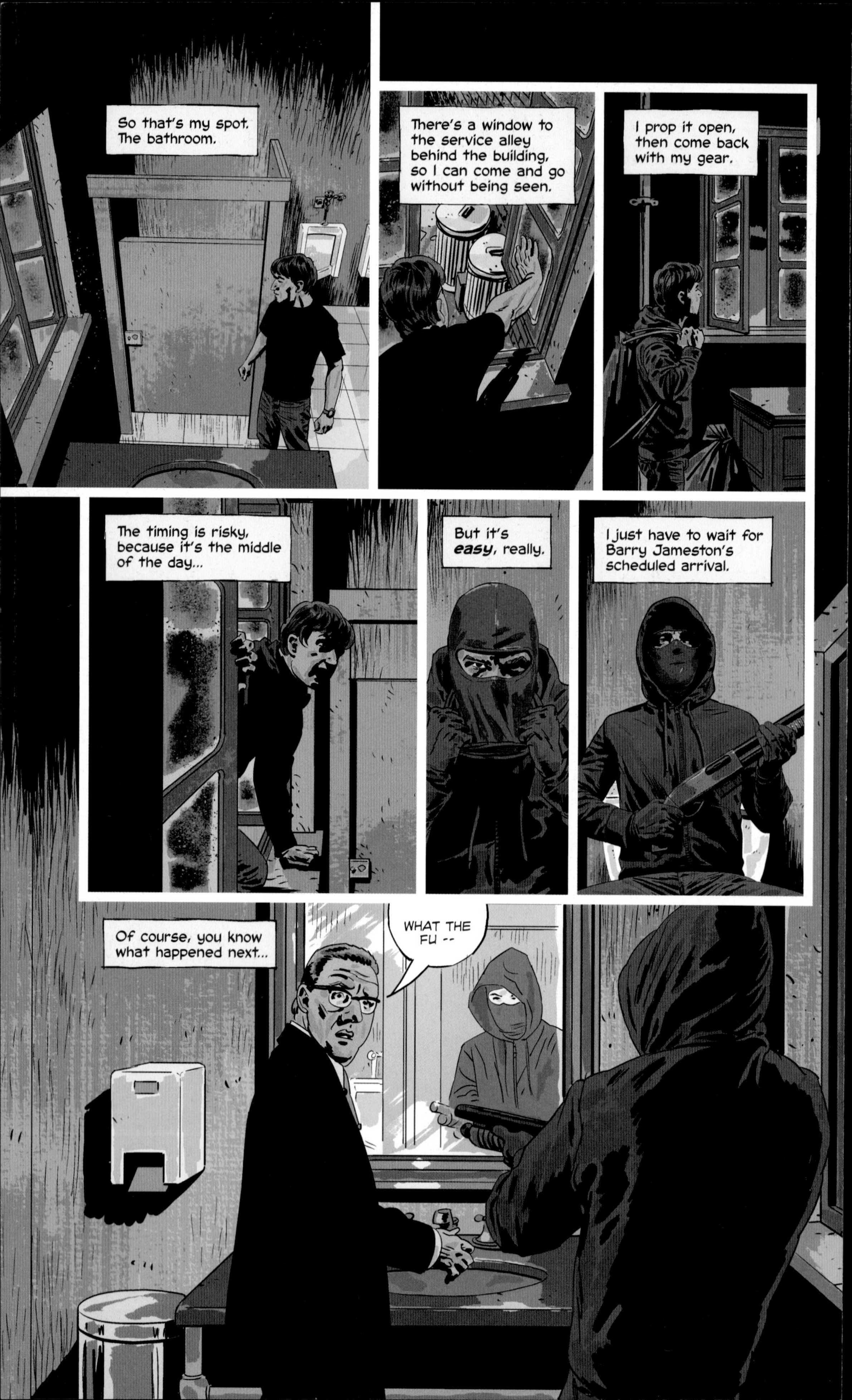
So that's my spot. The bathroom.
There's a window to the service alley behind the building, so I can come and go without being seen.
I prop it open, then come back with my gear.
The timing is risky, because it's the middle of the day...
But it's *easy*, really.
I just have to wait for Barry Jameston's scheduled arrival.
Of course, you know what happened next...
WHAT THE FU --

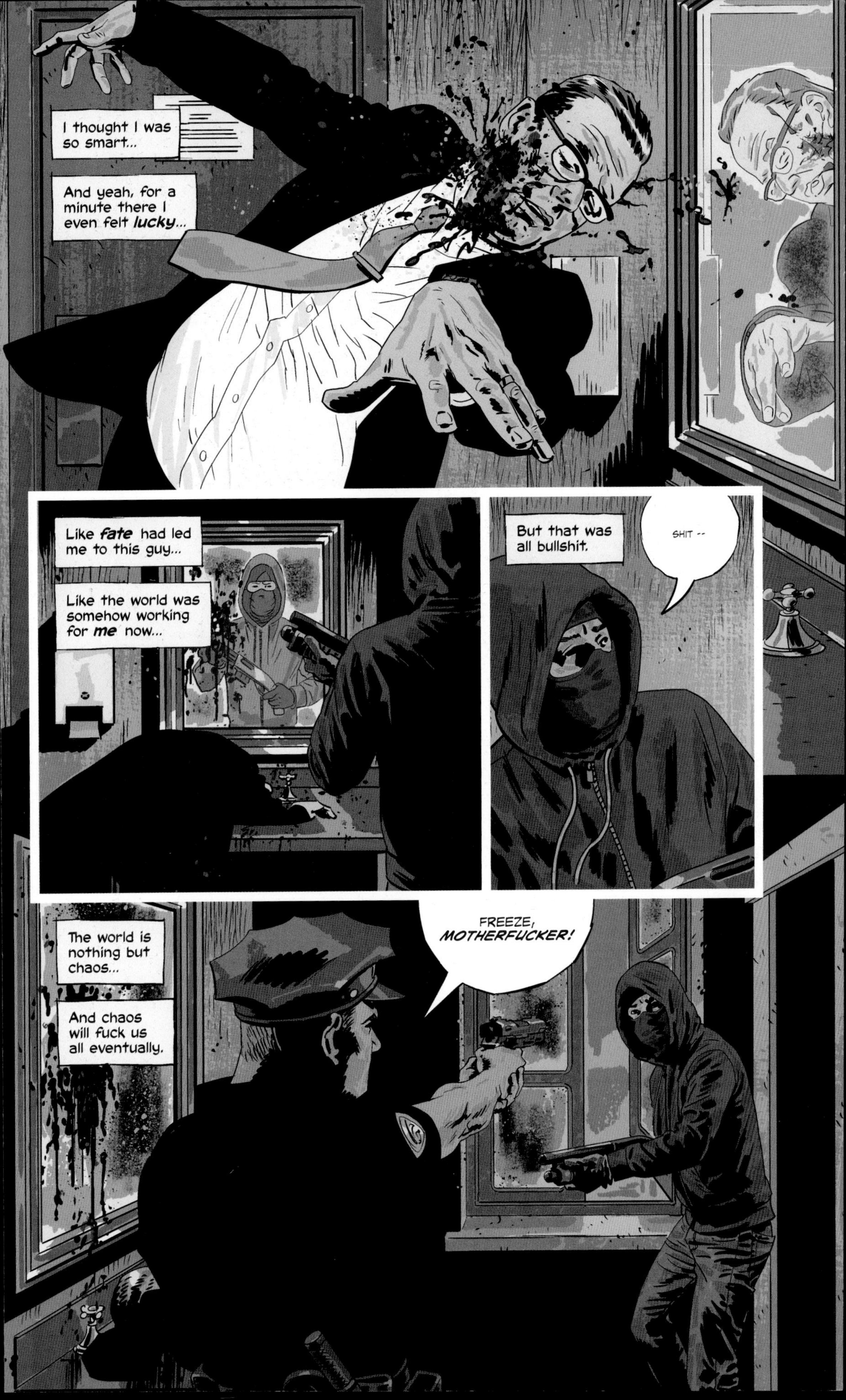
I thought I was so smart...
And yeah, for a minute there I even felt *lucky*...
Like *fate* had led me to this guy...
Like the world was somehow working for *me* now...
But that was all bullshit.
SHIT --
The world is nothing but chaos...
And chaos will fuck us all eventually.
FREEZE, *MOTHERFUCKER!*

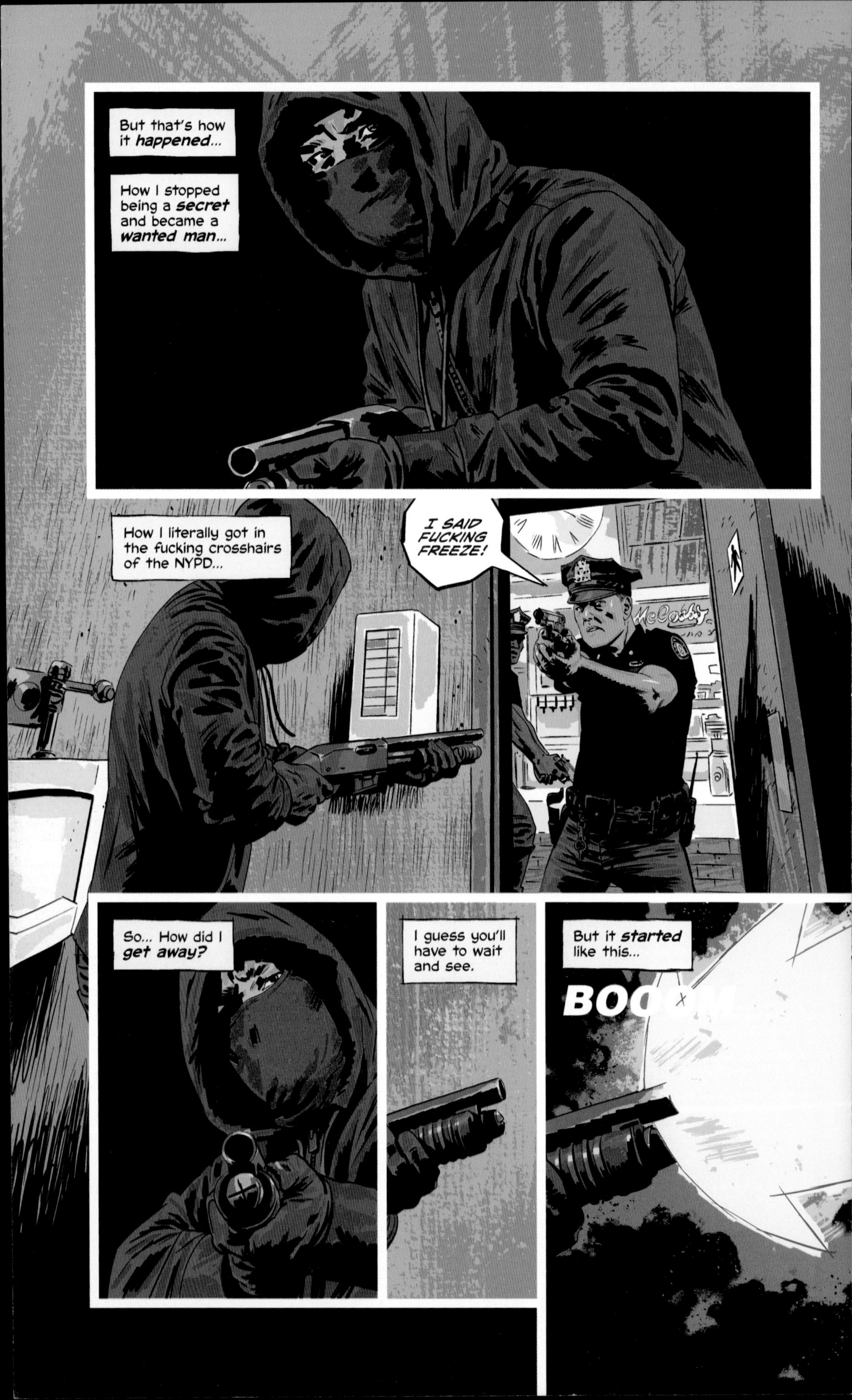
But that's how it *happened*...
How I stopped being a ***secret*** and became a ***wanted man***...
How I literally got in the fucking crosshairs of the NYPD...
I SAID FUCKING FREEZE!
So... How did I ***get away?***
I guess you'll have to wait and see.
But it ***started*** like this...

Here's something no one ever talks about, something that'll help you understand how I got through the next two minutes of my life...

That cop and I were in a stand-off, so you'd think I was ***panicking***, right? But I wasn't.

In fact, I'd never felt more calm and in control than I did right at that moment.

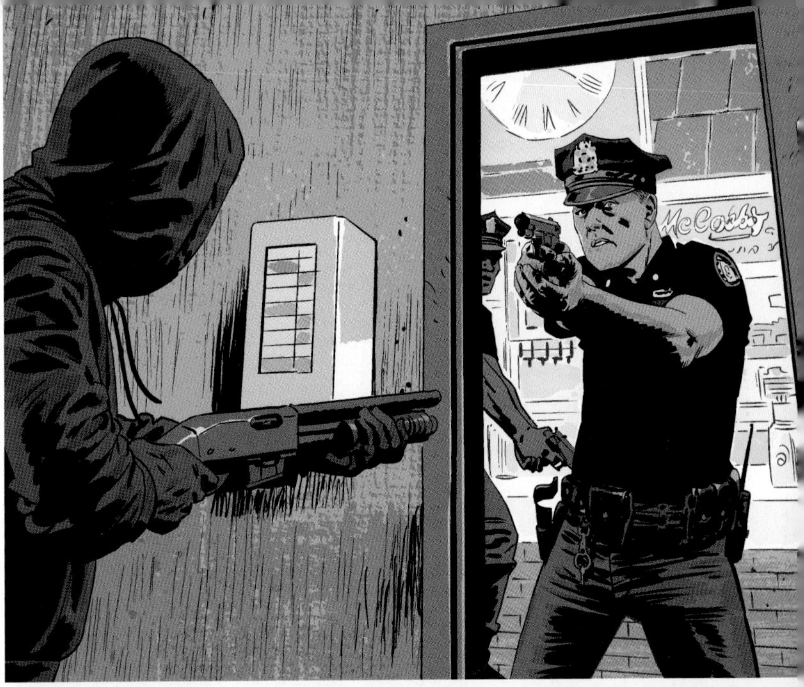

This was one of the ***secrets*** I was learning... When you break the rules you've been taught to follow your whole life, something ***strange*** happens.

Right up until the moment of no return, you're scared, trying to convince yourself not to do it, your heart just pounding in your throat...

But once you cross the line - pull a gun on someone or drive off in a stolen car or whatever - this strange ***calm*** comes over you.

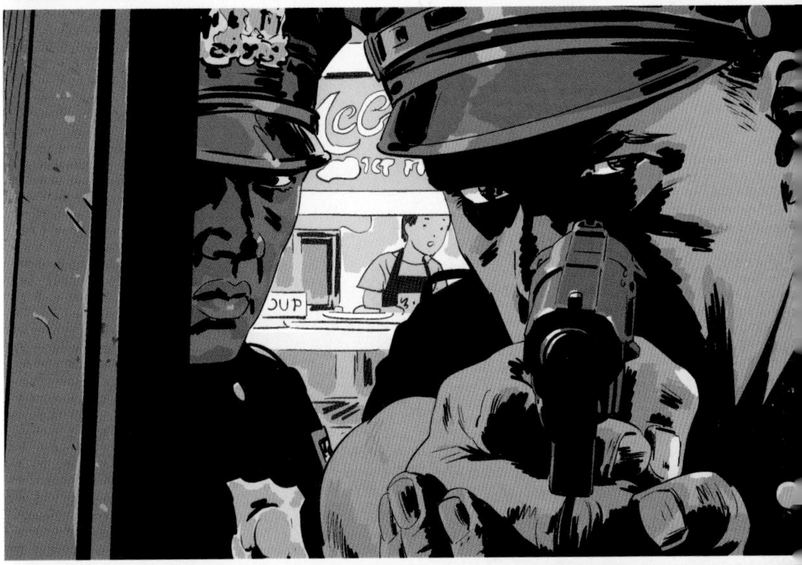

It's like all the rules we follow without thinking, knowing something bad will happen if we break them... You've just said ***fuck it*** to all of that.

So what is there to be afraid of?

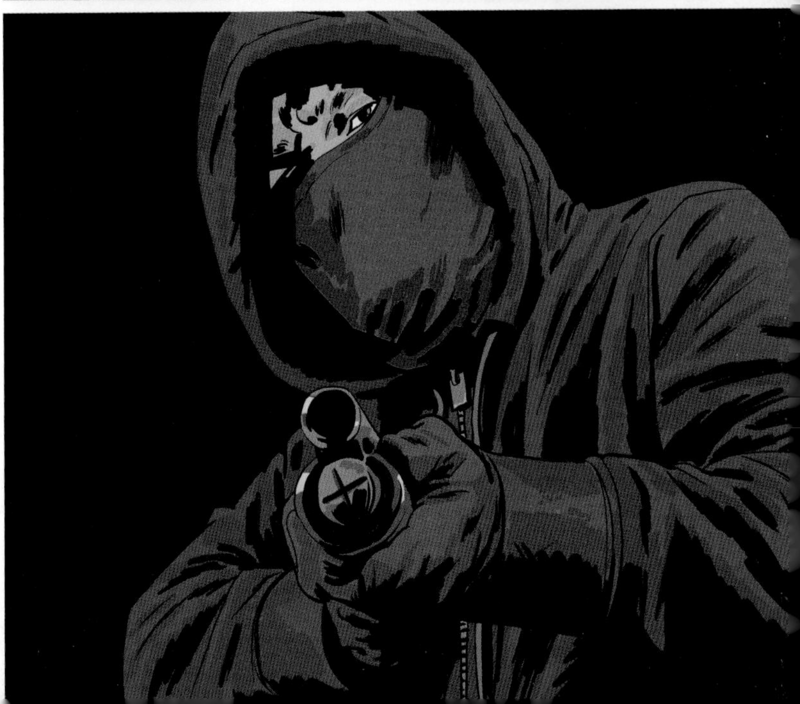

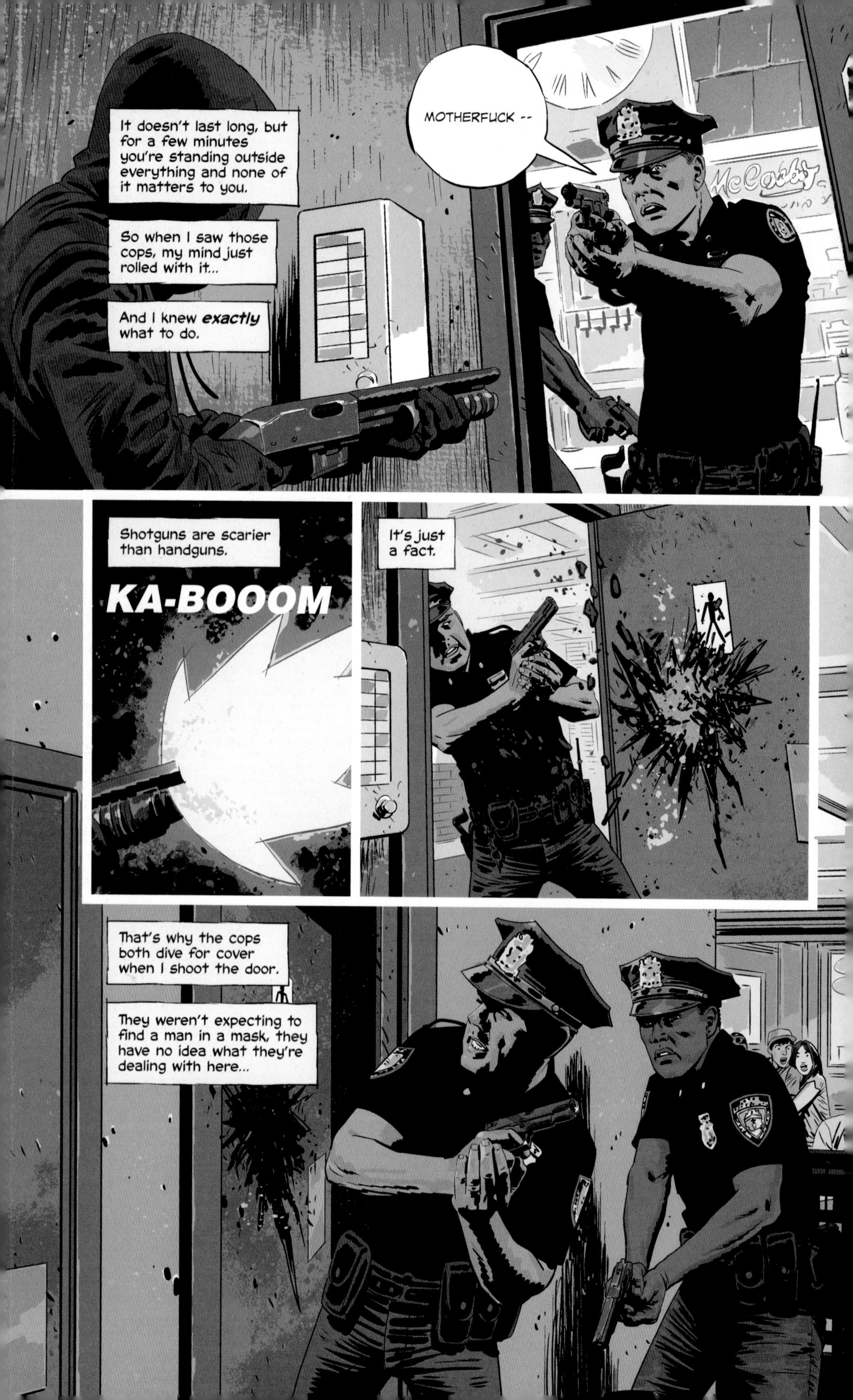
It doesn't last long, but for a few minutes you're standing outside everything and none of it matters to you.
So when I saw those cops, my mind just rolled with it...
And I knew *exactly* what to do.
MOTHERFUCK --
Shotguns are scarier than handguns.
KA-BOOOM
It's just a fact.
That's why the cops both dive for cover when I shoot the door.
They weren't expecting to find a man in a mask, they have no idea what they're dealing with here...

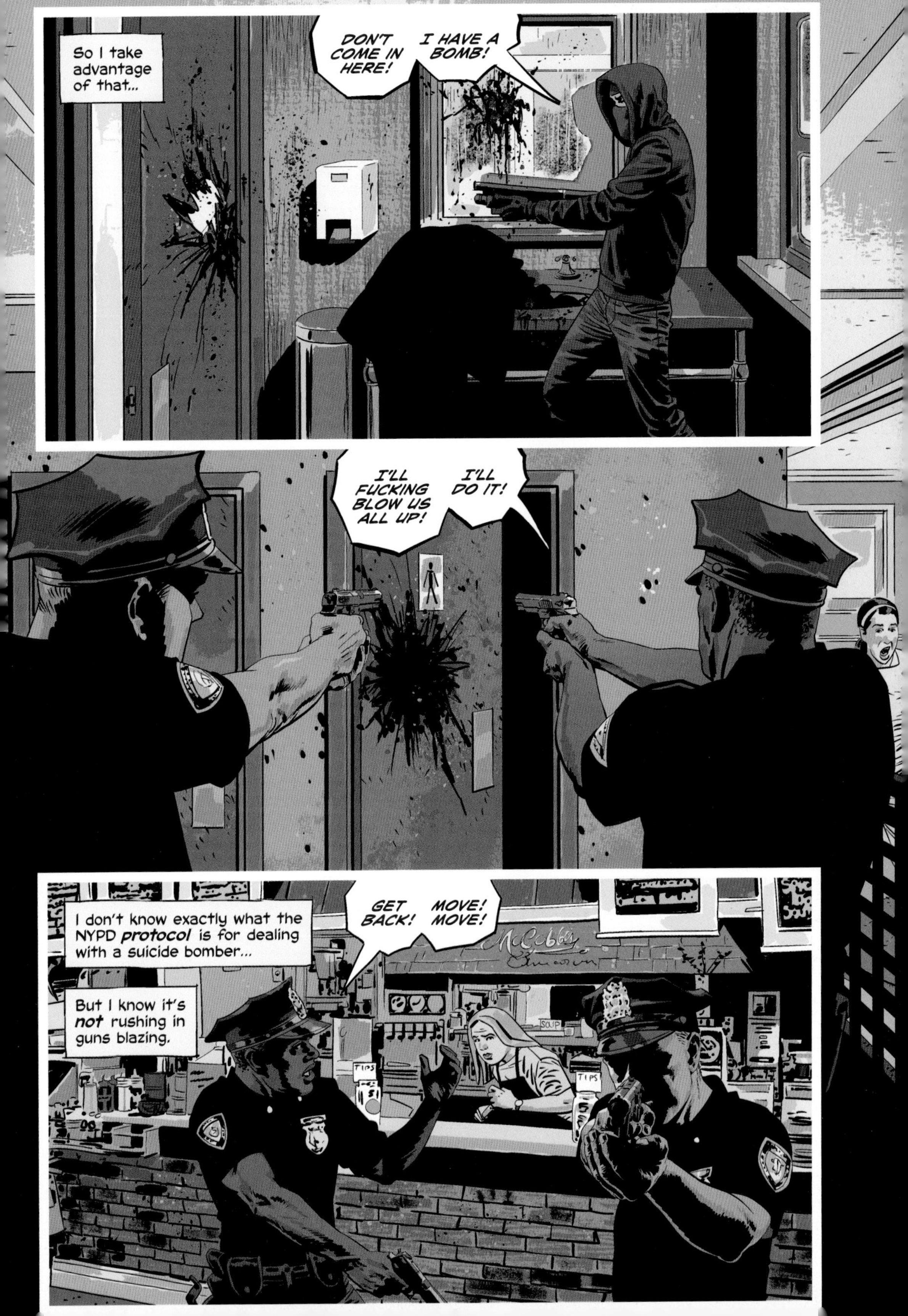
So I take advantage of that...
DON'T COME IN HERE!
I HAVE A BOMB!
I'LL FUCKING BLOW US ALL UP!
I'LL DO IT!
I don't know exactly what the NYPD *protocol* is for dealing with a suicide bomber...
GET BACK!
MOVE! MOVE!
But I know it's ***not*** rushing in guns blazing.
SOUP
TIPS
TIPS

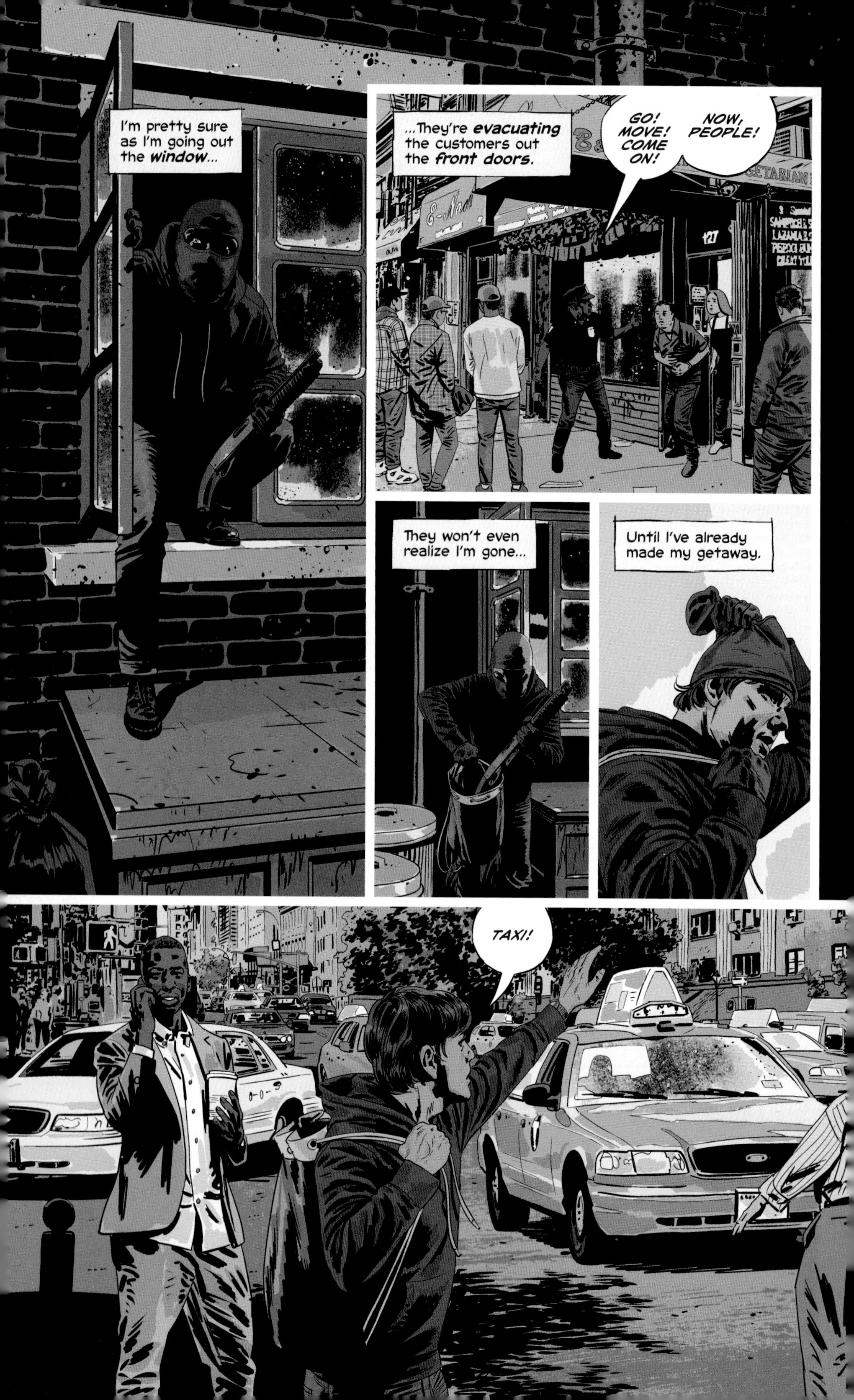
I'm pretty sure as I'm going out the *window*...
...They're *evacuating* the customers out the *front doors*.
GO! MOVE! COME ON!
NOW, PEOPLE!
127
They won't even realize I'm gone...
Until I've already made my getaway.
TAXI!

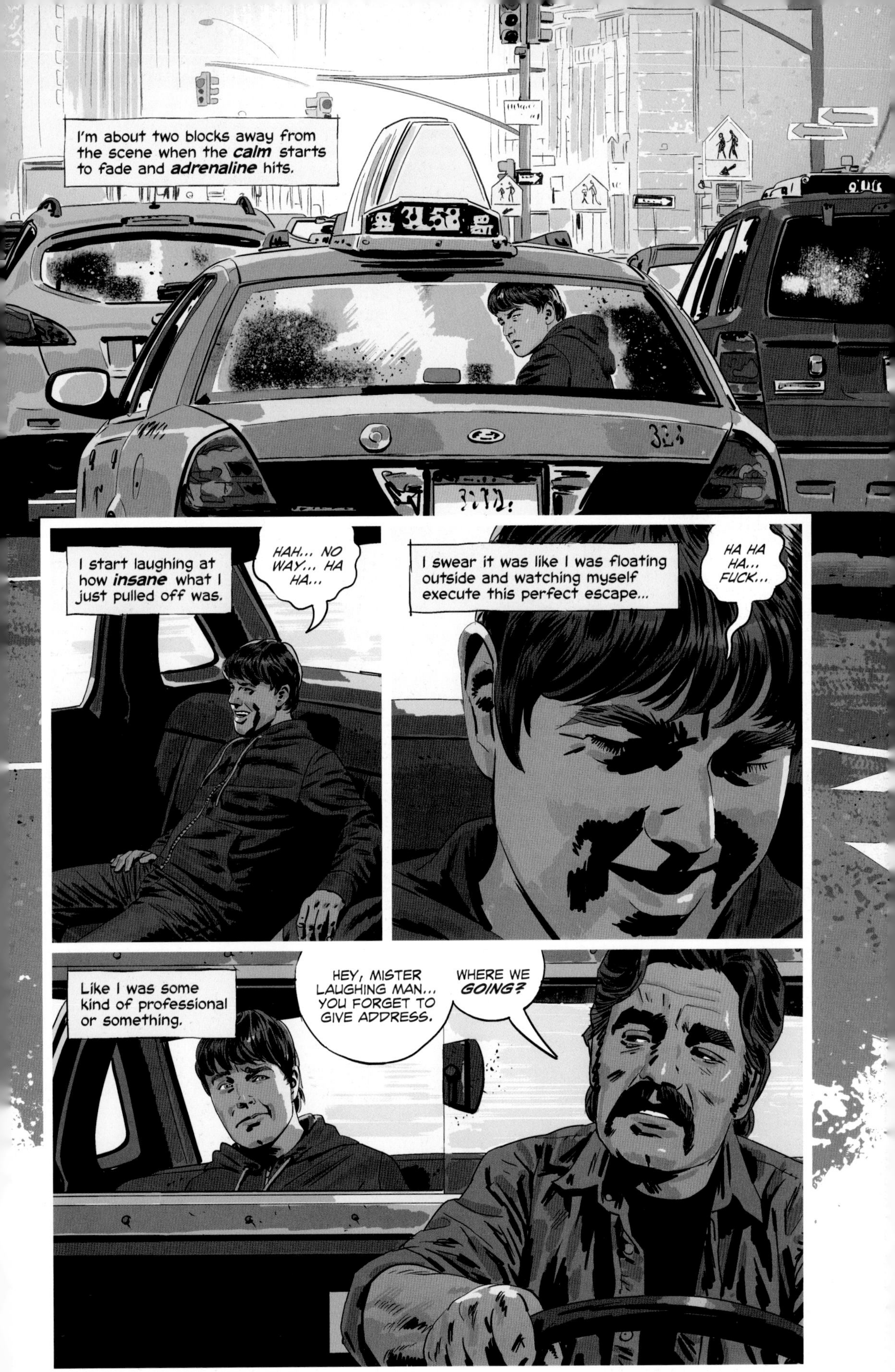
I'm about two blocks away from the scene when the *calm* starts to fade and *adrenaline* hits.
I start laughing at how *insane* what I just pulled off was.
HAH... NO WAY... HA HA...
I swear it was like I was floating outside and watching myself execute this perfect escape...
HA HA HA... FUCK...
Like I was some kind of professional or something.
HEY, MISTER LAUGHING MAN... YOU FORGET TO GIVE ADDRESS.
WHERE WE *GOING?*

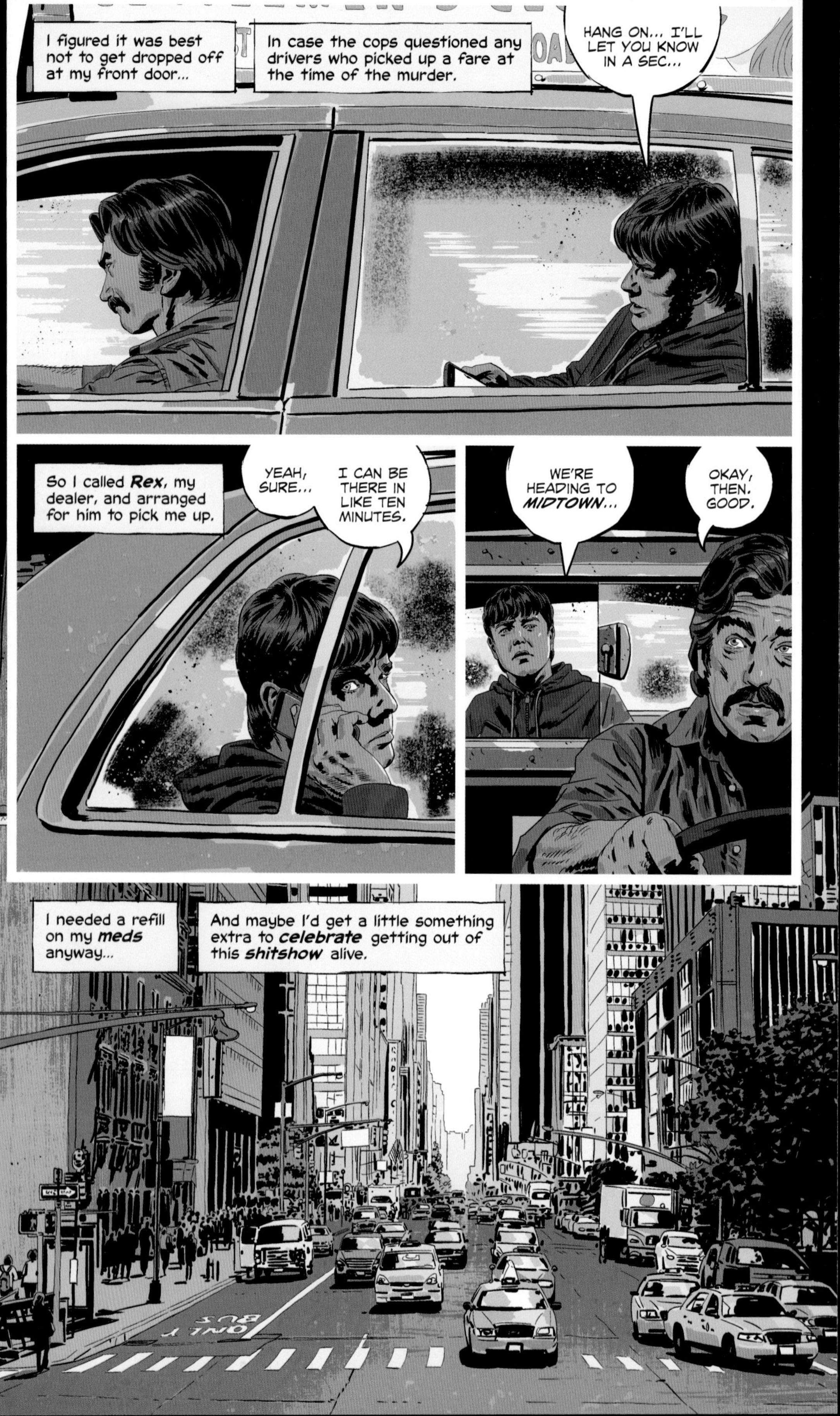

I figured it was best not to get dropped off at my front door...
In case the cops questioned any drivers who picked up a fare at the time of the murder.
HANG ON... I'LL LET YOU KNOW IN A SEC...
So I called *Rex*, my dealer, and arranged for him to pick me up.
YEAH, SURE...
I CAN BE THERE IN LIKE TEN MINUTES.
WE'RE HEADING TO *MIDTOWN*...
OKAY, THEN. GOOD.
I needed a refill on my *meds* anyway...
And maybe I'd get a little something extra to *celebrate* getting out of this *shitshow* alive.
ONLY BUS

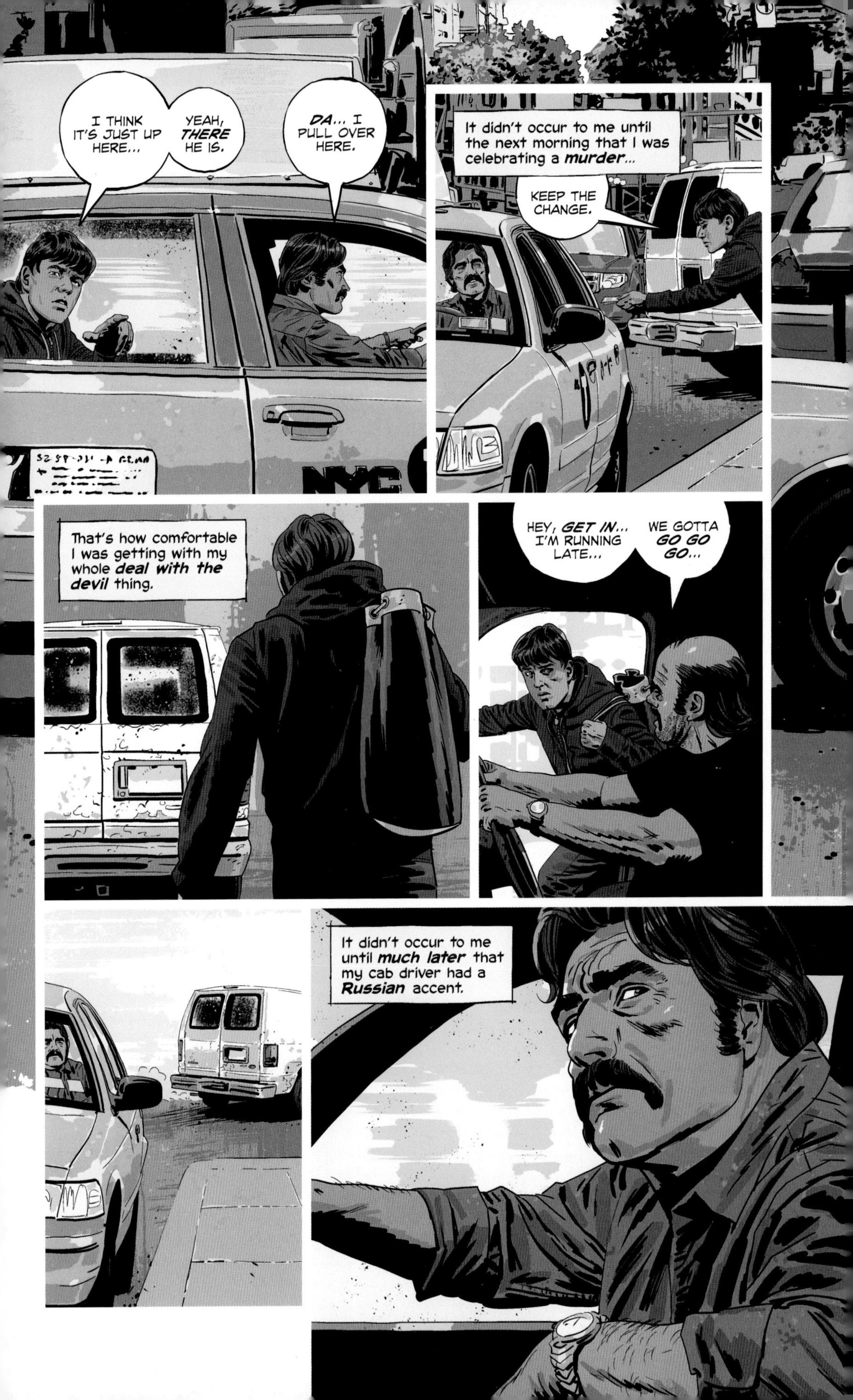
I THINK IT'S JUST UP HERE...
YEAH, *THERE* HE IS.
DA... I PULL OVER HERE.
It didn't occur to me until the next morning that I was celebrating a ***murder***...
KEEP THE CHANGE.
That's how comfortable I was getting with my whole ***deal with the devil*** thing.
HEY, ***GET IN***... I'M RUNNING LATE...
WE GOTTA ***GO GO GO***...
It didn't occur to me until ***much later*** that my cab driver had a ***Russian*** accent.
NYC

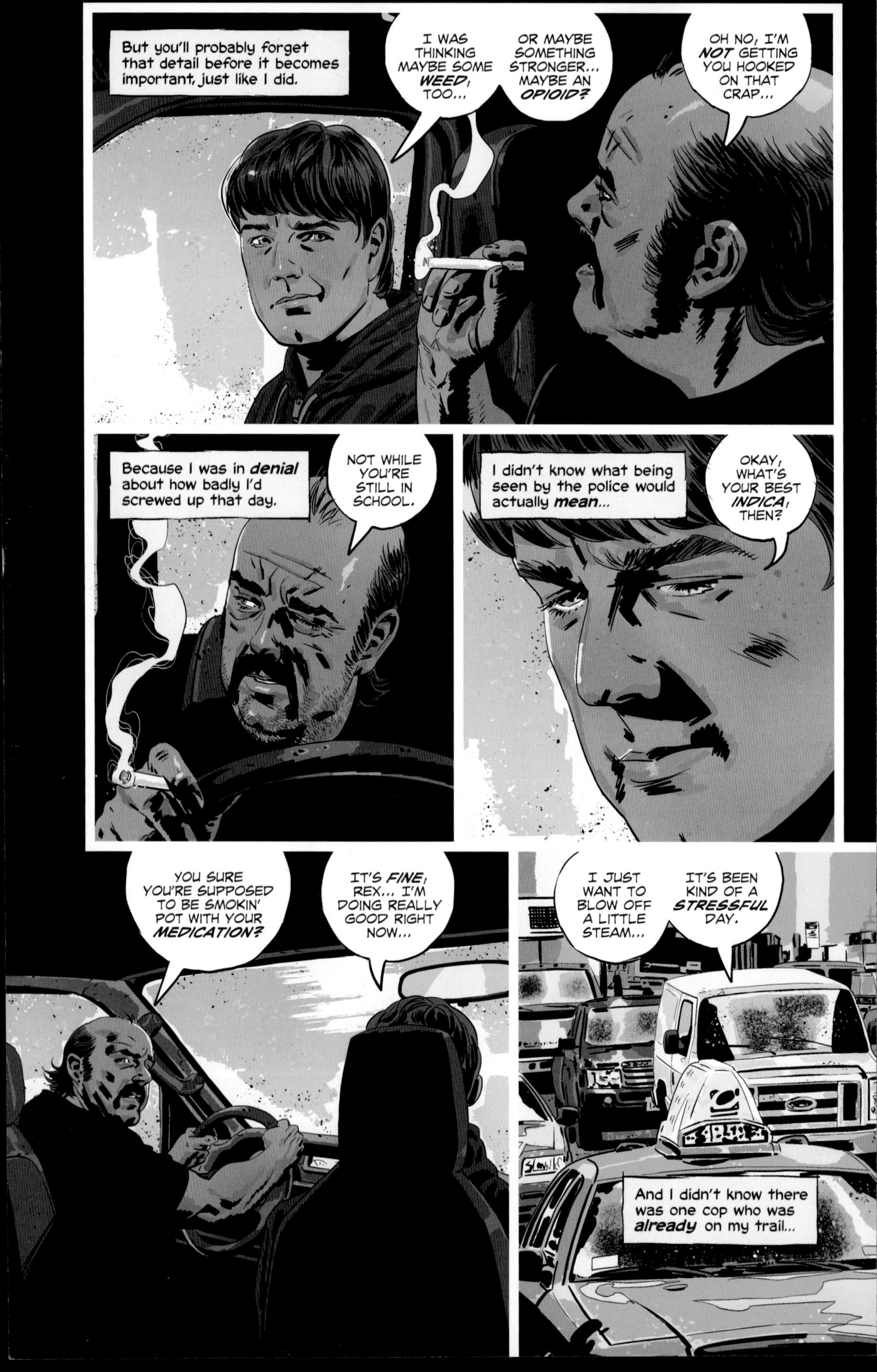
But you'll probably forget that detail before it becomes important, just like I did.
I WAS THINKING MAYBE SOME *WEED*, TOO...
OR MAYBE SOMETHING STRONGER... MAYBE AN *OPIOID?*
OH NO, I'M *NOT* GETTING YOU HOOKED ON THAT CRAP...
Because I was in *denial* about how badly I'd screwed up that day.
NOT WHILE YOU'RE STILL IN SCHOOL.
I didn't know what being seen by the police would actually *mean*...
OKAY, WHAT'S YOUR BEST *INDICA*, THEN?
YOU SURE YOU'RE SUPPOSED TO BE SMOKIN' POT WITH YOUR *MEDICATION?*
IT'S *FINE*, REX... I'M DOING REALLY GOOD RIGHT NOW...
I JUST WANT TO BLOW OFF A LITTLE STEAM...
IT'S BEEN KIND OF A *STRESSFUL* DAY.
And I didn't know there was one cop who was *already* on my trail...

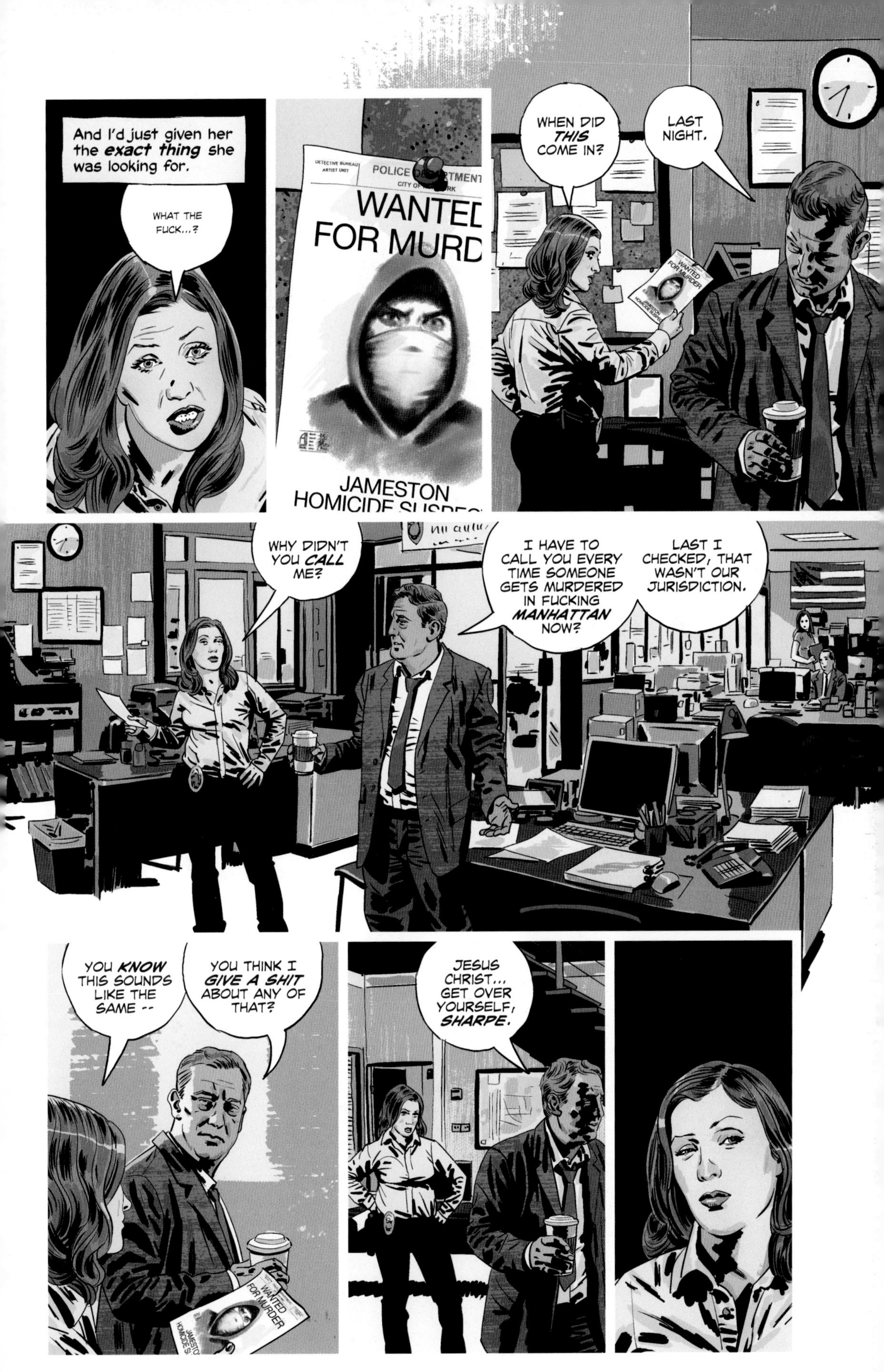
And I'd just given her the exact thing she was looking for.
WHAT THE FUCK...?
DETECTIVE BUREAU ARTIST UNIT
POLICE DEPARTMENT
WANTED FOR MURD
JAMESTON HOMICIDE SUSPEC
WHEN DID THIS COME IN?
LAST NIGHT.
WHY DIDN'T YOU CALL ME?
I HAVE TO CALL YOU EVERY TIME SOMEONE GETS MURDERED IN FUCKING MANHATTAN NOW?
LAST I CHECKED, THAT WASN'T OUR JURISDICTION.
YOU KNOW THIS SOUNDS LIKE THE SAME --
YOU THINK I GIVE A SHIT ABOUT ANY OF THAT?
JESUS CHRIST... GET OVER YOURSELF, SHARPE.

Lily Sharpe was the detective on the night shift in ***Port Chester*** when I shot Mark McLaren - my first target.

She was also the one who found Mark's secret laptop full of ***kiddie porn*** and linked him to an entire ring of child molesters.

But as it turns out, that was pretty much the ***high point*** of Lily's time in the Port Chester PD so far.

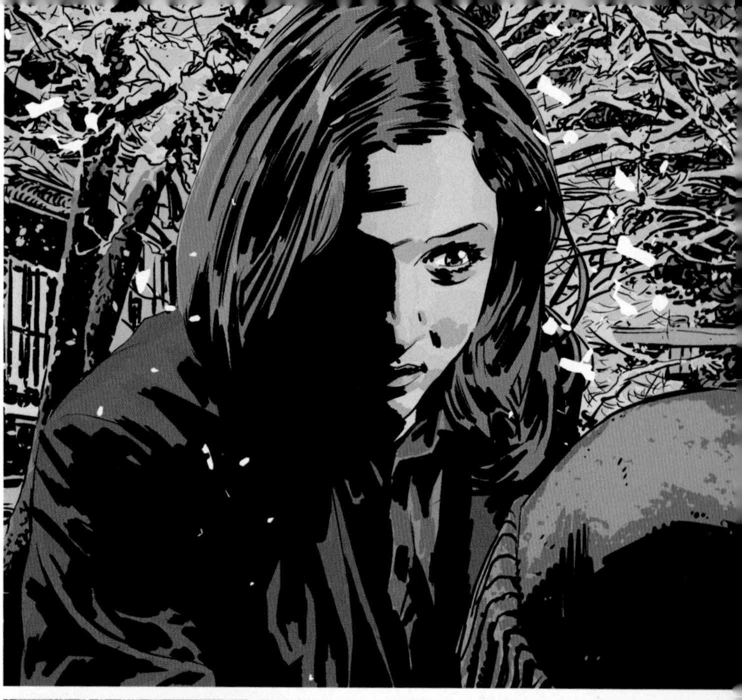

Lily had been hired after a scandal. The Chief had made a big show of bringing in ***new faces***, like he was revamping the department.

So she knew exactly how she'd be seen by the rest of the squad - as an outside hire, someone there for political reasons.

She knew they'd resent that, but she took the job anyway.

The money was better and she didn't care what anyone thought about her.

If they wanted to be retro-cliché chauvinist assholes, that was their problem, not hers.

No, the thing that really bothered Lily Sharpe was ***apathy***, which is most of what you see from the government.

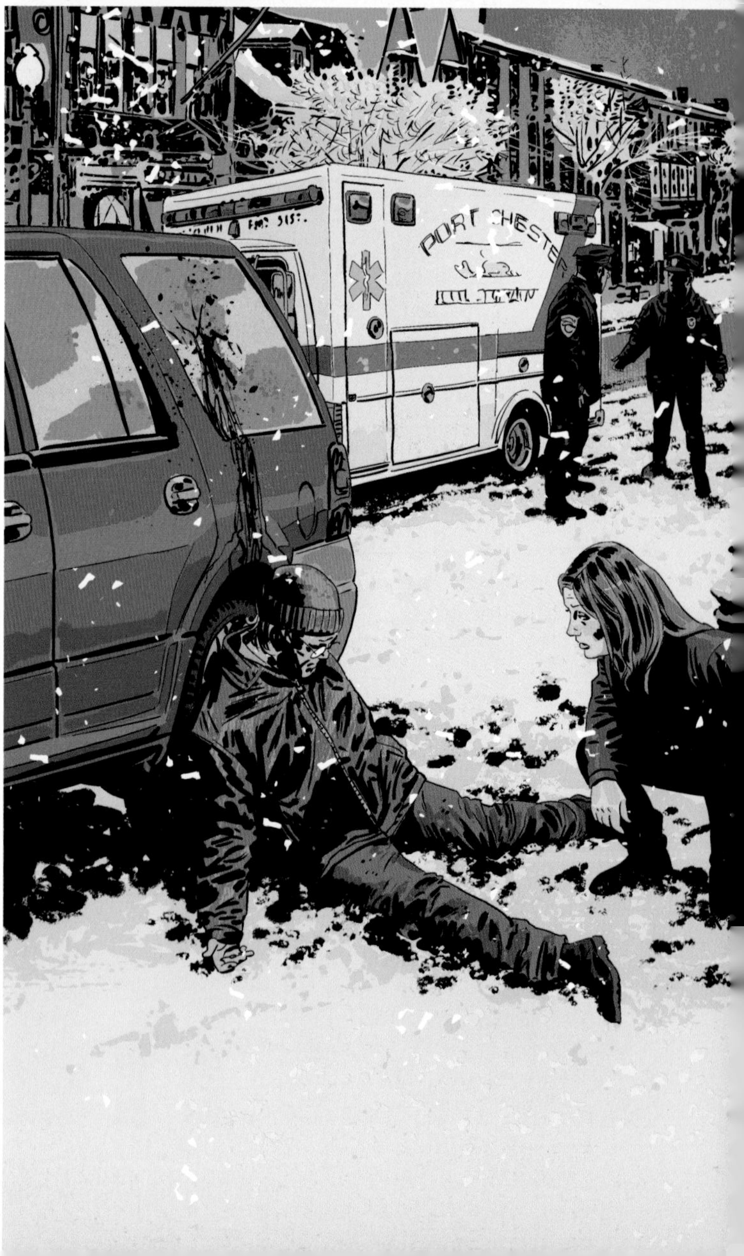
PORT CHESTER

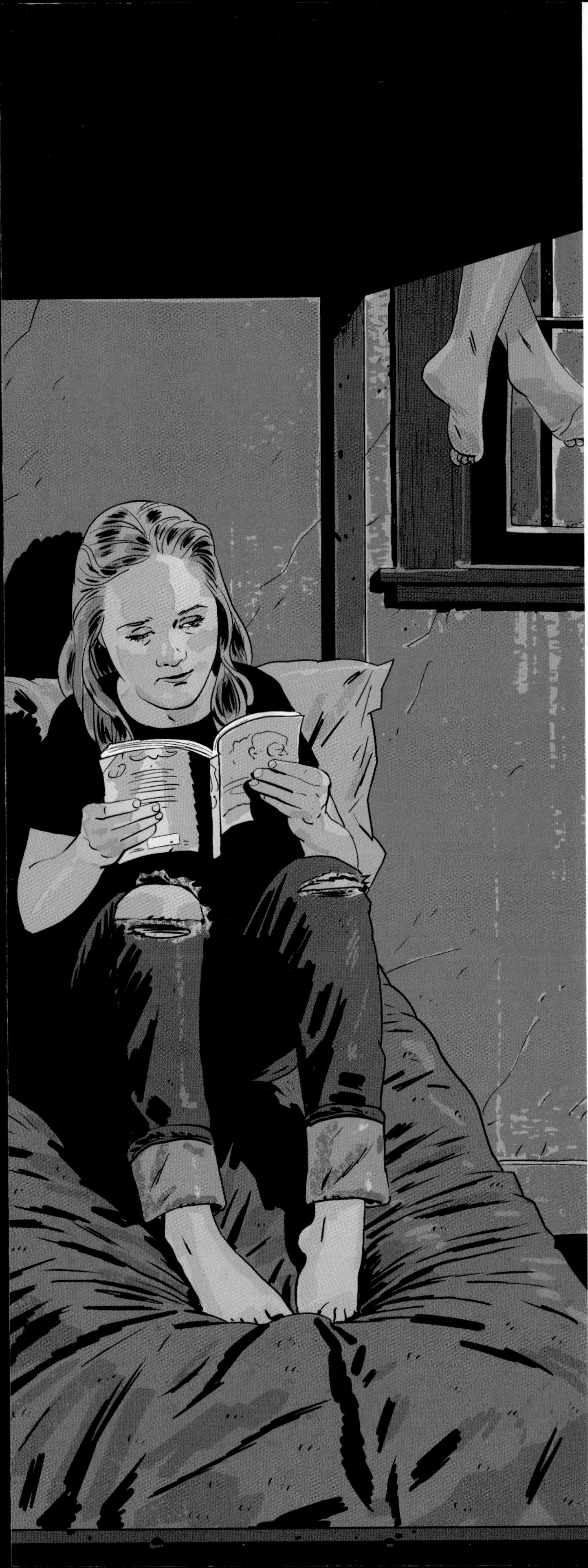

Lily was raised in ***foster care***, so she'd been dealing with the broken parts of our system since she was a kid.

And she'd seen that government apathy too many times.

On the faces of social workers who sent her back to group homes...

On the faces of judges and lawyers...

And even the IRS agent who decided to audit her last year.

And yeah, she'd seen corruption and incompetence all over the place, too, but even that didn't bother her as much as that ***look***...

The one that says "I don't give a shit" and "I'm not listening" at the same time.

It's a special kind of laziness unique to government work, that inability to care.

There's just something about being part of the system that makes you feel like giving up, I guess...

And Lily had spent her whole life fighting that feeling.

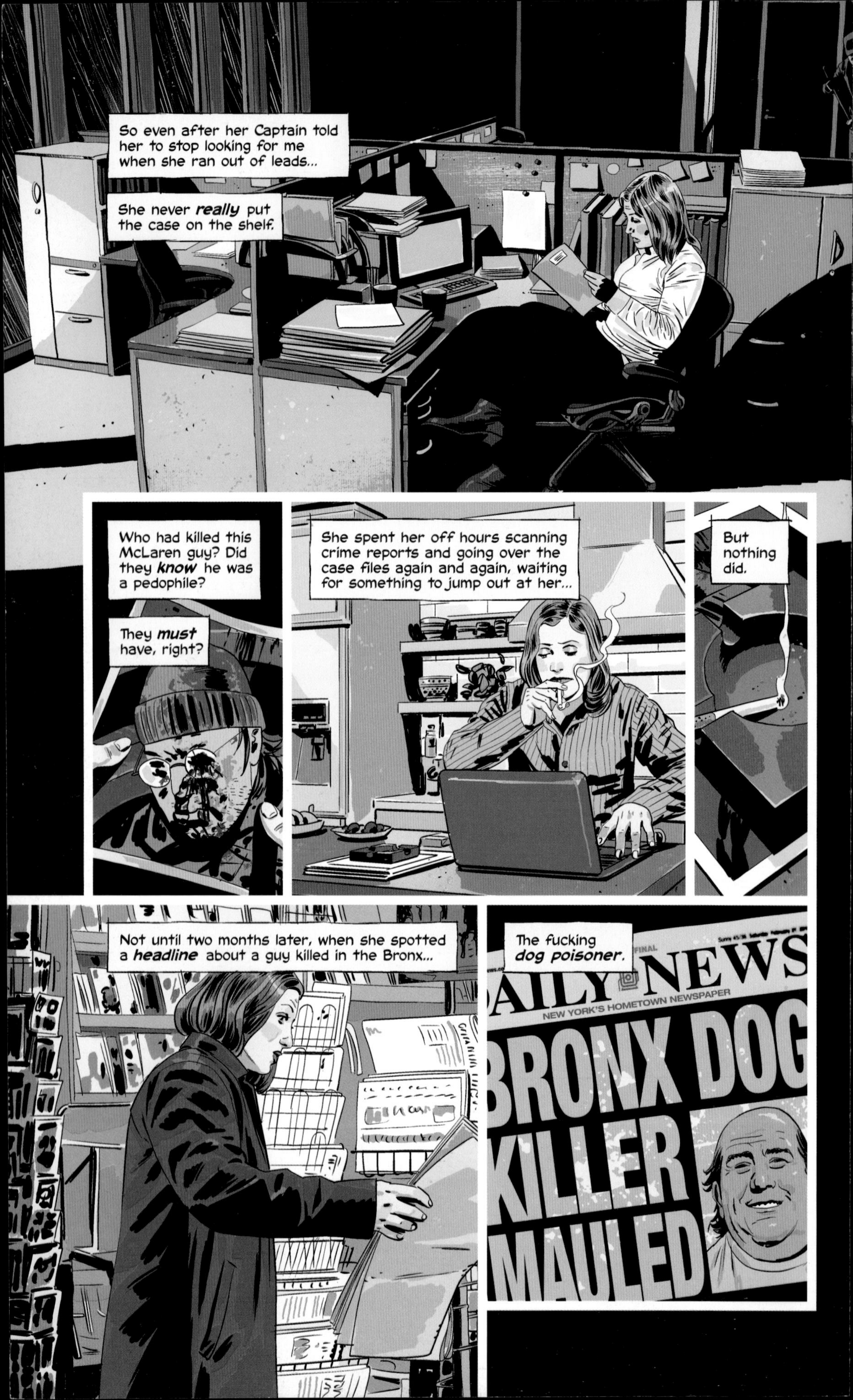

So even after her Captain told her to stop looking for me when she ran out of leads...
She never *really* put the case on the shelf.
Who had killed this McLaren guy? Did they *know* he was a pedophile?
They *must* have, right?
She spent her off hours scanning crime reports and going over the case files again and again, waiting for something to jump out at her...
But nothing did.
Not until two months later, when she spotted a *headline* about a guy killed in the Bronx...
The fucking *dog poisoner*.
FINAL
AILY NEWS
NEW YORK'S HOMETOWN NEWSPAPER
BRONX DOG KILLER MAULED

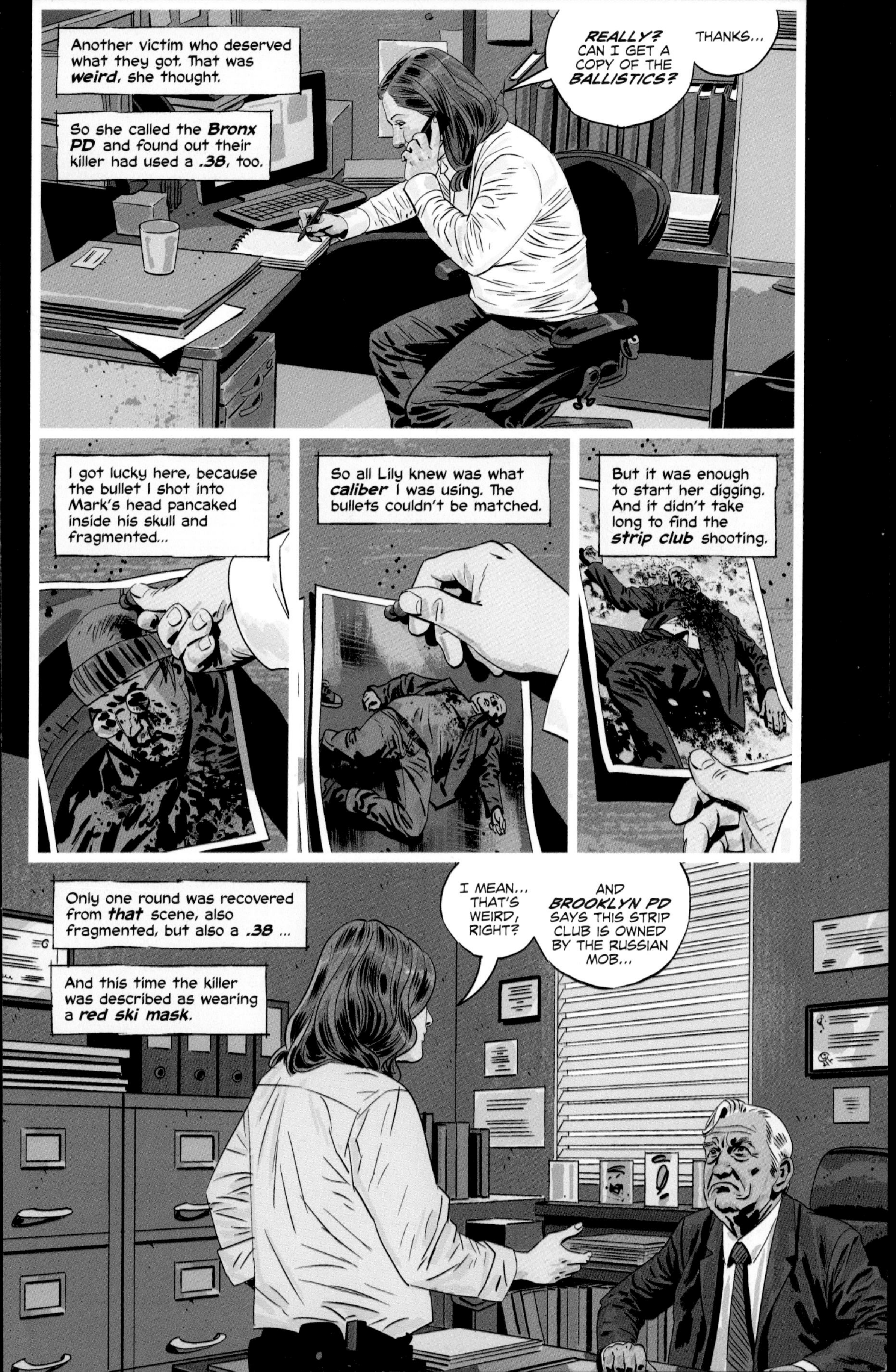

Another victim who deserved what they got. That was *weird*, she thought.
So she called the *Bronx PD* and found out their killer had used a *.38*, too.
REALLY? CAN I GET A COPY OF THE *BALLISTICS?*
THANKS...
I got lucky here, because the bullet I shot into Mark's head pancaked inside his skull and fragmented...
So all Lily knew was what *caliber* I was using. The bullets couldn't be matched.
But it was enough to start her digging. And it didn't take long to find the *strip club* shooting.
Only one round was recovered from *that* scene, also fragmented, but also a *.38* ...
And this time the killer was described as wearing a *red ski mask*.
I MEAN... THAT'S WEIRD, RIGHT?
AND *BROOKLYN PD* SAYS THIS STRIP CLUB IS OWNED BY THE RUSSIAN MOB...

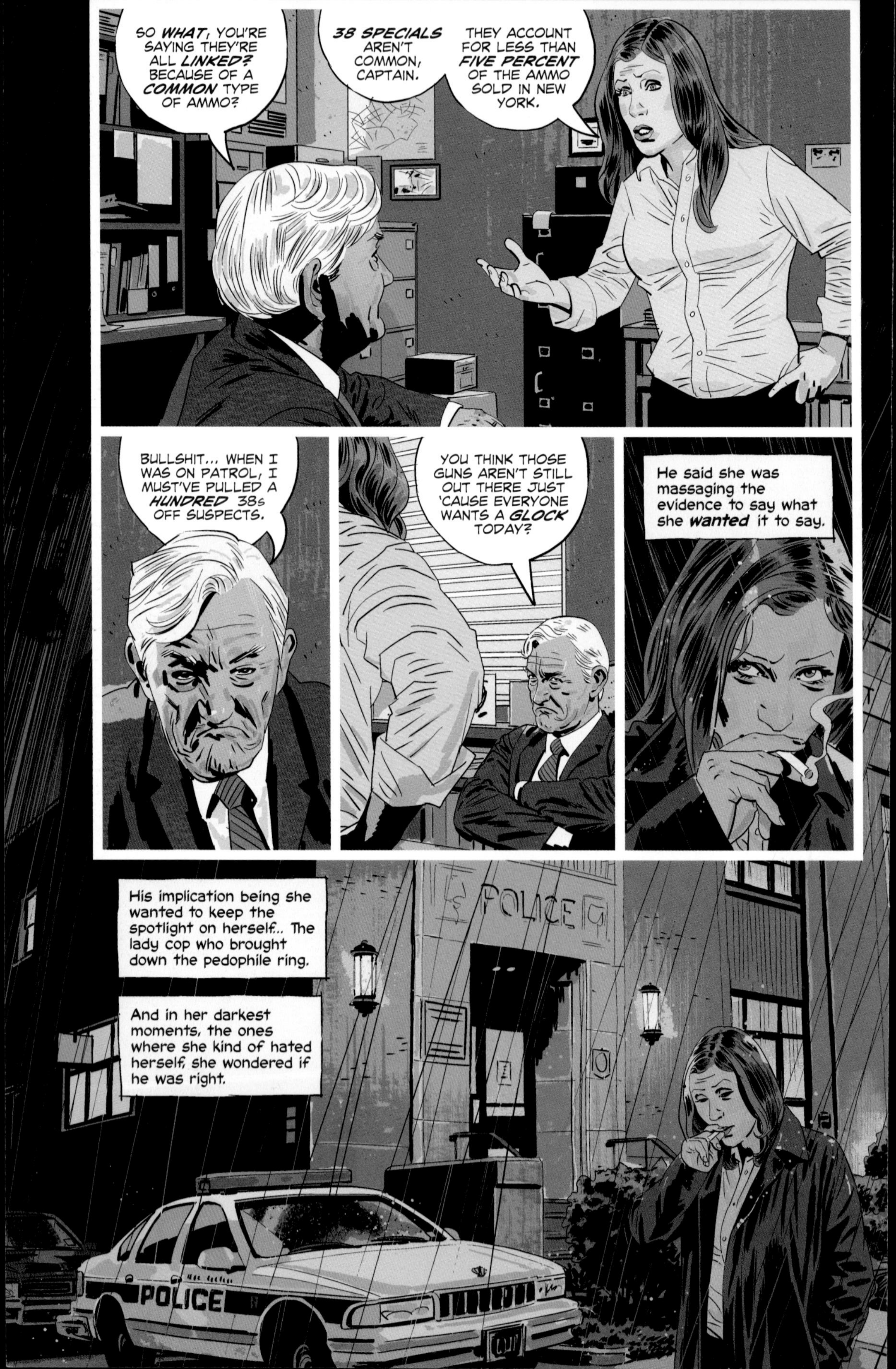
SO WHAT, YOU'RE SAYING THEY'RE ALL LINKED? BECAUSE OF A COMMON TYPE OF AMMO?
38 SPECIALS AREN'T COMMON, CAPTAIN.
THEY ACCOUNT FOR LESS THAN FIVE PERCENT OF THE AMMO SOLD IN NEW YORK.
BULLSHIT... WHEN I WAS ON PATROL, I MUST'VE PULLED A HUNDRED 38s OFF SUSPECTS.
YOU THINK THOSE GUNS AREN'T STILL OUT THERE JUST 'CAUSE EVERYONE WANTS A GLOCK TODAY?
He said she was massaging the evidence to say what she wanted it to say.
His implication being she wanted to keep the spotlight on herself.. The lady cop who brought down the pedophile ring.
And in her darkest moments, the ones where she kind of hated herself, she wondered if he was right.
POLICE
POLICE

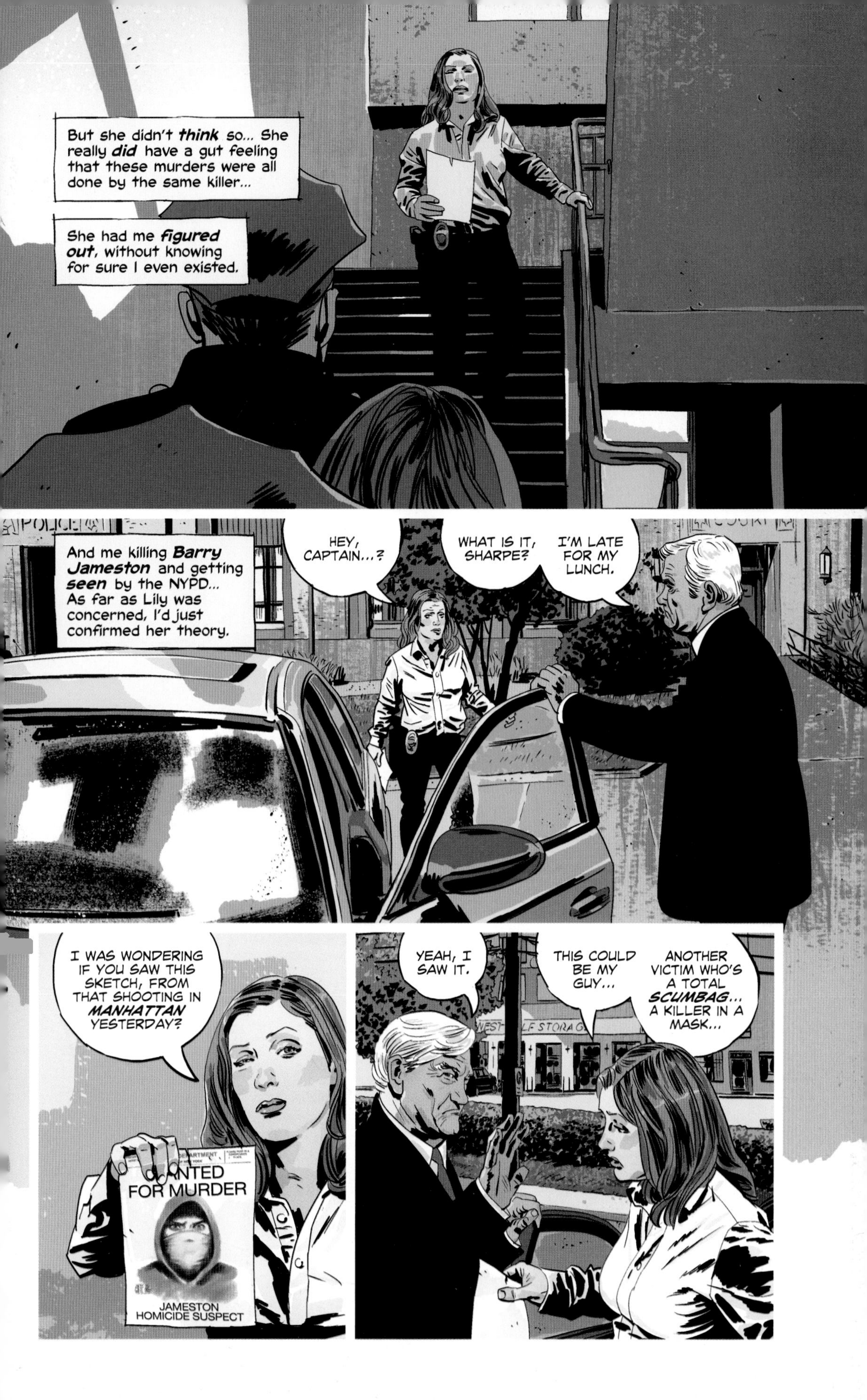
But she didn't *think* so... She really *did* have a gut feeling that these murders were all done by the same killer...
She had me *figured out*, without knowing for sure I even existed.
And me killing *Barry Jameston* and getting *seen* by the NYPD... As far as Lily was concerned, I'd just confirmed her theory.
HEY, CAPTAIN...?
WHAT IS IT, SHARPE?
I'M LATE FOR MY LUNCH.
I WAS WONDERING IF YOU SAW THIS SKETCH, FROM THAT SHOOTING IN *MANHATTAN* YESTERDAY?
FOR MURDER
JAMESTON
HOMICIDE SUSPECT
YEAH, I SAW IT.
THIS COULD BE MY GUY...
ANOTHER VICTIM WHO'S A TOTAL *SCUMBAG*... A KILLER IN A MASK...

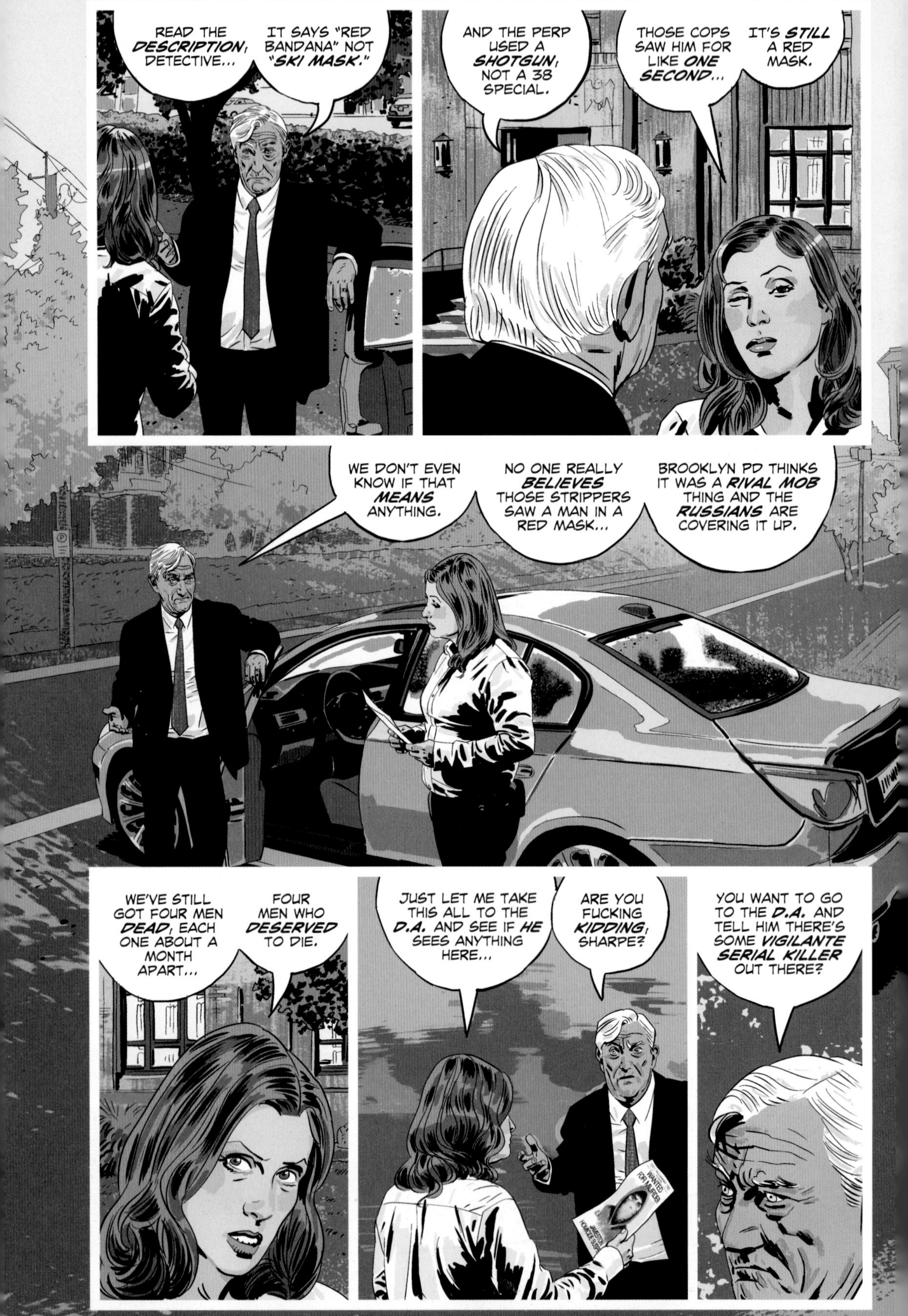
READ THE DESCRIPTION, DETECTIVE...
IT SAYS "RED BANDANA" NOT "SKI MASK."
AND THE PERP USED A SHOTGUN, NOT A 38 SPECIAL.
THOSE COPS SAW HIM FOR LIKE ONE SECOND...
IT'S STILL A RED MASK.
WE DON'T EVEN KNOW IF THAT MEANS ANYTHING.
NO ONE REALLY BELIEVES THOSE STRIPPERS SAW A MAN IN A RED MASK...
BROOKLYN PD THINKS IT WAS A RIVAL MOB THING AND THE RUSSIANS ARE COVERING IT UP.
WE'VE STILL GOT FOUR MEN DEAD, EACH ONE ABOUT A MONTH APART...
FOUR MEN WHO DESERVED TO DIE.
JUST LET ME TAKE THIS ALL TO THE D.A. AND SEE IF HE SEES ANYTHING HERE...
ARE YOU FUCKING KIDDING, SHARPE?
YOU WANT TO GO TO THE D.A. AND TELL HIM THERE'S SOME VIGILANTE SERIAL KILLER OUT THERE?
WANTED FOR MURDER

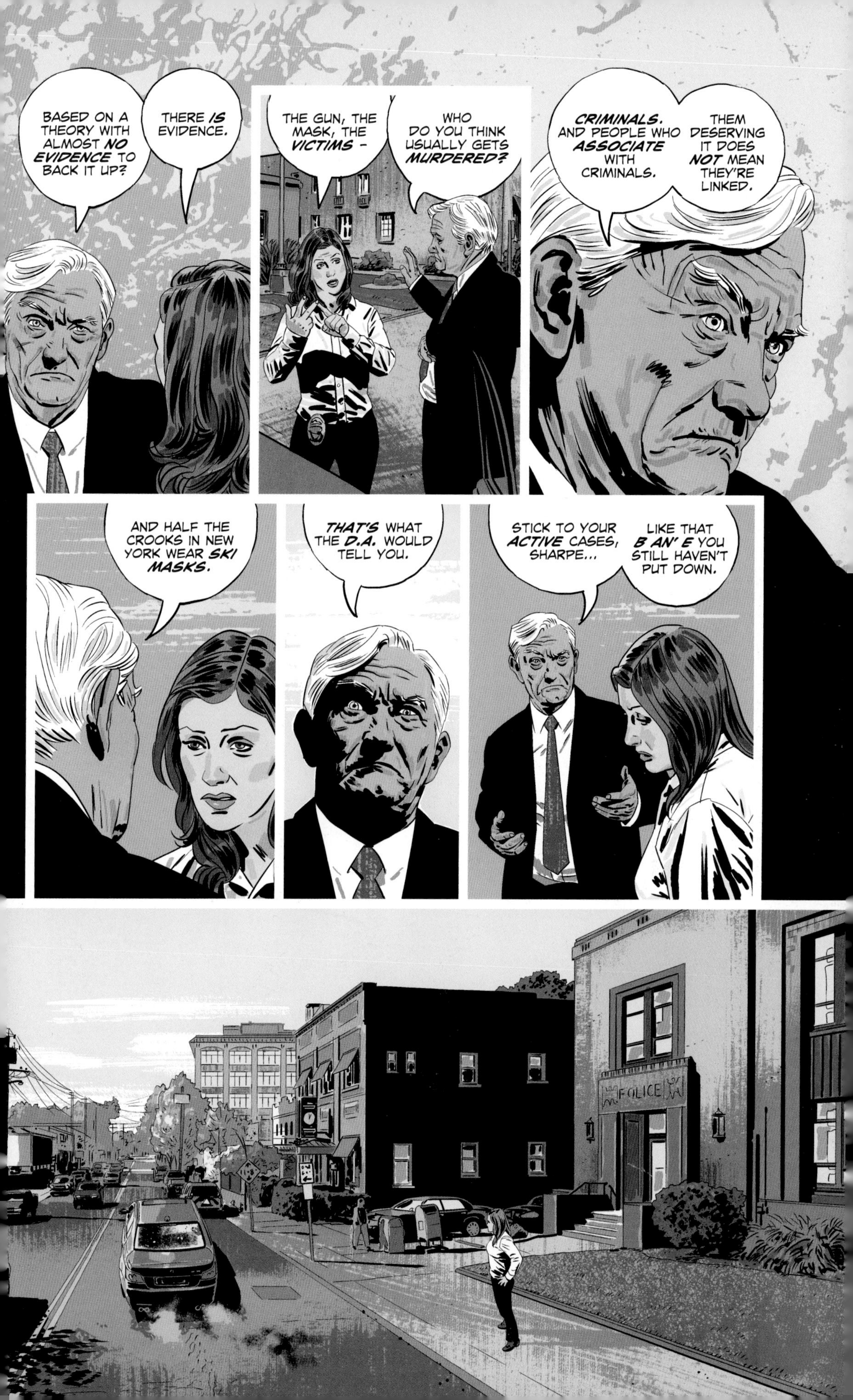
BASED ON A THEORY WITH ALMOST NO EVIDENCE TO BACK IT UP?
THERE IS EVIDENCE.
THE GUN, THE MASK, THE VICTIMS -
WHO DO YOU THINK USUALLY GETS MURDERED?
CRIMINALS. AND PEOPLE WHO ASSOCIATE WITH CRIMINALS.
THEM DESERVING IT DOES NOT MEAN THEY'RE LINKED.
AND HALF THE CROOKS IN NEW YORK WEAR SKI MASKS.
THAT'S WHAT THE D.A. WOULD TELL YOU.
STICK TO YOUR ACTIVE CASES, SHARPE...
LIKE THAT B AN' E YOU STILL HAVEN'T PUT DOWN.
POLICE

So yeah, it was ultimately the apathy that made Lily do what she did.

Because if the system is frustrating to deal with from the outside, it's ten times ***more*** frustrating when you're on the ***inside*** trying to get someone to listen to you.

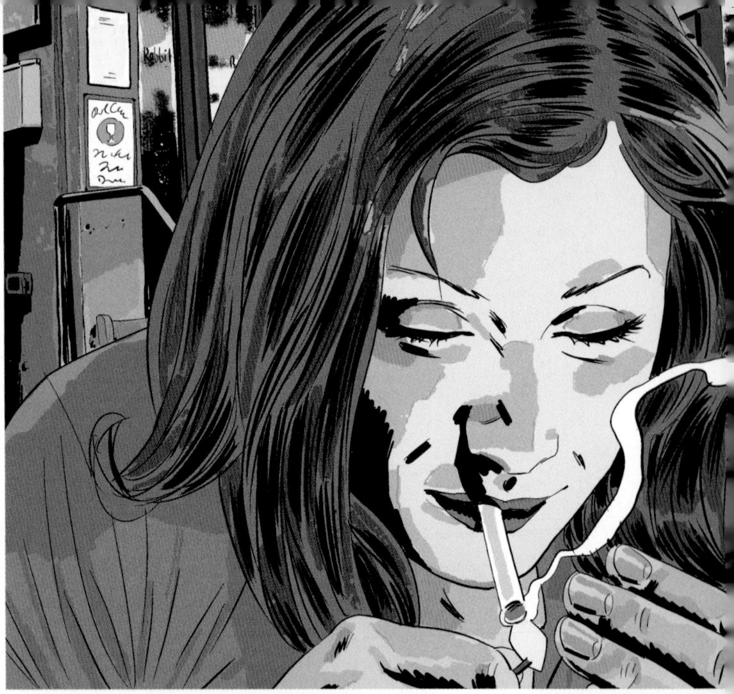

And Lily had been frustrated for too long.

Too many idiot bosses patting her ass...

Too much red tape...

And interdepartmental feuding...

Too many glass ceilings...

And way too many times when the ***man in charge*** wouldn't listen to her.

So fuck it, then. She was onto something and if her Captain was too lazy or stupid to see it, then he could suck her dick.

Metaphorically.

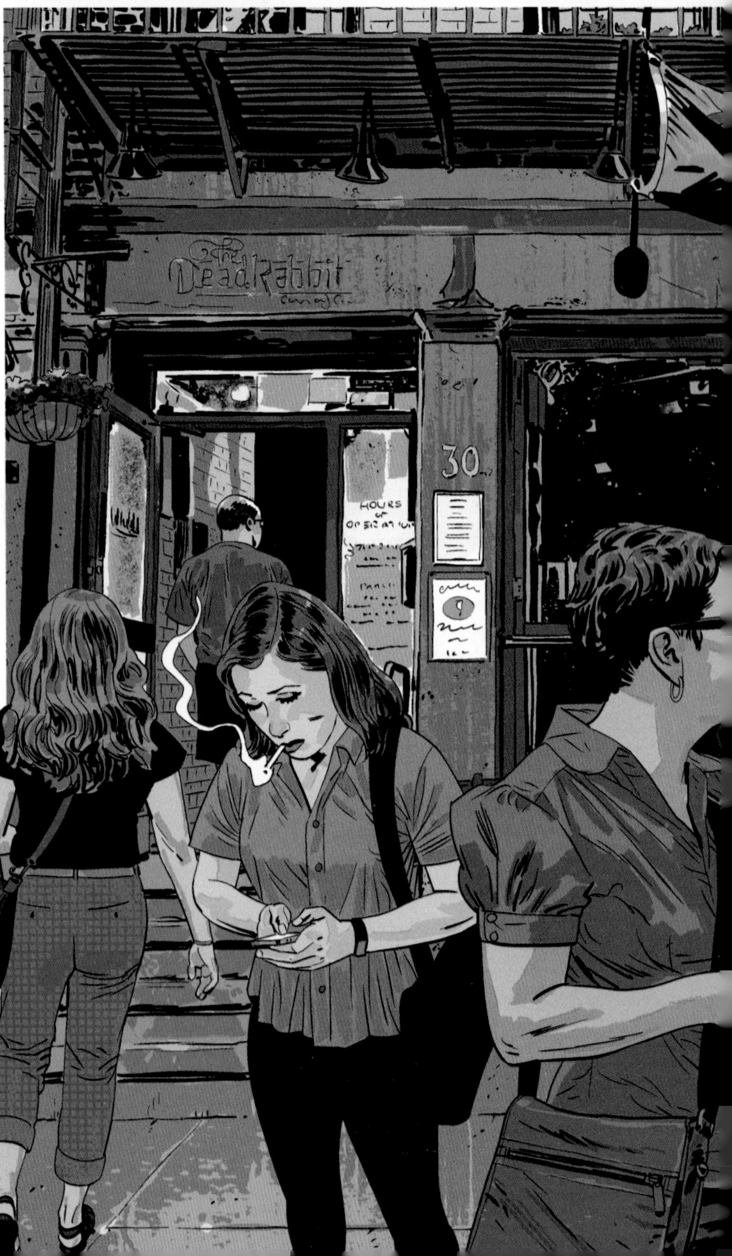
The Dead Rabbit
30
HOURS

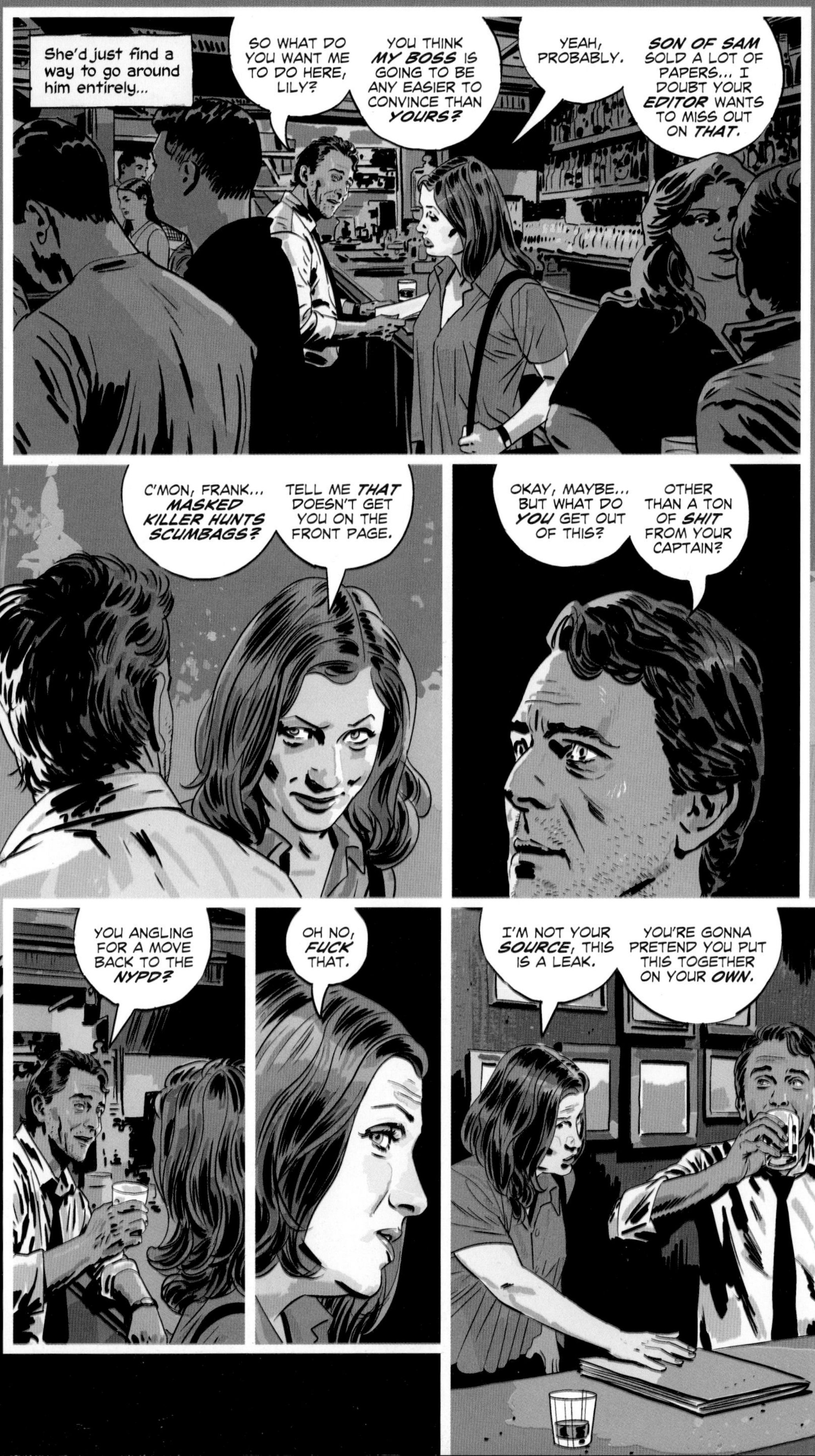

She'd just find a way to go around him entirely...
SO WHAT DO YOU WANT ME TO DO HERE, LILY?
YOU THINK MY BOSS IS GOING TO BE ANY EASIER TO CONVINCE THAN YOURS?
YEAH, PROBABLY.
SON OF SAM SOLD A LOT OF PAPERS... I DOUBT YOUR EDITOR WANTS TO MISS OUT ON THAT.
C'MON, FRANK... MASKED KILLER HUNTS SCUMBAGS?
TELL ME THAT DOESN'T GET YOU ON THE FRONT PAGE.
OKAY, MAYBE... BUT WHAT DO YOU GET OUT OF THIS?
OTHER THAN A TON OF SHIT FROM YOUR CAPTAIN?
YOU ANGLING FOR A MOVE BACK TO THE NYPD?
OH NO, FUCK THAT.
I'M NOT YOUR SOURCE, THIS IS A LEAK.
YOU'RE GONNA PRETEND YOU PUT THIS TOGETHER ON YOUR OWN.

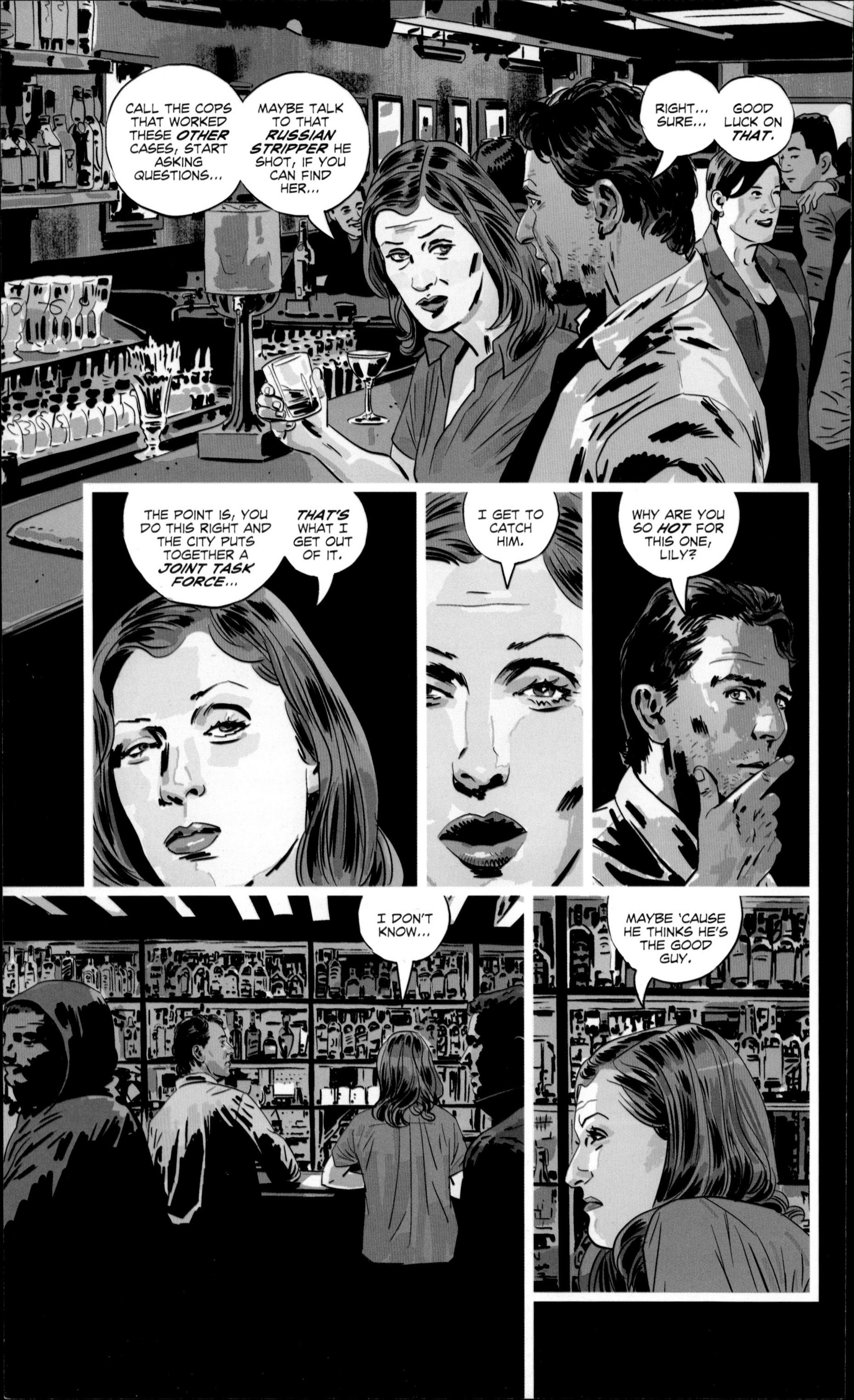
CALL THE COPS THAT WORKED THESE OTHER CASES, START ASKING QUESTIONS...
MAYBE TALK TO THAT RUSSIAN STRIPPER HE SHOT, IF YOU CAN FIND HER...
RIGHT... SURE...
GOOD LUCK ON THAT.
THE POINT IS, YOU DO THIS RIGHT AND THE CITY PUTS TOGETHER A JOINT TASK FORCE...
THAT'S WHAT I GET OUT OF IT.
I GET TO CATCH HIM.
WHY ARE YOU SO HOT FOR THIS ONE, LILY?
I DON'T KNOW...
MAYBE 'CAUSE HE THINKS HE'S THE GOOD GUY.

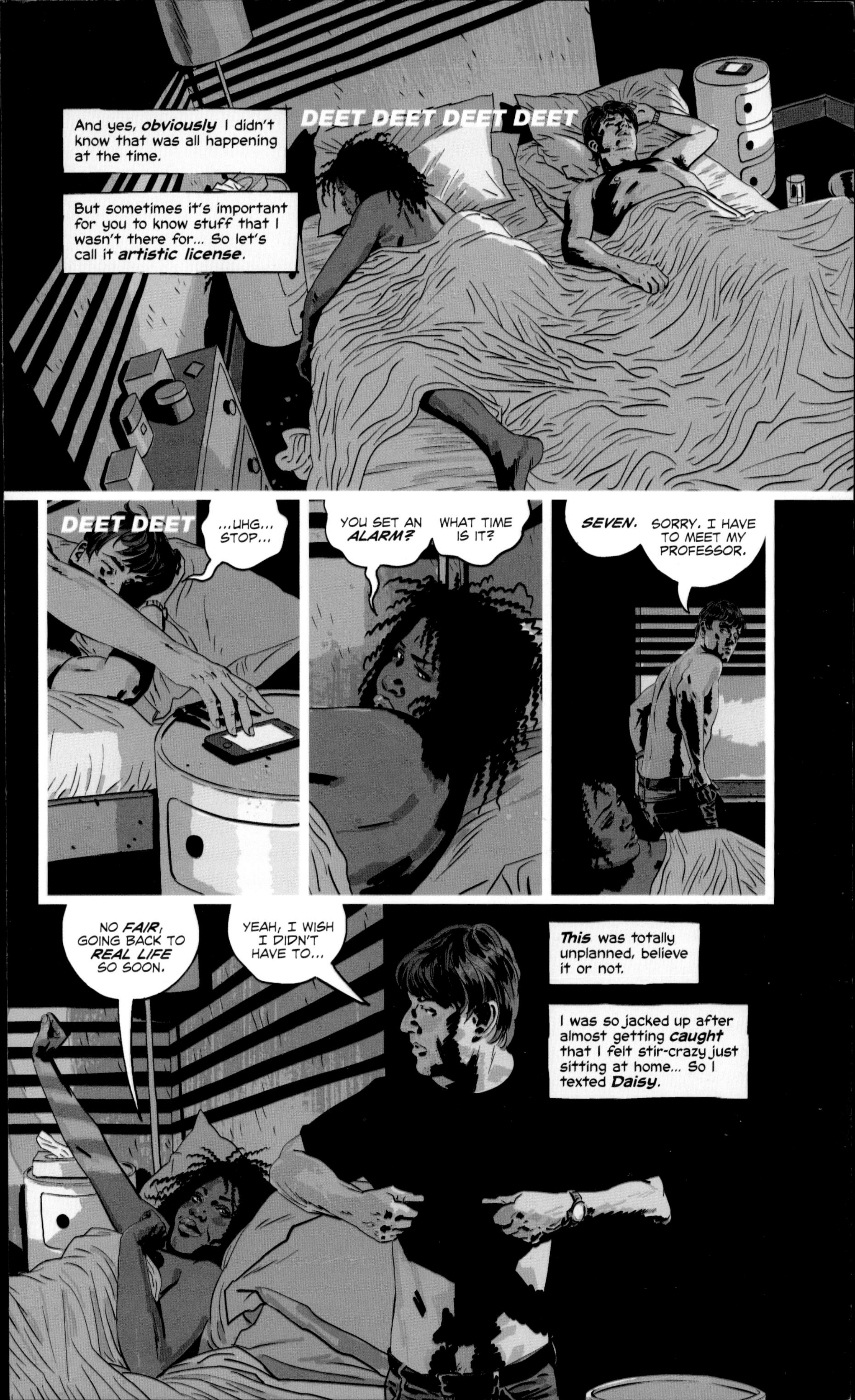
And yes, obviously I didn't know that was all happening at the time.
DEET DEET DEET DEET
But sometimes it's important for you to know stuff that I wasn't there for... So let's call it artistic license.
DEET DEET
...UHG... STOP...
YOU SET AN ALARM?
WHAT TIME IS IT?
SEVEN.
SORRY. I HAVE TO MEET MY PROFESSOR.
NO FAIR, GOING BACK TO REAL LIFE SO SOON.
YEAH, I WISH I DIDN'T HAVE TO...
This was totally unplanned, believe it or not.
I was so jacked up after almost getting caught that I felt stir-crazy just sitting at home... So I texted Daisy.

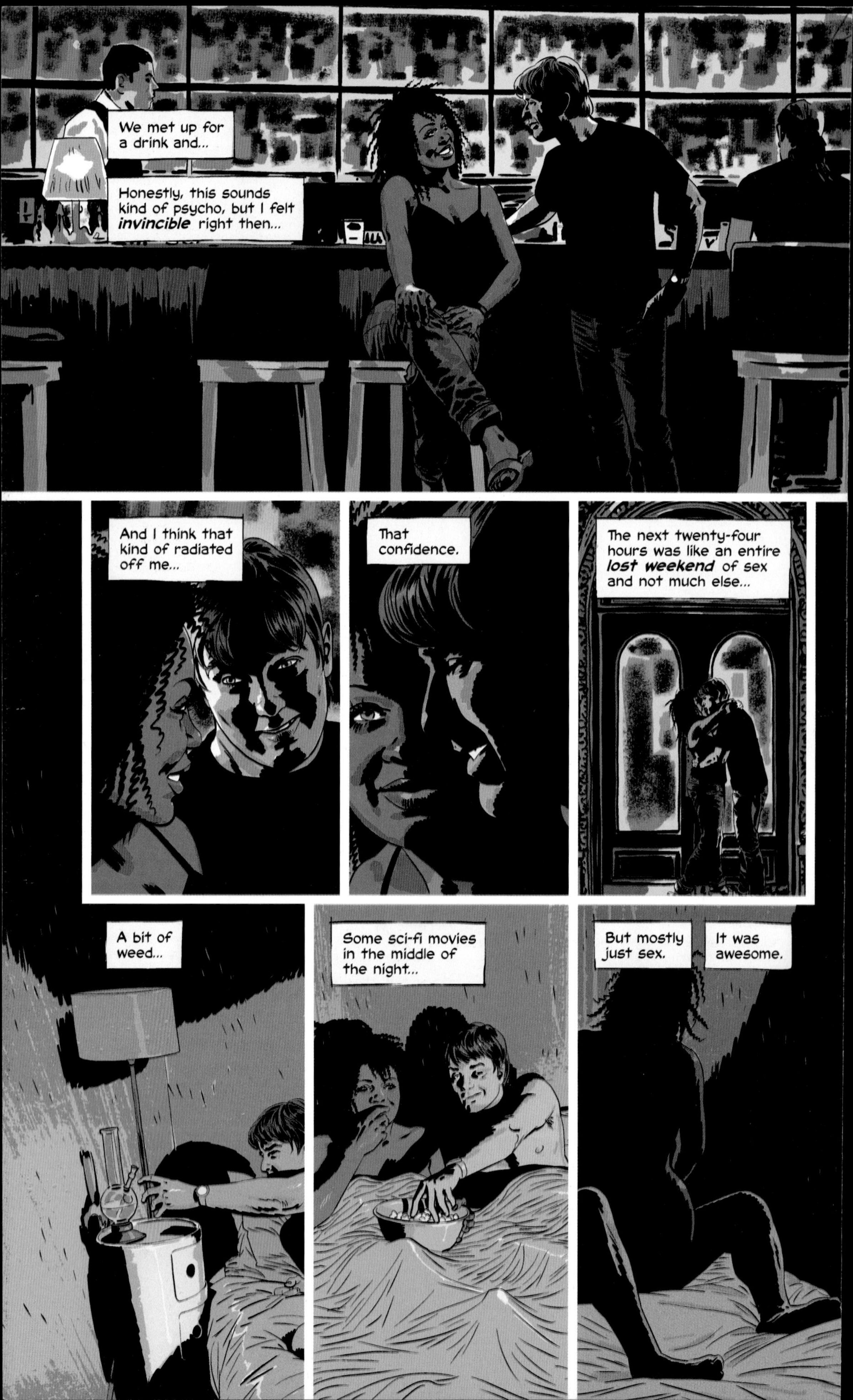
We met up for a drink and...
Honestly, this sounds kind of psycho, but I felt ***invincible*** right then...
And I think that kind of radiated off me...
That confidence.
The next twenty-four hours was like an entire ***lost weekend*** of sex and not much else...
A bit of weed...
Some sci-fi movies in the middle of the night...
But mostly just sex.
It was awesome.

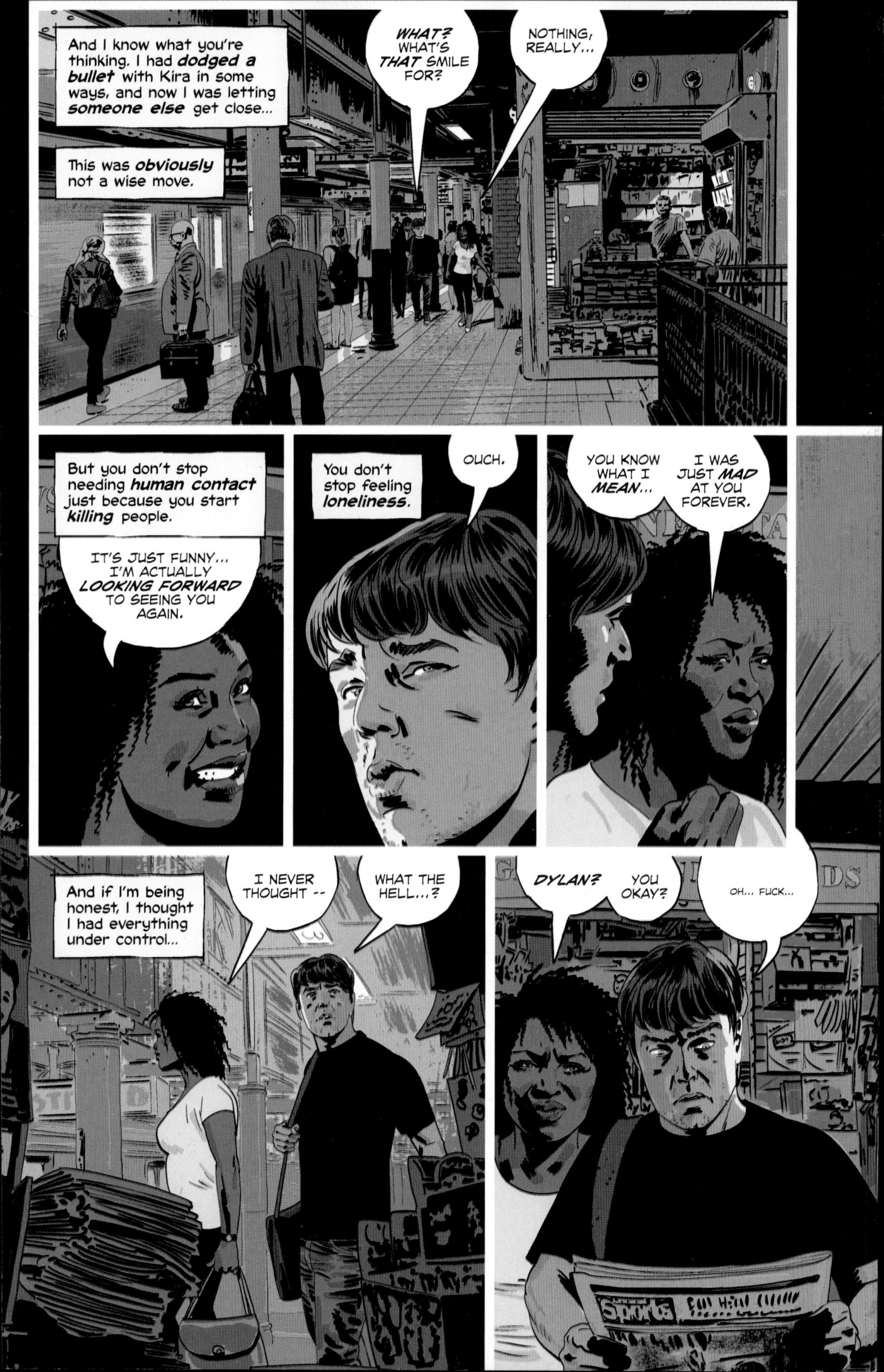
And I know what you're thinking. I had *dodged a bullet* with Kira in some ways, and now I was letting *someone else* get close...
This was *obviously* not a wise move.
WHAT? WHAT'S *THAT* SMILE FOR?
NOTHING, REALLY...
But you don't stop needing *human contact* just because you start *killing* people.
IT'S JUST FUNNY... I'M ACTUALLY *LOOKING FORWARD* TO SEEING YOU AGAIN.
You don't stop feeling *loneliness*.
OUCH.
YOU KNOW WHAT I *MEAN*...
I WAS JUST *MAD* AT YOU FOREVER.
And if I'm being honest, I thought I had everything under control...
I NEVER THOUGHT --
WHAT THE HELL...?
DYLAN?
YOU OKAY?
OH... FUCK...
Sports

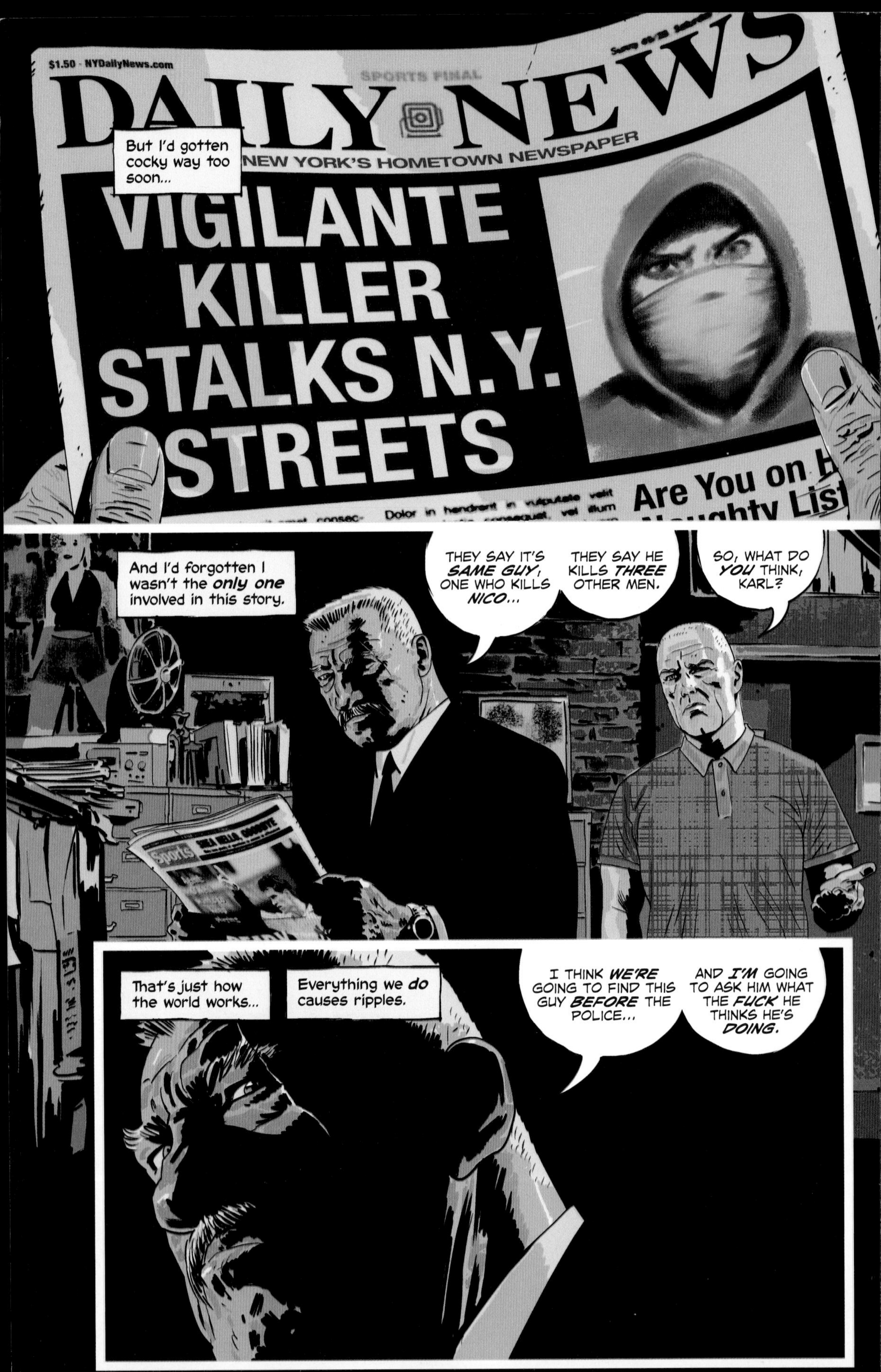

$1.50 - NYDailyNews.com
SPORTS FINAL
DAILY NEWS
But I'd gotten cocky way too soon...
NEW YORK'S HOMETOWN NEWSPAPER
VIGILANTE KILLER STALKS N.Y. STREETS
And I'd forgotten I wasn't the *only one* involved in this story.
THEY SAY IT'S *SAME GUY*, ONE WHO KILLS *NICO*...
THEY SAY HE KILLS *THREE* OTHER MEN.
SO, WHAT DO *YOU* THINK, KARL?
That's just how the world works...
Everything we *do* causes ripples.
I THINK *WE'RE* GOING TO FIND THIS GUY *BEFORE* THE POLICE...
AND *I'M* GOING TO ASK HIM WHAT THE *FUCK* HE THINKS HE'S *DOING*.

What Kira Sees

On the shelf where we kept our
photo albums there was a book my
Mom called The Family Book of
the Dead.

Among its dozen or so
pages were the faces
of those we'd lost along
the way...

There was my grandfather's older brother, Del, who was run over by a car in 1922, at age eleven.

And the twins, Wendy and Gwendy, who would have been my fourth cousins twice removed. They died in the influenza pandemic of 1918.

My great-great-granduncle, Philo, had moved West in the late 1800s and been killed by bandits on the road.

Once when my father was drunk, he told me Philo had actually been hung as a horse thief, but he denied it later.

My Grandpa Jimmy had survived Korea, but his helicopter went down in the early days of the Vietnam War.

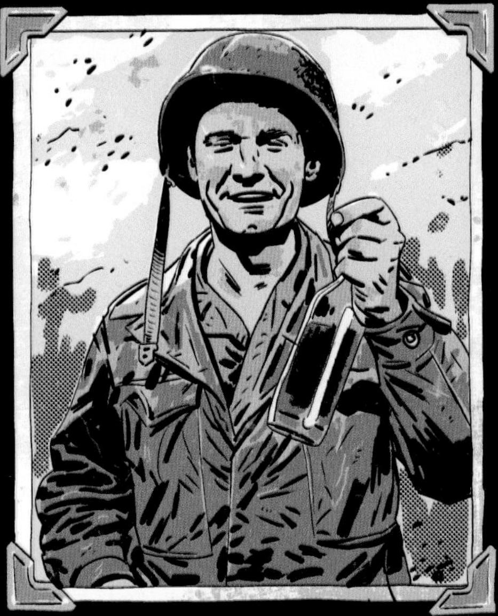

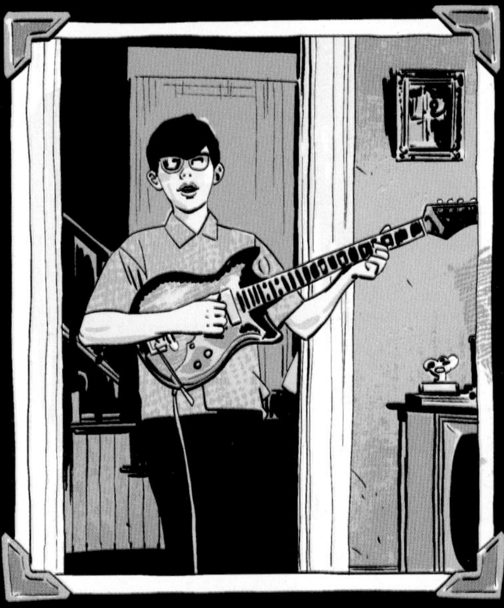

A few years after that Mom's brother, my uncle Jack, fell from a tree and fractured his collarbone. The fracture got infected and he died before the doctors even knew he was in danger.

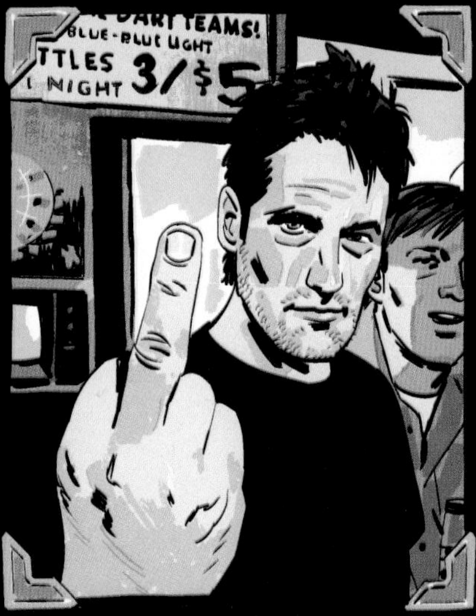
TEAMS!
BLUE-BLUE LIGHT
TTLES 3/$5
NIGHT

And of course, my dad, who had died of pancreatic cancer when I was sixteen. Mom got mad at me when I put his picture in the book.

She said I was "missing the point" and I said she didn't want to be reminded of what she'd done to him.

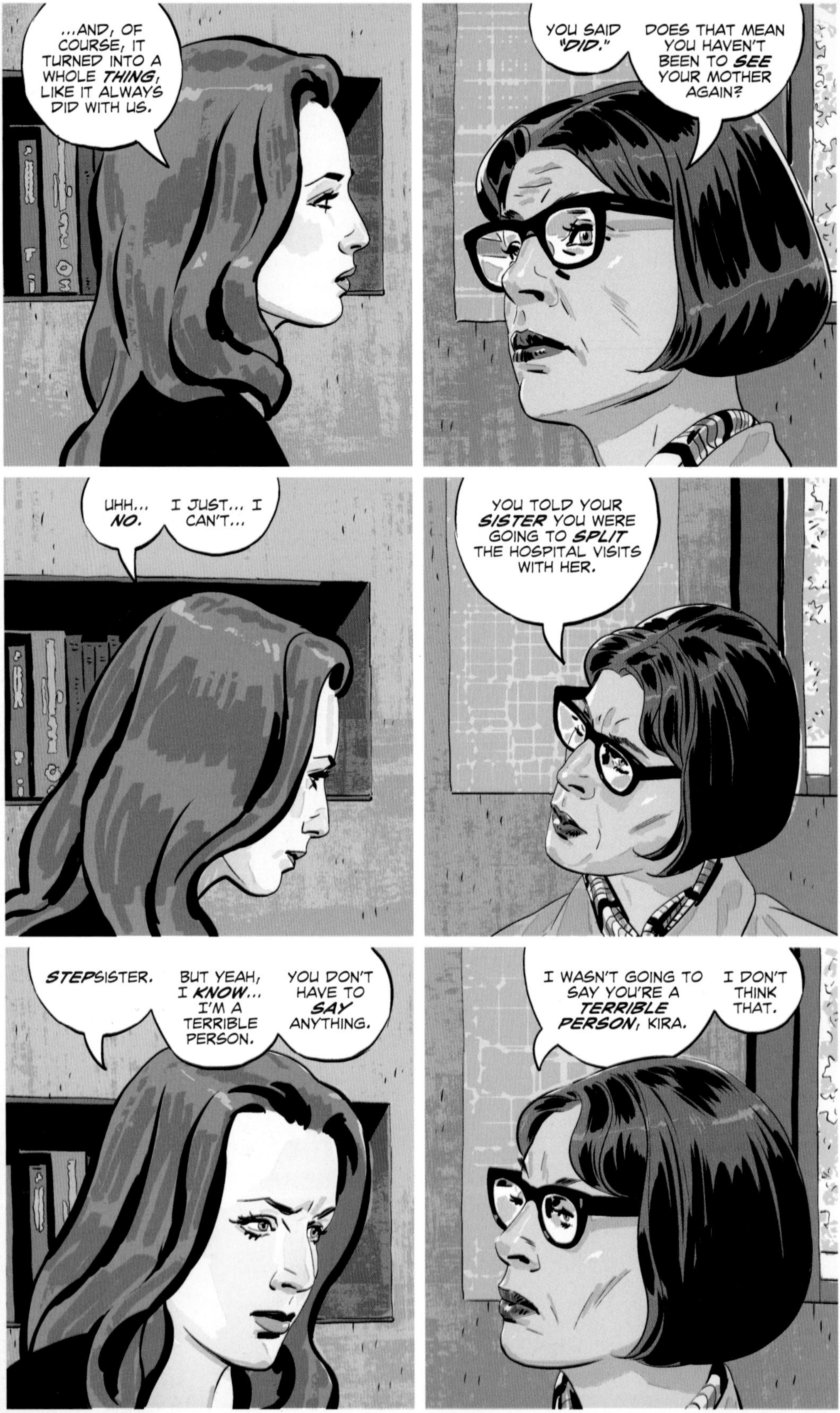
...AND, OF COURSE, IT TURNED INTO A WHOLE THING, LIKE IT ALWAYS DID WITH US.
YOU SAID "DID."
DOES THAT MEAN YOU HAVEN'T BEEN TO SEE YOUR MOTHER AGAIN?
UHH... NO.
I JUST... I CAN'T...
YOU TOLD YOUR SISTER YOU WERE GOING TO SPLIT THE HOSPITAL VISITS WITH HER.
STEPSISTER.
BUT YEAH, I KNOW... I'M A TERRIBLE PERSON.
YOU DON'T HAVE TO SAY ANYTHING.
I WASN'T GOING TO SAY YOU'RE A TERRIBLE PERSON, KIRA.
I DON'T THINK THAT.

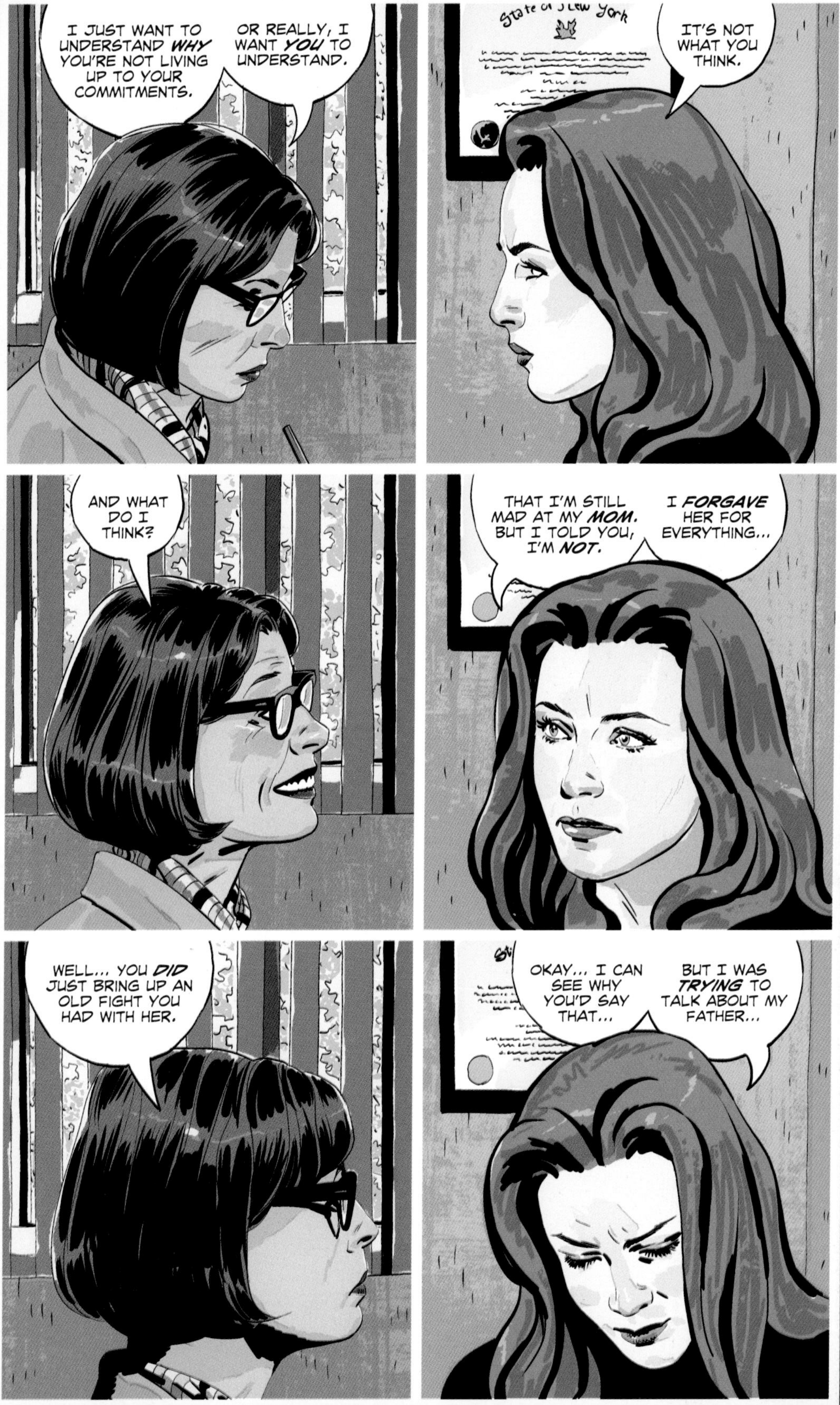

I JUST WANT TO UNDERSTAND WHY YOU'RE NOT LIVING UP TO YOUR COMMITMENTS.
OR REALLY, I WANT YOU TO UNDERSTAND.
State of New York
IT'S NOT WHAT YOU THINK.
AND WHAT DO I THINK?
THAT I'M STILL MAD AT MY MOM. BUT I TOLD YOU, I'M NOT.
I FORGAVE HER FOR EVERYTHING...
WELL... YOU DID JUST BRING UP AN OLD FIGHT YOU HAD WITH HER.
OKAY... I CAN SEE WHY YOU'D SAY THAT...
BUT I WAS TRYING TO TALK ABOUT MY FATHER...

After she left him, Dad would park across the street in the middle of the night and watch the shadows moving in my mother's bedroom windows.

One night, just after three in the morning, he started honking his horn over and over again.

He didn't stop until Mom ran out into the street in her nightgown, screaming at him.

I remember it was raining that night, and she stood there in it for a long time after he drove away.

Until her boyfriend came out and got her.

If you look at *pictures* of my Mom and Dad from the early days, when they were young lovers starting a family...

...And *pictures* from just before the divorce, you can't really tell that anything has changed.

Mom's got her usual fake smile and Dad looks uncomfortable and out of place. It's the same as it always was.

There's nothing in these pictures to make you think she's cheating on him with her art teacher. No evidence that she's already plotting her escape.

I always thought that made it even more tragic.

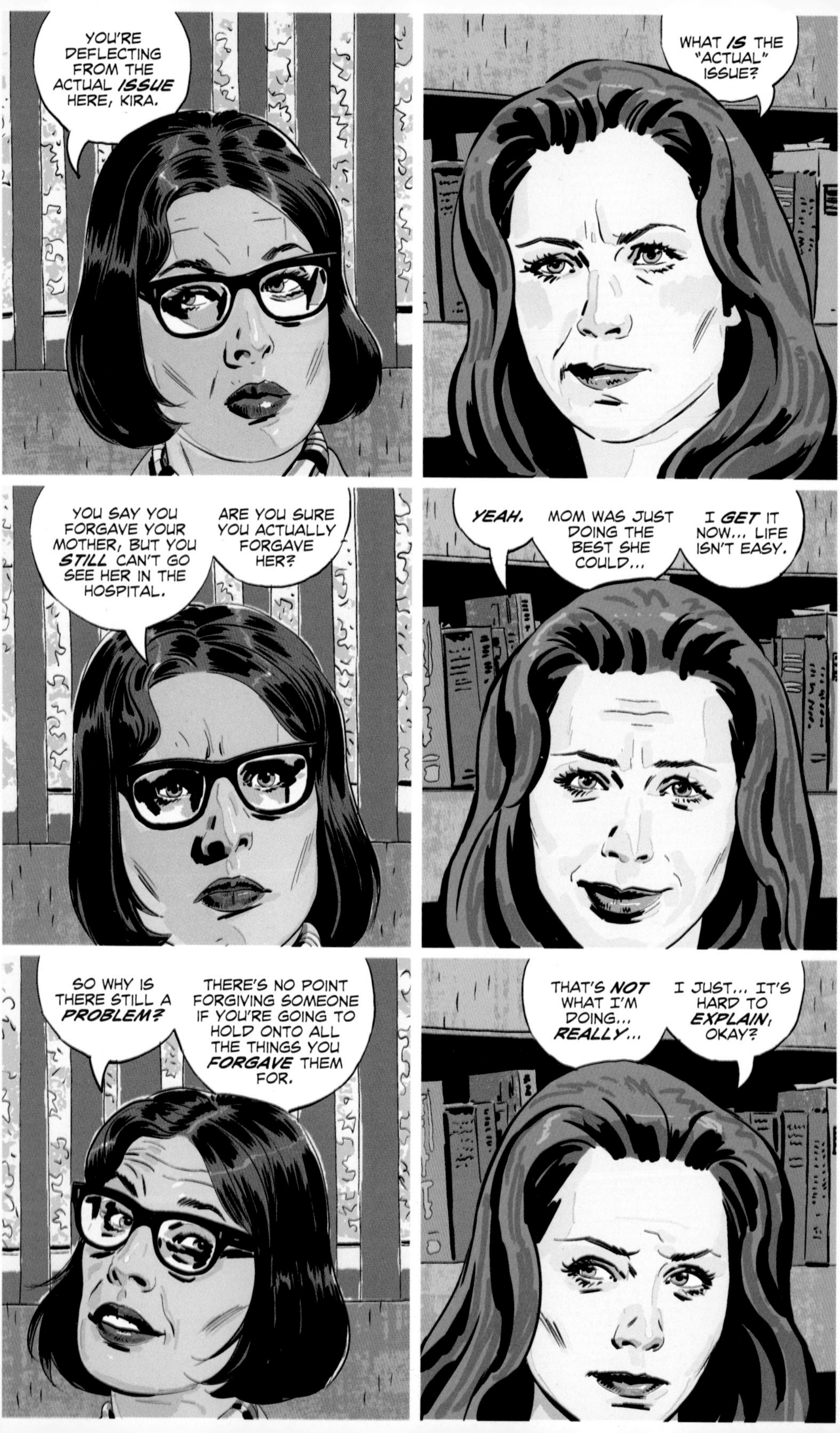
YOU'RE DEFLECTING FROM THE ACTUAL ISSUE HERE, KIRA.
WHAT IS THE "ACTUAL" ISSUE?
YOU SAY YOU FORGAVE YOUR MOTHER, BUT YOU STILL CAN'T GO SEE HER IN THE HOSPITAL.
ARE YOU SURE YOU ACTUALLY FORGAVE HER?
YEAH.
MOM WAS JUST DOING THE BEST SHE COULD...
I GET IT NOW... LIFE ISN'T EASY.
SO WHY IS THERE STILL A PROBLEM?
THERE'S NO POINT FORGIVING SOMEONE IF YOU'RE GOING TO HOLD ONTO ALL THE THINGS YOU FORGAVE THEM FOR.
THAT'S NOT WHAT I'M DOING... REALLY...
I JUST... IT'S HARD TO EXPLAIN, OKAY?

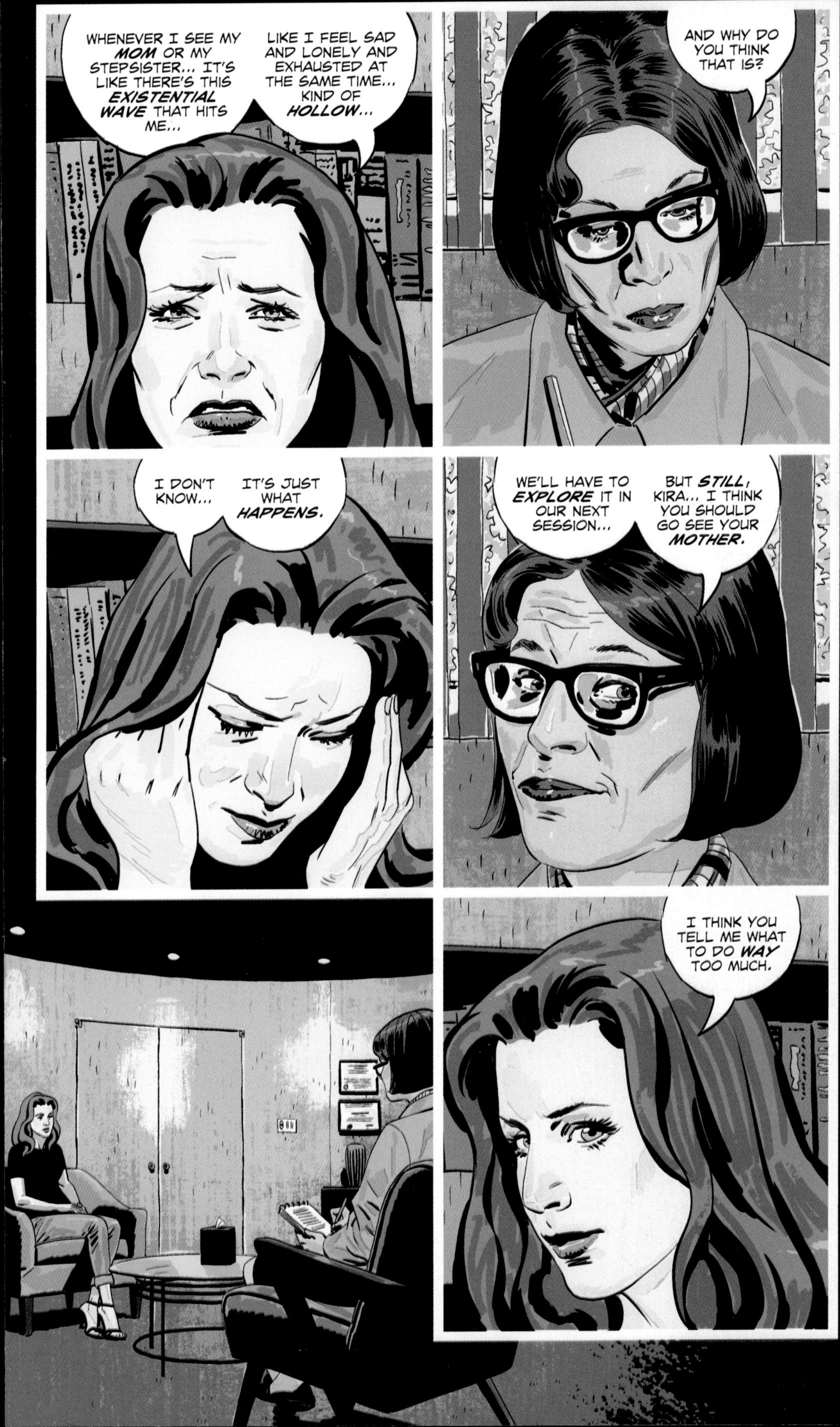
WHENEVER I SEE MY MOM OR MY STEPSISTER... IT'S LIKE THERE'S THIS EXISTENTIAL WAVE THAT HITS ME...
LIKE I FEEL SAD AND LONELY AND EXHAUSTED AT THE SAME TIME... KIND OF HOLLOW...
AND WHY DO YOU THINK THAT IS?
I DON'T KNOW...
IT'S JUST WHAT HAPPENS.
WE'LL HAVE TO EXPLORE IT IN OUR NEXT SESSION...
BUT STILL, KIRA... I THINK YOU SHOULD GO SEE YOUR MOTHER.
I THINK YOU TELL ME WHAT TO DO WAY TOO MUCH.

When my Dad was in the hospital, sometimes he would drift into these aimless reveries. About his life, his memories, his fears.

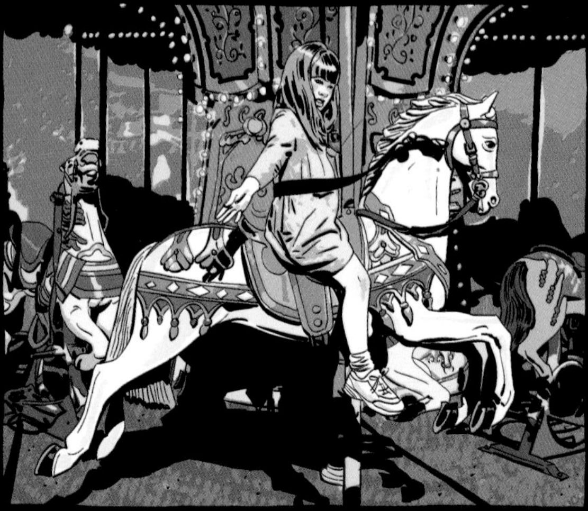

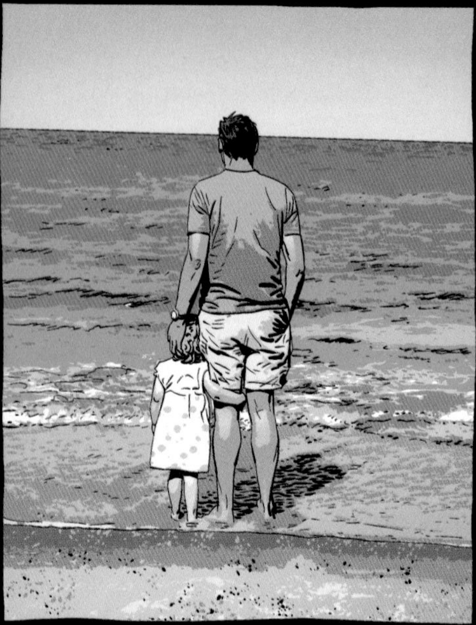

And one night as he talked, he looked at me with so much loneliness in his eyes and said, "My whole life I just felt like the most unlovable person in the world."

I told him not to say things like that, I told him everybody loved him, and I held his hand until he fell asleep.

Then I went out to my stepsister's car in the parking lot and cried for an hour.

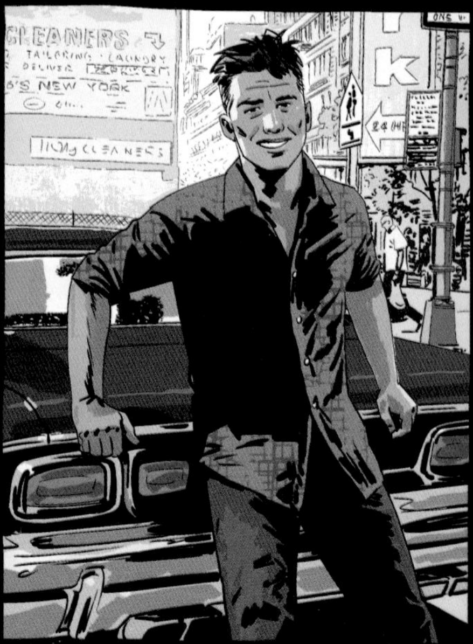
CLEANERS
NEW YORK

When Dad died his second wife went through his things and found a bunch of unmailed love letters to my Mom. She gave them to me at his funeral.

I sat up late that night reading them, feeling so sad for him. It was like he saw something in her that just wasn't there.

But I guess everyone saw whatever they were looking for in my mom most of the time.

I burned the letters and never told Mom about them. I didn't think she deserved to know he'd never gotten over her.

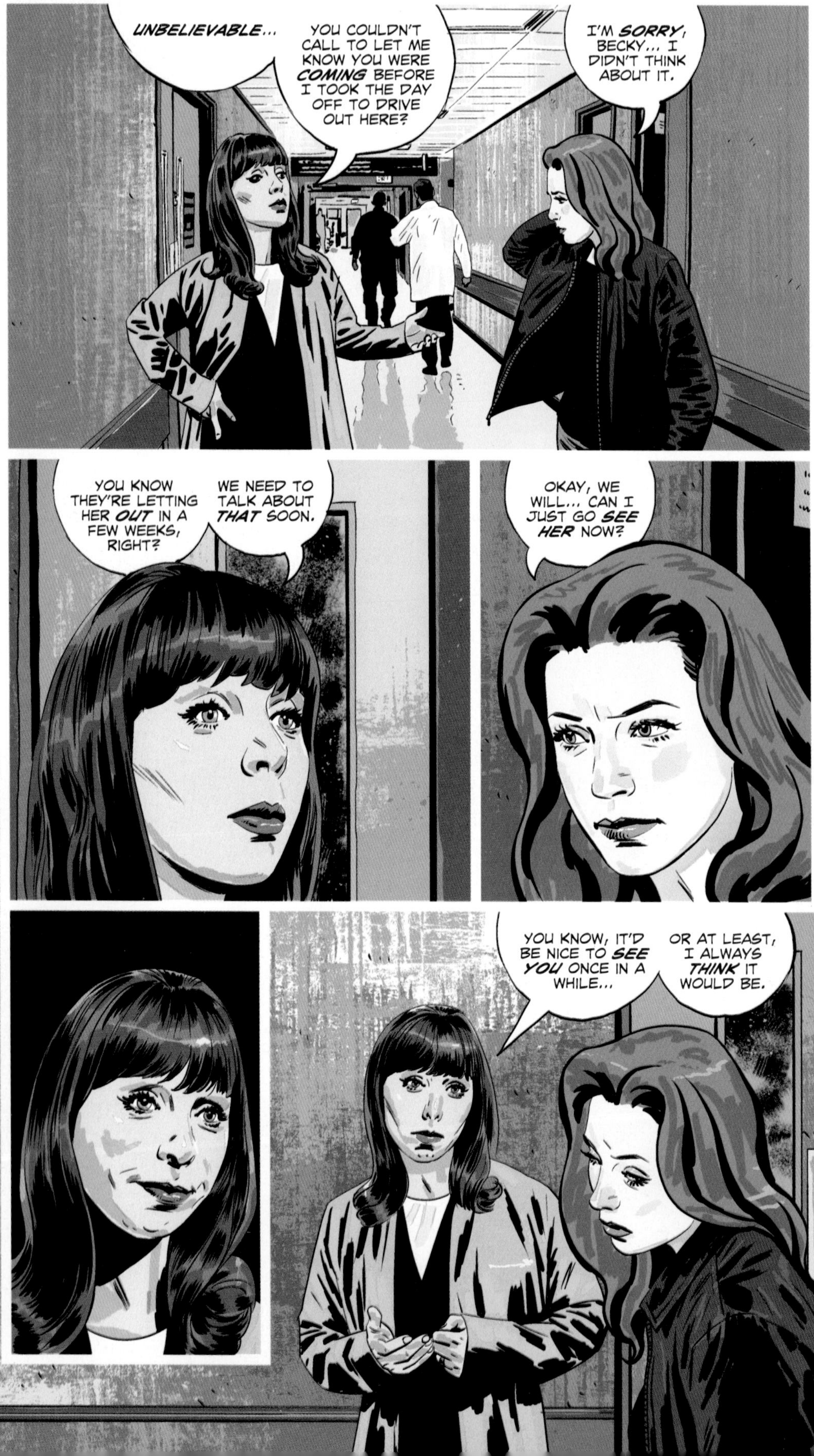
UNBELIEVABLE...
YOU COULDN'T CALL TO LET ME KNOW YOU WERE COMING BEFORE I TOOK THE DAY OFF TO DRIVE OUT HERE?
I'M SORRY, BECKY... I DIDN'T THINK ABOUT IT.
YOU KNOW THEY'RE LETTING HER OUT IN A FEW WEEKS, RIGHT?
WE NEED TO TALK ABOUT THAT SOON.
OKAY, WE WILL... CAN I JUST GO SEE HER NOW?
YOU KNOW, IT'D BE NICE TO SEE YOU ONCE IN A WHILE...
OR AT LEAST, I ALWAYS THINK IT WOULD BE.

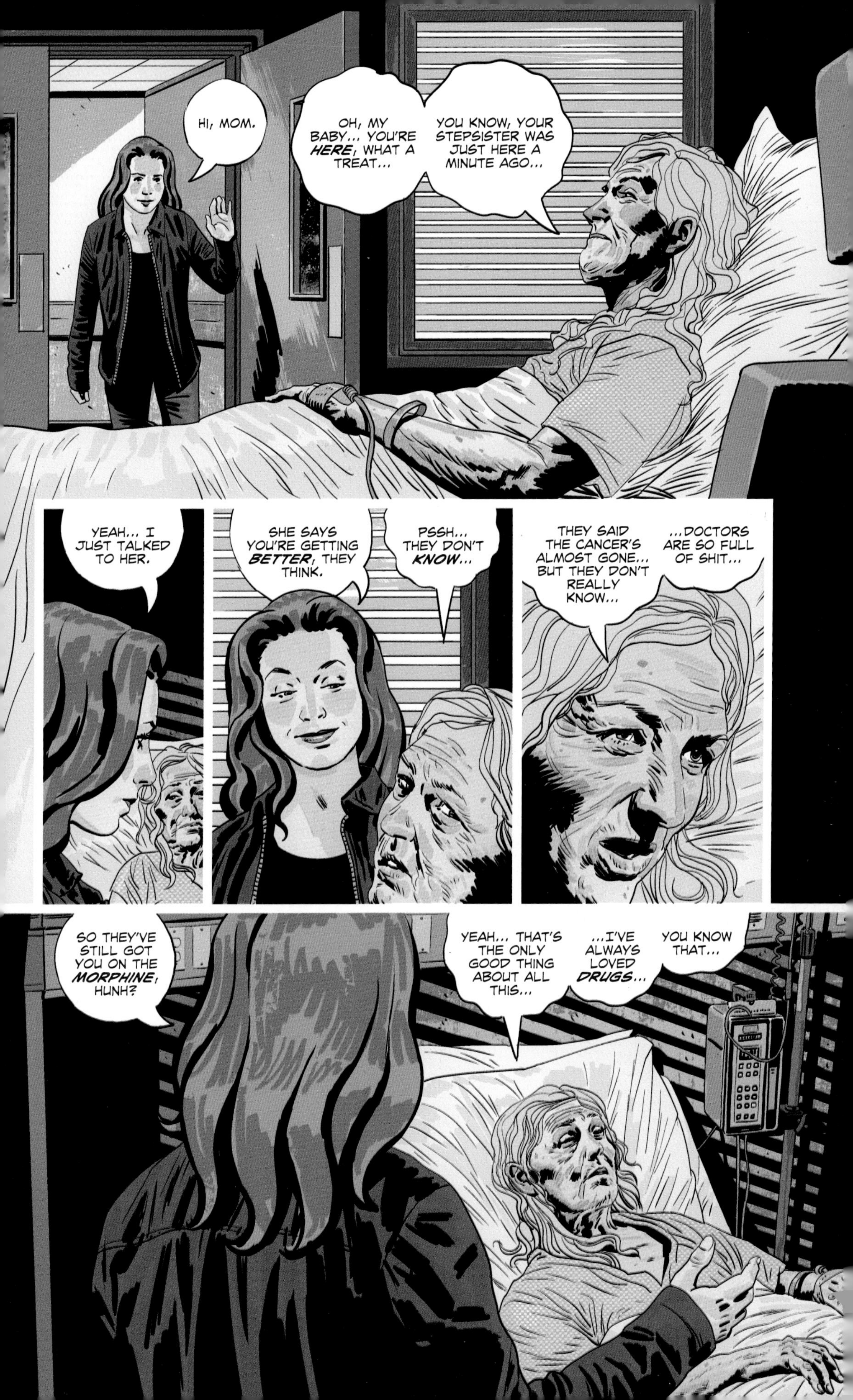
HI, MOM.
OH, MY BABY... YOU'RE HERE, WHAT A TREAT...
YOU KNOW, YOUR STEPSISTER WAS JUST HERE A MINUTE AGO...
YEAH... I JUST TALKED TO HER.
SHE SAYS YOU'RE GETTING BETTER, THEY THINK.
PSSH... THEY DON'T KNOW...
THEY SAID THE CANCER'S ALMOST GONE... BUT THEY DON'T REALLY KNOW...
...DOCTORS ARE SO FULL OF SHIT...
SO THEY'VE STILL GOT YOU ON THE MORPHINE, HUNH?
YEAH... THAT'S THE ONLY GOOD THING ABOUT ALL THIS...
...I'VE ALWAYS LOVED DRUGS...
YOU KNOW THAT...

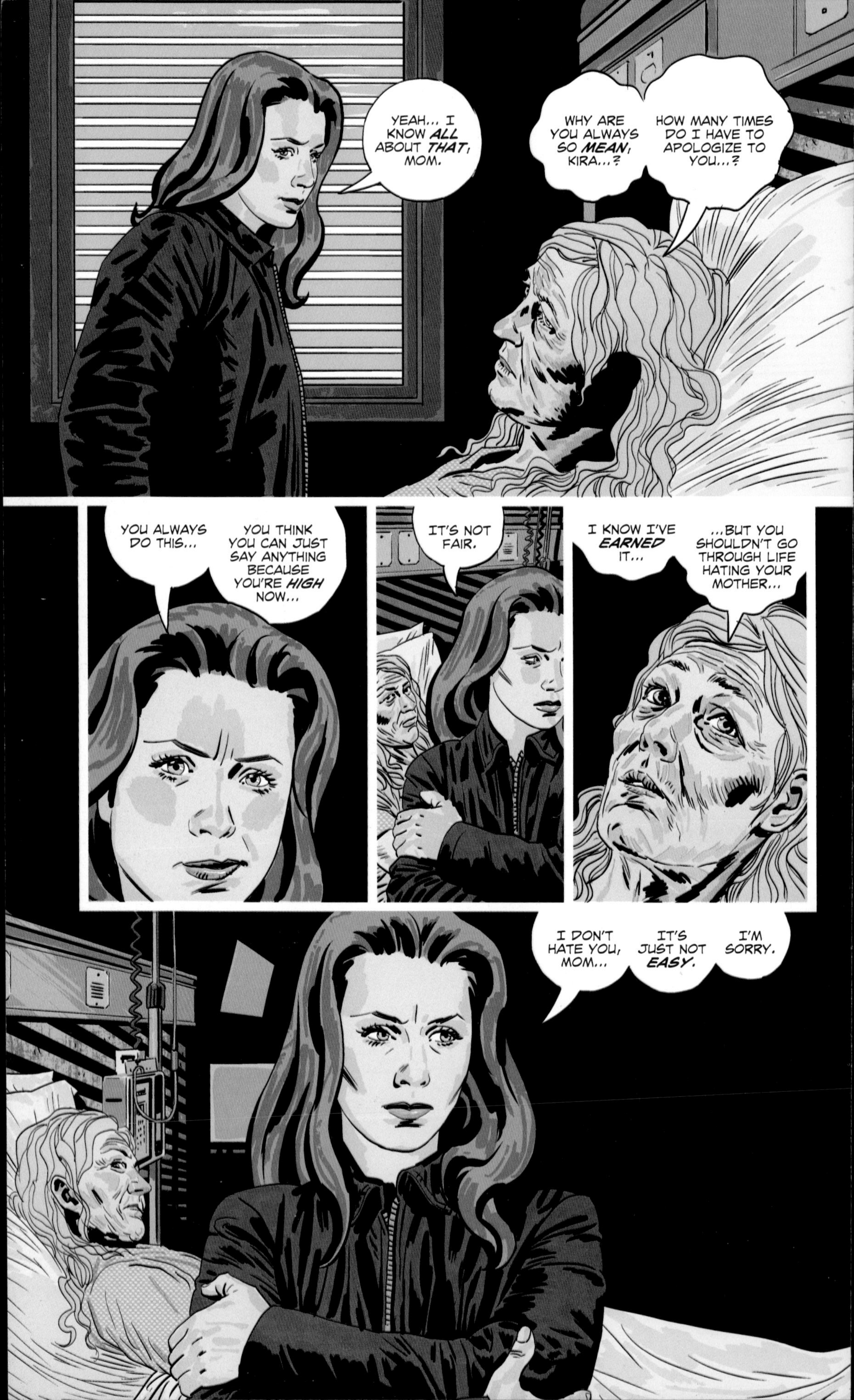
YEAH... I KNOW ALL ABOUT THAT, MOM.
WHY ARE YOU ALWAYS SO MEAN, KIRA...?
HOW MANY TIMES DO I HAVE TO APOLOGIZE TO YOU...?
YOU ALWAYS DO THIS...
YOU THINK YOU CAN JUST SAY ANYTHING BECAUSE YOU'RE HIGH NOW...
IT'S NOT FAIR.
I KNOW I'VE EARNED IT...
...BUT YOU SHOULDN'T GO THROUGH LIFE HATING YOUR MOTHER...
I DON'T HATE YOU, MOM...
IT'S JUST NOT EASY.
I'M SORRY.

Mom grew up in a small town in West Virginia, and she was the only one in four generations of her family to leave. My cousins are still back there, living in the sticks.

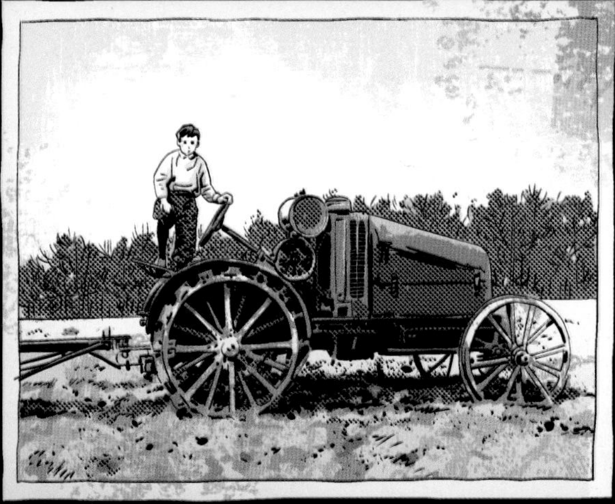

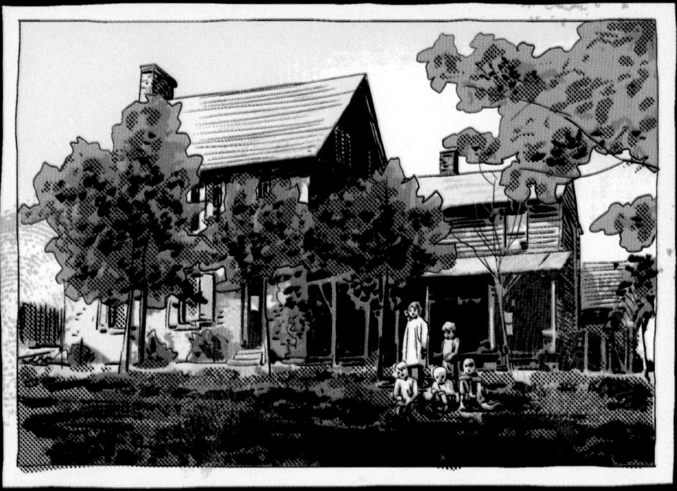

The few conversations I've had with them the past few years makes me feel like they're living in a totally different century than me.

So I'm always grateful that Mom and Dad got out of there when she was pregnant with me. That took courage.

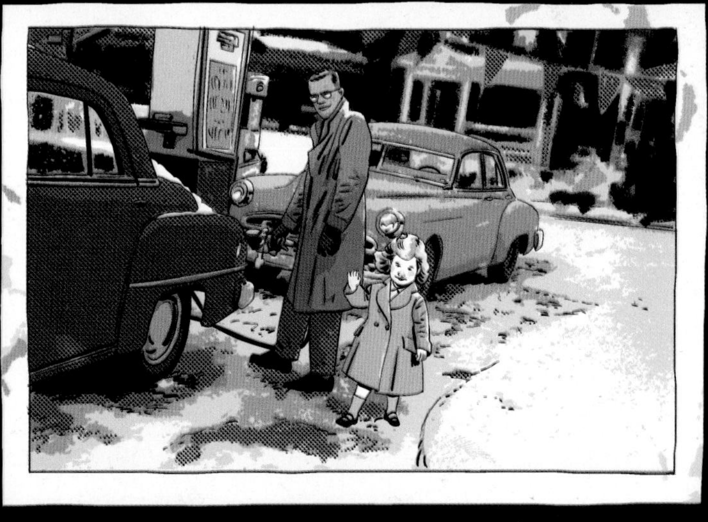

And it must have felt scary, to be discovering the world at the same time you're becoming a mother.

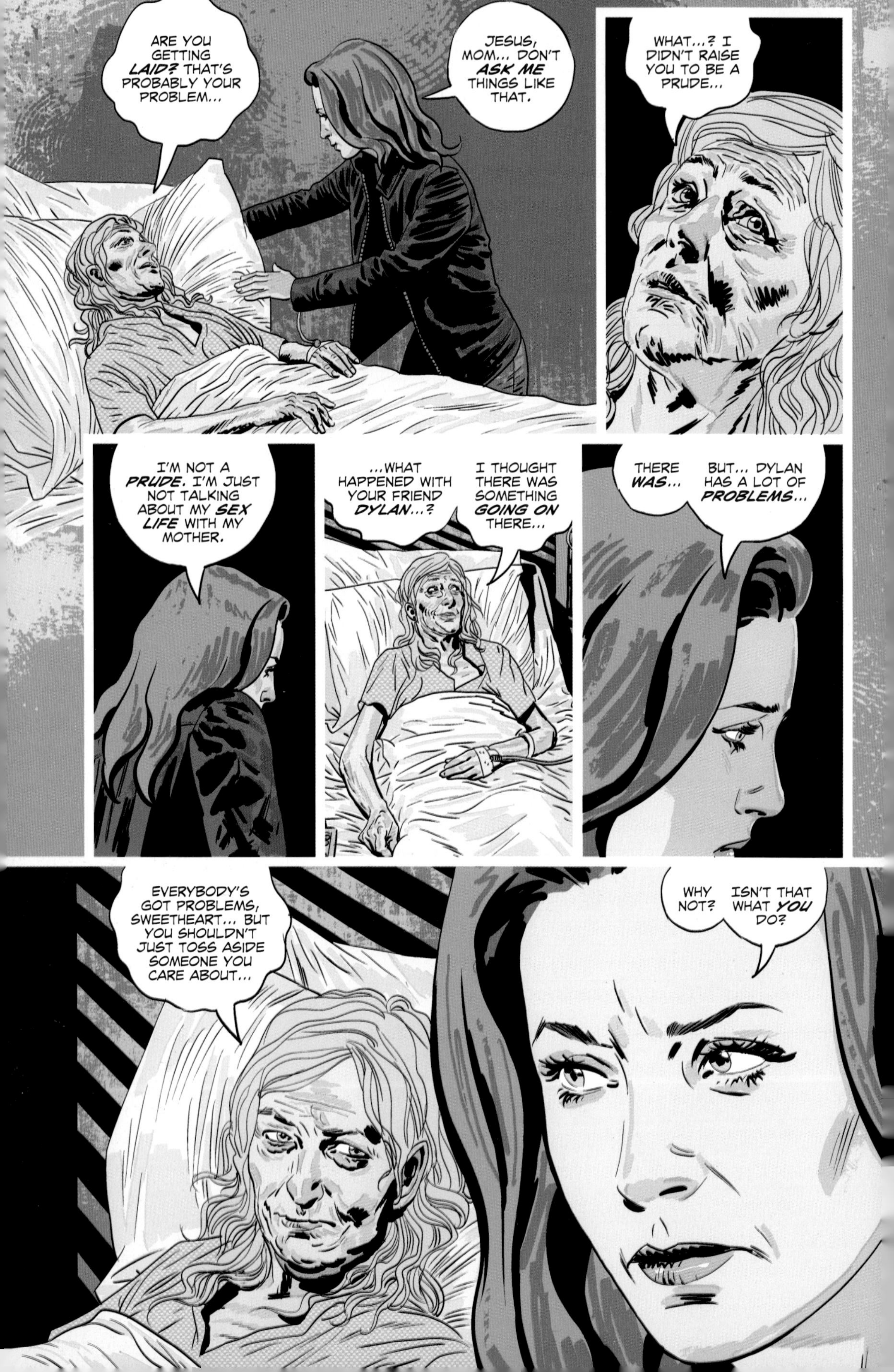
ARE YOU GETTING LAID? THAT'S PROBABLY YOUR PROBLEM...
JESUS, MOM... DON'T ASK ME THINGS LIKE THAT.
WHAT...? I DIDN'T RAISE YOU TO BE A PRUDE...
I'M NOT A PRUDE. I'M JUST NOT TALKING ABOUT MY SEX LIFE WITH MY MOTHER.
...WHAT HAPPENED WITH YOUR FRIEND DYLAN...?
I THOUGHT THERE WAS SOMETHING GOING ON THERE...
THERE WAS...
BUT... DYLAN HAS A LOT OF PROBLEMS...
EVERYBODY'S GOT PROBLEMS, SWEETHEART... BUT YOU SHOULDN'T JUST TOSS ASIDE SOMEONE YOU CARE ABOUT...
WHY NOT?
ISN'T THAT WHAT YOU DO?

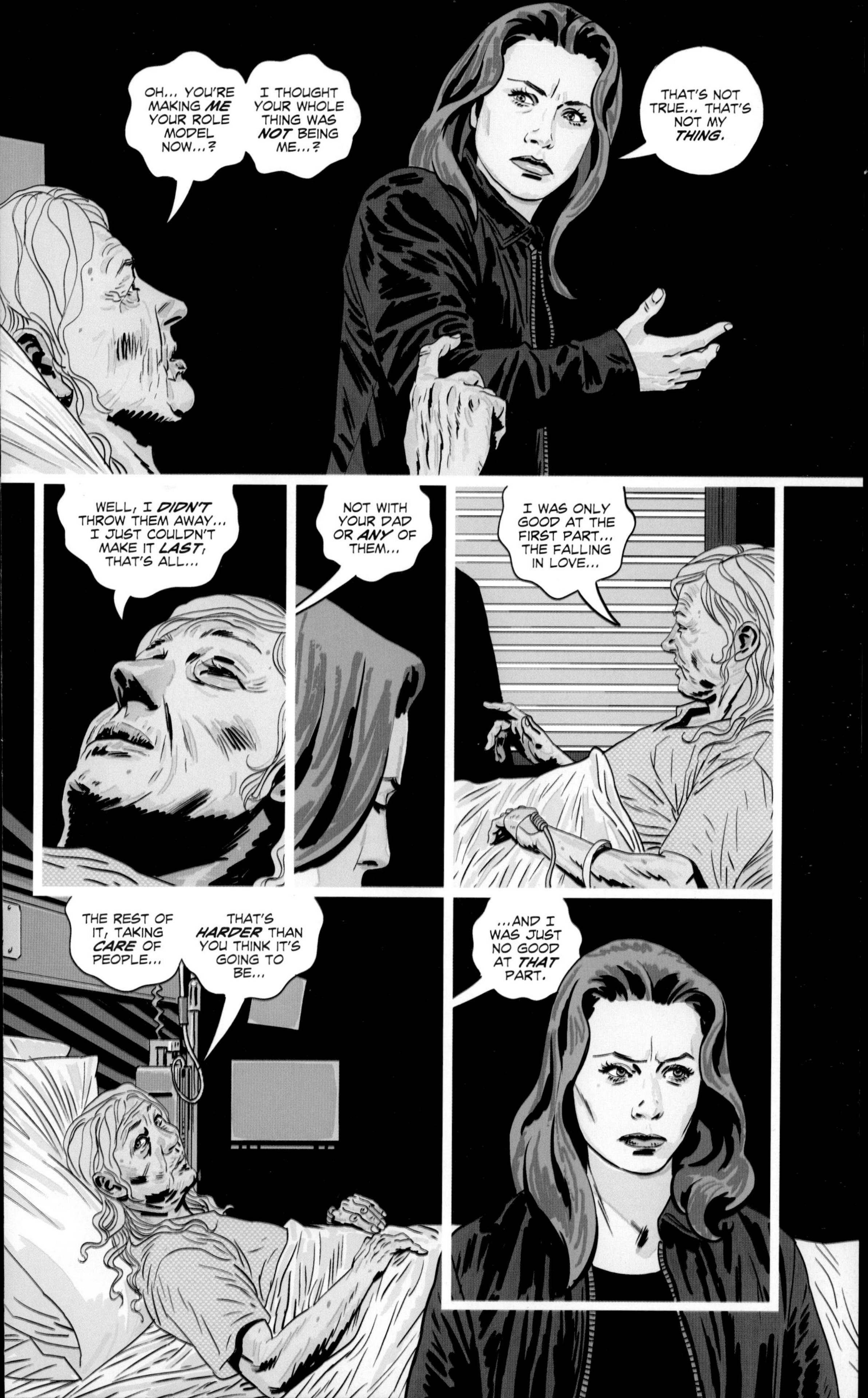
OH... YOU'RE MAKING *ME* YOUR ROLE MODEL NOW...?
I THOUGHT YOUR WHOLE THING WAS *NOT* BEING ME...?
THAT'S NOT TRUE... THAT'S NOT MY *THING.*
WELL, I *DIDN'T* THROW THEM AWAY... I JUST COULDN'T MAKE IT *LAST,* THAT'S ALL...
NOT WITH YOUR DAD OR *ANY* OF THEM...
I WAS ONLY GOOD AT THE FIRST PART... THE FALLING IN LOVE...
THE REST OF IT, TAKING *CARE* OF PEOPLE...
THAT'S *HARDER* THAN YOU THINK IT'S GOING TO BE...
...AND I WAS JUST NO GOOD AT *THAT* PART.

Dylan and I weren't really friends at first, we were just part of the same group. But one night we all ended up at this hipster karaoke bar and Dylan took a dare and sang a Joni Mitchell song.

At first he was doing it like a joke, because no guy can hit her vocal range. But then the song took him over and he really started belting it out.

He got to this part that goes "You've got tombs in your eyes" and I saw something crack inside him, like some hidden pain was seeping out.

I don't think he meant to reveal himself. Music just does that to you sometimes.

Later, we sat on some steps and had one of those talks where it's like you've always known each other. Where you talk about family curses and suicides.

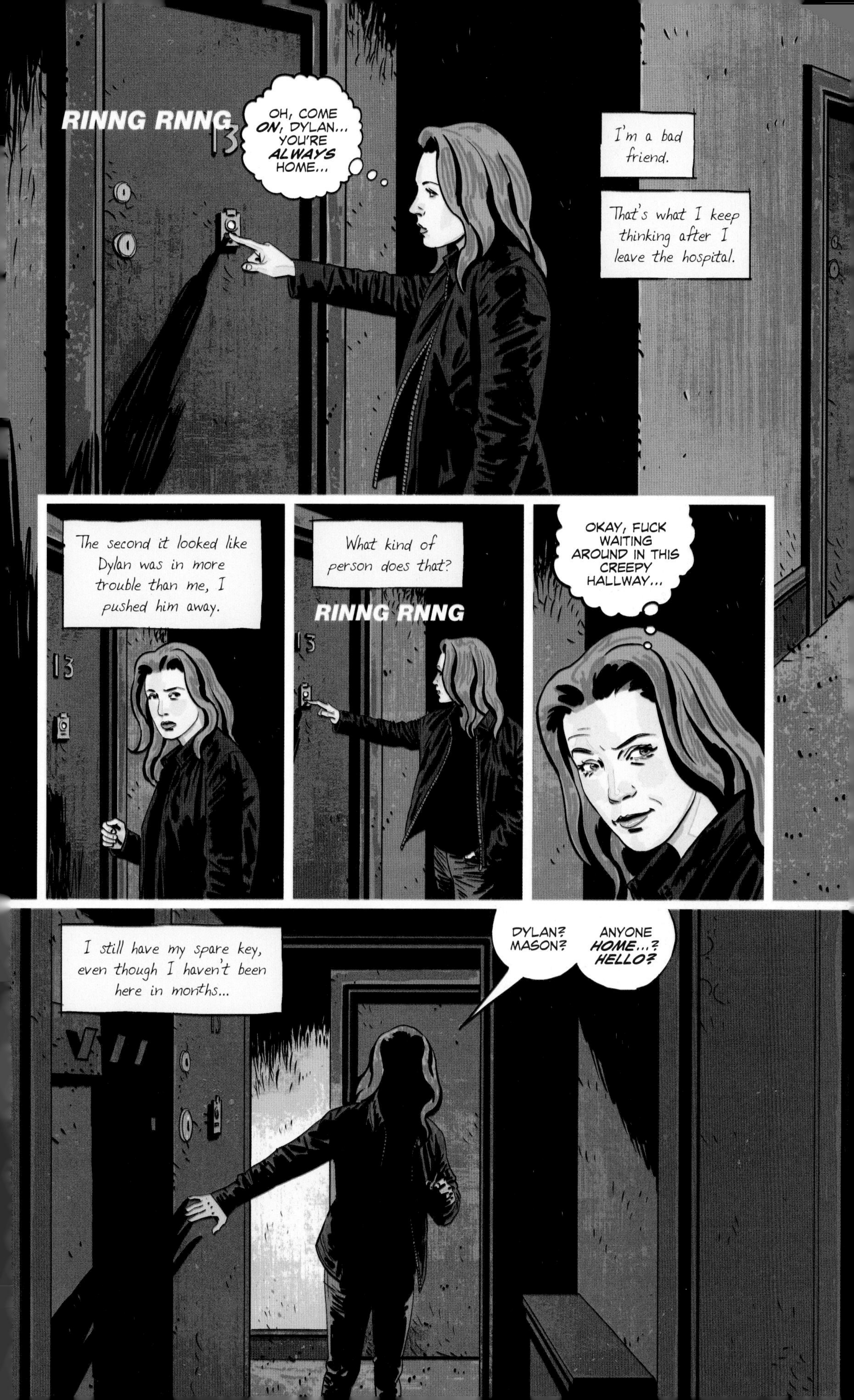
RINNG RNNG
OH, COME ON, DYLAN... YOU'RE ALWAYS HOME...
I'm a bad friend.
That's what I keep thinking after I leave the hospital.
The second it looked like Dylan was in more trouble than me, I pushed him away.
What kind of person does that?
RINNG RNNG
OKAY, FUCK WAITING AROUND IN THIS CREEPY HALLWAY...
I still have my spare key, even though I haven't been here in months...
DYLAN? MASON?
ANYONE HOME...? HELLO?

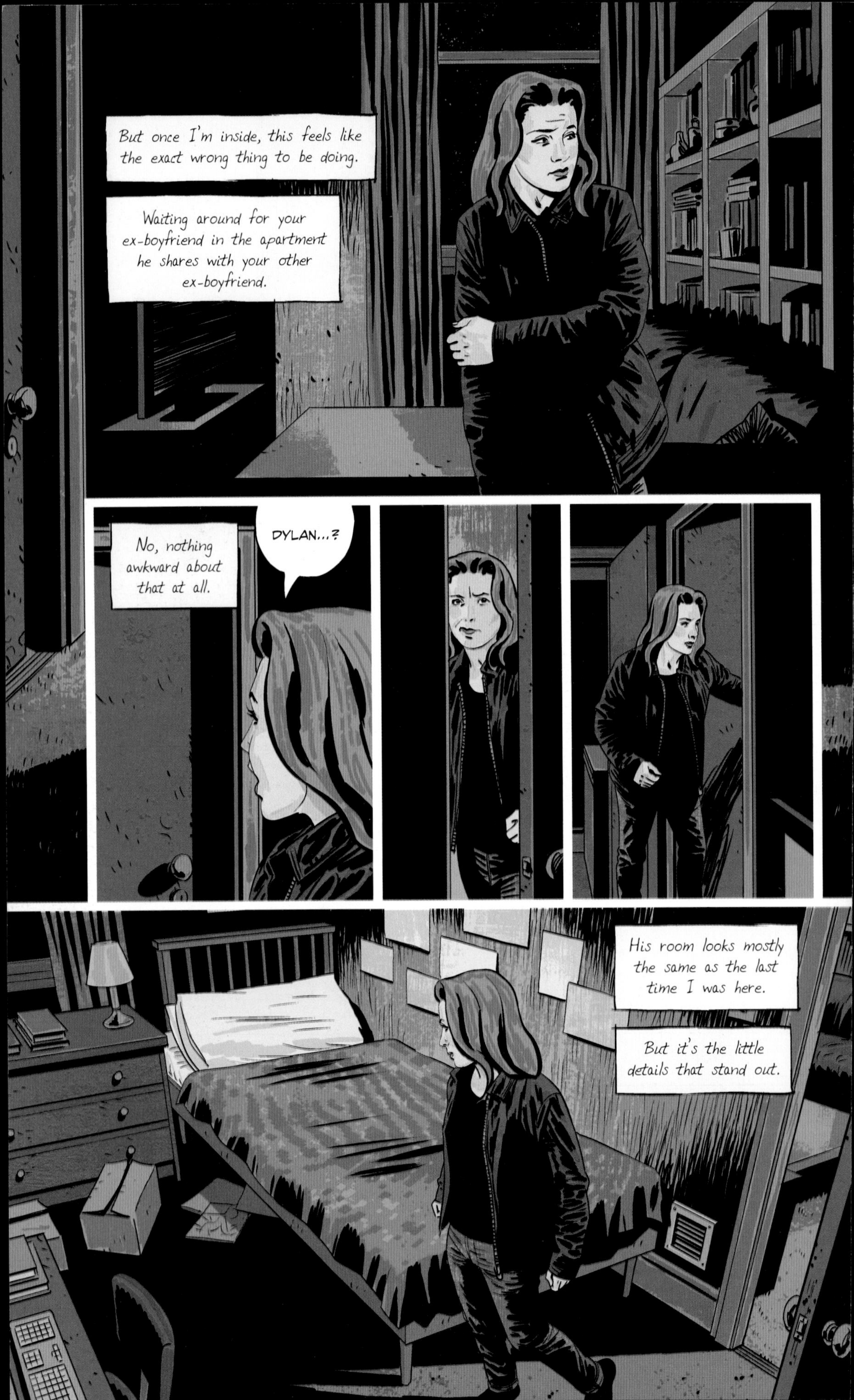
But once I'm inside, this feels like the exact wrong thing to be doing.
Waiting around for your ex-boyfriend in the apartment he shares with your other ex-boyfriend.
No, nothing awkward about that at all.
DYLAN...?
His room looks mostly the same as the last time I was here.
But it's the little details that stand out.

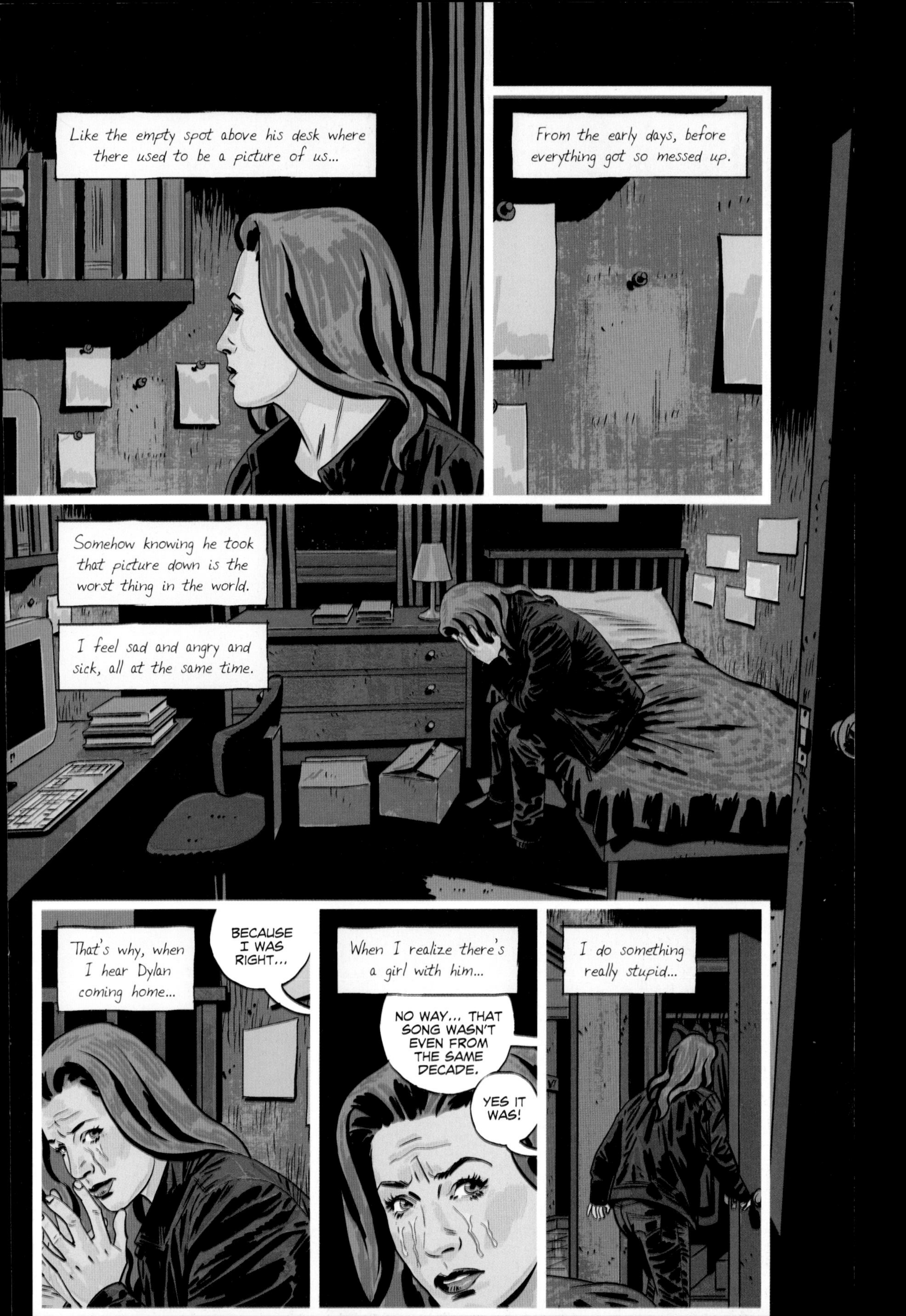
Like the empty spot above his desk where there used to be a picture of us...
From the early days, before everything got so messed up.
Somehow knowing he took that picture down is the worst thing in the world.
I feel sad and angry and sick, all at the same time.
That's why, when I hear Dylan coming home...
BECAUSE I WAS RIGHT...
When I realize there's a girl with him...
NO WAY... THAT SONG WASN'T EVEN FROM THE SAME DECADE.
YES IT WAS!
I do something really stupid...

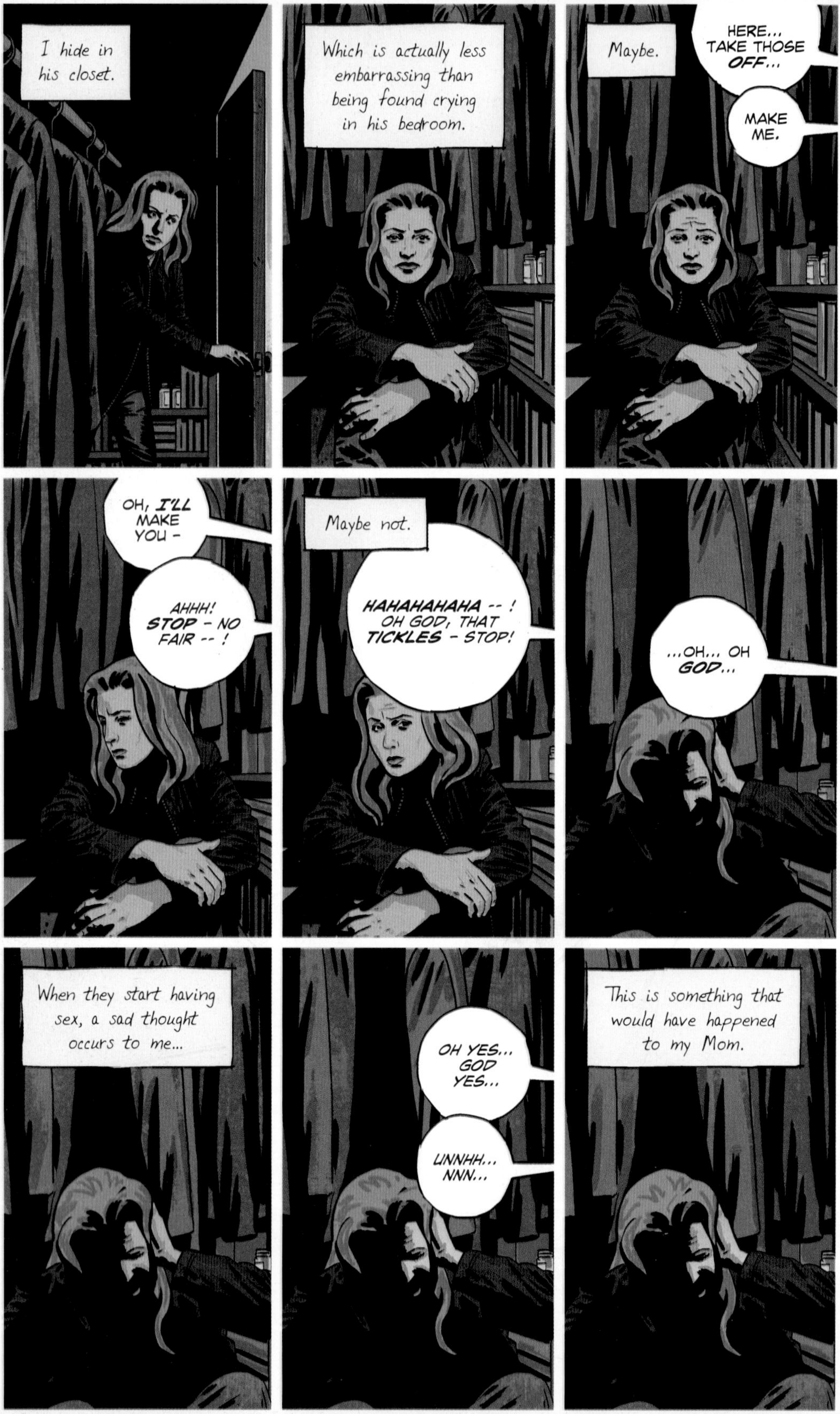
I hide in his closet.
Which is actually less embarrassing than being found crying in his bedroom.
Maybe.
HERE... TAKE THOSE OFF...
MAKE ME.
OH, I'LL MAKE YOU -
AHHH! STOP - NO FAIR -- !
Maybe not.
HAHAHAHAHA -- ! OH GOD, THAT TICKLES - STOP!
...OH... OH GOD...
When they start having sex, a sad thought occurs to me...
OH YES... GOD YES...
UNNHH... NNN...
This is something that would have happened to my Mom.

Hiding in a closet while the man she probably loves has sex with another woman...

NNN... RIGHT THERE... NNNHHH...

Feeling alone and angry...

UHHH... UHH...

Blaming herself for fucking it all up.

HH... HHHH...

!!!

My poor, stupid, selfish Mom.

Shrshu...

WHAT THE HELL...?

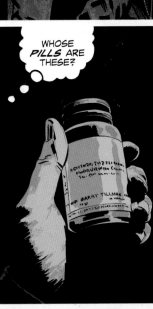

WHOSE PILLS ARE THESE?

Sometimes when I think about my family, all I can see are the thousand little wounds that made us who we are.

The ones lost to time and death, and those of us still here, continuing the cycle.

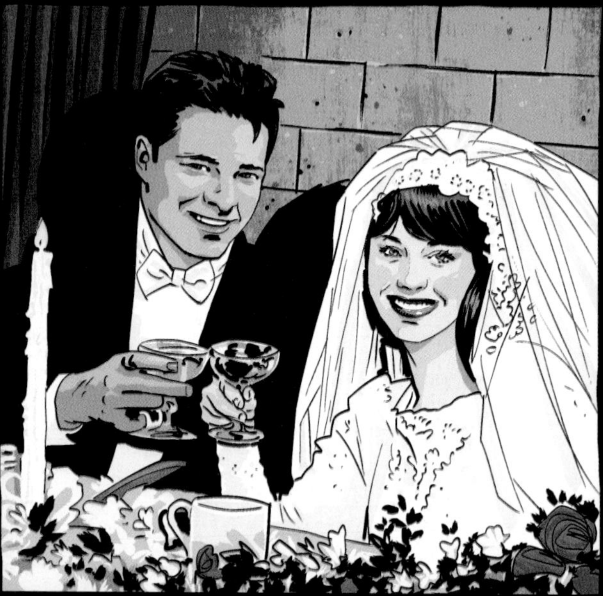

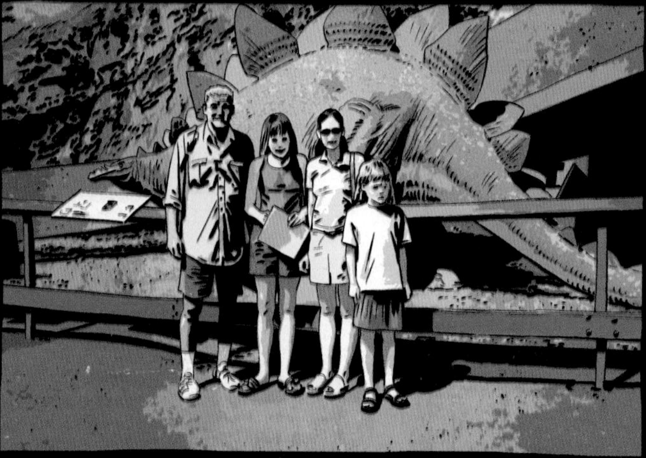

I see us moving forward, diminishing over time, until there's nothing left but a distant shared pain...

And knowing looks that say, I know what you've been through, I was there...

I wear those chains, too.

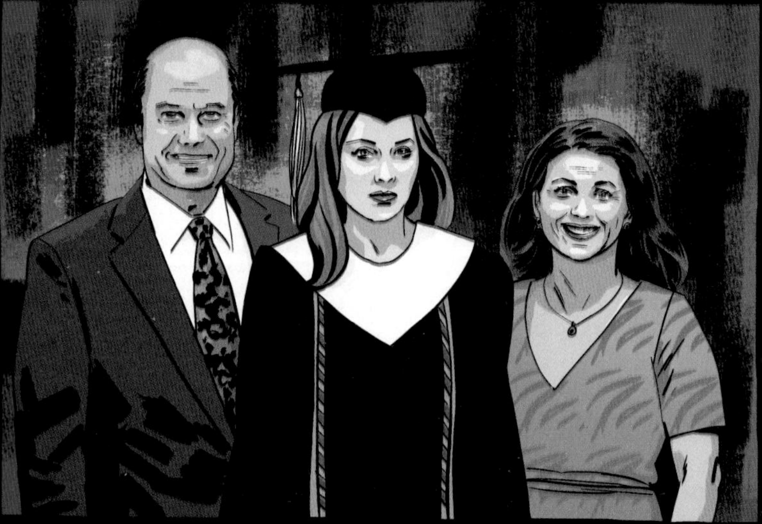

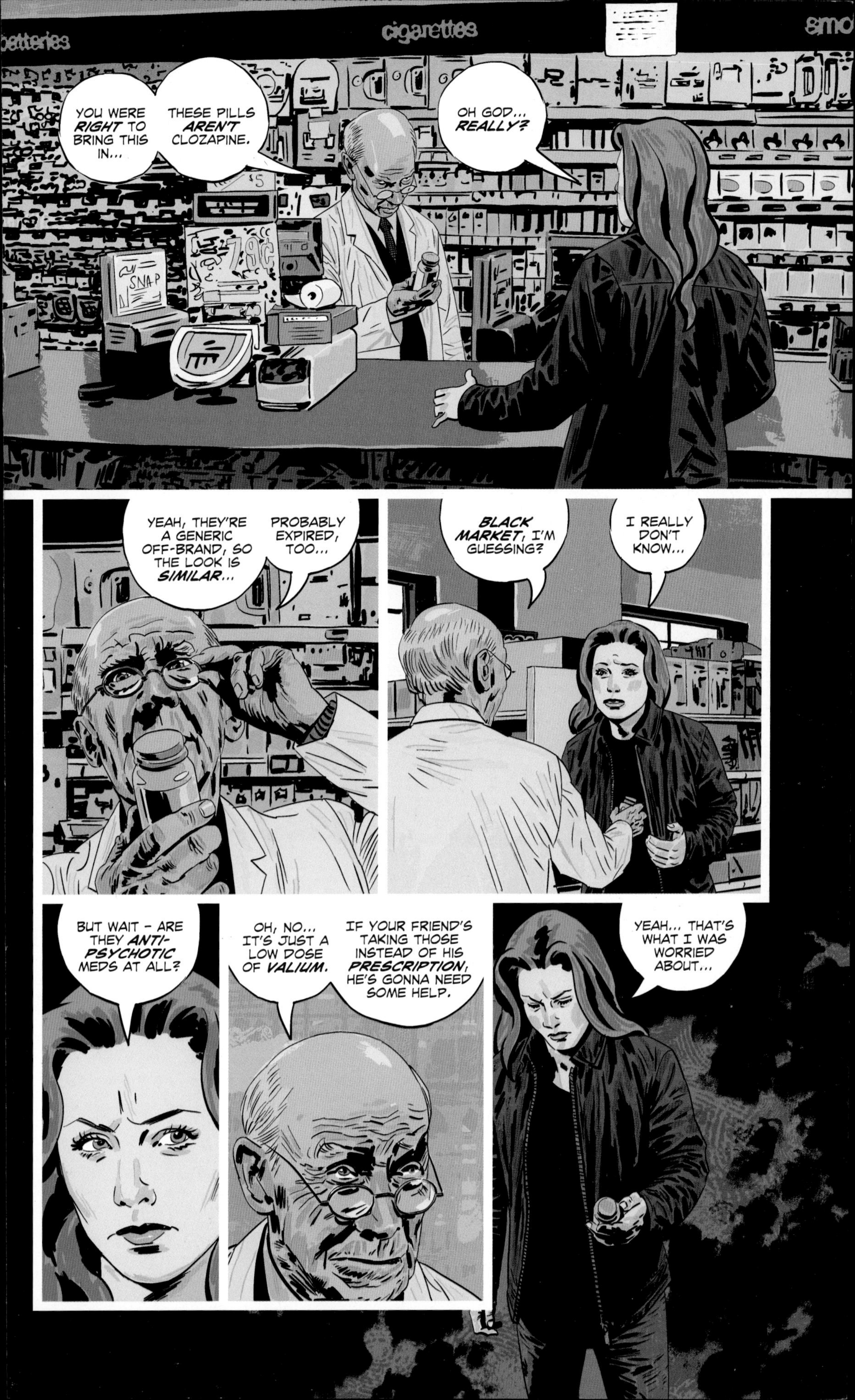

battteries
cigarettes
YOU WERE RIGHT TO BRING THIS IN...
THESE PILLS AREN'T CLOZAPINE.
OH GOD... REALLY?
YEAH, THEY'RE A GENERIC OFF-BRAND, SO THE LOOK IS SIMILAR...
PROBABLY EXPIRED, TOO...
BLACK MARKET, I'M GUESSING?
I REALLY DON'T KNOW...
BUT WAIT - ARE THEY ANTI-PSYCHOTIC MEDS AT ALL?
OH, NO... IT'S JUST A LOW DOSE OF VALIUM.
IF YOUR FRIEND'S TAKING THOSE INSTEAD OF HIS PRESCRIPTION, HE'S GONNA NEED SOME HELP.
YEAH... THAT'S WHAT I WAS WORRIED ABOUT...

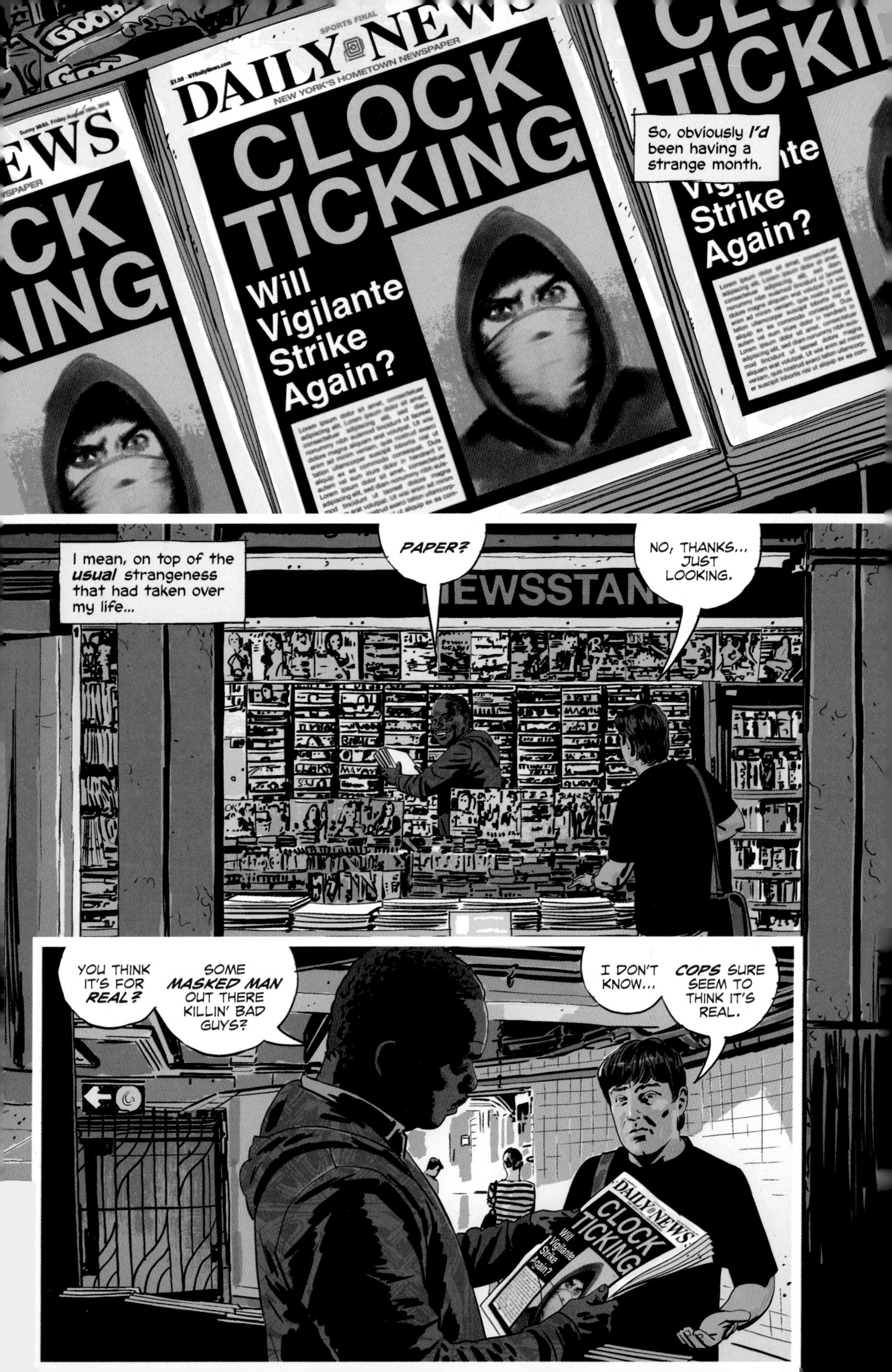
SPORTS FINAL
DAILY NEWS
$1.50 · NYDailyNews.com
NEW YORK'S HOMETOWN NEWSPAPER
CLOCK TICKING
Will Vigilante Strike Again?
So, obviously *I'd* been having a strange month.
I mean, on top of the *usual* strangeness that had taken over my life...
PAPER?
NO, THANKS... JUST LOOKING.
NEWSSTAN
YOU THINK IT'S FOR *REAL?*
SOME *MASKED MAN* OUT THERE KILLIN' BAD GUYS?
I DON'T KNOW...
COPS SURE SEEM TO THINK IT'S REAL.
DAILY NEWS
CLOCK TICKING
Will Vigilante Strike Again?

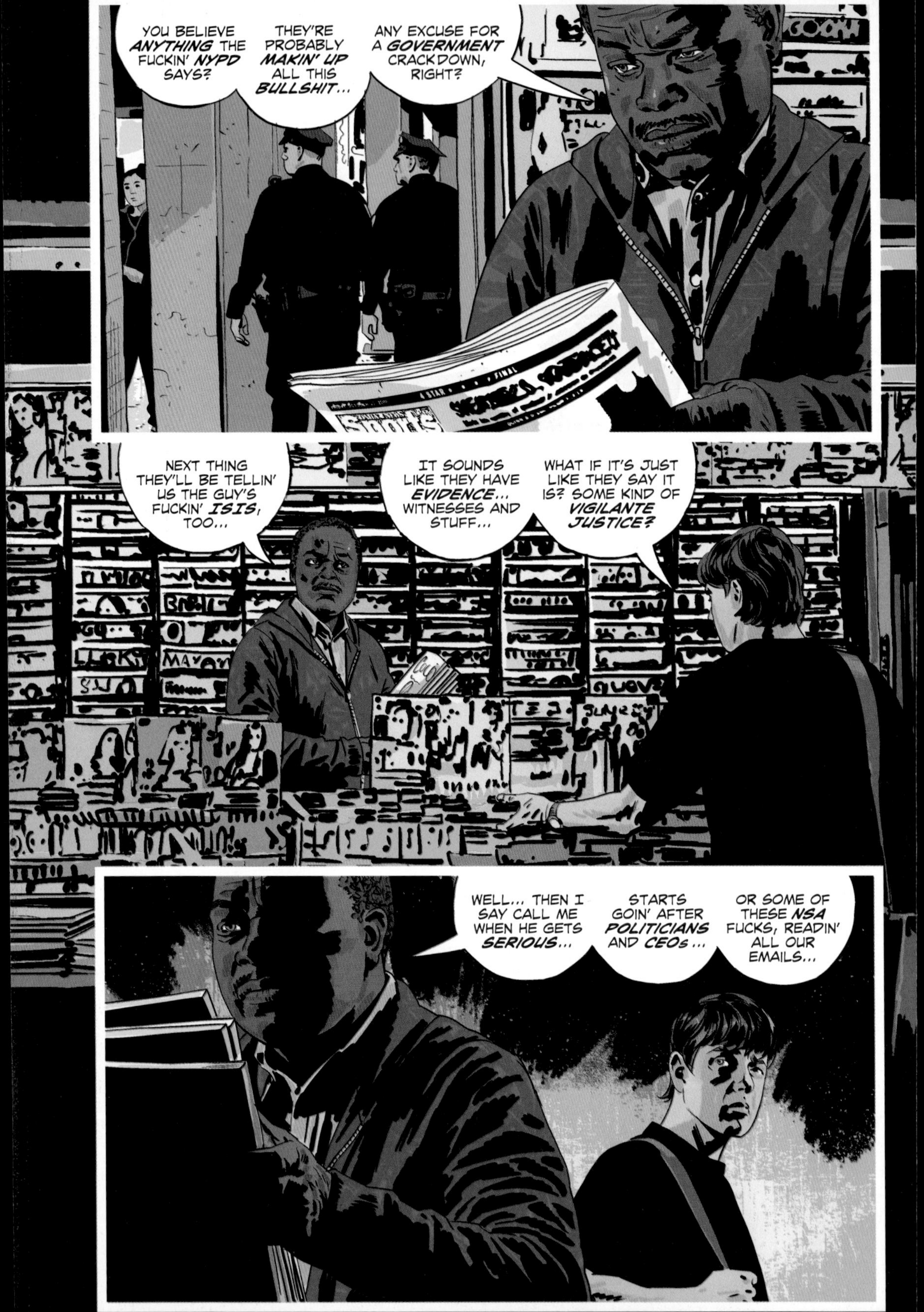
YOU BELIEVE ANYTHING THE FUCKIN' NYPD SAYS?
THEY'RE PROBABLY MAKIN' UP ALL THIS BULLSHIT...
ANY EXCUSE FOR A GOVERNMENT CRACKDOWN, RIGHT?
NEXT THING THEY'LL BE TELLIN' US THE GUY'S FUCKIN' ISIS, TOO...
IT SOUNDS LIKE THEY HAVE EVIDENCE... WITNESSES AND STUFF...
WHAT IF IT'S JUST LIKE THEY SAY IT IS? SOME KIND OF VIGILANTE JUSTICE?
WELL... THEN I SAY CALL ME WHEN HE GETS SERIOUS...
STARTS GOIN' AFTER POLITICIANS AND CEOs...
OR SOME OF THESE NSA FUCKS, READIN' ALL OUR EMAILS...

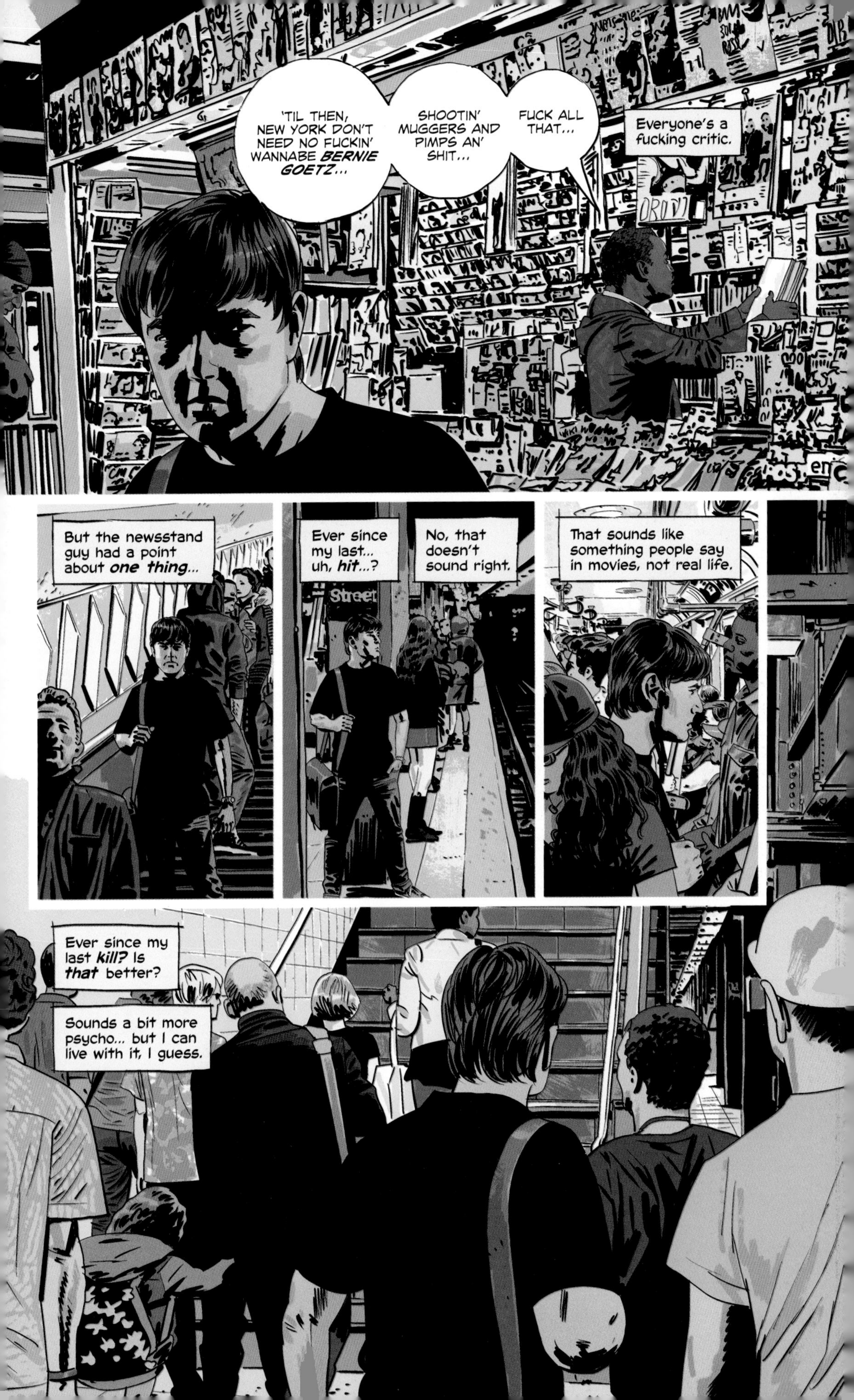
'TIL THEN, NEW YORK DON'T NEED NO FUCKIN' WANNABE ***BERNIE GOETZ***...
SHOOTIN' MUGGERS AND PIMPS AN' SHIT...
FUCK ALL THAT...
Everyone's a fucking critic.
But the newsstand guy had a point about ***one thing***...
Ever since my last... uh, ***hit***...?
No, that doesn't sound right.
That sounds like something people say in movies, not real life.
Ever since my last ***kill?*** Is ***that*** better?
Sounds a bit more psycho... but I can live with it, I guess.

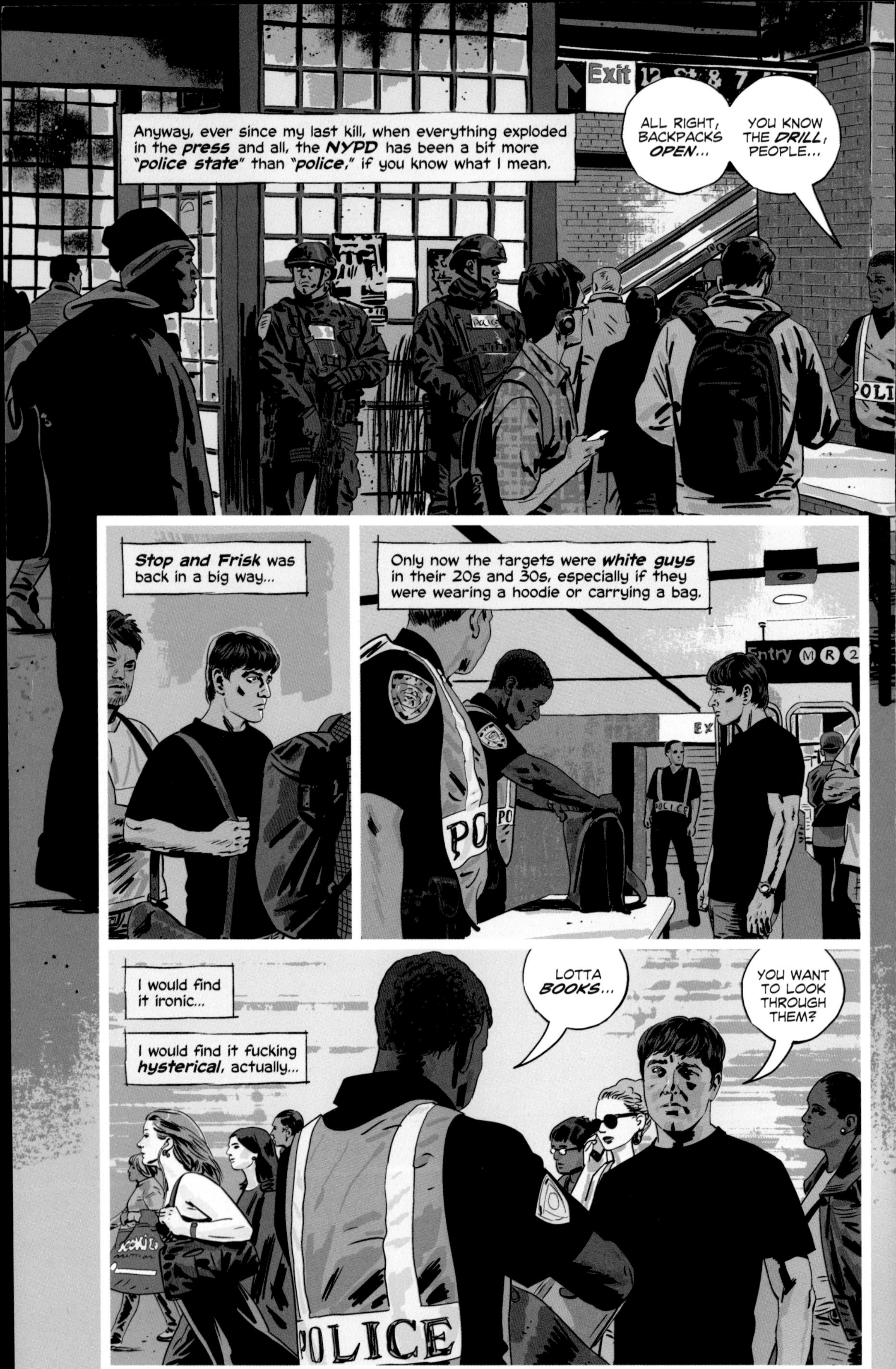

Exit 12 St & 7
Anyway, ever since my last kill, when everything exploded in the *press* and all, the *NYPD* has been a bit more "*police state*" than "*police*," if you know what I mean.
ALL RIGHT, BACKPACKS *OPEN*...
YOU KNOW THE *DRILL*, PEOPLE...
Stop and Frisk was back in a big way...
Only now the targets were *white guys* in their 20s and 30s, especially if they were wearing a hoodie or carrying a bag.
Entry M R
POLICE
I would find it ironic...
I would find it fucking *hysterical*, actually...
LOTTA *BOOKS*...
YOU WANT TO LOOK THROUGH THEM?
POLICE

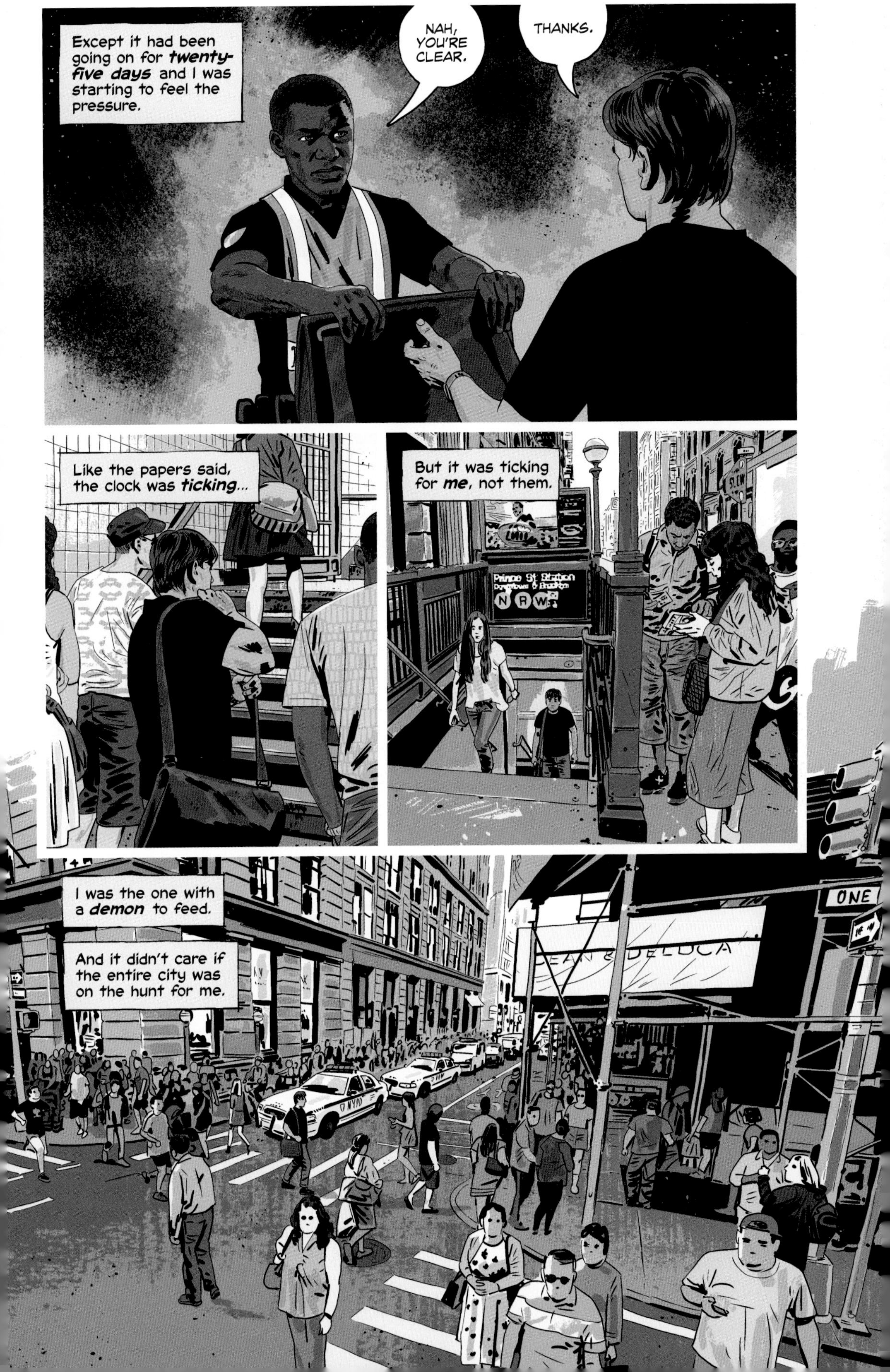

Except it had been going on for ***twenty-five days*** and I was starting to feel the pressure.
NAH, YOU'RE CLEAR.
THANKS.
Like the papers said, the clock was ***ticking***...
But it was ticking for ***me***, not them.
Prince St Station
I was the one with a ***demon*** to feed.
And it didn't care if the entire city was on the hunt for me.
ONE
NYPD

And it really did feel like that, honestly.

Like any sane person, I had a healthy fear of the NYPD, but I hadn't expected them to be so competent.

Suddenly, it was like they were this finely tuned machine...

Increased patrols, military gear, random checkpoints...

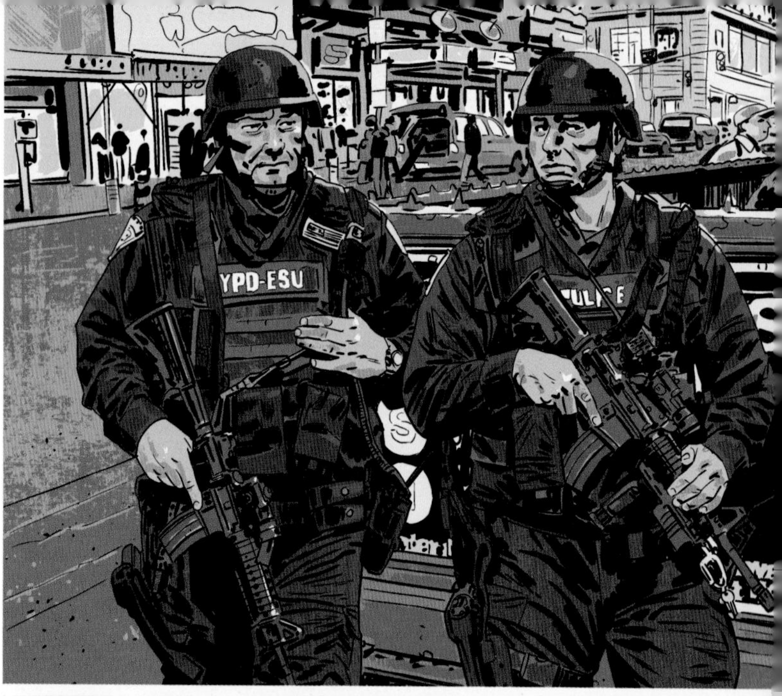
NYPD-ESU

And at first, I kind of enjoyed the show.

Seeing the entire city respond to the actions of a single person...

And actually being that person?

That kind of power was awesome.

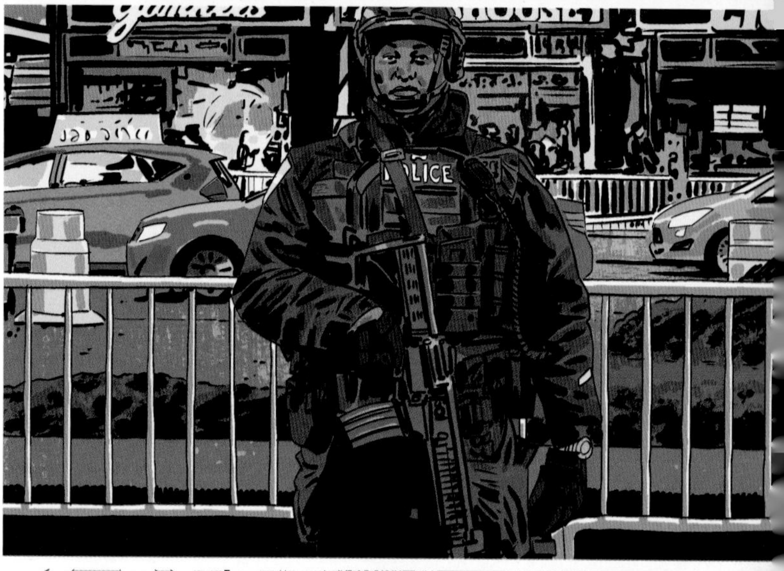
POLICE

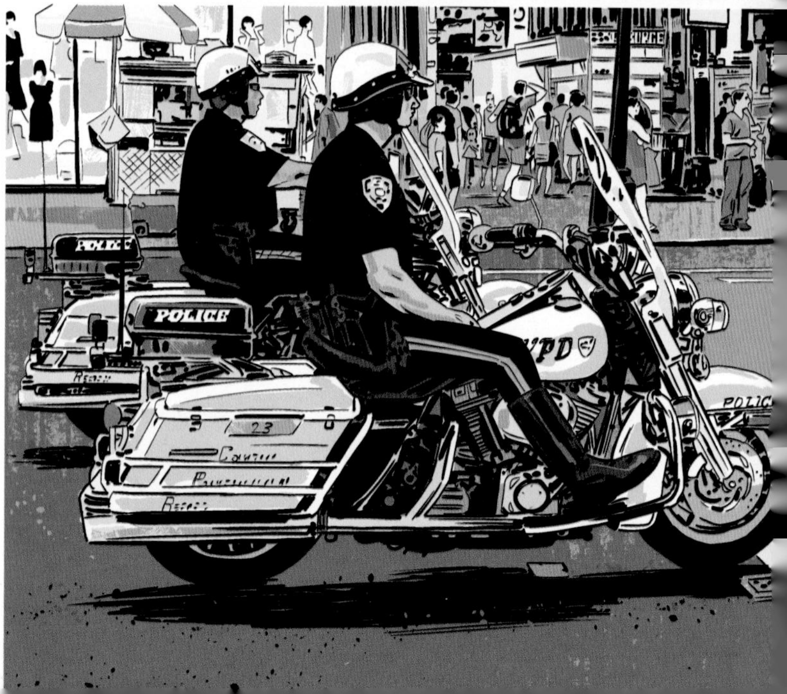
POLICE
NYPD

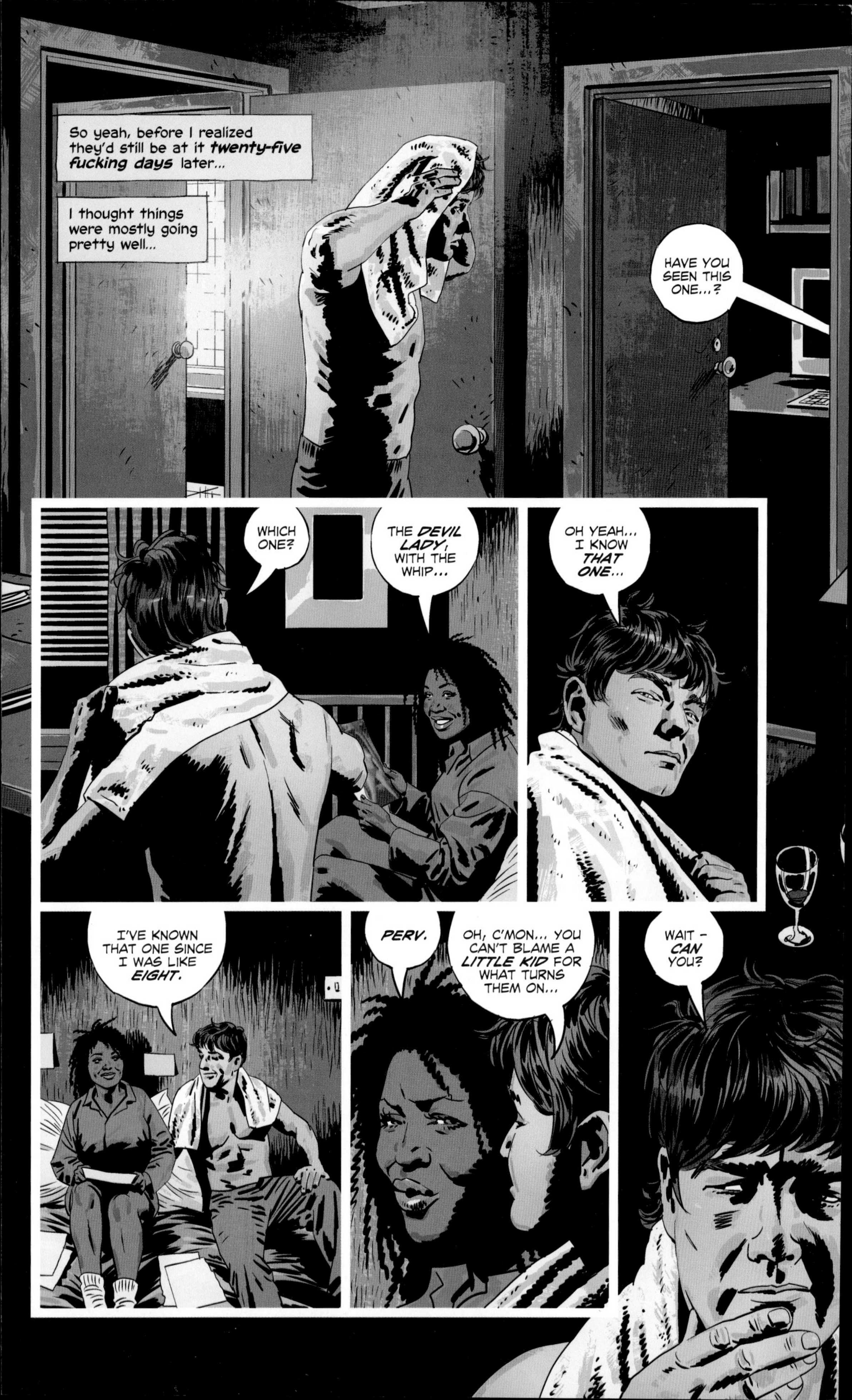
So yeah, before I realized they'd still be at it *twenty-five fucking days* later...
I thought things were mostly going pretty well...
HAVE YOU SEEN THIS ONE...?
WHICH ONE?
THE *DEVIL LADY*, WITH THE WHIP...
OH YEAH... I KNOW *THAT ONE*...
I'VE KNOWN THAT ONE SINCE I WAS LIKE *EIGHT*.
PERV.
OH, C'MON... YOU CAN'T BLAME A *LITTLE KID* FOR WHAT TURNS THEM ON...
WAIT - *CAN* YOU?

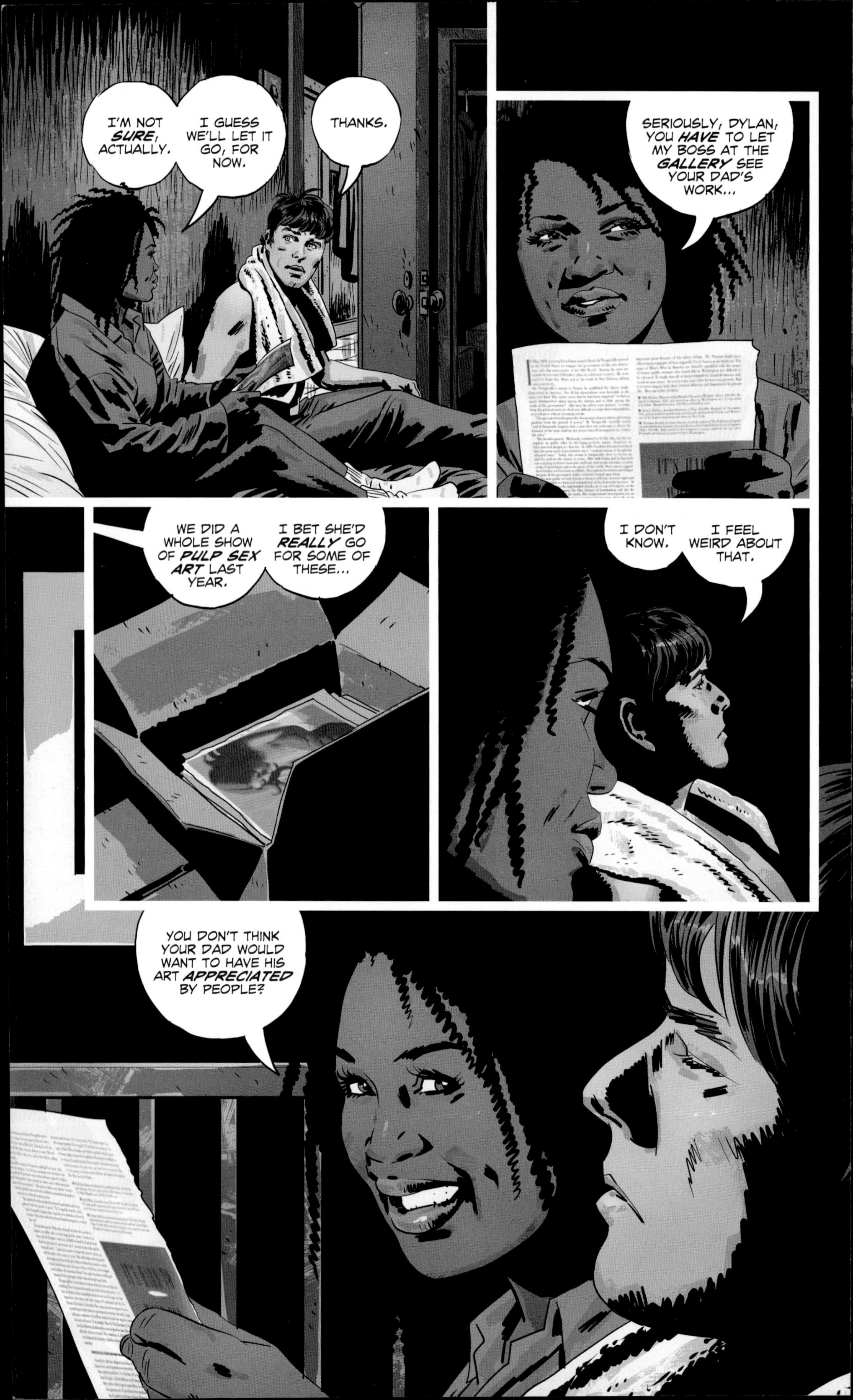
I'M NOT SURE, ACTUALLY.
I GUESS WE'LL LET IT GO, FOR NOW.
THANKS.
SERIOUSLY, DYLAN, YOU HAVE TO LET MY BOSS AT THE GALLERY SEE YOUR DAD'S WORK...
WE DID A WHOLE SHOW OF PULP SEX ART LAST YEAR.
I BET SHE'D REALLY GO FOR SOME OF THESE...
I DON'T KNOW.
I FEEL WEIRD ABOUT THAT.
YOU DON'T THINK YOUR DAD WOULD WANT TO HAVE HIS ART APPRECIATED BY PEOPLE?

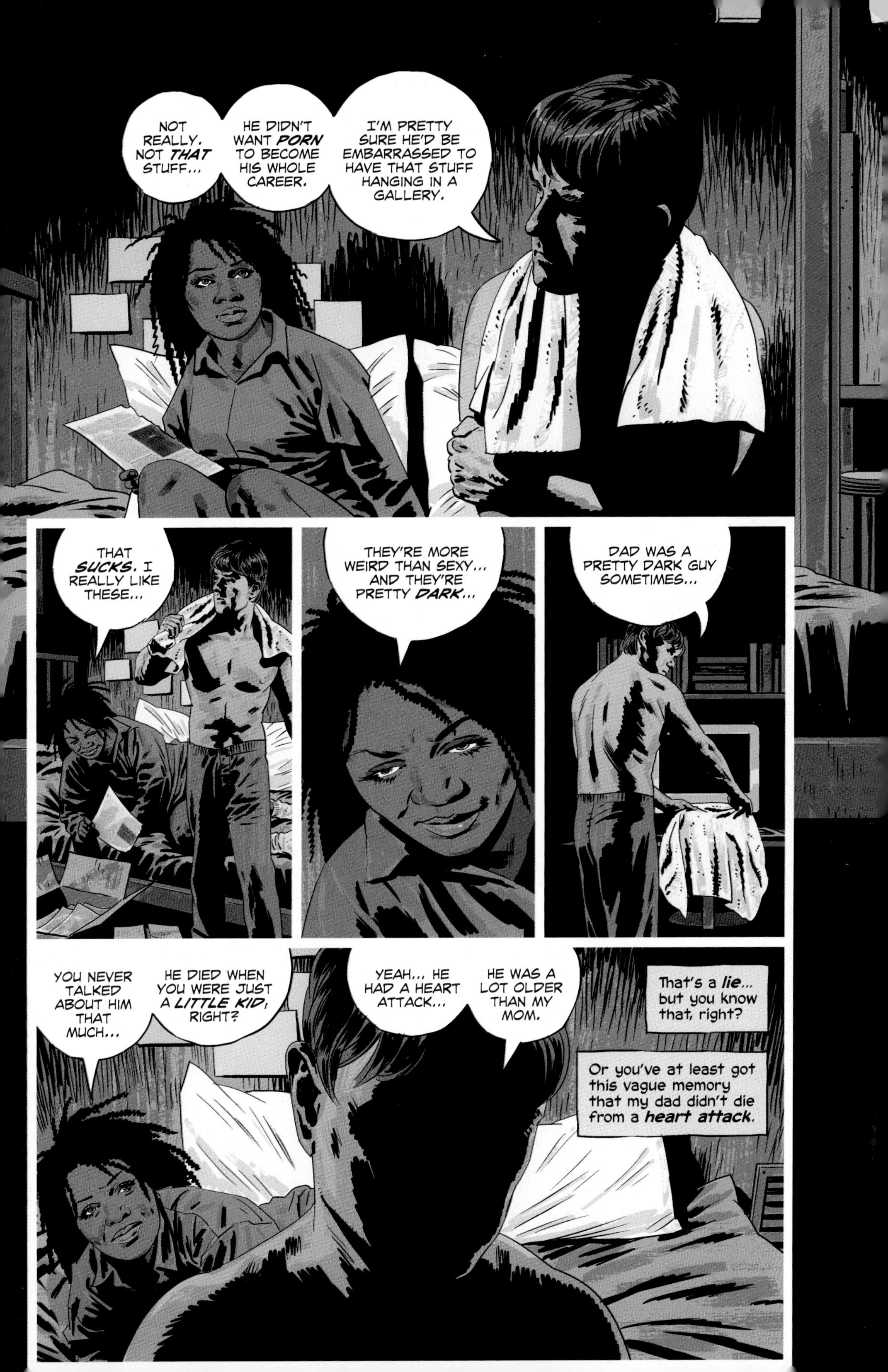
NOT REALLY. NOT *THAT* STUFF...
HE DIDN'T WANT *PORN* TO BECOME HIS WHOLE CAREER.
I'M PRETTY SURE HE'D BE EMBARRASSED TO HAVE THAT STUFF HANGING IN A GALLERY.
THAT *SUCKS.* I REALLY LIKE THESE...
THEY'RE MORE WEIRD THAN SEXY... AND THEY'RE PRETTY *DARK*...
DAD WAS A PRETTY DARK GUY SOMETIMES...
YOU NEVER TALKED ABOUT HIM THAT MUCH...
HE DIED WHEN YOU WERE JUST A *LITTLE KID*, RIGHT?
YEAH... HE HAD A HEART ATTACK...
HE WAS A LOT OLDER THAN MY MOM.
That's a *lie*... but you know that, right?
Or you've at least got this vague memory that my dad didn't die from a **heart attack**.

That's because I mentioned a while back that my dad had killed himself.

What he actually ***did*** was, he sent my mom to get his prescription filled at the pharmacy...

And then he sat down on the couch, put his gun in his mouth, and blew his brains out.

So why couldn't I say that to Daisy? Why did I make up a ***story*** instead?

By this point, we'd been spending almost every night together for a couple of weeks. Things were good.

So why didn't I open up?

I think it was because on some level, as good as it was, everything with me and Daisy also felt a bit ***unreal***.

Like our relationship was part of this fiction I was writing around myself now...

To cover up my secret life.

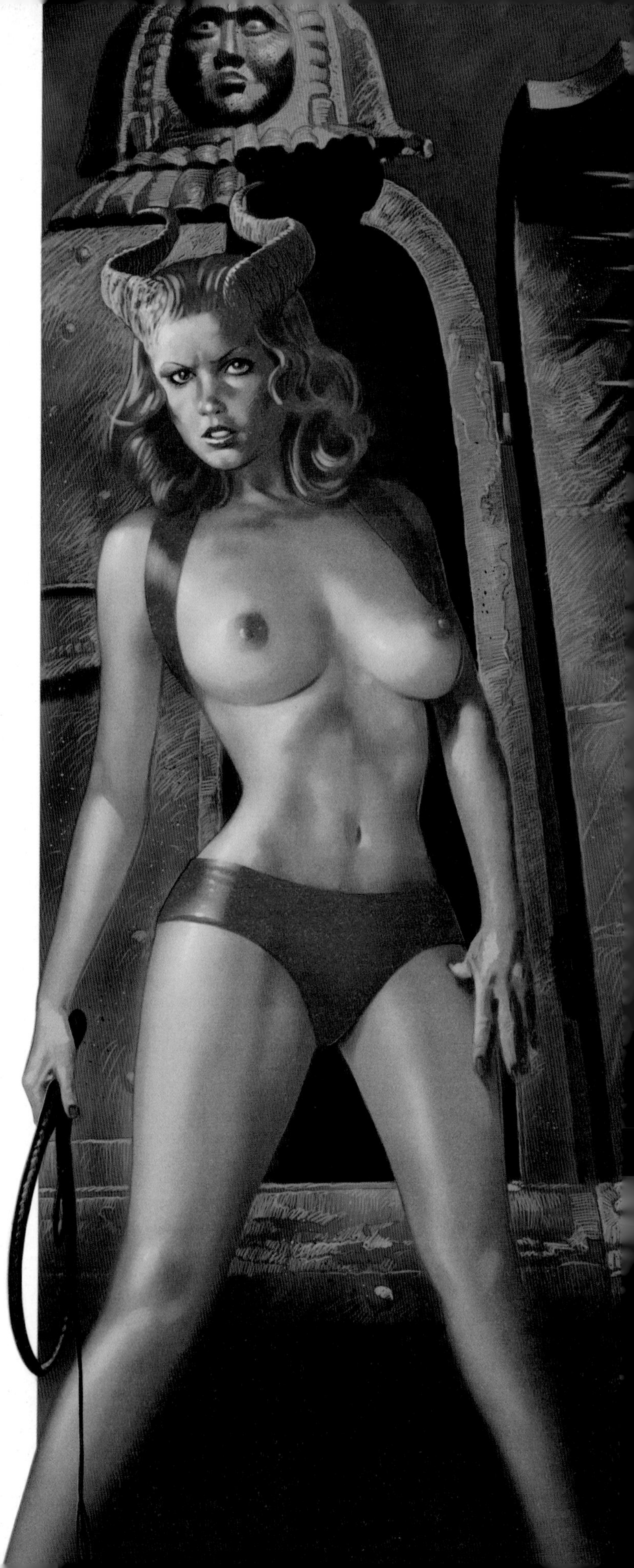

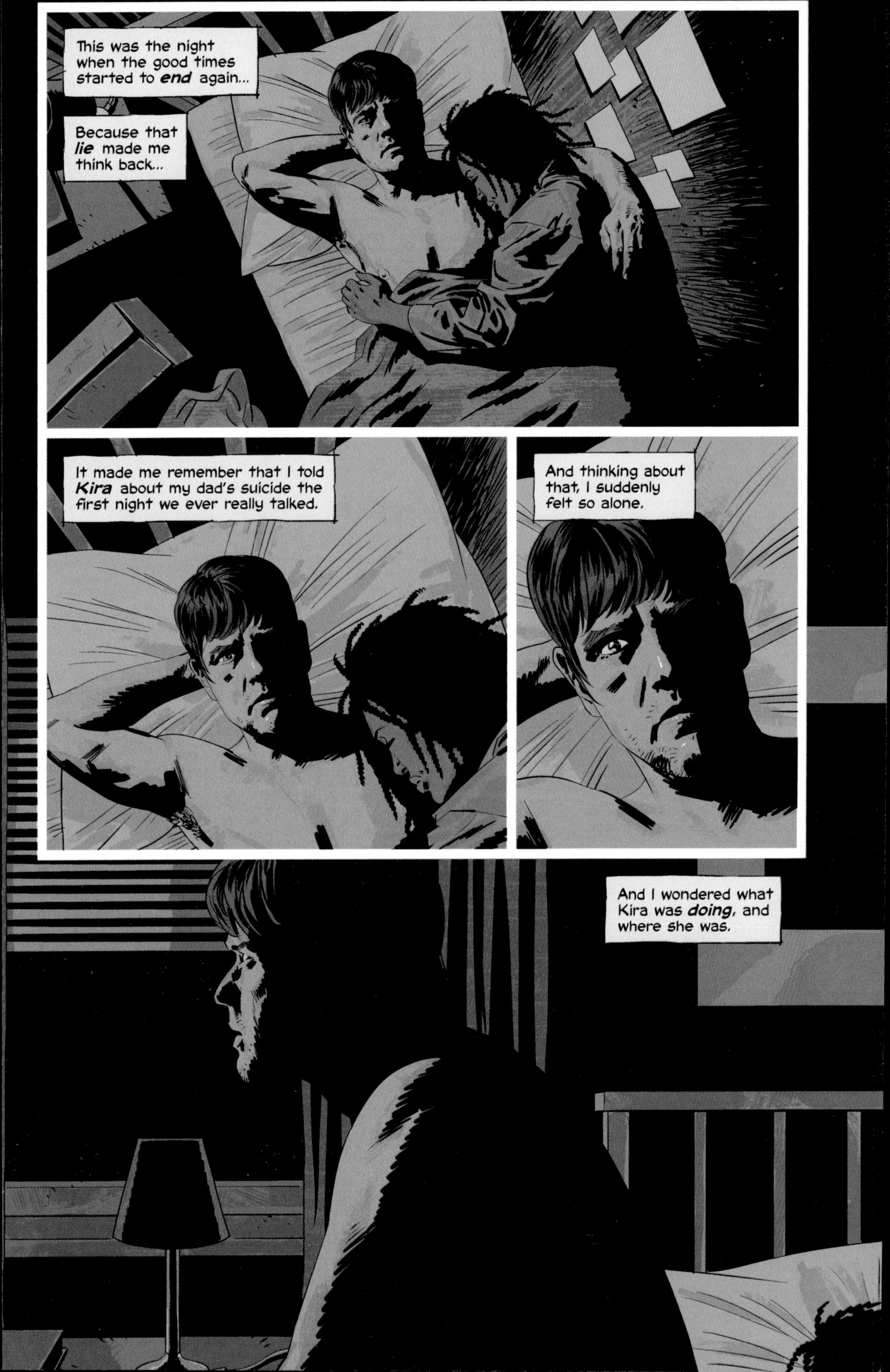
This was the night when the good times started to ***end*** again...
Because that ***lie*** made me think back...
It made me remember that I told ***Kira*** about my dad's suicide the first night we ever really talked.
And thinking about that, I suddenly felt so alone.
And I wondered what Kira was ***doing,*** and where she was.

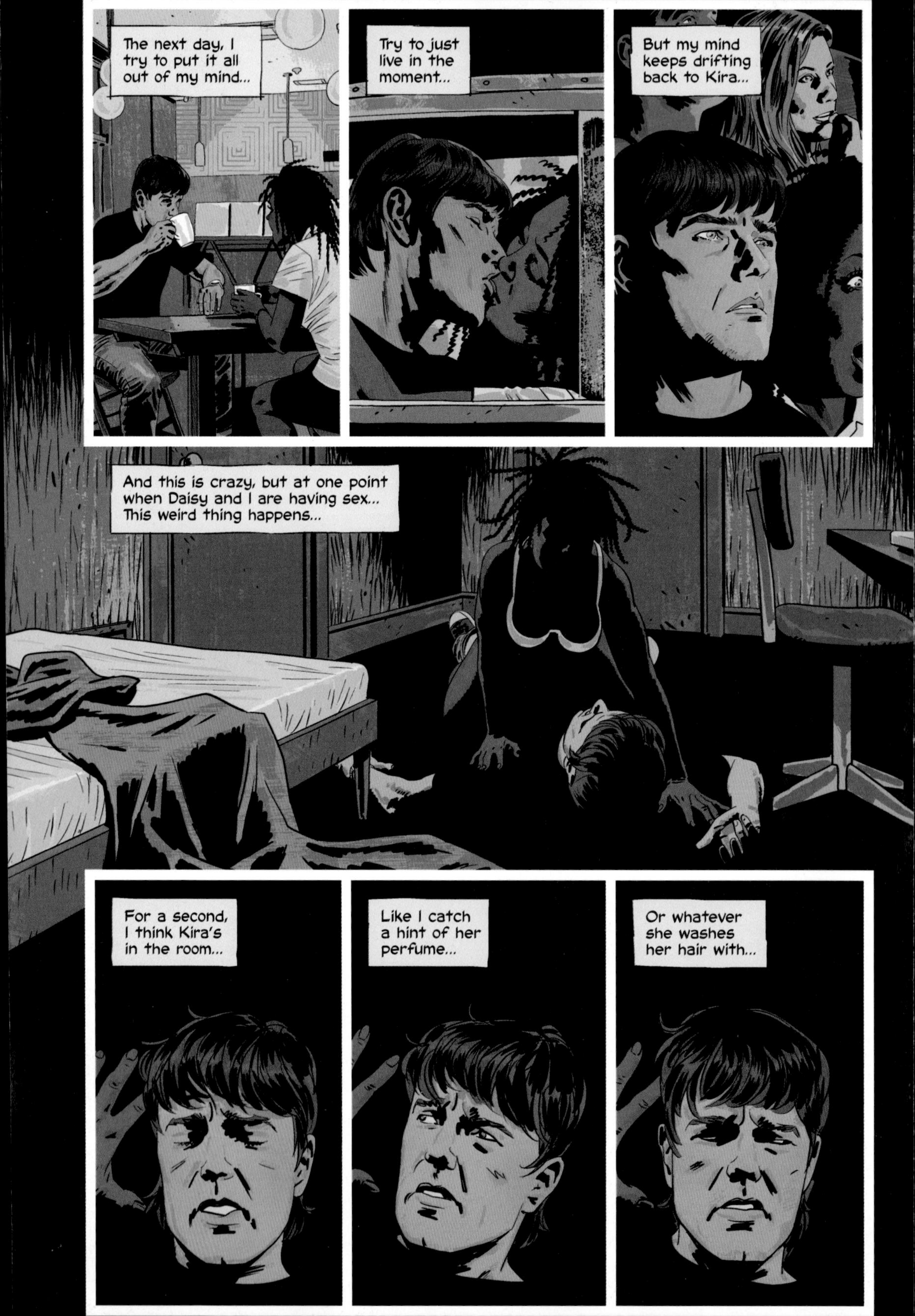
The next day, I try to put it all out of my mind...
Try to just live in the moment...
But my mind keeps drifting back to Kira...
And this is crazy, but at one point when Daisy and I are having sex... This weird thing happens...
For a second, I think Kira's in the room...
Like I catch a hint of her perfume...
Or whatever she washes her hair with...

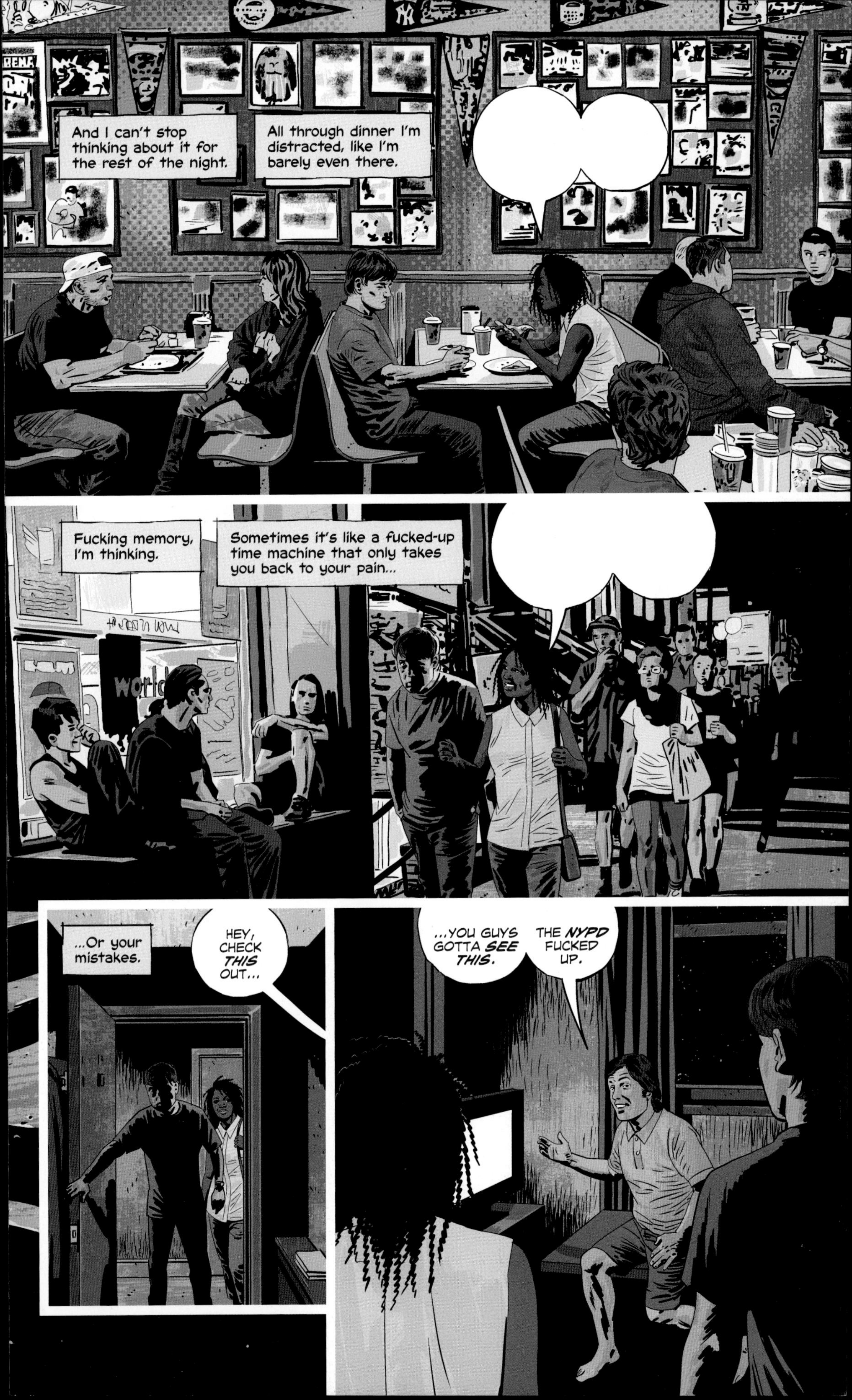
And I can't stop thinking about it for the rest of the night.
All through dinner I'm distracted, like I'm barely even there.
Fucking memory, I'm thinking.
Sometimes it's like a fucked-up time machine that only takes you back to your pain...
...Or your mistakes.
HEY, CHECK *THIS* OUT...
...YOU GUYS GOTTA *SEE THIS*.
THE *NYPD* FUCKED UP.

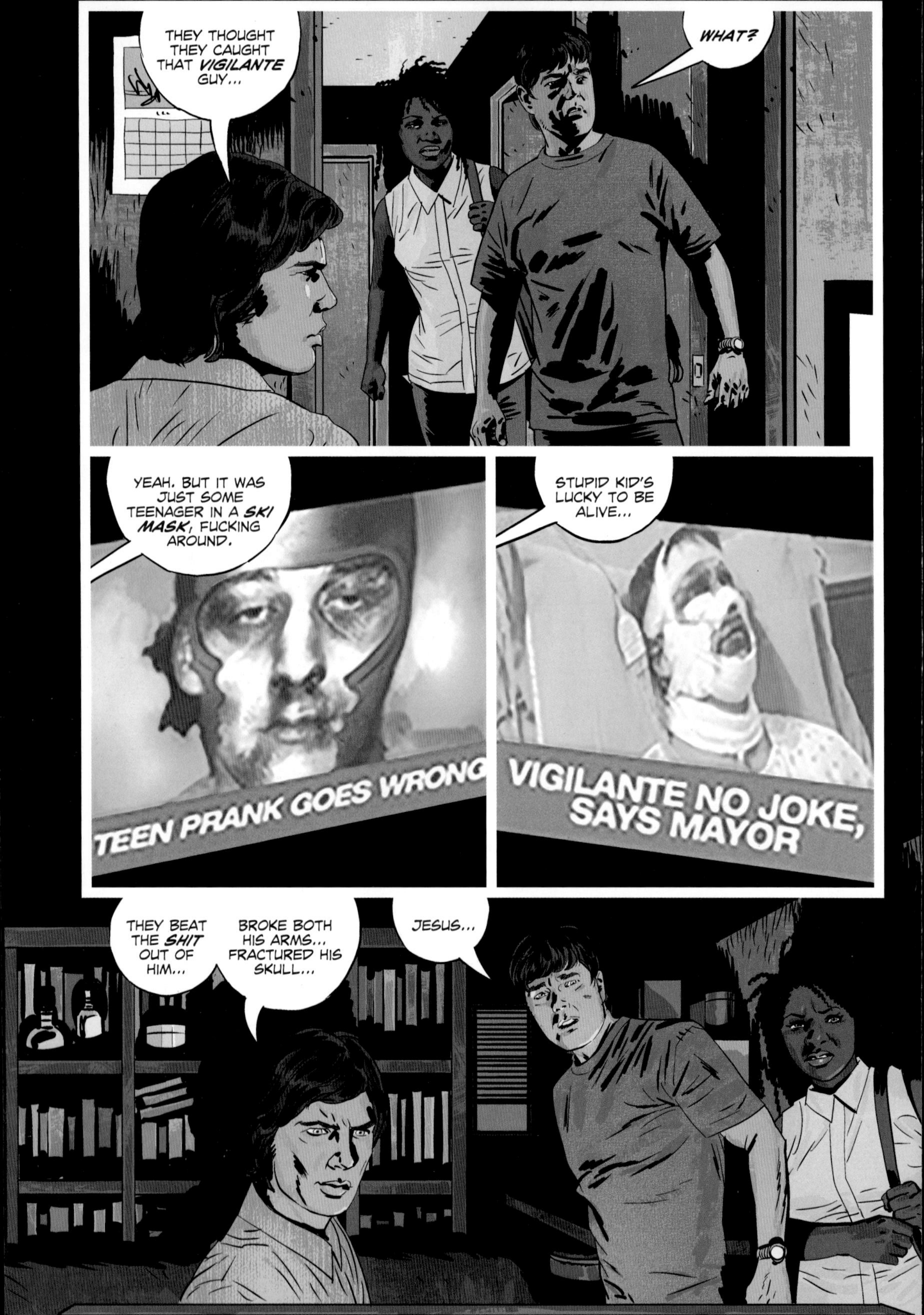
THEY THOUGHT THEY CAUGHT THAT VIGILANTE GUY...
WHAT?
YEAH. BUT IT WAS JUST SOME TEENAGER IN A SKI MASK, FUCKING AROUND.
TEEN PRANK GOES WRONG
STUPID KID'S LUCKY TO BE ALIVE...
VIGILANTE NO JOKE, SAYS MAYOR
THEY BEAT THE SHIT OUT OF HIM...
BROKE BOTH HIS ARMS... FRACTURED HIS SKULL...
JESUS...

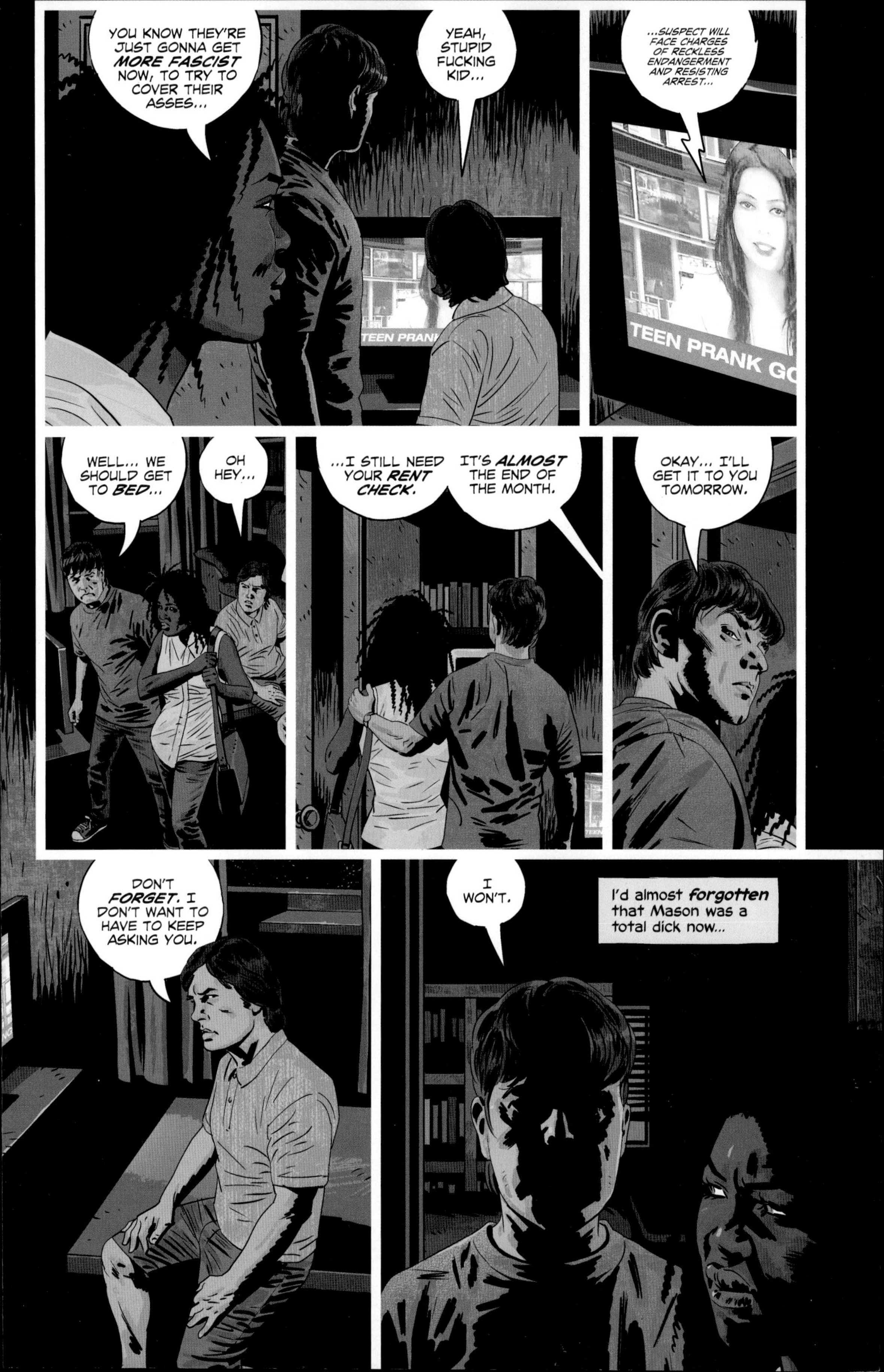
YOU KNOW THEY'RE JUST GONNA GET MORE FASCIST NOW, TO TRY TO COVER THEIR ASSES...
YEAH, STUPID FUCKING KID...
...SUSPECT WILL FACE CHARGES OF RECKLESS ENDANGERMENT AND RESISTING ARREST...
TEEN PRANK GO
WELL... WE SHOULD GET TO BED...
OH HEY...
...I STILL NEED YOUR RENT CHECK.
IT'S ALMOST THE END OF THE MONTH.
OKAY... I'LL GET IT TO YOU TOMORROW.
DON'T FORGET. I DON'T WANT TO HAVE TO KEEP ASKING YOU.
I WON'T.
I'd almost forgotten that Mason was a total dick now...

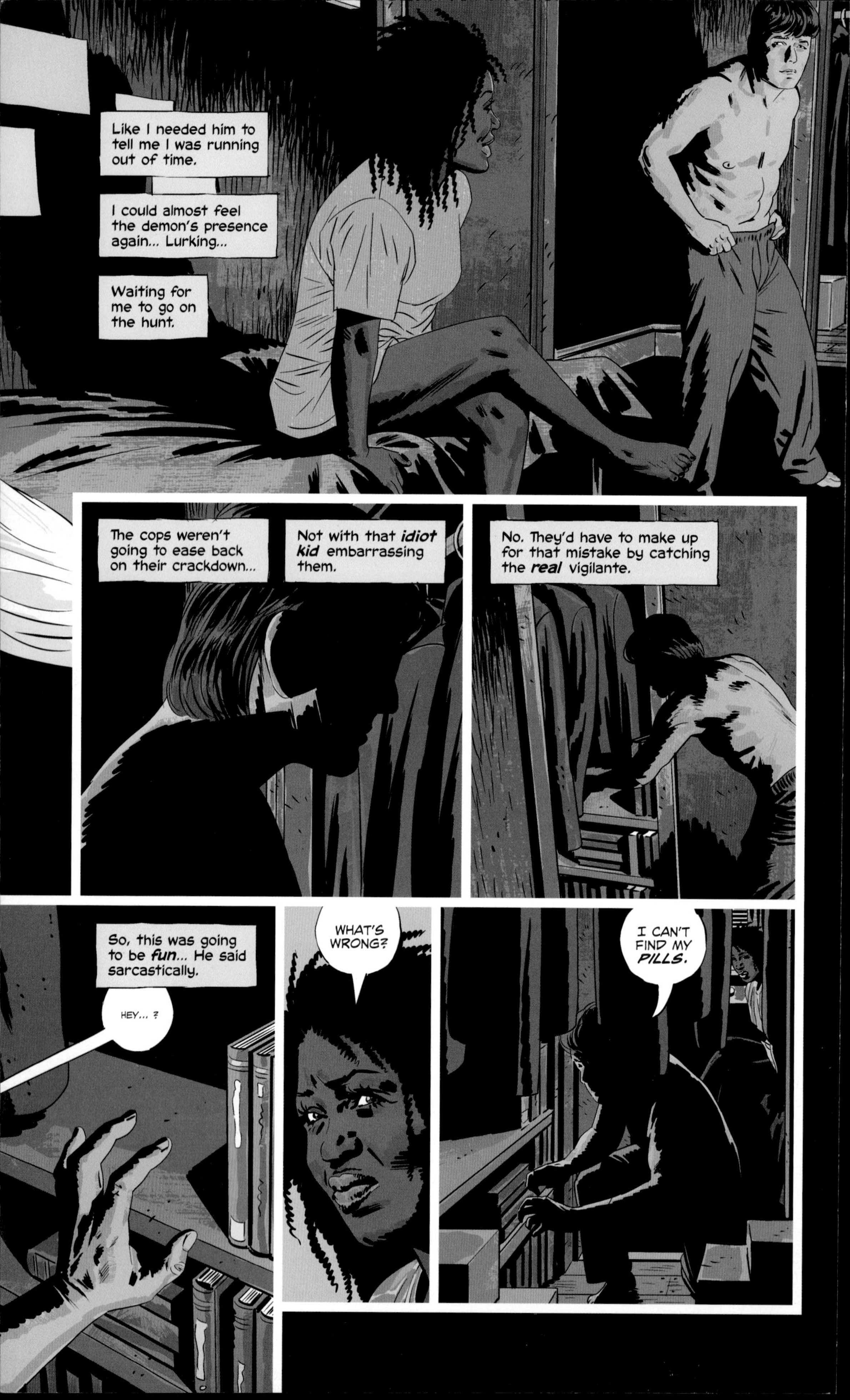
Like I needed him to tell me I was running out of time.
I could almost feel the demon's presence again... Lurking...
Waiting for me to go on the hunt.
The cops weren't going to ease back on their crackdown...
Not with that *idiot kid* embarrassing them.
No. They'd have to make up for that mistake by catching the *real* vigilante.
So, this was going to be *fun*... He said sarcastically.
HEY... ?
WHAT'S WRONG?
I CAN'T FIND MY *PILLS*.

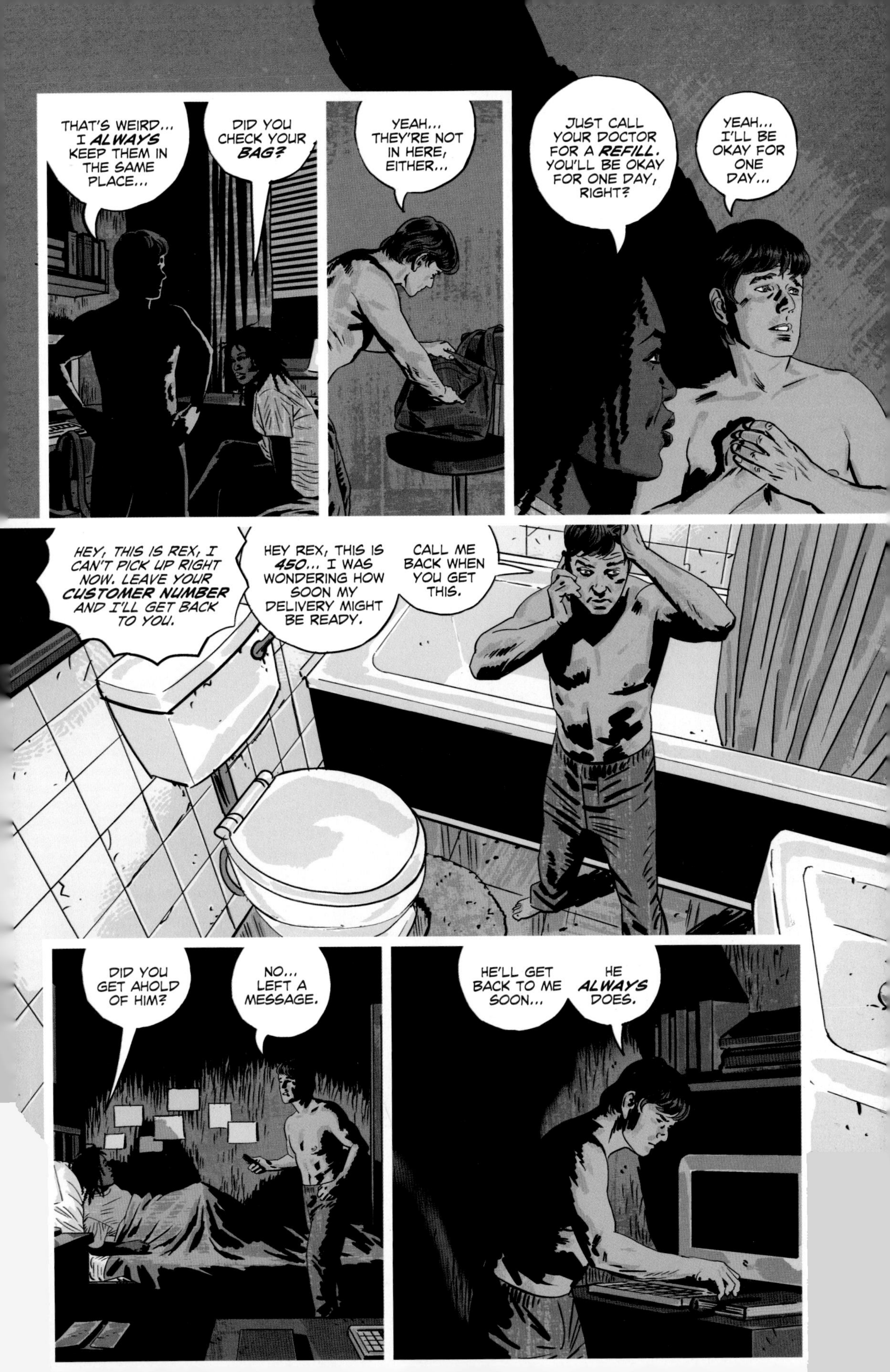
THAT'S WEIRD... I ALWAYS KEEP THEM IN THE SAME PLACE...
DID YOU CHECK YOUR BAG?
YEAH... THEY'RE NOT IN HERE, EITHER...
JUST CALL YOUR DOCTOR FOR A REFILL. YOU'LL BE OKAY FOR ONE DAY, RIGHT?
YEAH... I'LL BE OKAY FOR ONE DAY...
HEY, THIS IS REX, I CAN'T PICK UP RIGHT NOW. LEAVE YOUR CUSTOMER NUMBER AND I'LL GET BACK TO YOU.
HEY REX, THIS IS 450... I WAS WONDERING HOW SOON MY DELIVERY MIGHT BE READY.
CALL ME BACK WHEN YOU GET THIS.
DID YOU GET AHOLD OF HIM?
NO... LEFT A MESSAGE.
HE'LL GET BACK TO ME SOON...
HE ALWAYS DOES.

But Rex doesn't call me back that night or the next morning.

It's not like him, but I've got other things on my mind most of the day anyway...

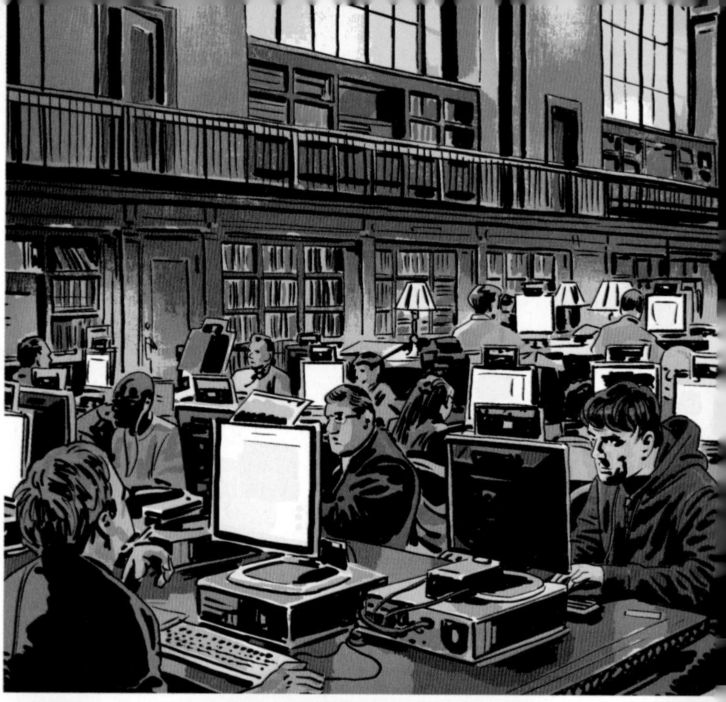

The past few weeks, I'd gotten pretty paranoid about my ***research***.

We all know the government is monitoring our phone calls and internet searches... But how closely?

Like, is it an unsorted mass of data, or can they put a murder victim's name into some ***algorithm*** and find out exactly who looked them up online?

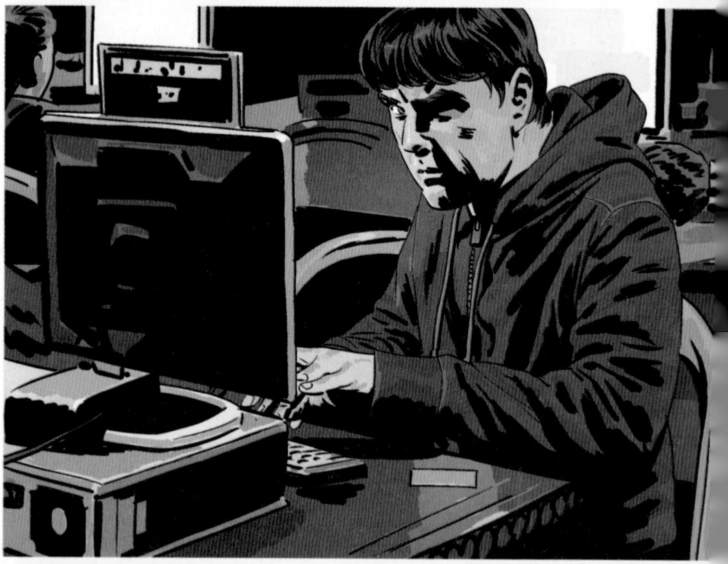

I didn't know, obviously, but it still felt safer using the computers at the library.

I'd switch from one to another every half hour or so... And I made sure not to get seen too well on the security cameras.

It was the best I could do to be ***anonymous*** without trying to become some kind of ***darknet*** hacker or something...

Which, let's face it, I was never going to be.

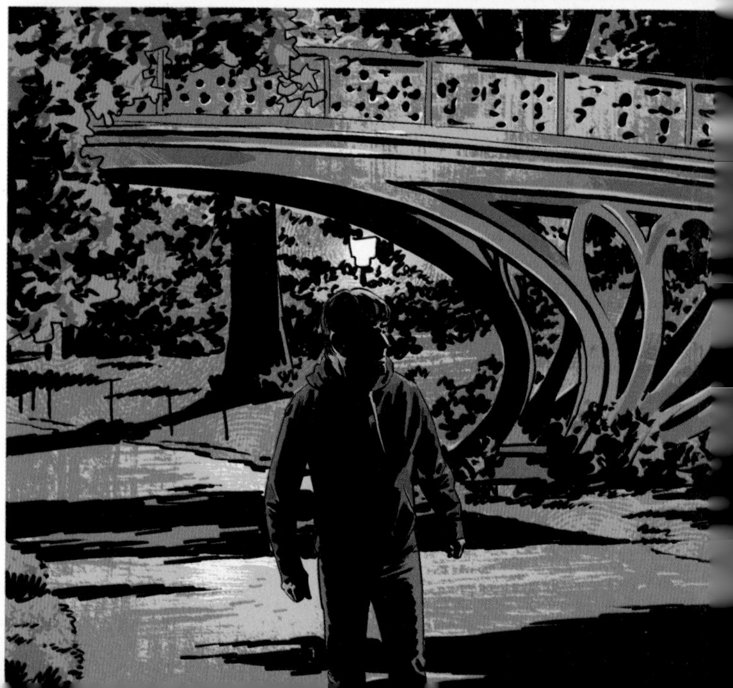

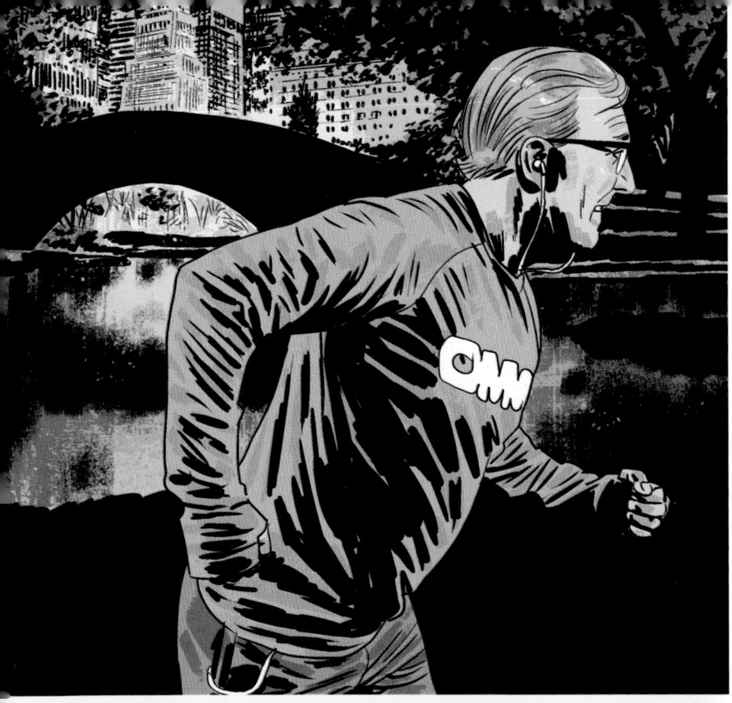

There weren't any ***deep investigative skills*** involved in finding this month's target, that's for sure...

I was just scanning local news when I stumbled across a story that made me sick... About a ***lobbyist*** named ***Gideon Prince.***

Lobbyists aren't all bad, of course. Some lobby for human rights or the environment.

But most of the time, they work for big business and what they do is, they pay a lot of money to politicians to pass laws or repeal regulations...

So the corporations they work for can do ***whatever the fuck*** they want.

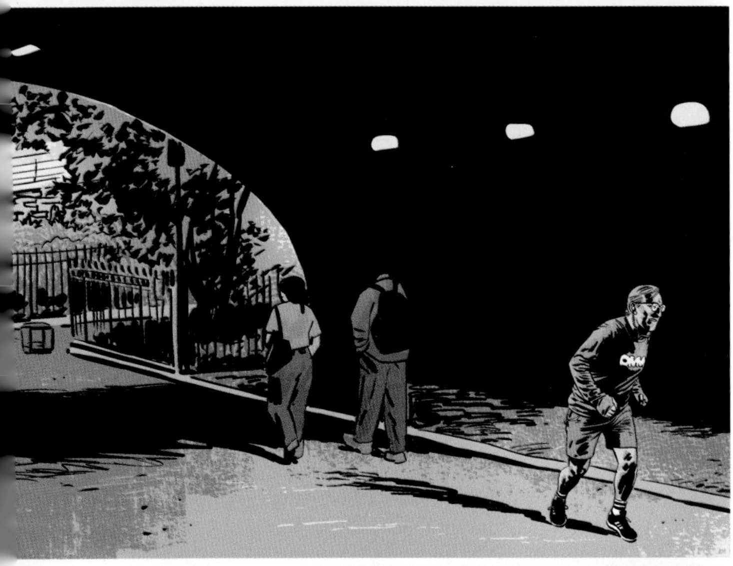

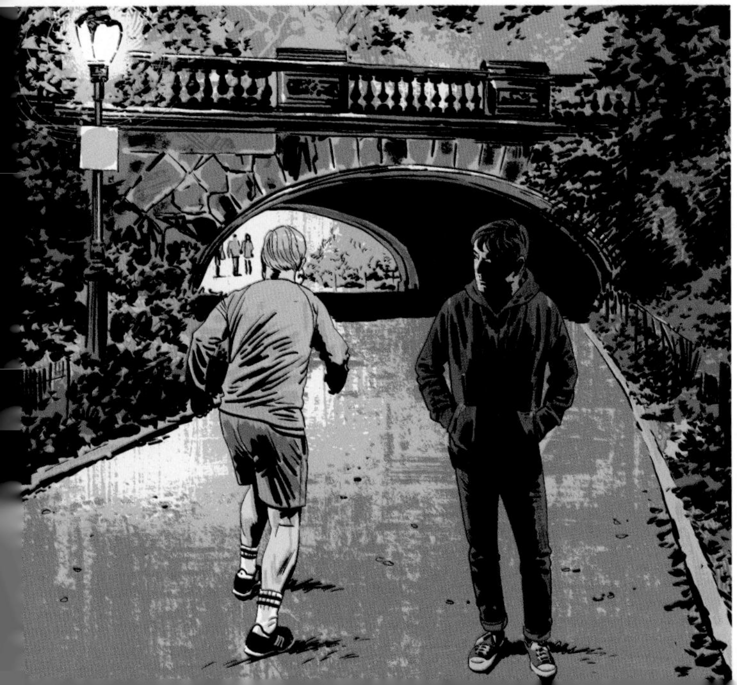

Gideon Prince was the kind of lobbyist who helped put ***poison*** in your drinking water and then laughed about it to his buddies.

And what I mean is, he'd done that ***exact*** thing.

His company had contaminated the water in a small town in Kentucky and when people were getting sick, he was caught on tape joking about it...

"Better get a job so you can afford ***bottled water***, Jethro."

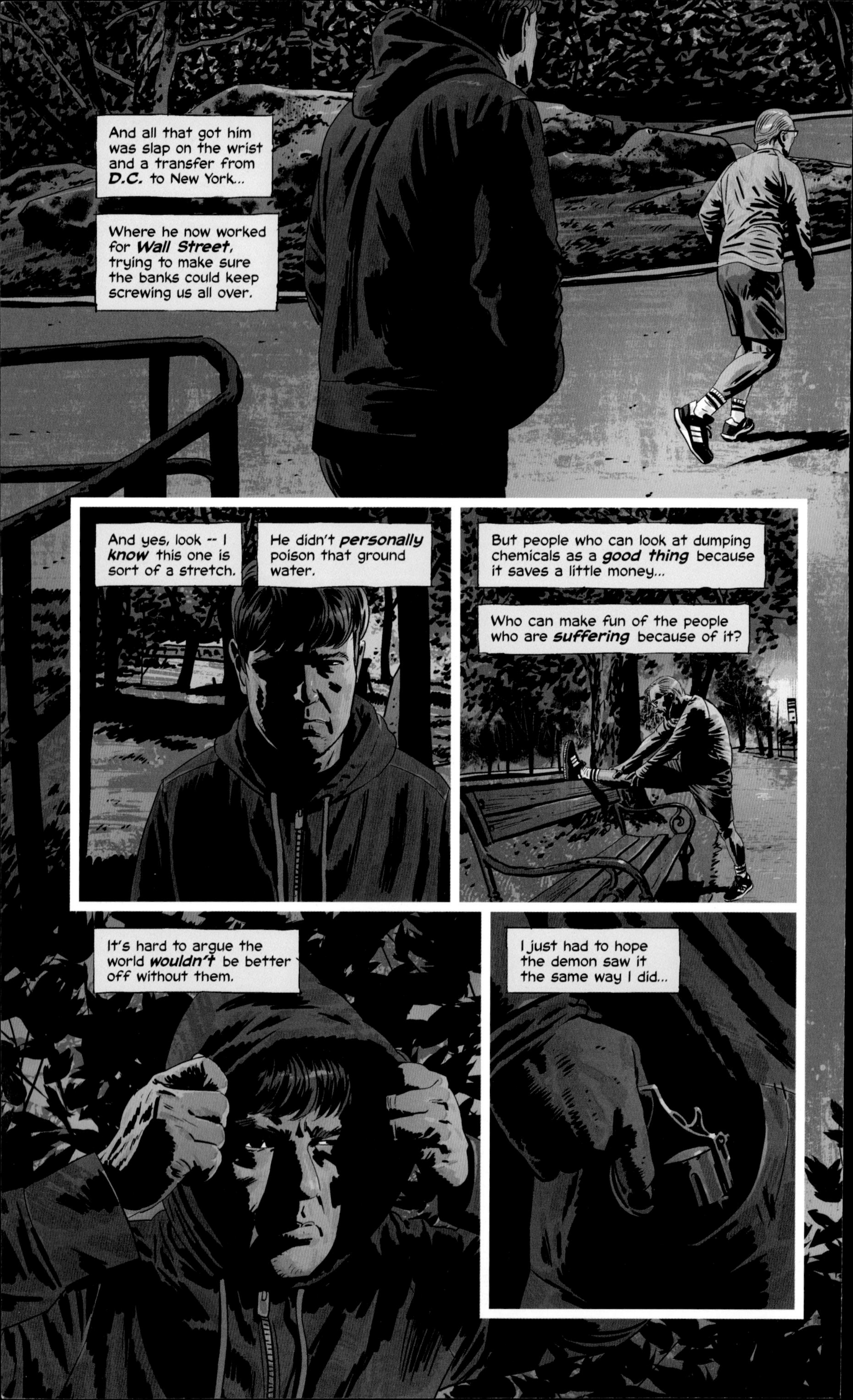
And all that got him was slap on the wrist and a transfer from D.C. to New York...
Where he now worked for Wall Street, trying to make sure the banks could keep screwing us all over.
And yes, look -- I know this one is sort of a stretch.
He didn't personally poison that ground water.
But people who can look at dumping chemicals as a good thing because it saves a little money...
Who can make fun of the people who are suffering because of it?
It's hard to argue the world wouldn't be better off without them.
I just had to hope the demon saw it the same way I did...

But, of course, it couldn't be that simple...

No... There just had to be a bunch of *cops* patrolling the park tonight.

And they just had to be right in front of us on the path.

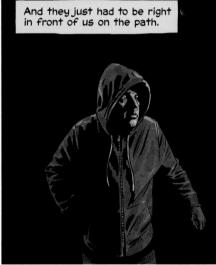

Shit... There was no way I could do this...

I had to think of something. I had to --

HEY... ?

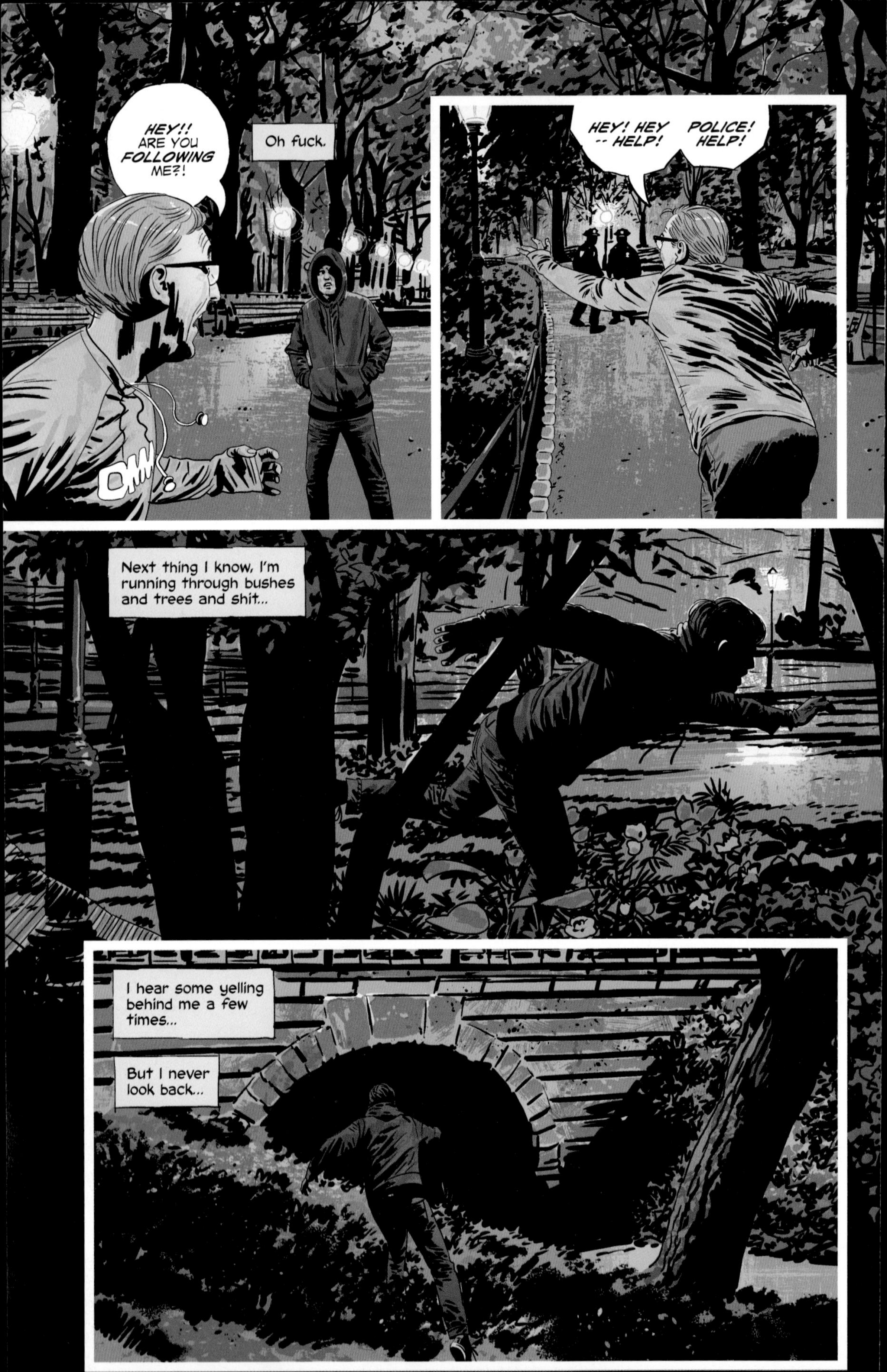
HEY!! ARE YOU FOLLOWING ME?!
Oh fuck.
OMW
HEY! HEY -- HELP!
POLICE! HELP!
Next thing I know, I'm running through bushes and trees and shit...
I hear some yelling behind me a few times...
But I never look back...

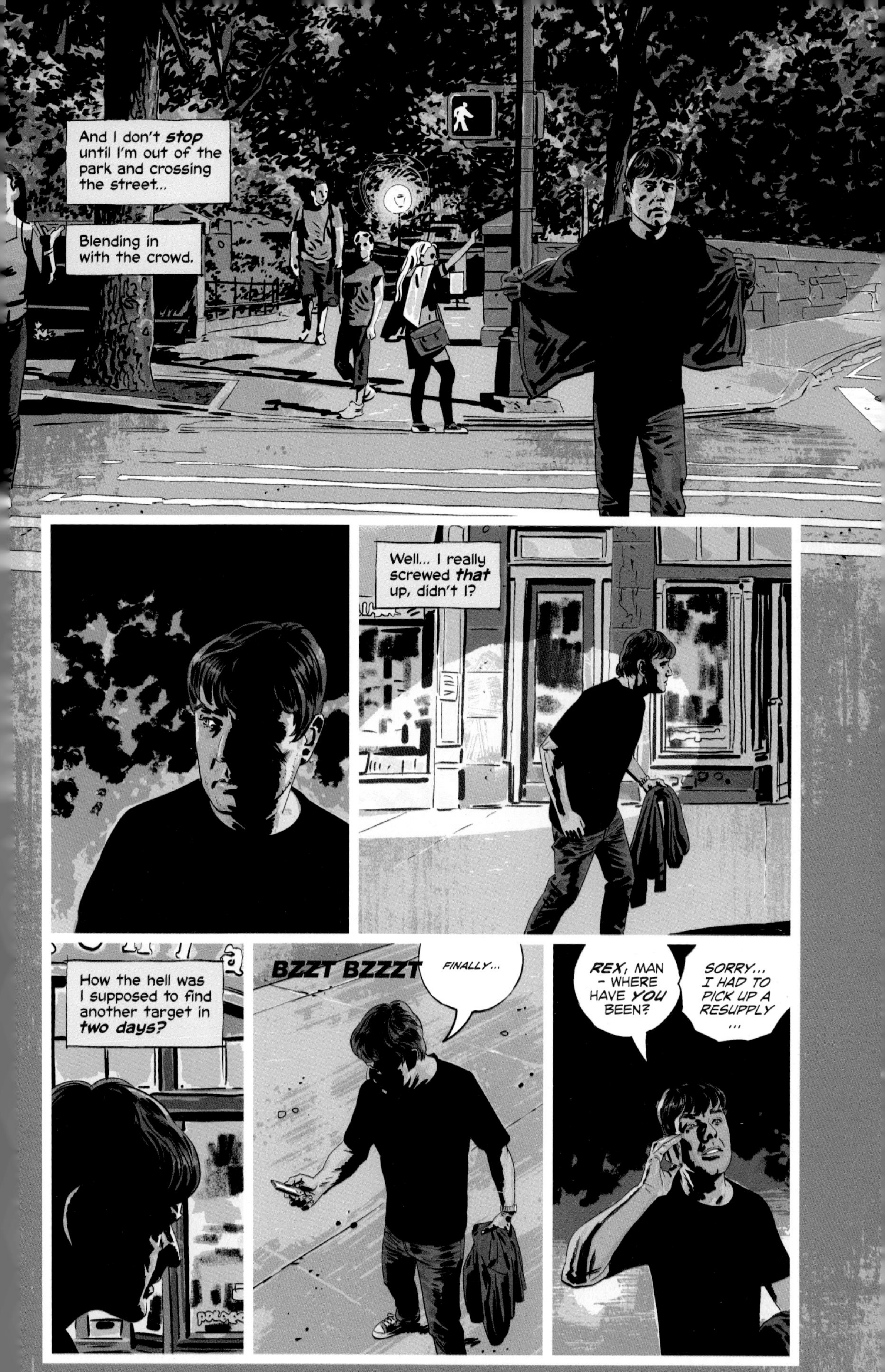
And I don't *stop* until I'm out of the park and crossing the street...
Blending in with the crowd.
Well... I really screwed *that* up, didn't I?
How the hell was I supposed to find another target in *two days?*
BZZT BZZZT
FINALLY...
REX, MAN – WHERE HAVE *YOU* BEEN?
SORRY... I HAD TO PICK UP A RESUPPLY ...

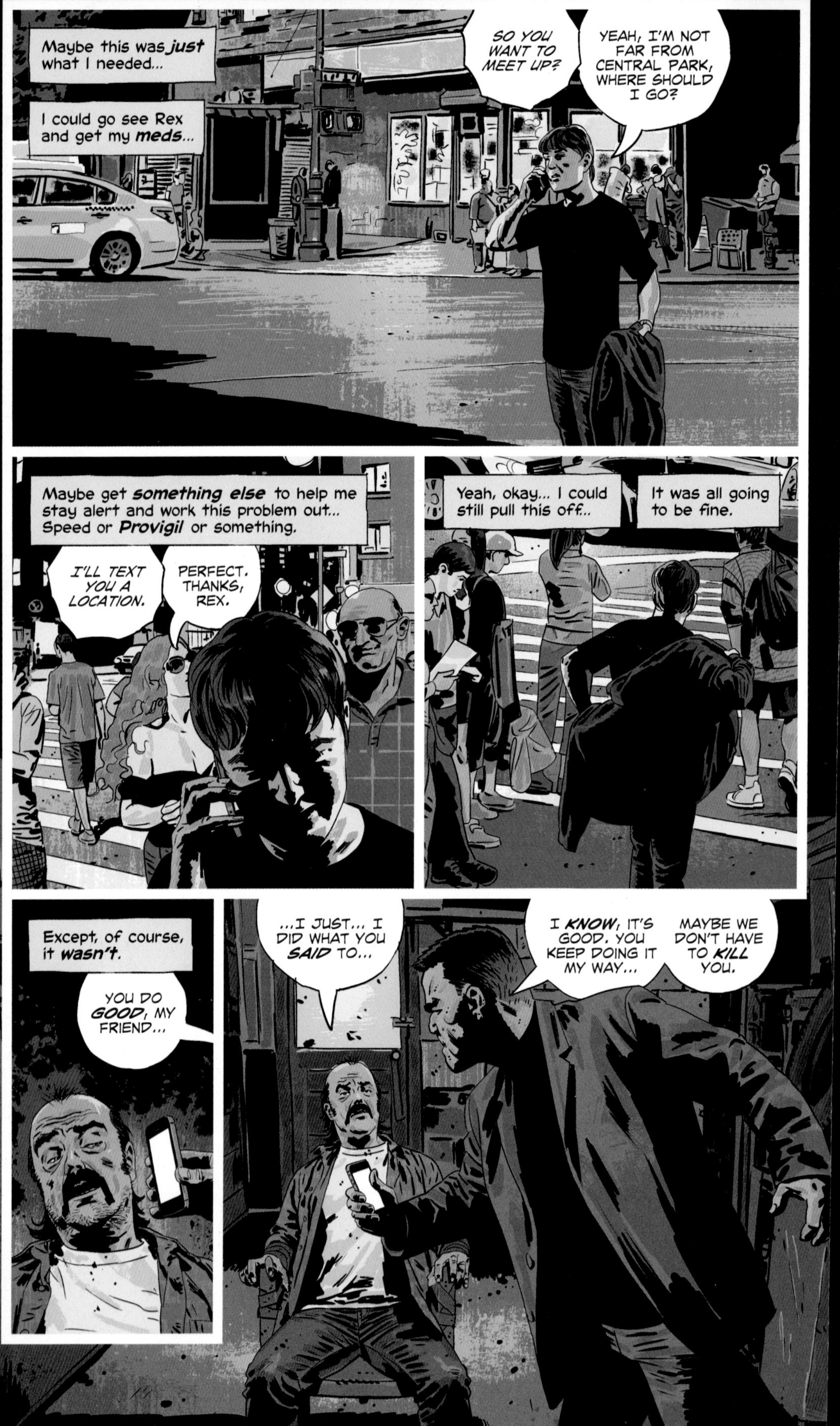
Maybe this was just what I needed...
I could go see Rex and get my meds...
SO YOU WANT TO MEET UP?
YEAH, I'M NOT FAR FROM CENTRAL PARK, WHERE SHOULD I GO?
Maybe get something else to help me stay alert and work this problem out... Speed or Provigil or something.
I'LL TEXT YOU A LOCATION.
PERFECT. THANKS, REX.
Yeah, okay... I could still pull this off...
It was all going to be fine.
Except, of course, it wasn't.
YOU DO GOOD, MY FRIEND...
...I JUST... I DID WHAT YOU SAID TO...
I KNOW, IT'S GOOD. YOU KEEP DOING IT MY WAY...
MAYBE WE DON'T HAVE TO KILL YOU.

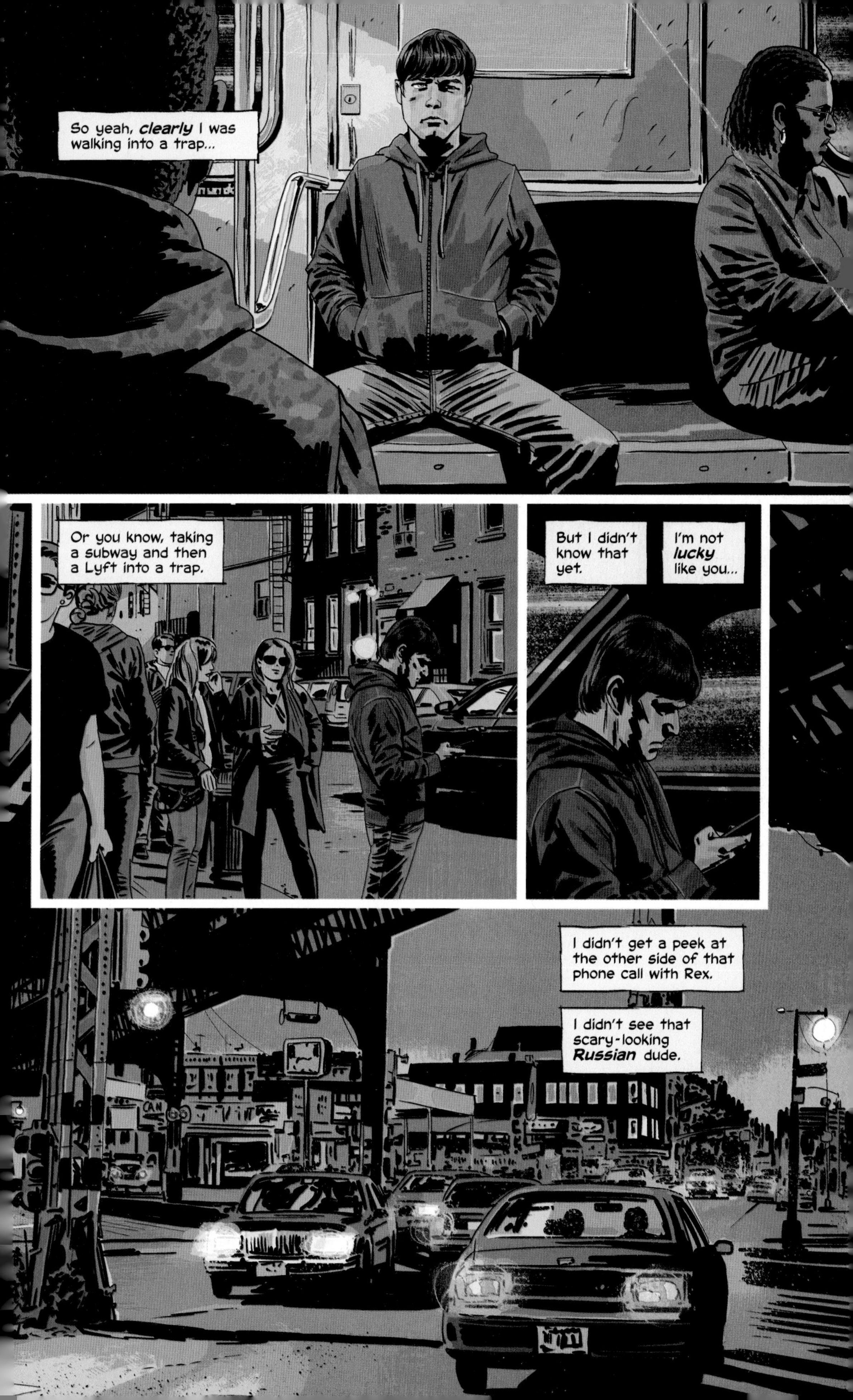
So yeah, *clearly* I was walking into a trap...
Or you know, taking a subway and then a Lyft into a trap.
But I didn't know that yet.
I'm not *lucky* like you...
I didn't get a peek at the other side of that phone call with Rex.
I didn't see that scary-looking *Russian* dude.

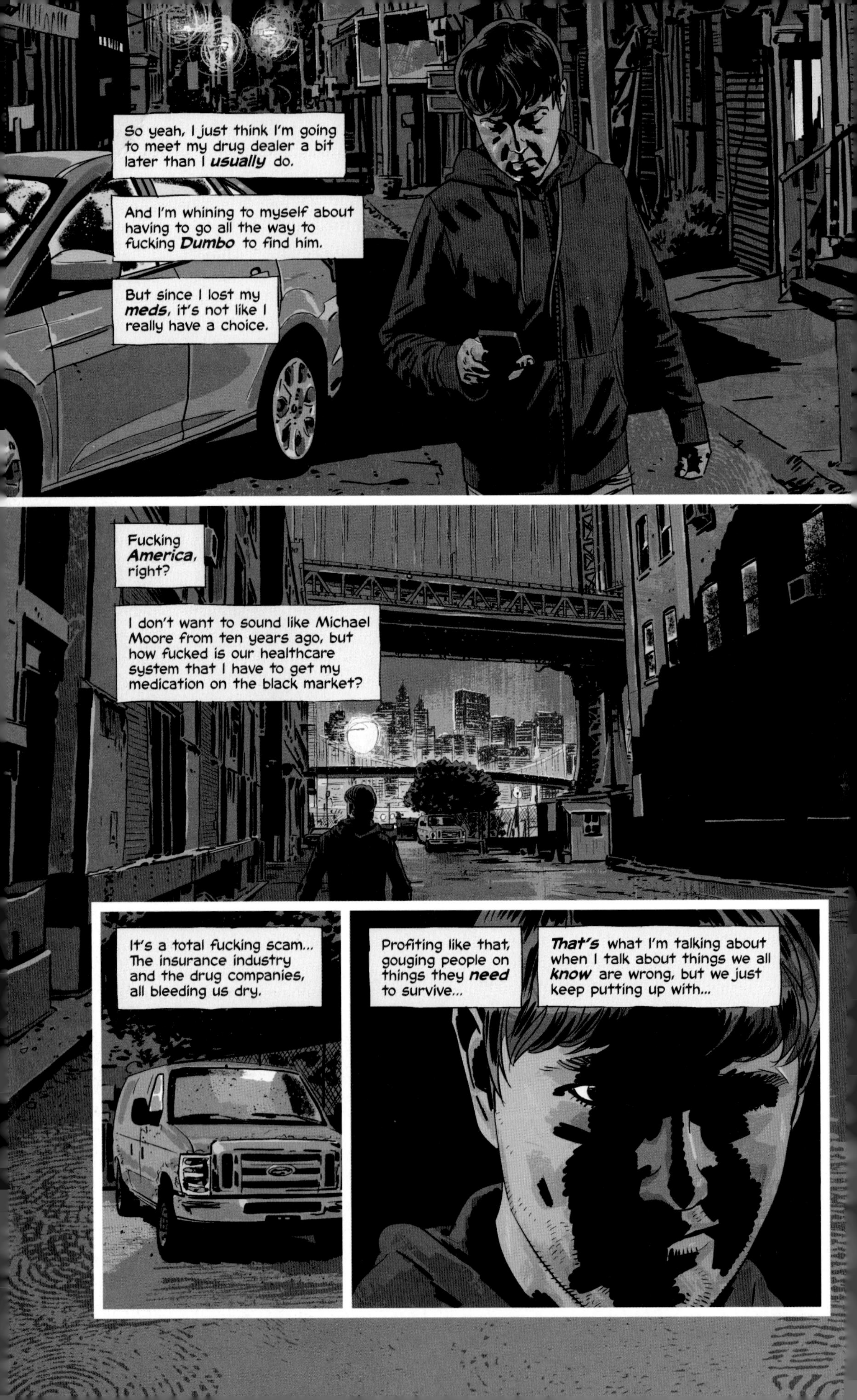

So yeah, I just think I'm going to meet my drug dealer a bit later than I *usually* do.
And I'm whining to myself about having to go all the way to fucking *Dumbo* to find him.
But since I lost my *meds*, it's not like I really have a choice.
Fucking *America*, right?
I don't want to sound like Michael Moore from ten years ago, but how fucked is our healthcare system that I have to get my medication on the black market?
It's a total fucking scam... The insurance industry and the drug companies, all bleeding us dry.
Profiting like that, gouging people on things they *need* to survive...
That's what I'm talking about when I talk about things we all *know* are wrong, but we just keep putting up with...

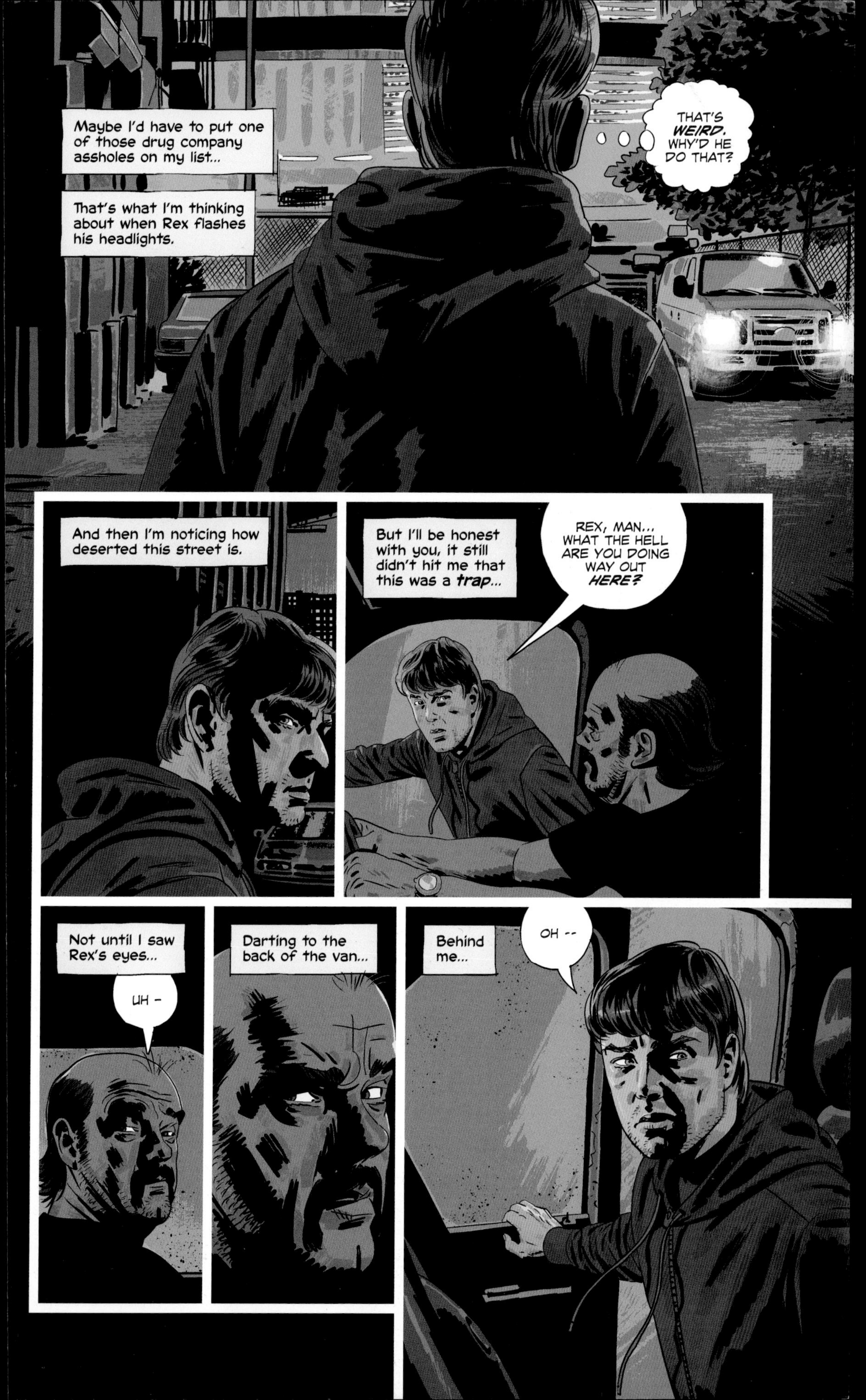
Maybe I'd have to put one of those drug company assholes on my list...
That's what I'm thinking about when Rex flashes his headlights.
THAT'S WEIRD. WHY'D HE DO THAT?
And then I'm noticing how deserted this street is.
But I'll be honest with you, it still didn't hit me that this was a trap...
REX, MAN... WHAT THE HELL ARE YOU DOING WAY OUT HERE?
Not until I saw Rex's eyes...
UH -
Darting to the back of the van...
Behind me...
OH --

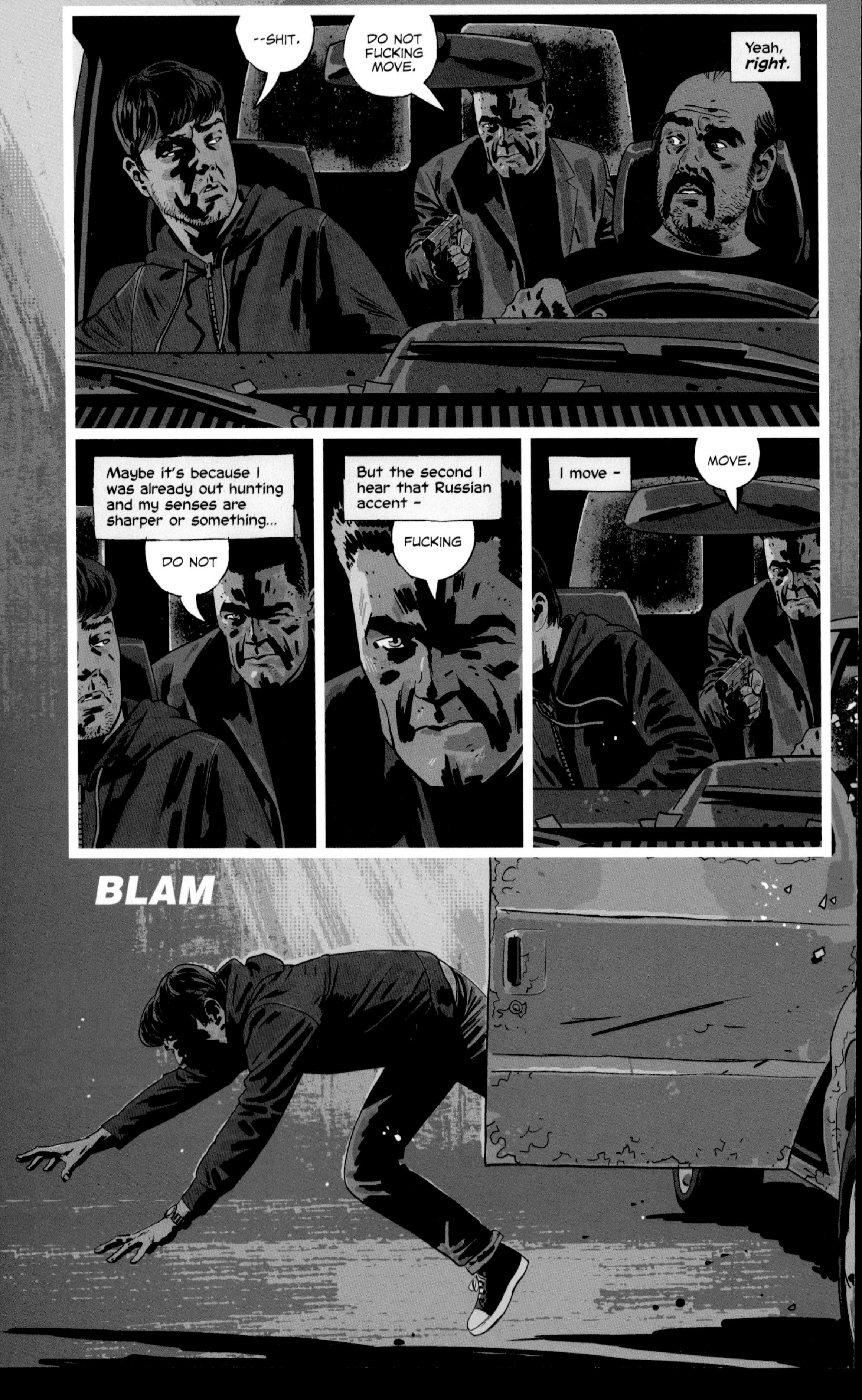
--SHIT.
DO NOT FUCKING MOVE.
Yeah, *right*.
Maybe it's because I was already out hunting and my senses are sharper or something...
DO NOT
But the second I hear that Russian accent -
FUCKING
I move -
MOVE.
BLAM

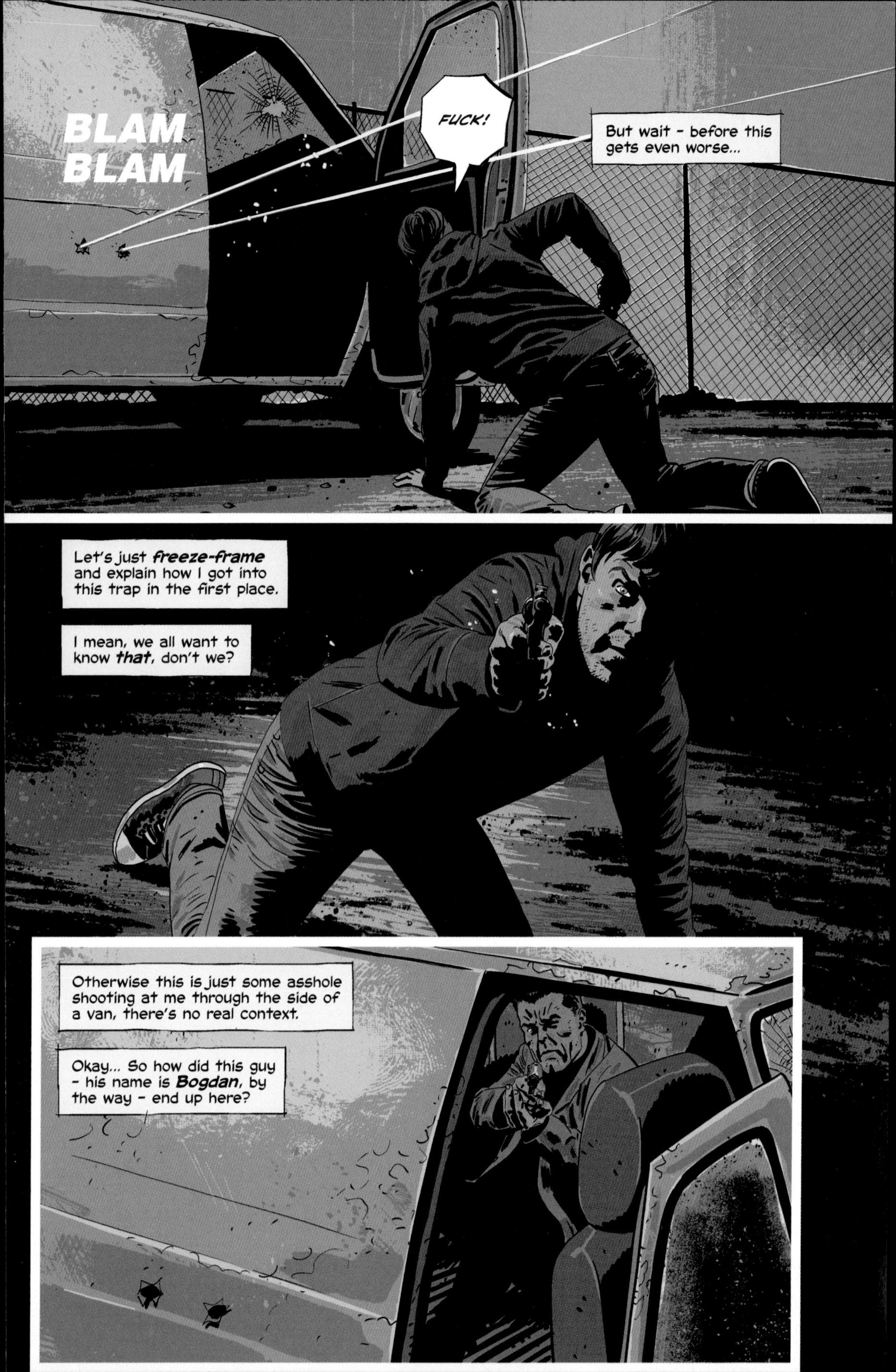
BLAM
BLAM
FUCK!
But wait - before this gets even worse...
Let's just *freeze-frame* and explain how I got into this trap in the first place.
I mean, we all want to know *that*, don't we?
Otherwise this is just some asshole shooting at me through the side of a van, there's no real context.
Okay... So how did this guy - his name is *Bogdan*, by the way - end up here?

Well, remember when I barely escaped from the NYPD and I thought I was all hot shit, until that got me splashed all over the news?

And remember how my getaway ***cab driver*** that day was a Russian?

No, of course you don't remember that. I even said at the time you probably wouldn't.

But anyway, he ***was***.

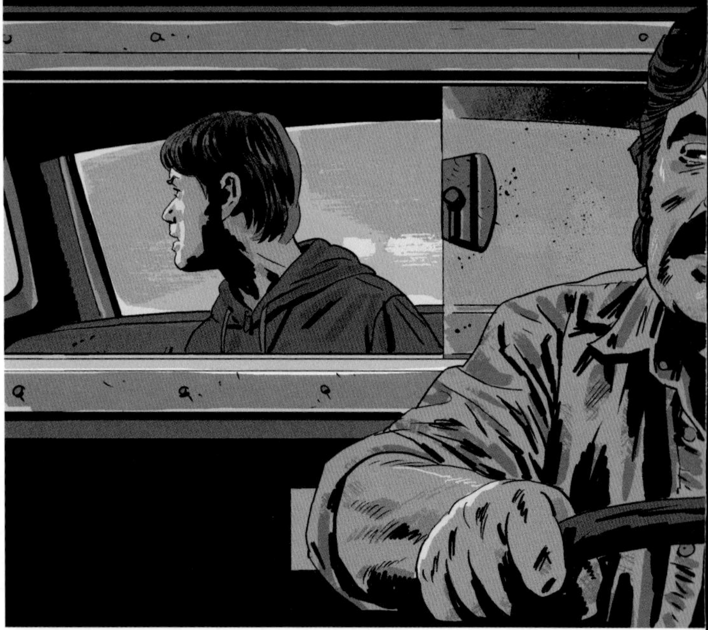

And it turns out if you kill one of their men - and shoot one of their strippers - the Russian mafia holds a grudge.

So when I was suddenly front-page news, the Russians sent that guy you just met, ***Bogdan***, to look for me.

Bogdan put the word out that they were paying for information on the masked vigilante...

And a few days later, my Russian cab driver came forward to tell him about a fare he'd picked up at the time of the shooting...

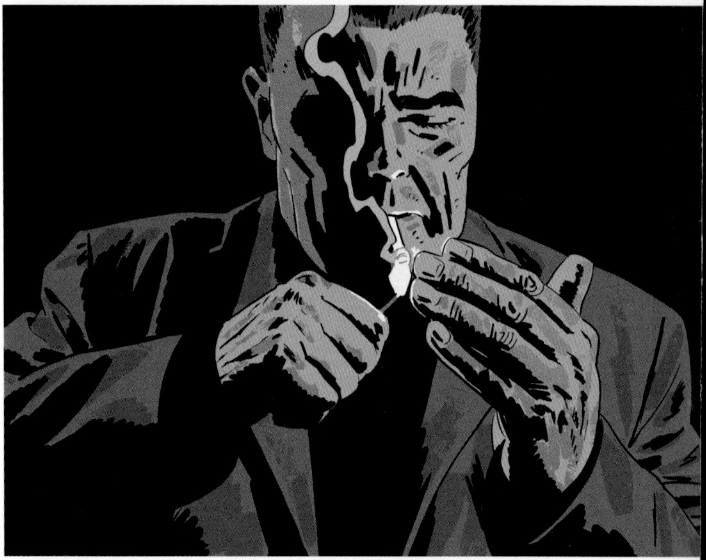

A young guy in a hoodie, who smelled like gunpowder.

The cabbie had made the connection when the police interviewed him earlier...

But the police weren't Russian, and they weren't offering him money.

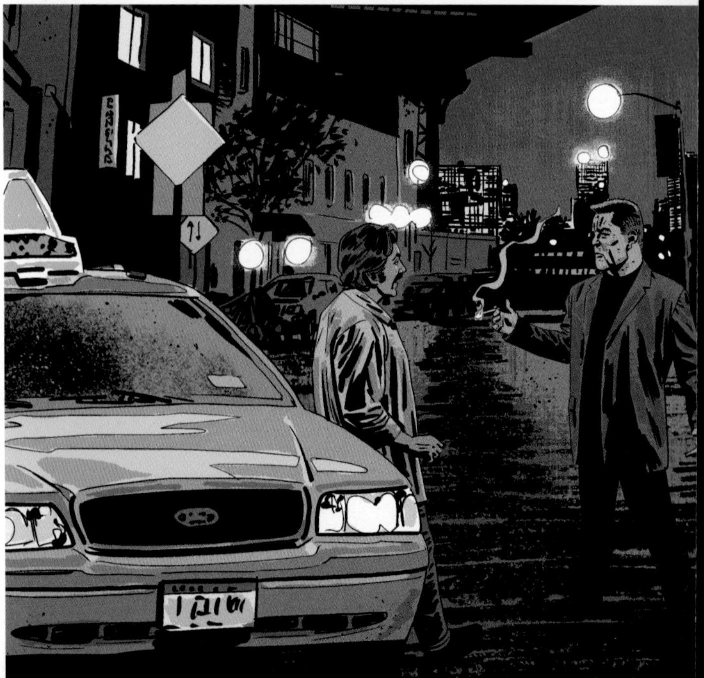

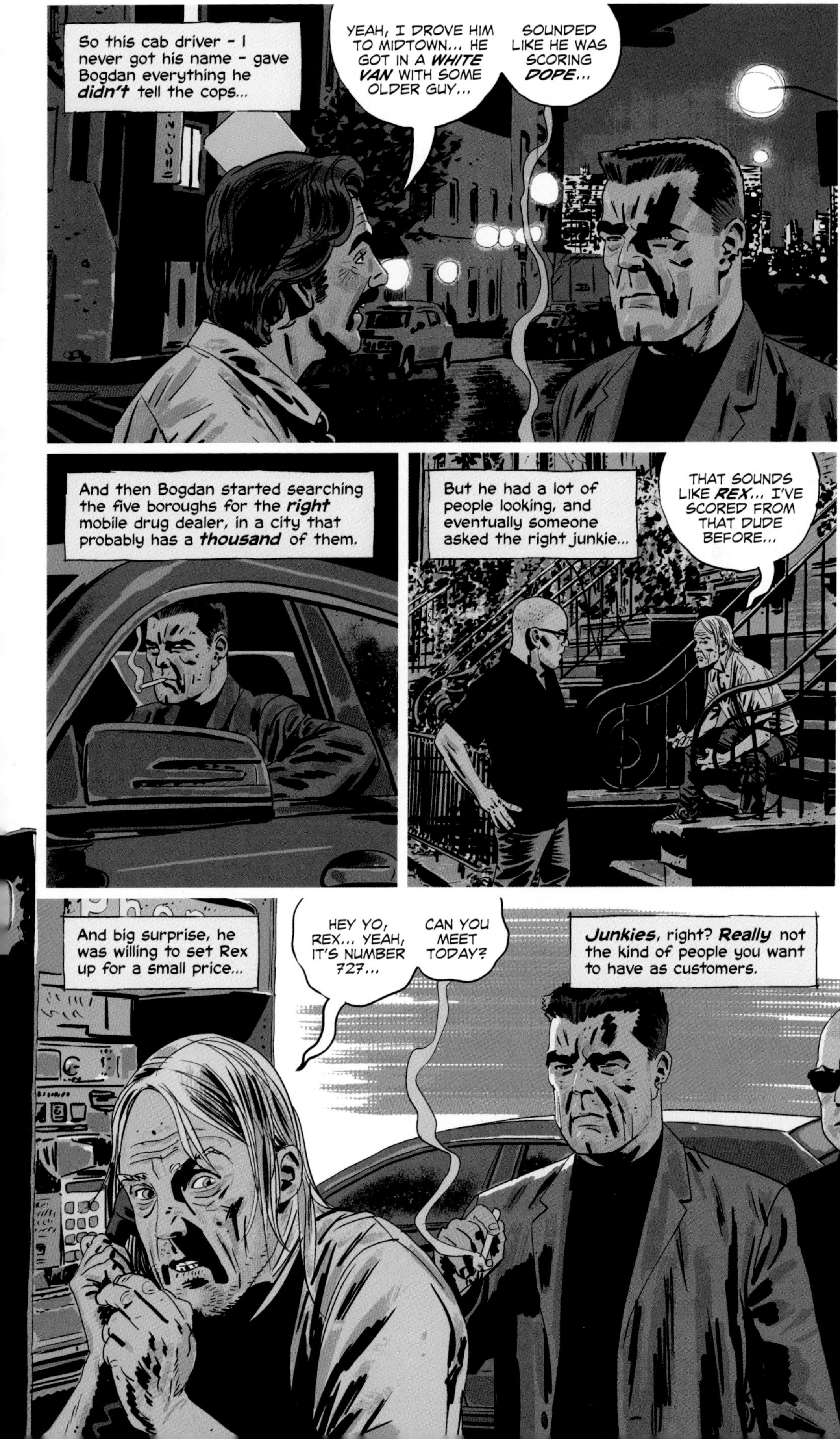
So this cab driver - I never got his name - gave Bogdan everything he didn't tell the cops...
YEAH, I DROVE HIM TO MIDTOWN... HE GOT IN A WHITE VAN WITH SOME OLDER GUY...
SOUNDED LIKE HE WAS SCORING DOPE...
And then Bogdan started searching the five boroughs for the right mobile drug dealer, in a city that probably has a thousand of them.
But he had a lot of people looking, and eventually someone asked the right junkie...
THAT SOUNDS LIKE REX... I'VE SCORED FROM THAT DUDE BEFORE...
And big surprise, he was willing to set Rex up for a small price...
HEY YO, REX... YEAH, IT'S NUMBER 727...
CAN YOU MEET TODAY?
Junkies, right? Really not the kind of people you want to have as customers.

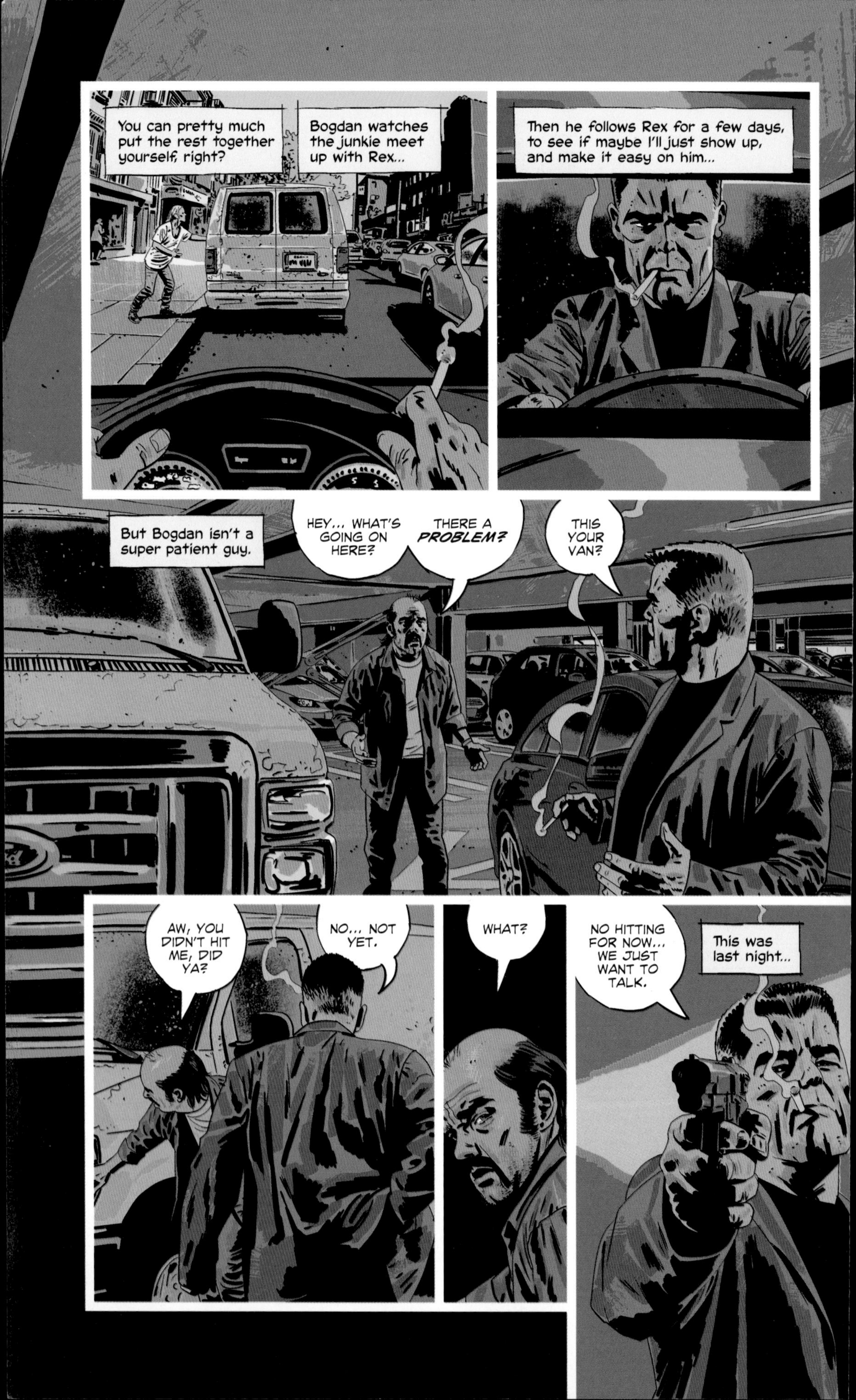
You can pretty much put the rest together yourself, right?
Bogdan watches the junkie meet up with Rex...
Then he follows Rex for a few days, to see if maybe I'll just show up, and make it easy on him...
But Bogdan isn't a super patient guy.
HEY... WHAT'S GOING ON HERE?
THERE A *PROBLEM?*
THIS YOUR VAN?
AW, YOU DIDN'T HIT ME, DID YA?
NO... NOT YET.
WHAT?
NO HITTING FOR NOW... WE JUST WANT TO TALK.
This was last night...

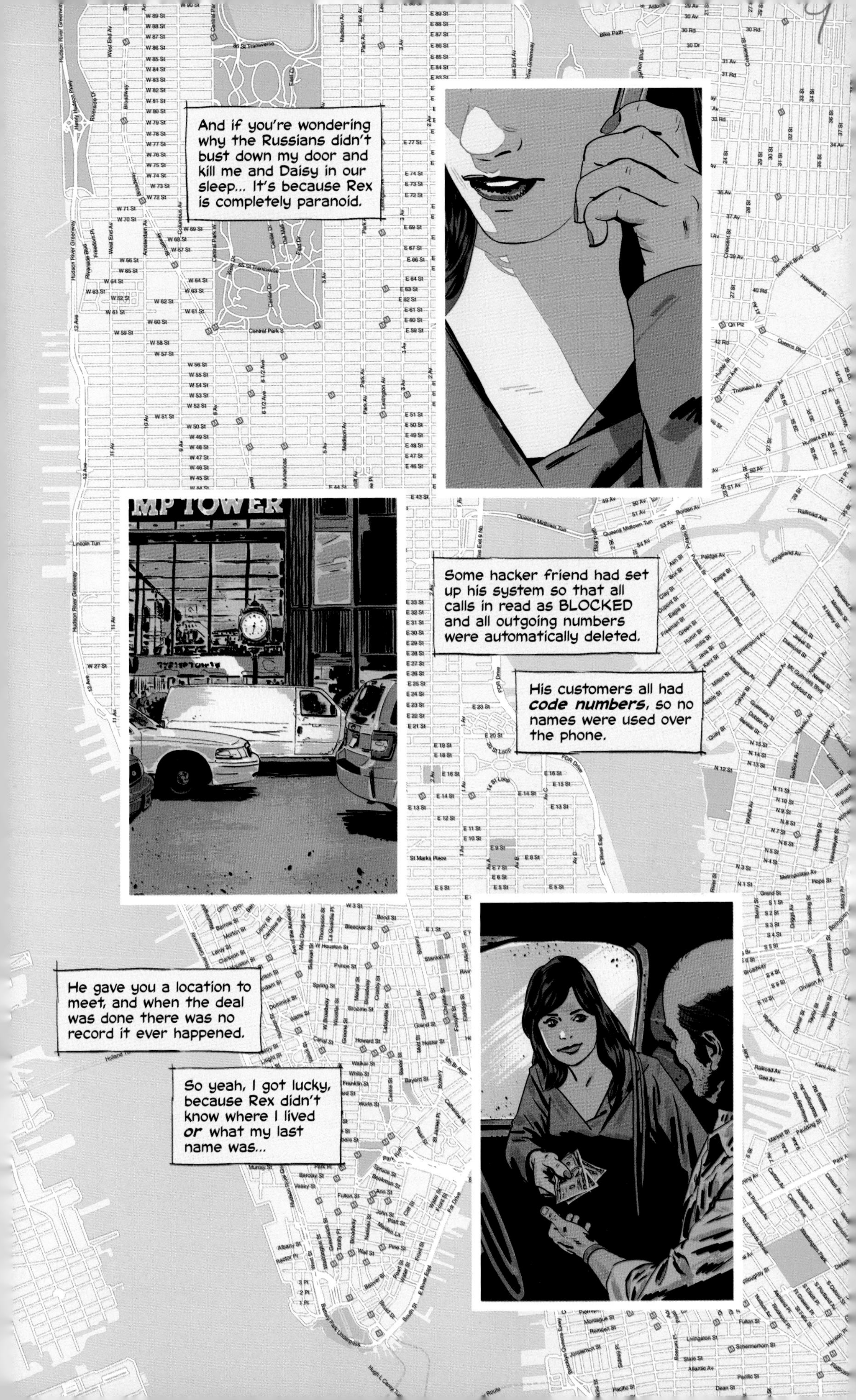
And if you're wondering why the Russians didn't bust down my door and kill me and Daisy in our sleep... It's because Rex is completely paranoid.
Some hacker friend had set up his system so that all calls in read as BLOCKED and all outgoing numbers were automatically deleted.
His customers all had ***code numbers***, so no names were used over the phone.
He gave you a location to meet, and when the deal was done there was no record it ever happened.
So yeah, I got lucky, because Rex didn't know where I lived ***or*** what my last name was...

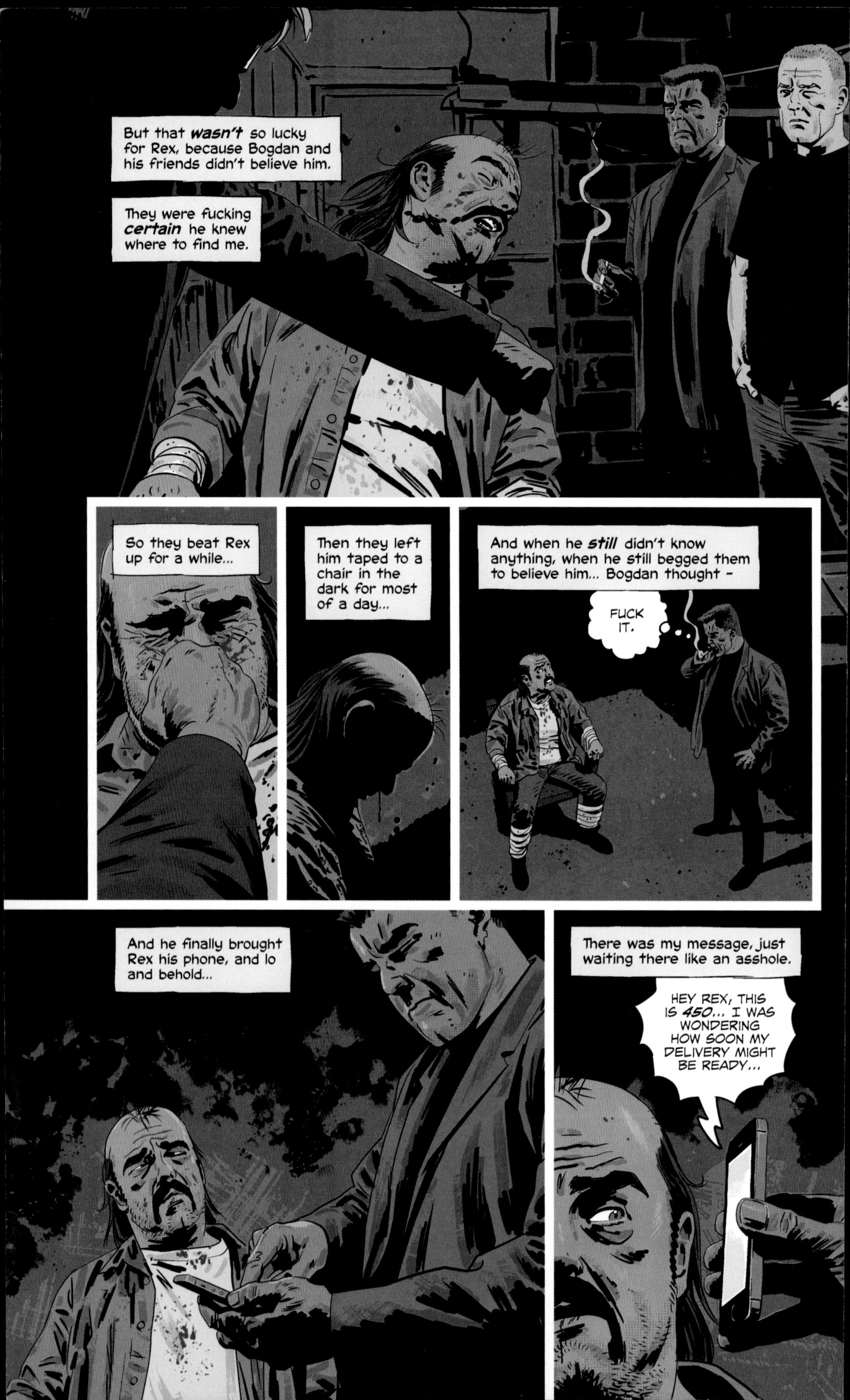

But that wasn't so lucky for Rex, because Bogdan and his friends didn't believe him.
They were fucking certain he knew where to find me.
So they beat Rex up for a while...
Then they left him taped to a chair in the dark for most of a day...
And when he still didn't know anything, when he still begged them to believe him... Bogdan thought –
FUCK IT.
And he finally brought Rex his phone, and lo and behold...
There was my message, just waiting there like an asshole.
HEY REX, THIS IS 450... I WAS WONDERING HOW SOON MY DELIVERY MIGHT BE READY...

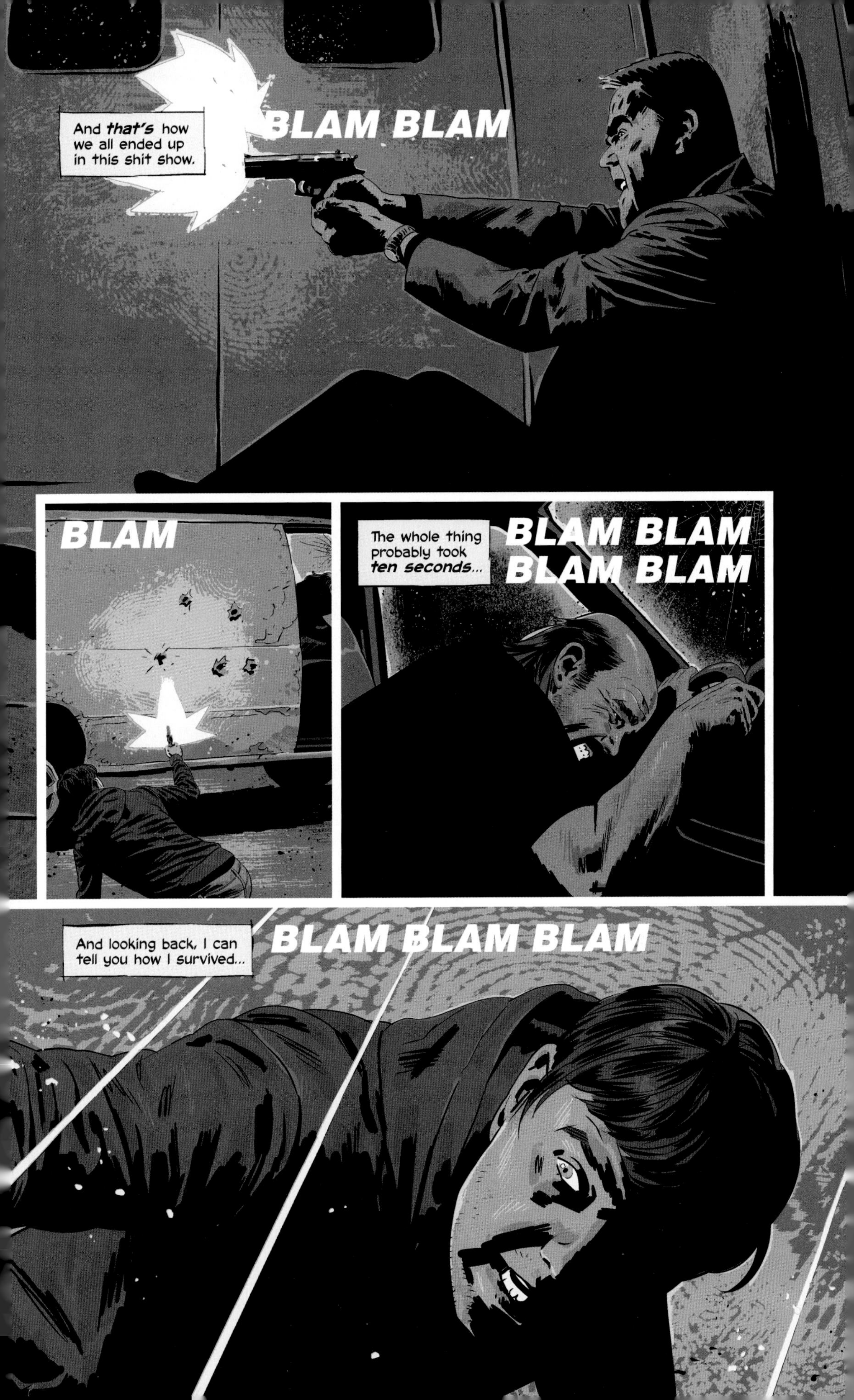
And *that's* how we all ended up in this shit show.
BLAM BLAM
BLAM
The whole thing probably took *ten seconds*...
BLAM BLAM
BLAM BLAM
And looking back, I can tell you how I survived...
BLAM BLAM BLAM

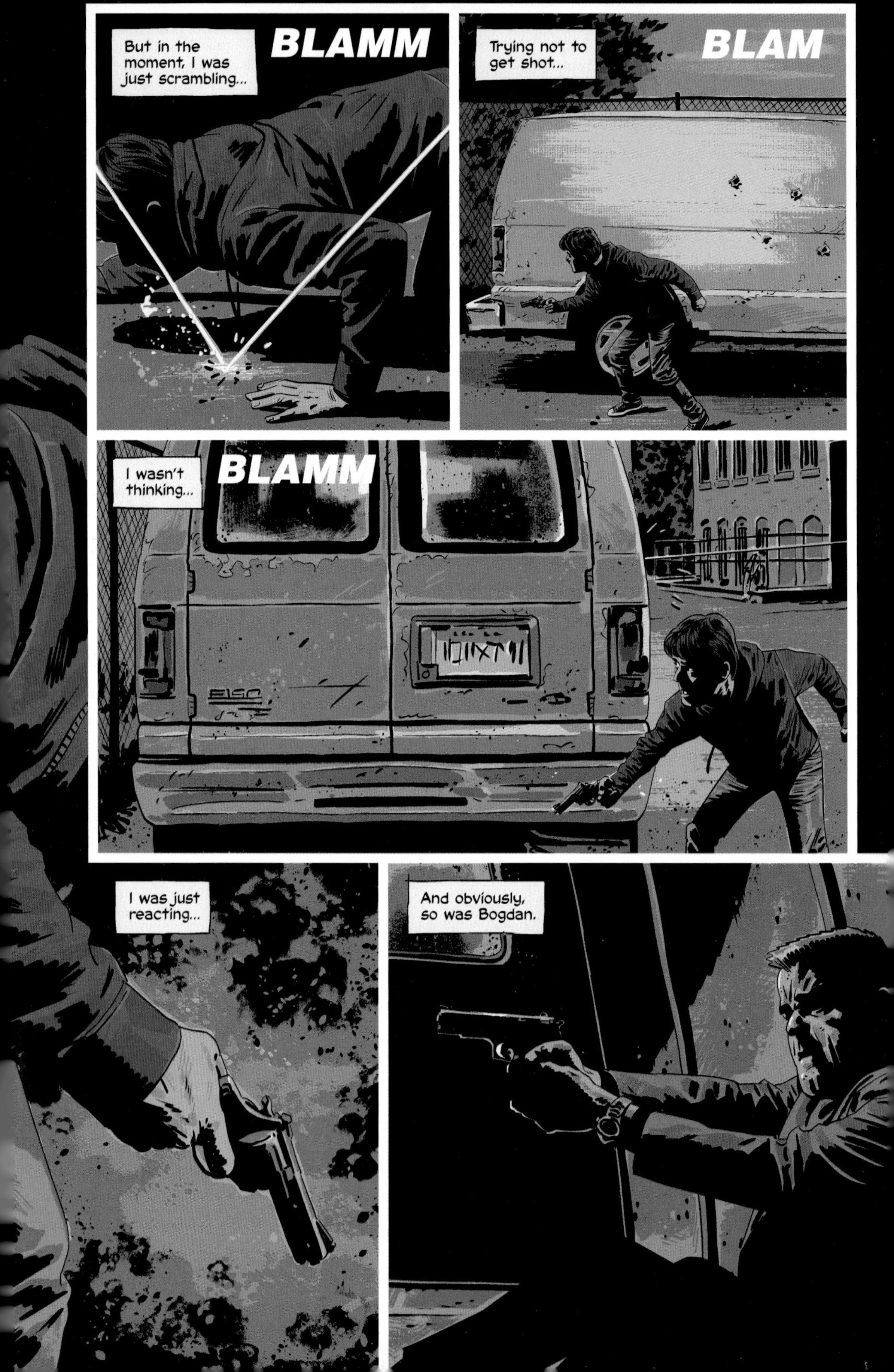
But in the moment, I was just scrambling...
BLAMM
Trying not to get shot...
BLAM
I wasn't thinking...
BLAMM
I was just reacting...
And obviously, so was Bogdan.

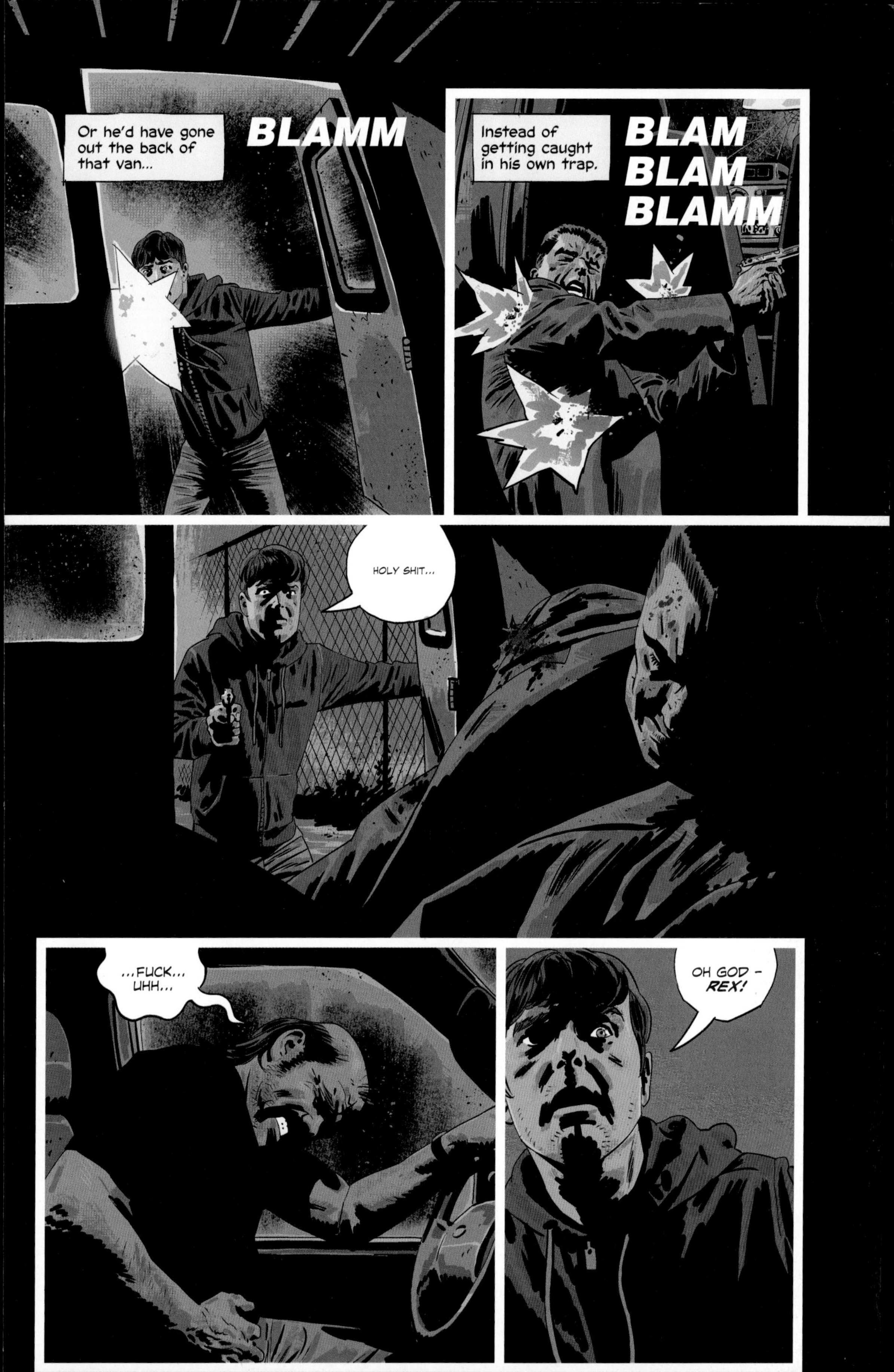
Or he'd have gone out the back of that van...
BLAMM
Instead of getting caught in his own trap.
BLAM
BLAM
BLAMM
HOLY SHIT...
...FUCK... UHH...
OH GOD - REX!

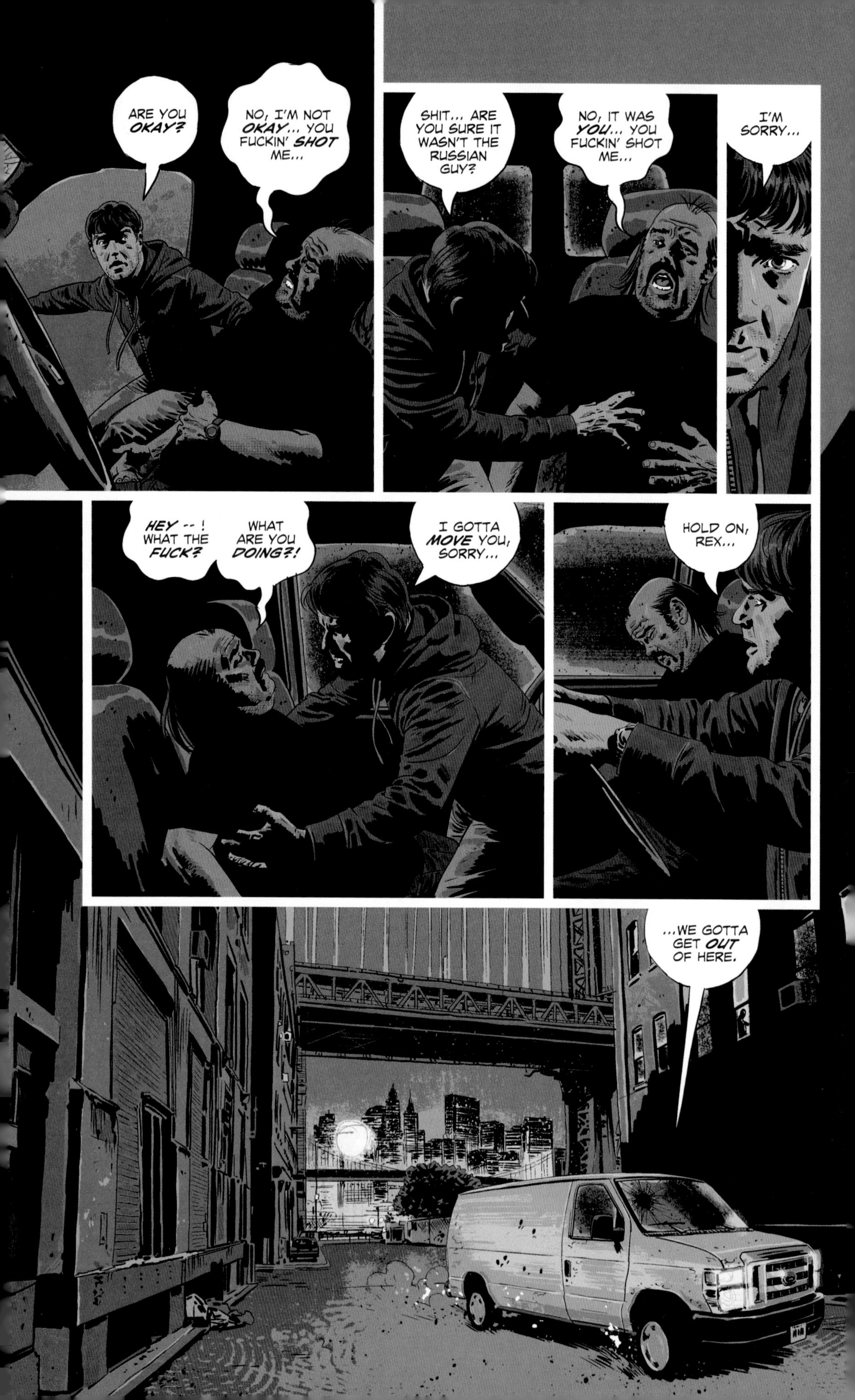
ARE YOU *OKAY?*
NO, I'M NOT *OKAY*... YOU FUCKIN' *SHOT* ME...
SHIT... ARE YOU SURE IT WASN'T THE RUSSIAN GUY?
NO, IT WAS *YOU*... YOU FUCKIN' SHOT ME...
I'M SORRY...
HEY -- ! WHAT THE *FUCK?*
WHAT ARE YOU *DOING?!*
I GOTTA *MOVE* YOU, SORRY...
HOLD ON, REX...
...WE GOTTA GET *OUT* OF HERE.

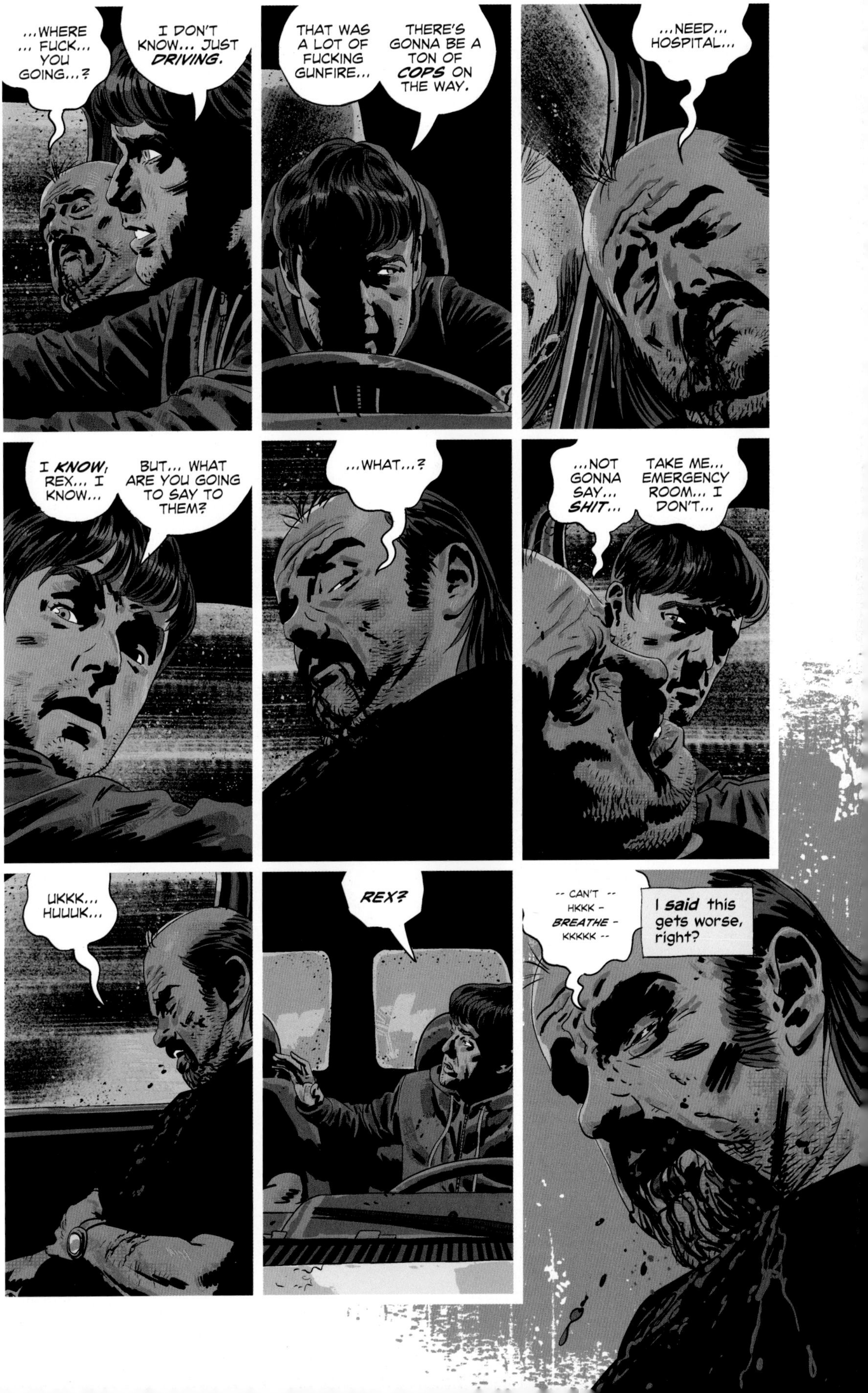
...WHERE ... FUCK... YOU GOING...?
I DON'T KNOW... JUST DRIVING.
THAT WAS A LOT OF FUCKING GUNFIRE...
THERE'S GONNA BE A TON OF COPS ON THE WAY.
...NEED... HOSPITAL...
I KNOW, REX... I KNOW...
BUT... WHAT ARE YOU GOING TO SAY TO THEM?
...WHAT...?
...NOT GONNA SAY... SHIT...
TAKE ME... EMERGENCY ROOM... I DON'T...
UKKK... HUUUK...
REX?
-- CAN'T -- HKKK - BREATHE - KKKKK --
I said this gets worse, right?

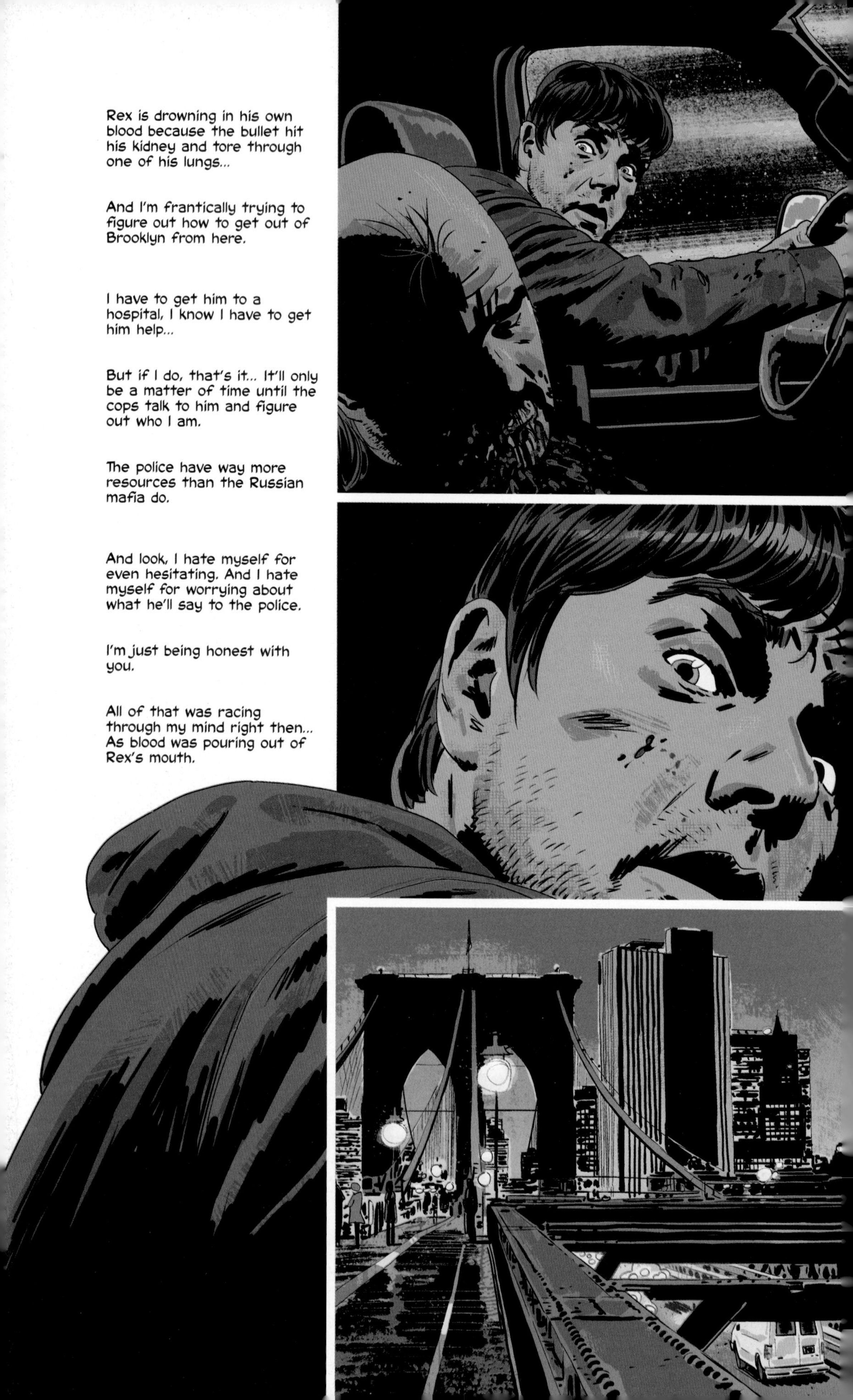
Rex is drowning in his own blood because the bullet hit his kidney and tore through one of his lungs...
And I'm frantically trying to figure out how to get out of Brooklyn from here.
I have to get him to a hospital, I know I have to get him help...
But if I do, that's it... It'll only be a matter of time until the cops talk to him and figure out who I am.
The police have way more resources than the Russian mafia do.
And look, I hate myself for even hesitating. And I hate myself for worrying about what he'll say to the police.
I'm just being honest with you.
All of that was racing through my mind right then... As blood was pouring out of Rex's mouth.

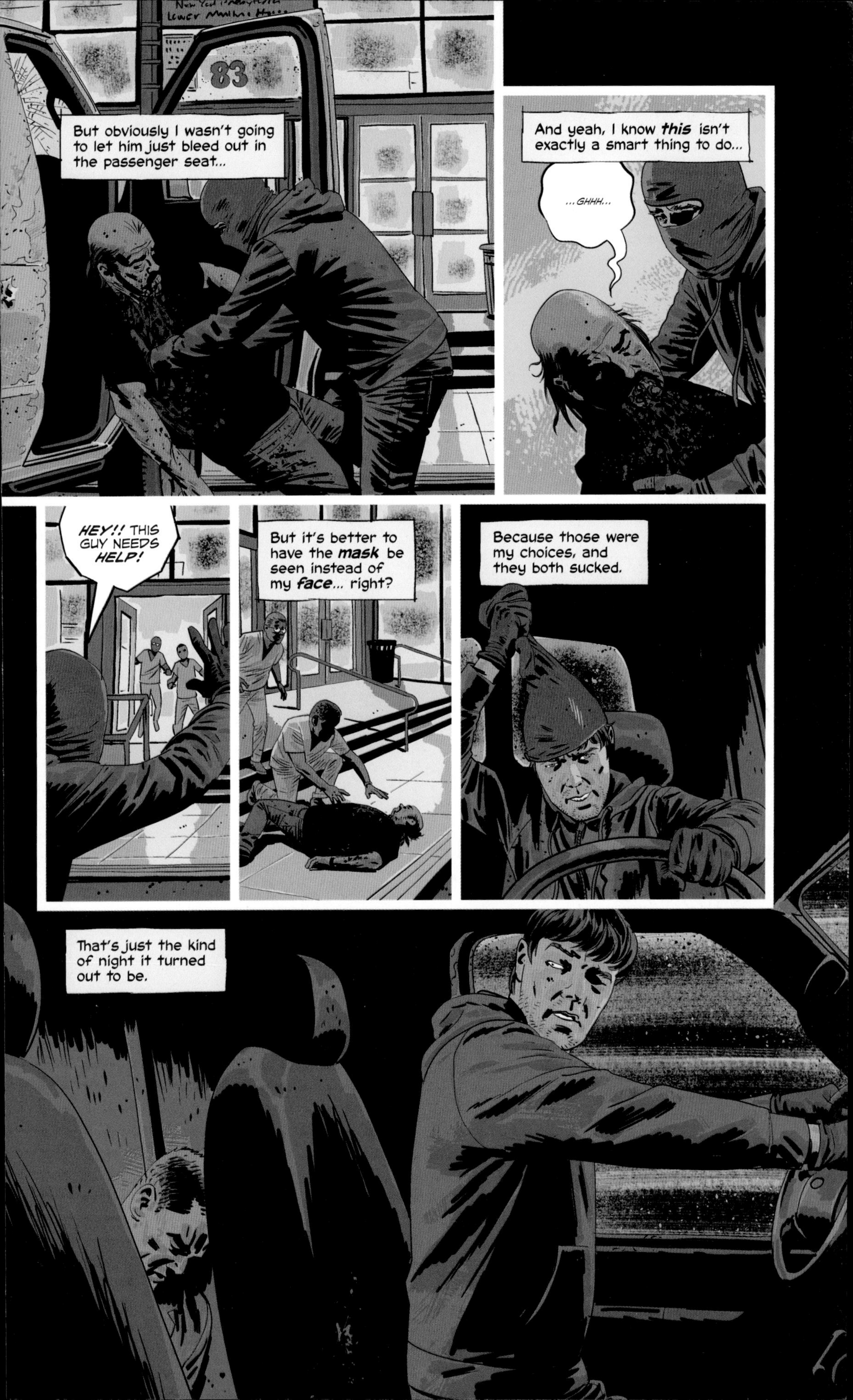

But obviously I wasn't going to let him just bleed out in the passenger seat...
And yeah, I know *this* isn't exactly a smart thing to do...
...GHHH...
HEY!! THIS GUY NEEDS *HELP!*
But it's better to have the *mask* be seen instead of my *face*... right?
Because those were my choices, and they both sucked.
That's just the kind of night it turned out to be.

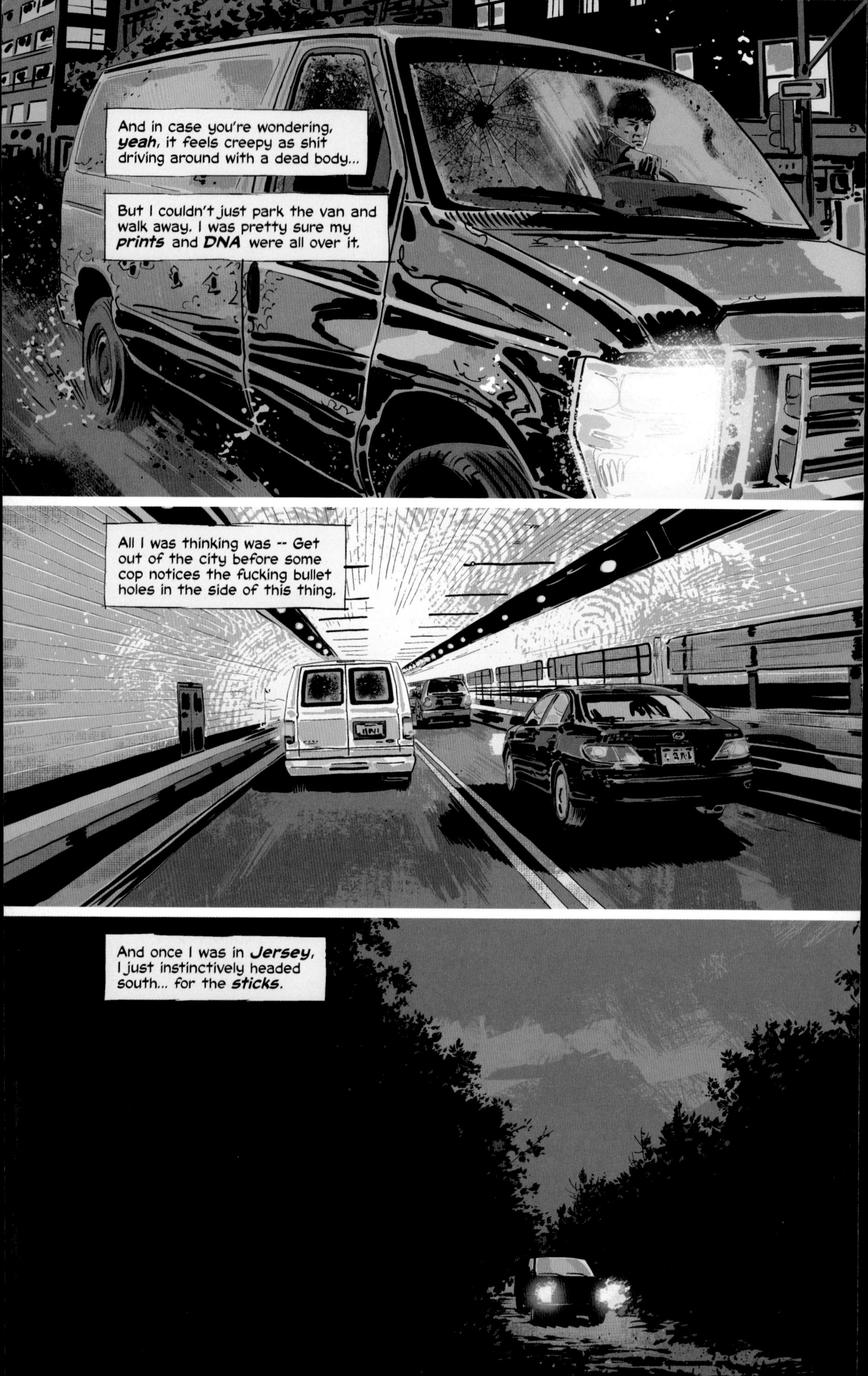
And in case you're wondering, *yeah*, it feels creepy as shit driving around with a dead body...
But I couldn't just park the van and walk away. I was pretty sure my *prints* and *DNA* were all over it.
All I was thinking was -- Get out of the city before some cop notices the fucking bullet holes in the side of this thing.
And once I was in *Jersey*, I just instinctively headed south... for the *sticks*.

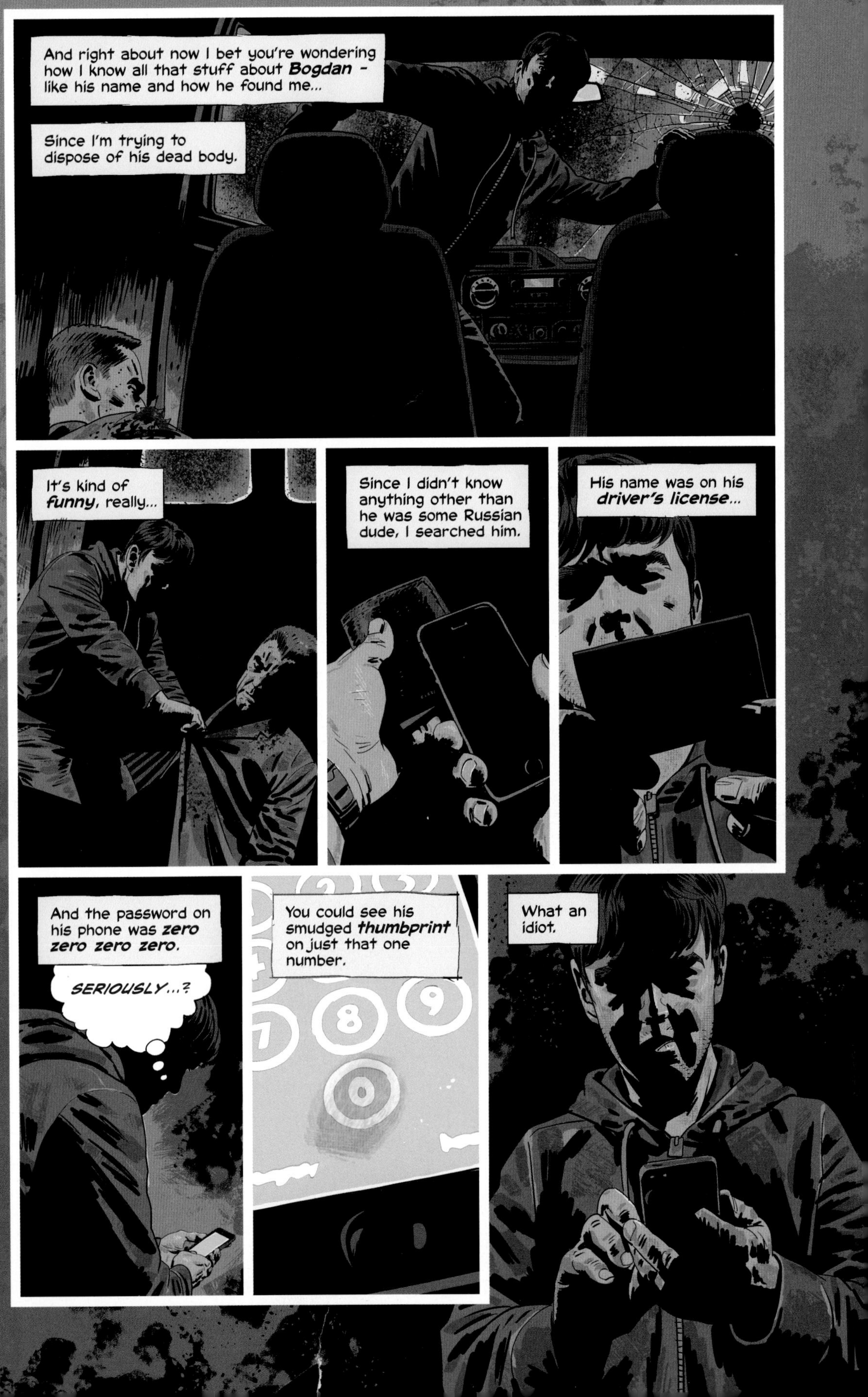
And right about now I bet you're wondering how I know all that stuff about *Bogdan* – like his name and how he found me...
Since I'm trying to dispose of his dead body.
It's kind of *funny*, really...
Since I didn't know anything other than he was some Russian dude, I searched him.
His name was on his *driver's license*...
And the password on his phone was *zero zero zero zero.*
SERIOUSLY...?
You could see his smudged *thumbprint* on just that one number.
What an idiot.

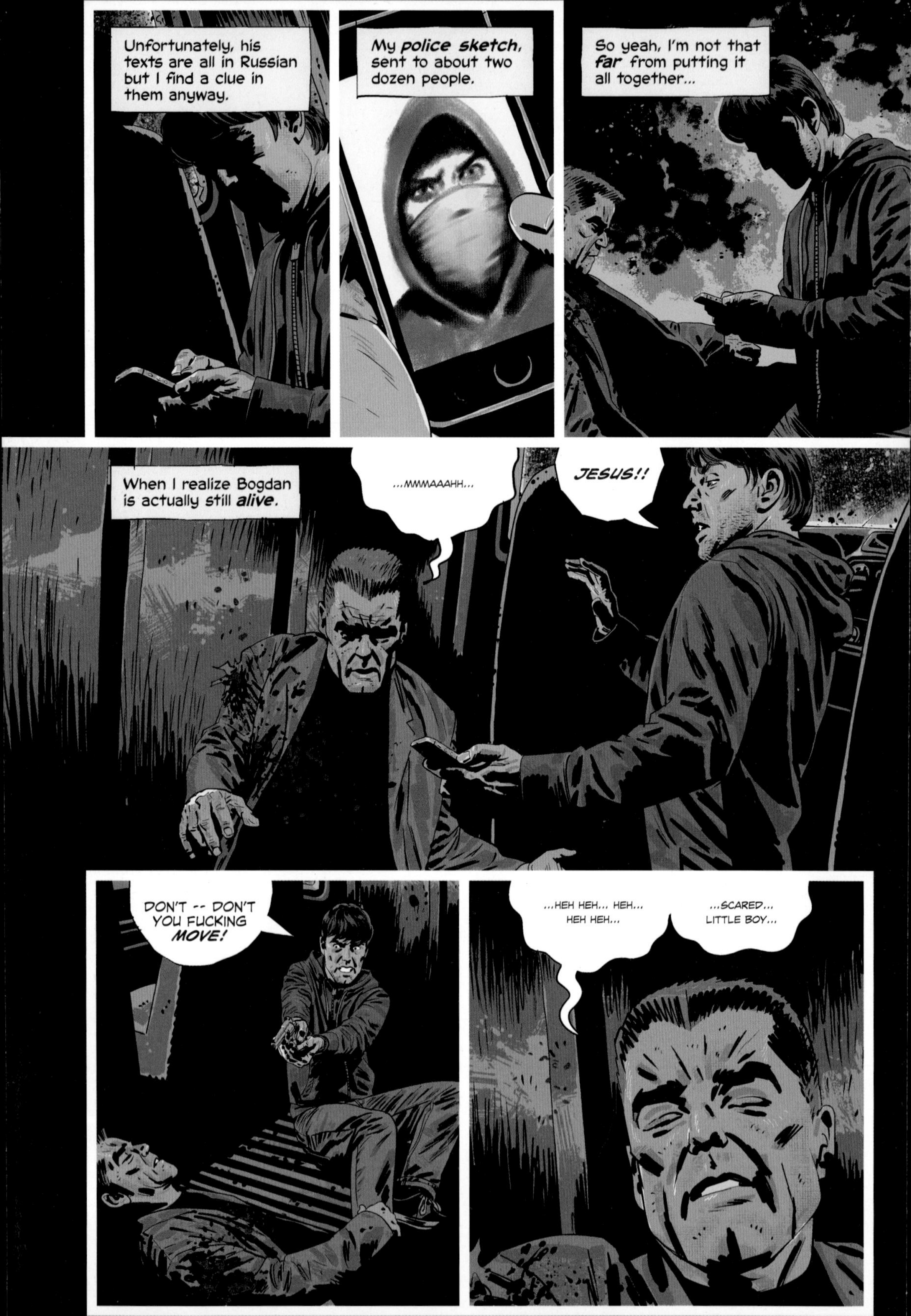
Unfortunately, his texts are all in Russian but I find a clue in them anyway.
My *police sketch*, sent to about two dozen people.
So yeah, I'm not that *far* from putting it all together...
When I realize Bogdan is actually still *alive*.
...MMMAAAHH...
JESUS!!
DON'T -- DON'T YOU FUCKING *MOVE!*
...HEH HEH... HEH... HEH HEH...
...SCARED... LITTLE BOY...

...DID YOU PISS... YOUR PANTS...?

SHUT UP.

HEH HEH... PUSSY...

So yeah, this is when I found out everything about *Bogdan*... After he woke up too weak to do anything but talk...

And even at death's door, every word out of his mouth still sounded like a threat.

I sat there holding a gun on him while he told me all that stuff I already told you...

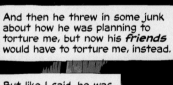

And then he threw in some junk about how he was planning to torture me, but now his *friends* would have to torture me, instead.

But like I said, he was *weak*... He probably figured he was dying...

And I guess he didn't want to die with a *question* left hanging...

WHY DO... YOU... DO THIS...?

DRESS UP IN MASK... KILL...

...WHAT... WE... DO TO YOU...?

I'm sure my answer isn't what he was expecting... But it's a relief actually, to be able to tell someone the truth.

I've been carrying this secret around for months, and it's not until I start telling this total stranger what happened to me that I realize how much it's been weighing me down.

It all comes pouring out... The suicide attempt, the deal with the demon, the people I've killed... Losing Kira...

Everything.

I think right up until I started describing the demon, Bogdan actually thought he might talk his way out of this...

But then I see that last shred of hope disappear... And I think, this must be what he looks like when he's scared.

For a second, I almost feel bad for him...

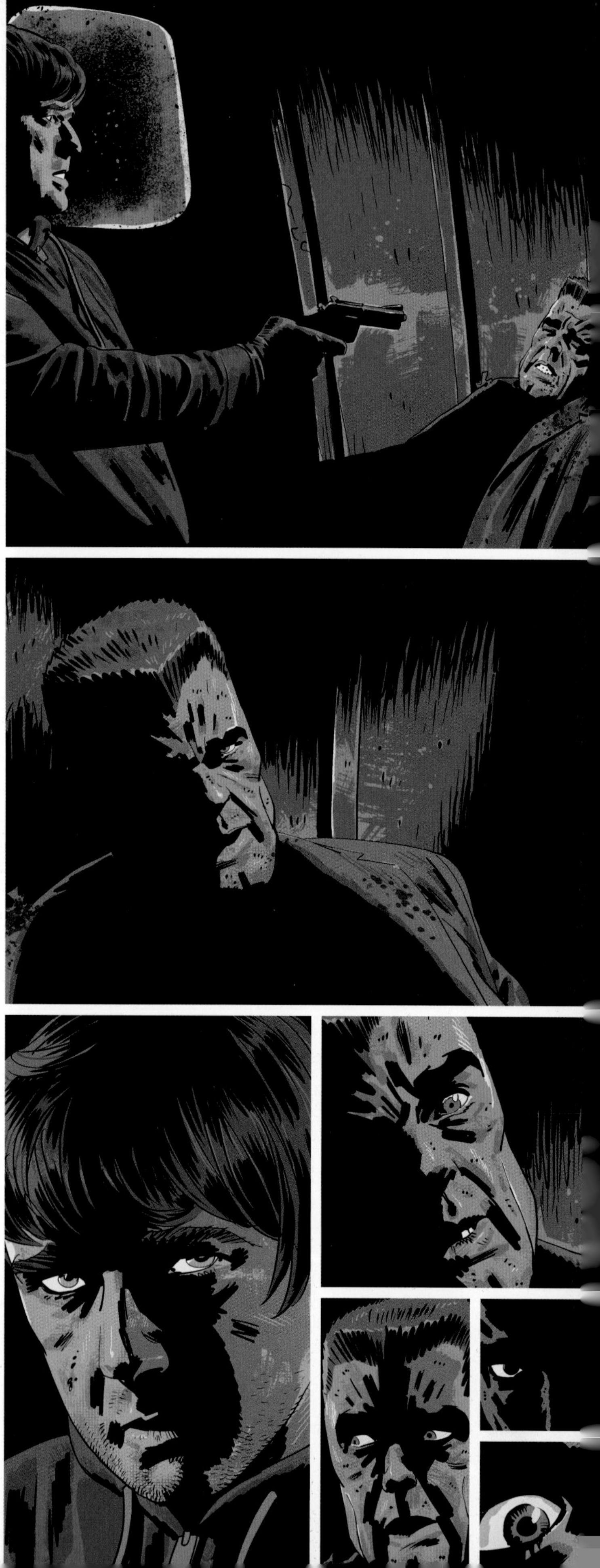

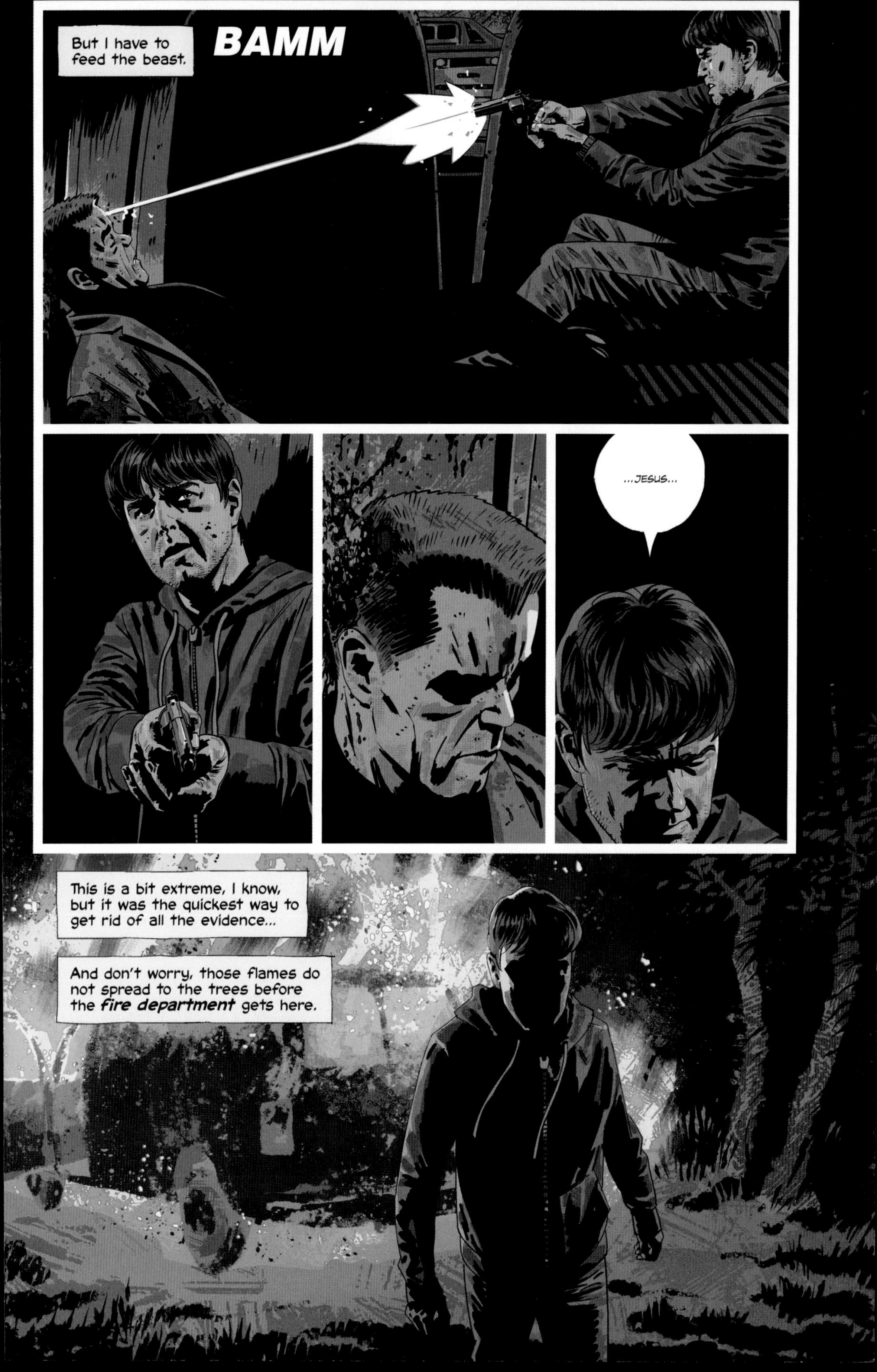
But I have to feed the beast.
BAMM
...JESUS...
This is a bit extreme, I know, but it was the quickest way to get rid of all the evidence...
And don't worry, those flames do not spread to the trees before the *fire department* gets here.

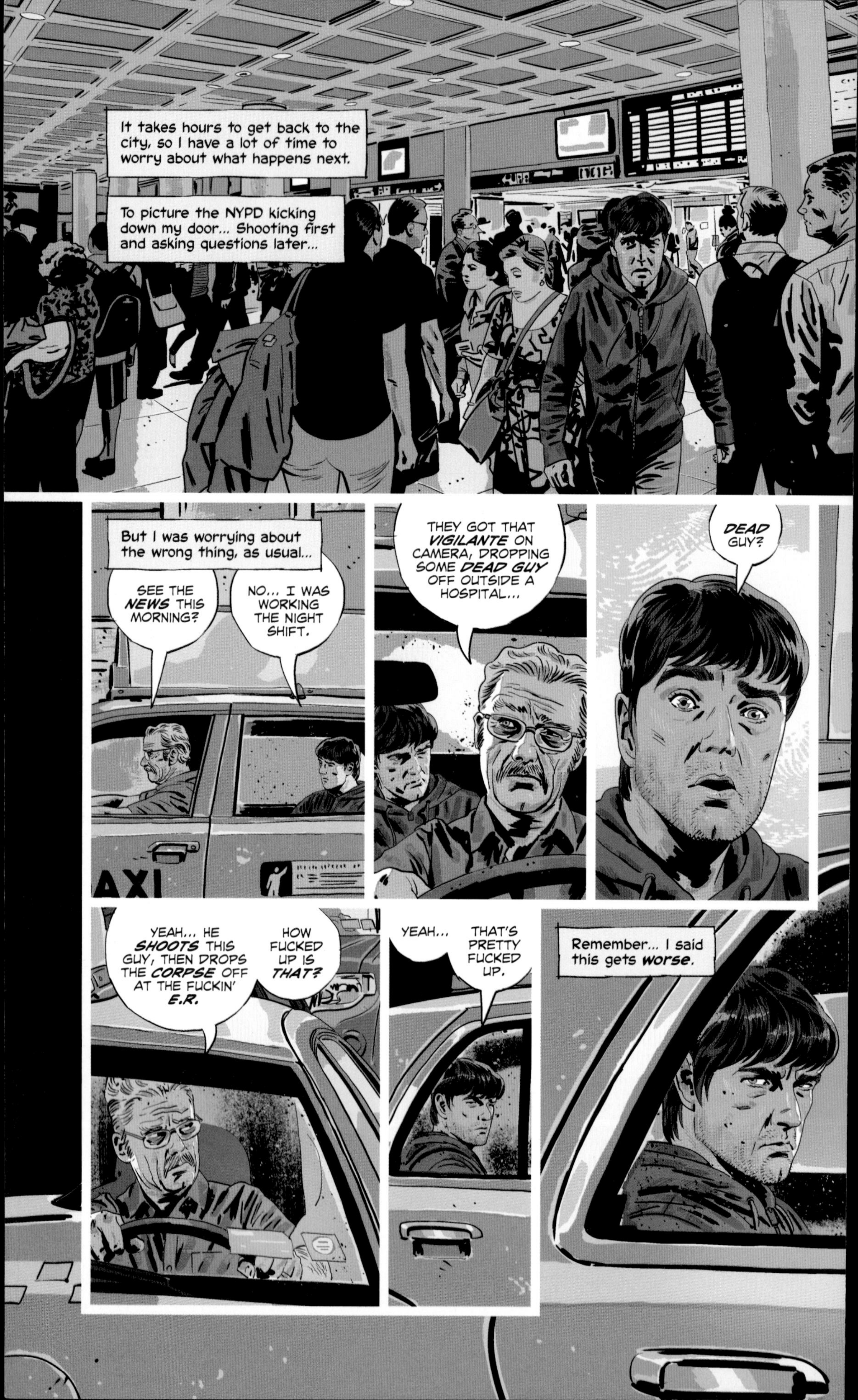
It takes hours to get back to the city, so I have a lot of time to worry about what happens next.
To picture the NYPD kicking down my door... Shooting first and asking questions later...
But I was worrying about the wrong thing, as usual...
SEE THE NEWS THIS MORNING?
NO... I WAS WORKING THE NIGHT SHIFT.
THEY GOT THAT VIGILANTE ON CAMERA, DROPPING SOME DEAD GUY OFF OUTSIDE A HOSPITAL...
DEAD GUY?
YEAH... HE SHOOTS THIS GUY, THEN DROPS THE CORPSE OFF AT THE FUCKIN' E.R.
HOW FUCKED UP IS THAT?
YEAH...
THAT'S PRETTY FUCKED UP.
Remember... I said this gets worse.

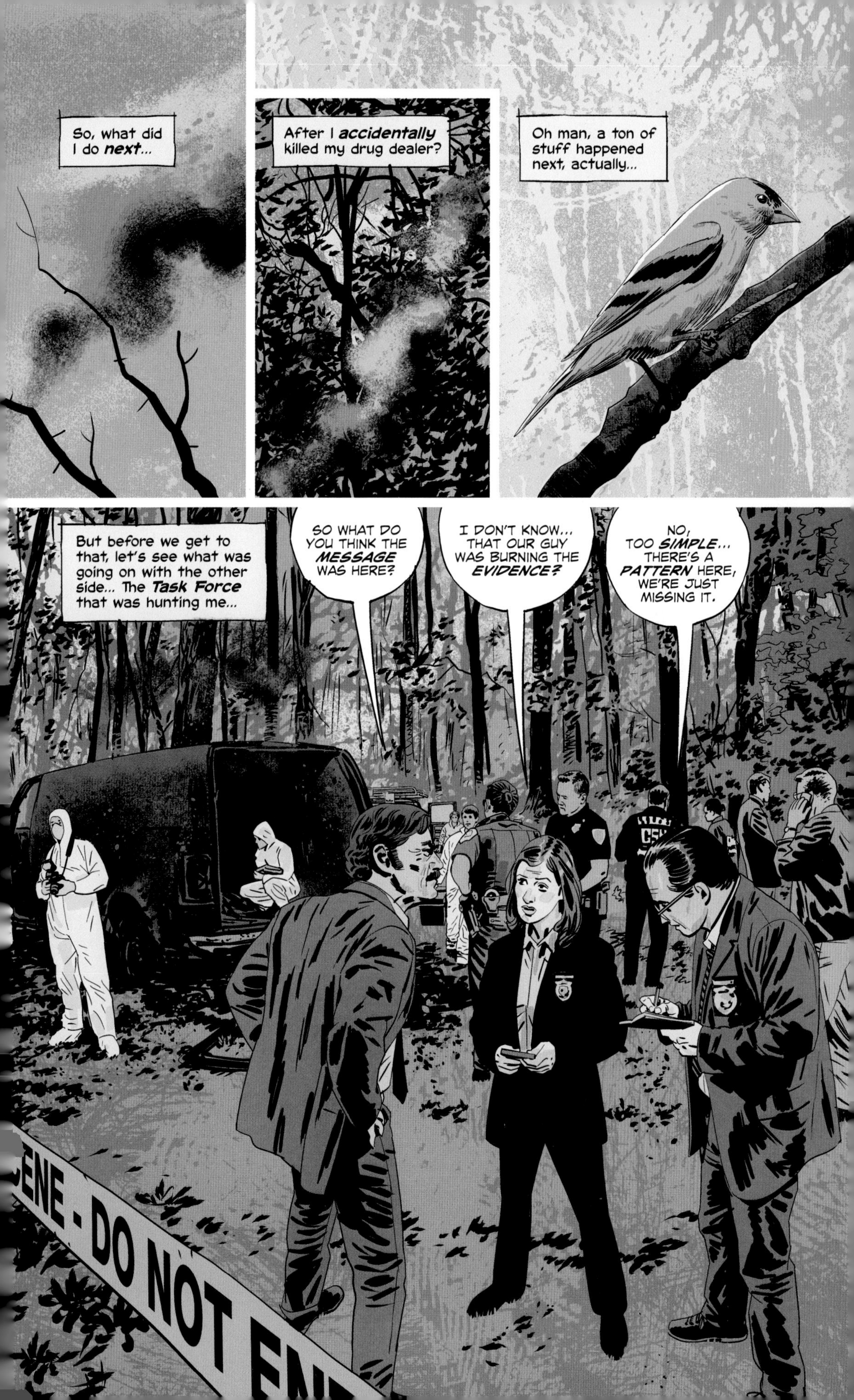
So, what did I do *next*...
After I *accidentally* killed my drug dealer?
Oh man, a ton of stuff happened next, actually...
But before we get to that, let's see what was going on with the other side... The *Task Force* that was hunting me...
SO WHAT DO YOU THINK THE *MESSAGE* WAS HERE?
I DON'T KNOW... THAT OUR GUY WAS BURNING THE *EVIDENCE?*
NO, TOO *SIMPLE*... THERE'S A *PATTERN* HERE, WE'RE JUST MISSING IT.
CSU
ENE - DO NOT EN

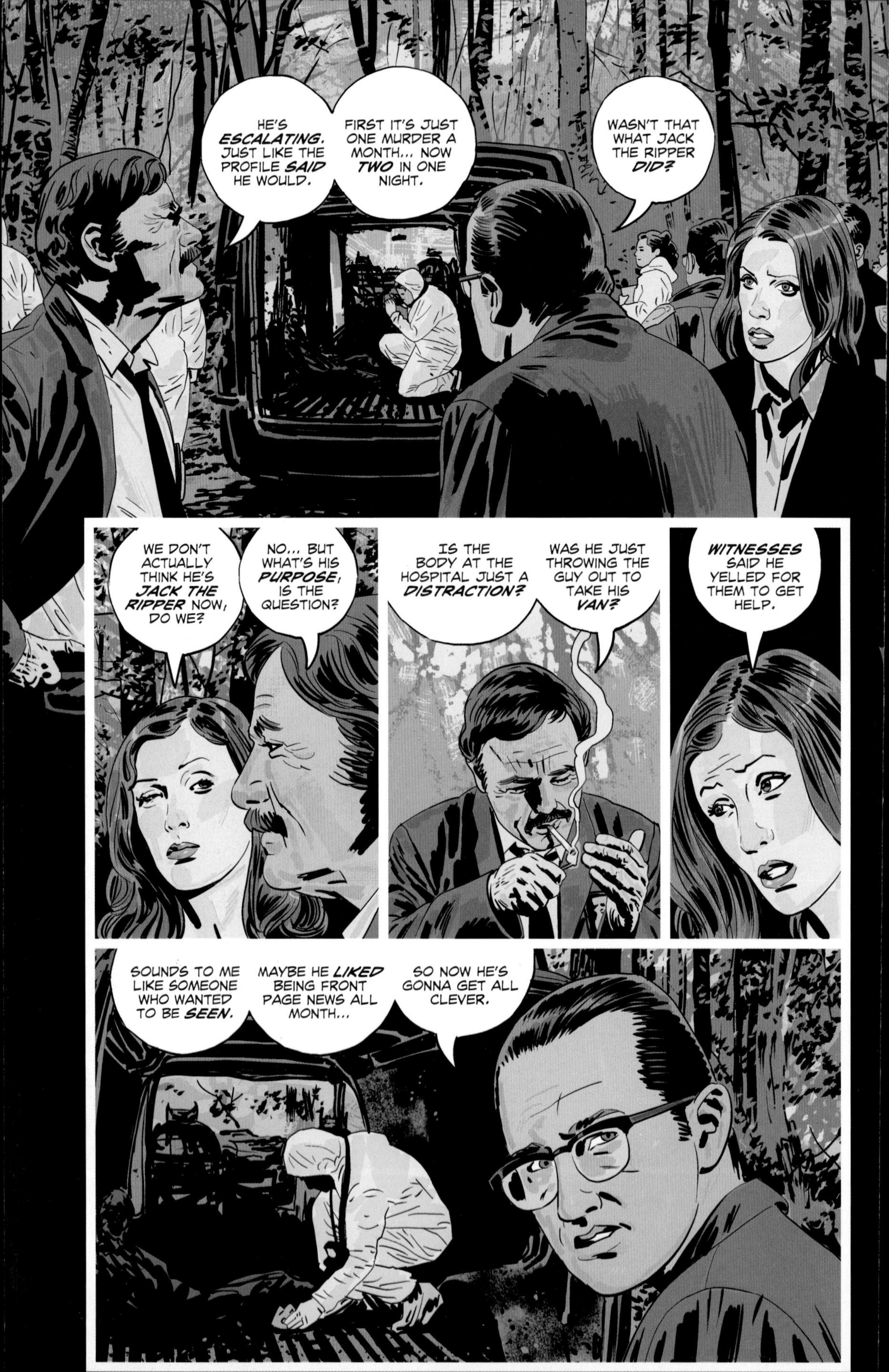
HE'S ESCALATING. JUST LIKE THE PROFILE SAID HE WOULD.
FIRST IT'S JUST ONE MURDER A MONTH... NOW TWO IN ONE NIGHT.
WASN'T THAT WHAT JACK THE RIPPER DID?
WE DON'T ACTUALLY THINK HE'S JACK THE RIPPER NOW, DO WE?
NO... BUT WHAT'S HIS PURPOSE, IS THE QUESTION?
IS THE BODY AT THE HOSPITAL JUST A DISTRACTION?
WAS HE JUST THROWING THE GUY OUT TO TAKE HIS VAN?
WITNESSES SAID HE YELLED FOR THEM TO GET HELP.
SOUNDS TO ME LIKE SOMEONE WHO WANTED TO BE SEEN.
MAYBE HE LIKED BEING FRONT PAGE NEWS ALL MONTH...
SO NOW HE'S GONNA GET ALL CLEVER.

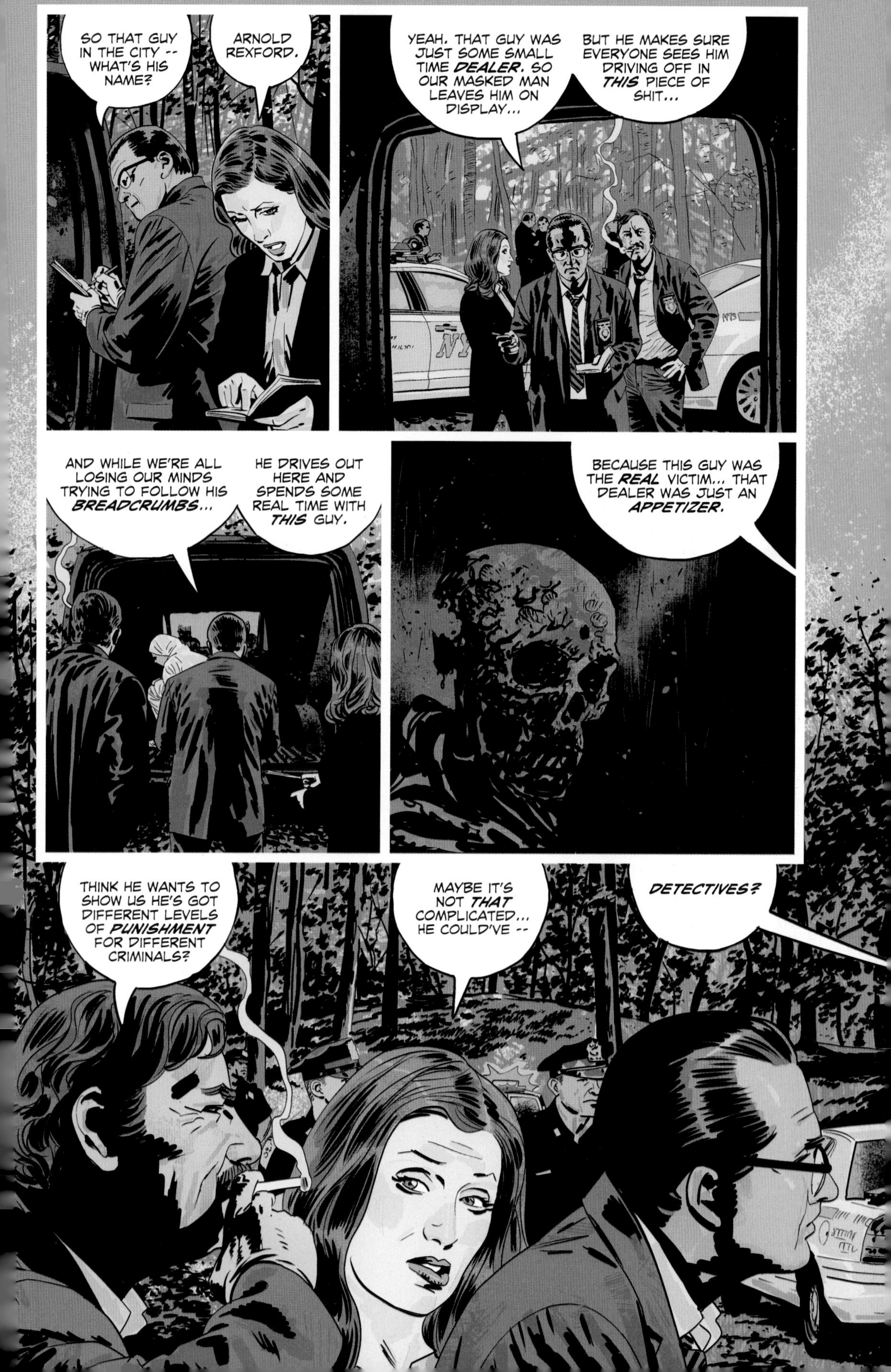
SO THAT GUY IN THE CITY -- WHAT'S HIS NAME?
ARNOLD REXFORD.
YEAH. THAT GUY WAS JUST SOME SMALL TIME DEALER. SO OUR MASKED MAN LEAVES HIM ON DISPLAY...
BUT HE MAKES SURE EVERYONE SEES HIM DRIVING OFF IN THIS PIECE OF SHIT...
AND WHILE WE'RE ALL LOSING OUR MINDS TRYING TO FOLLOW HIS BREADCRUMBS...
HE DRIVES OUT HERE AND SPENDS SOME REAL TIME WITH THIS GUY.
BECAUSE THIS GUY WAS THE REAL VICTIM... THAT DEALER WAS JUST AN APPETIZER.
THINK HE WANTS TO SHOW US HE'S GOT DIFFERENT LEVELS OF PUNISHMENT FOR DIFFERENT CRIMINALS?
MAYBE IT'S NOT THAT COMPLICATED... HE COULD'VE --
DETECTIVES?

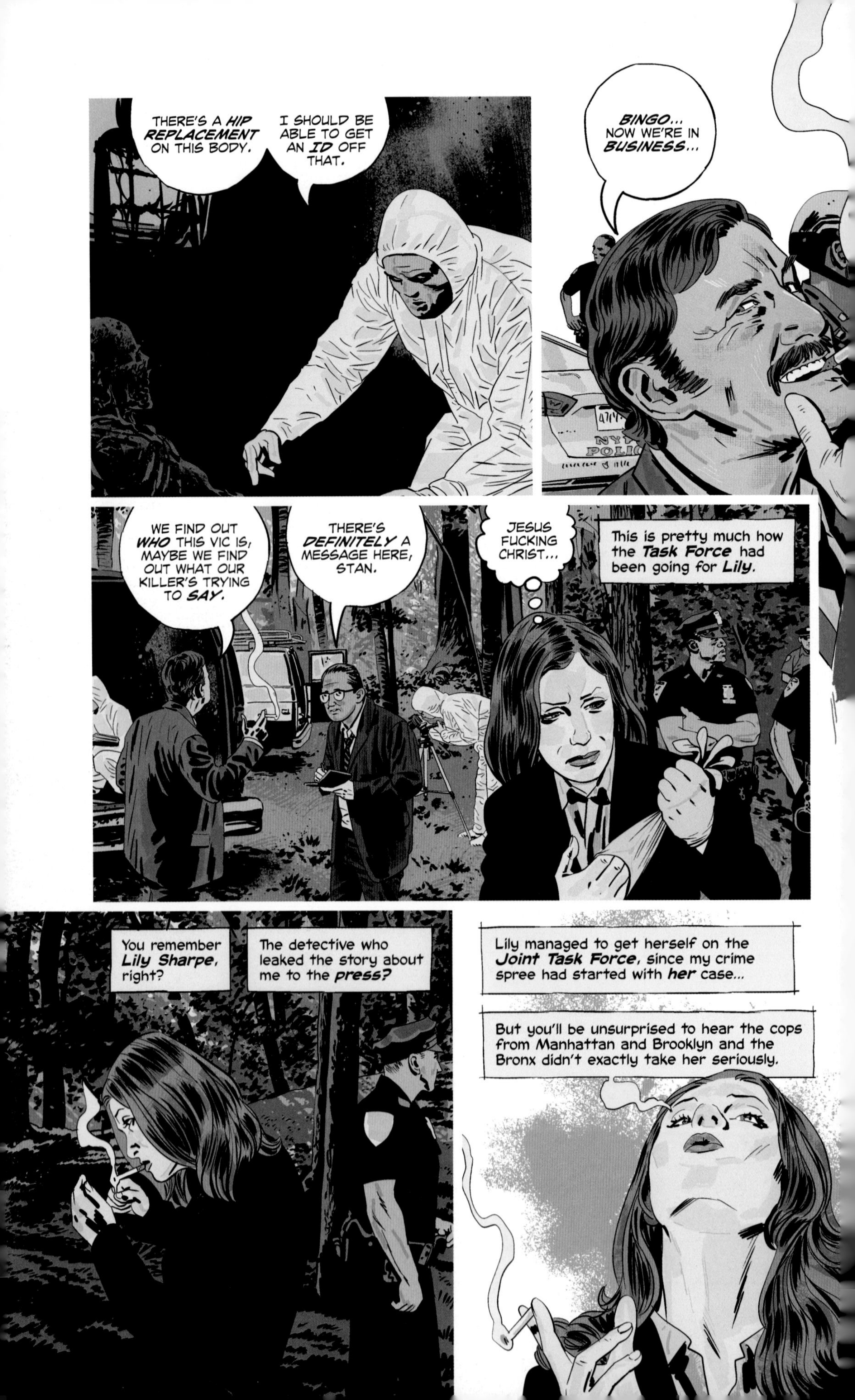
THERE'S A HIP REPLACEMENT ON THIS BODY.
I SHOULD BE ABLE TO GET AN ID OFF THAT.
BINGO... NOW WE'RE IN BUSINESS...
WE FIND OUT WHO THIS VIC IS, MAYBE WE FIND OUT WHAT OUR KILLER'S TRYING TO SAY.
THERE'S DEFINITELY A MESSAGE HERE, STAN.
JESUS FUCKING CHRIST...
This is pretty much how the Task Force had been going for Lily.
You remember Lily Sharpe, right?
The detective who leaked the story about me to the press?
Lily managed to get herself on the Joint Task Force, since my crime spree had started with her case...
But you'll be unsurprised to hear the cops from Manhattan and Brooklyn and the Bronx didn't exactly take her seriously.

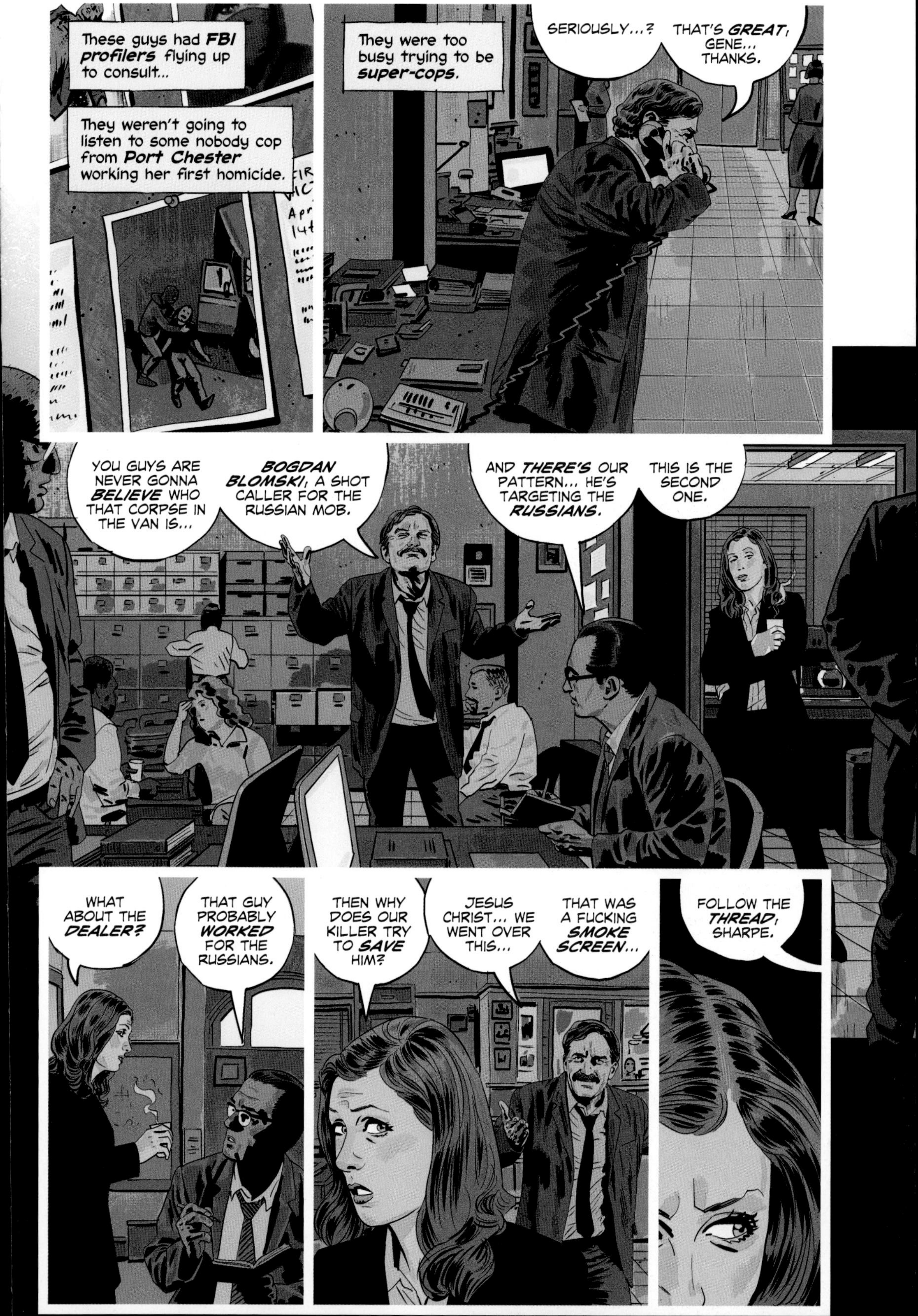
These guys had FBI profilers flying up to consult...
They weren't going to listen to some nobody cop from Port Chester working her first homicide.
They were too busy trying to be super-cops.
SERIOUSLY...?
THAT'S GREAT, GENE... THANKS.
YOU GUYS ARE NEVER GONNA BELIEVE WHO THAT CORPSE IN THE VAN IS...
BOGDAN BLOMSKI, A SHOT CALLER FOR THE RUSSIAN MOB.
AND THERE'S OUR PATTERN... HE'S TARGETING THE RUSSIANS.
THIS IS THE SECOND ONE.
WHAT ABOUT THE DEALER?
THAT GUY PROBABLY WORKED FOR THE RUSSIANS.
THEN WHY DOES OUR KILLER TRY TO SAVE HIM?
JESUS CHRIST... WE WENT OVER THIS...
THAT WAS A FUCKING SMOKE SCREEN...
FOLLOW THE THREAD, SHARPE.

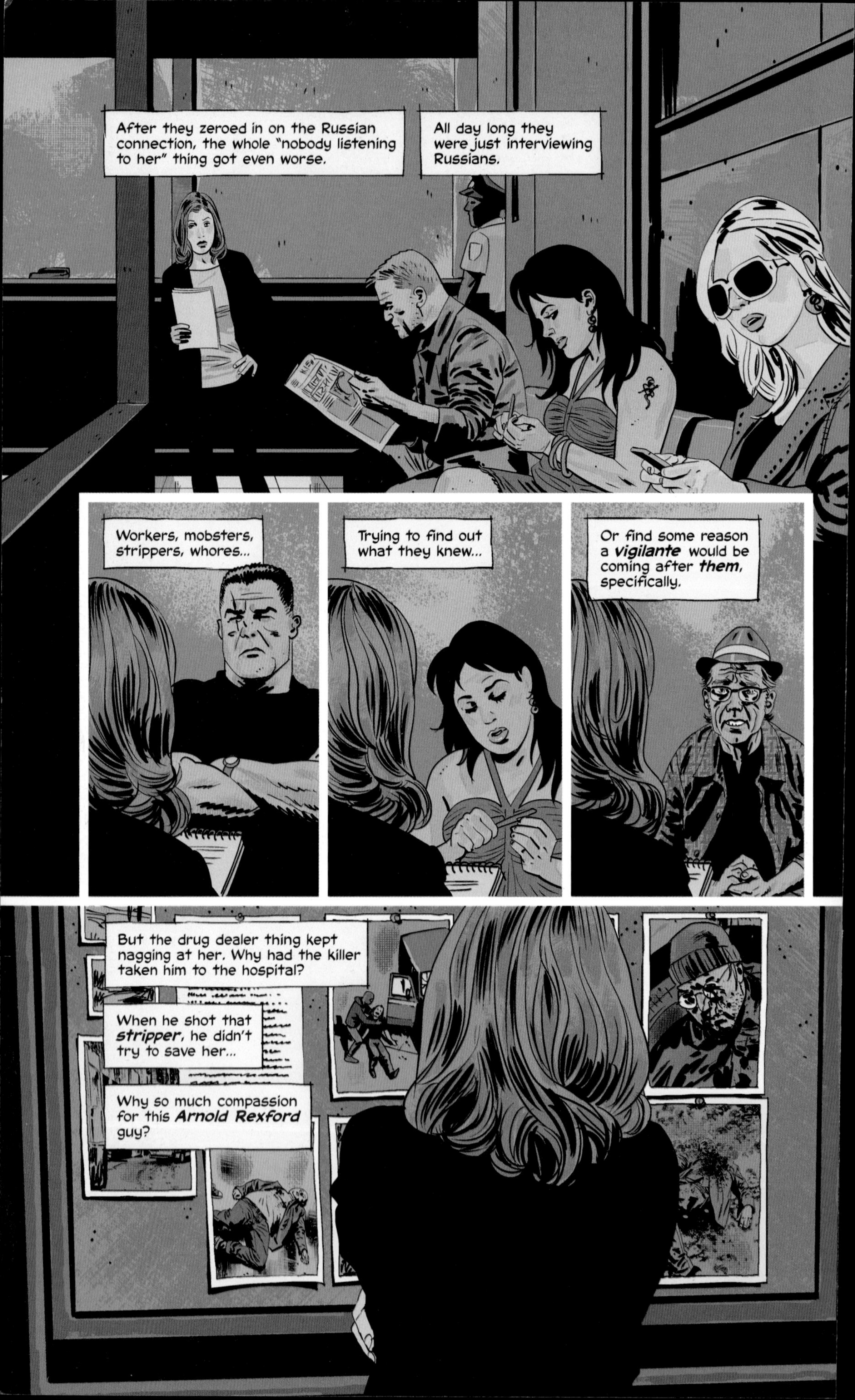
After they zeroed in on the Russian connection, the whole "nobody listening to her" thing got even worse.
All day long they were just interviewing Russians.
Workers, mobsters, strippers, whores...
Trying to find out what they knew...
Or find some reason a *vigilante* would be coming after *them*, specifically.
But the drug dealer thing kept nagging at her. Why had the killer taken him to the hospital?
When he shot that *stripper*, he didn't try to save her...
Why so much compassion for this *Arnold Rexford* guy?

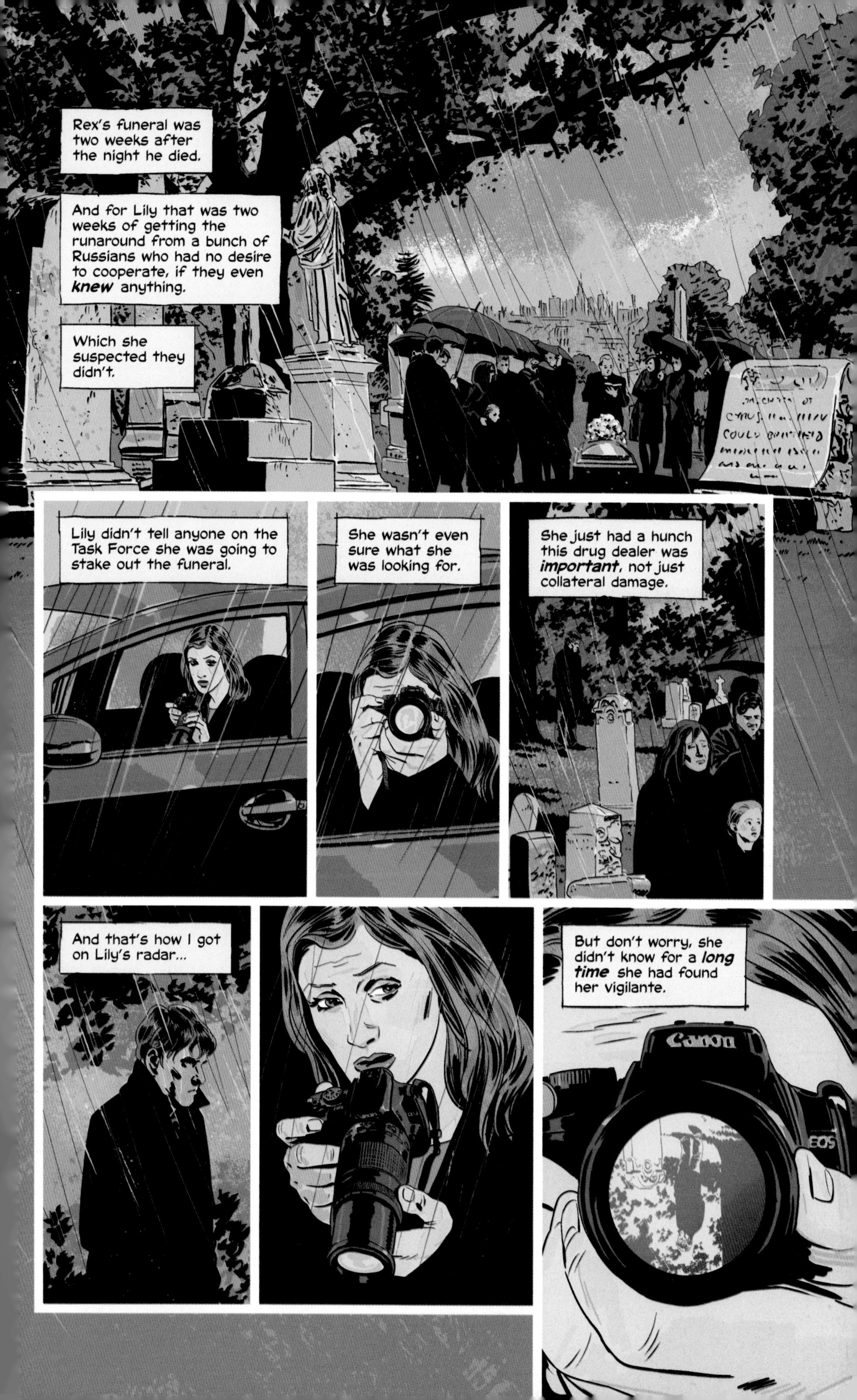
Rex's funeral was two weeks after the night he died.
And for Lily that was two weeks of getting the runaround from a bunch of Russians who had no desire to cooperate, if they even **knew** anything.
Which she suspected they didn't.
Lily didn't tell anyone on the Task Force she was going to stake out the funeral.
She wasn't even sure what she was looking for.
She just had a hunch this drug dealer was **important**, not just collateral damage.
And that's how I got on Lily's radar...
But don't worry, she didn't know for a **long time** she had found her vigilante.
Canon
EOS

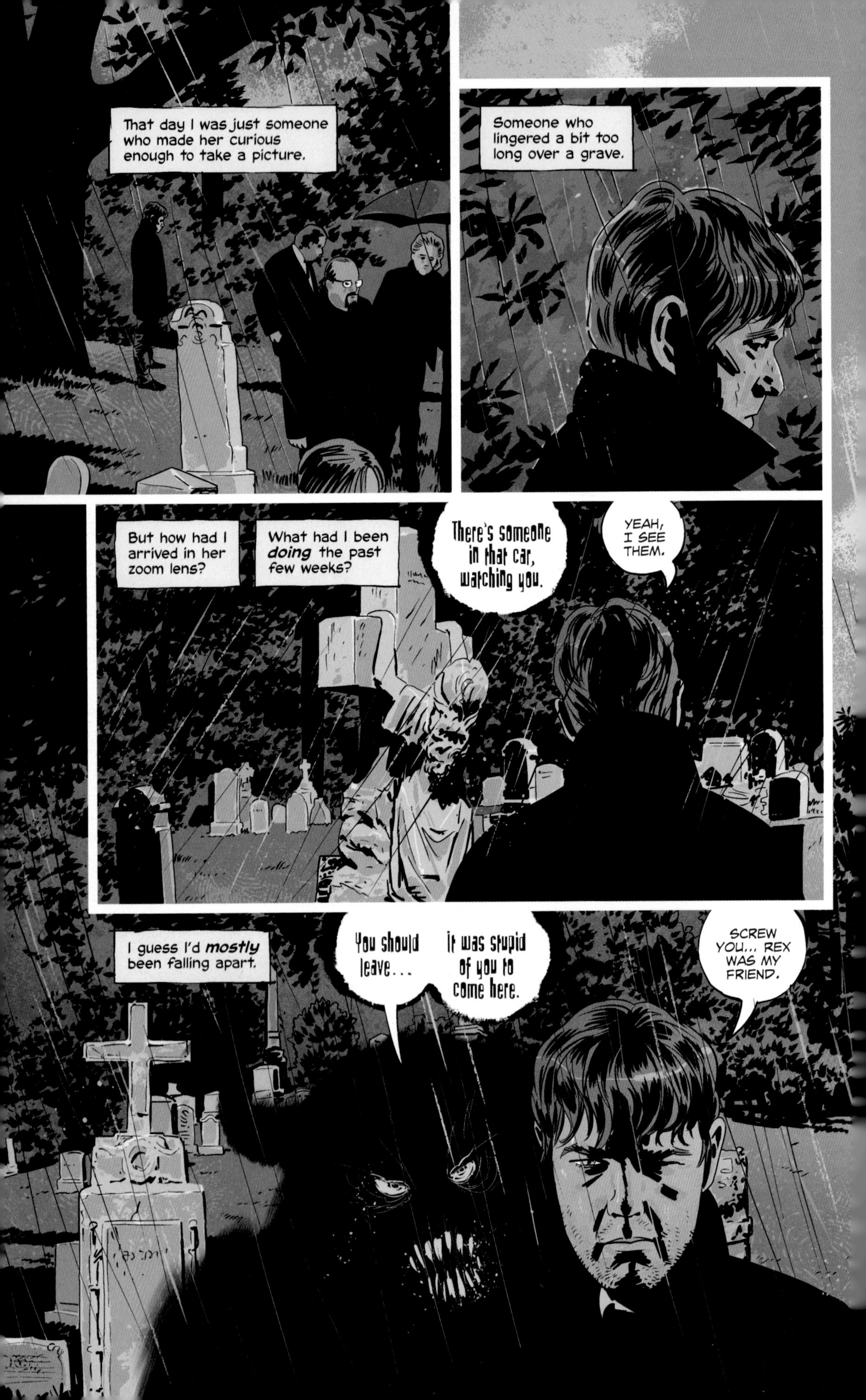

That day I was just someone who made her curious enough to take a picture.
Someone who lingered a bit too long over a grave.
But how had I arrived in her zoom lens?
What had I been *doing* the past few weeks?
There's someone in that car, watching you.
YEAH, I SEE THEM.
I guess I'd *mostly* been falling apart.
You should leave...
it was stupid of you to come here.
SCREW YOU... REX WAS MY FRIEND.

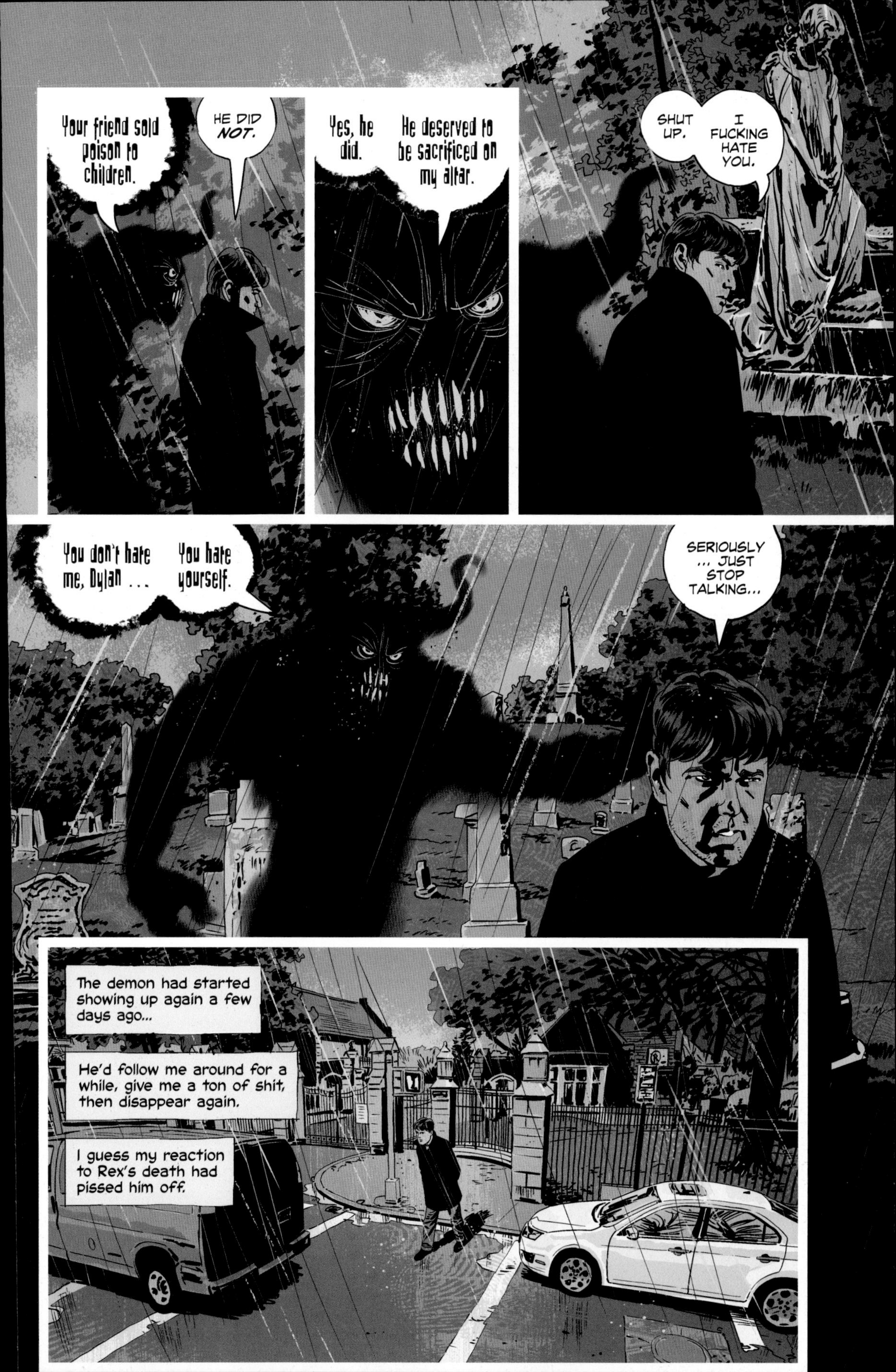
Your friend sold poison to children.
HE DID NOT.
Yes, he did.
He deserved to be sacrificed on my altar.
SHUT UP.
I FUCKING HATE YOU.
You don't hate me, Dylan . . .
You hate yourself.
SERIOUSLY ... JUST STOP TALKING...
The demon had started showing up again a few days ago...
He'd follow me around for a while, give me a ton of shit, then disappear again.
I guess my reaction to Rex's death had pissed him off.

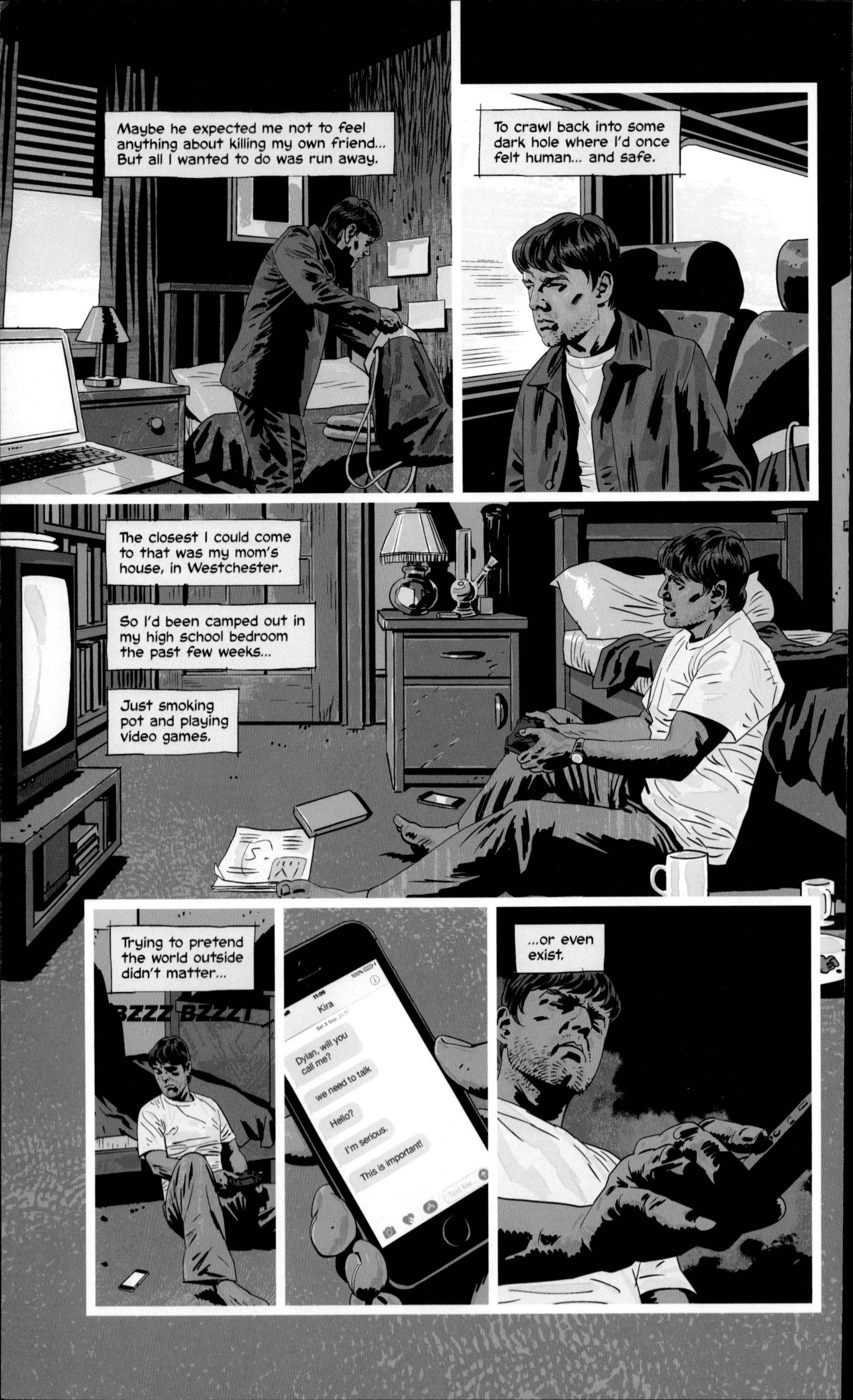
Maybe he expected me not to feel anything about killing my own friend... But all I wanted to do was run away.
To crawl back into some dark hole where I'd once felt human... and safe.
The closest I could come to that was my mom's house, in Westchester.
So I'd been camped out in my high school bedroom the past few weeks...
Just smoking pot and playing video games.
Trying to pretend the world outside didn't matter...
BZZZ BZZZT
Kira
Dylan, will you call me?
we need to talk
Hello?
I'm serious.
This is important!
...or even exist.

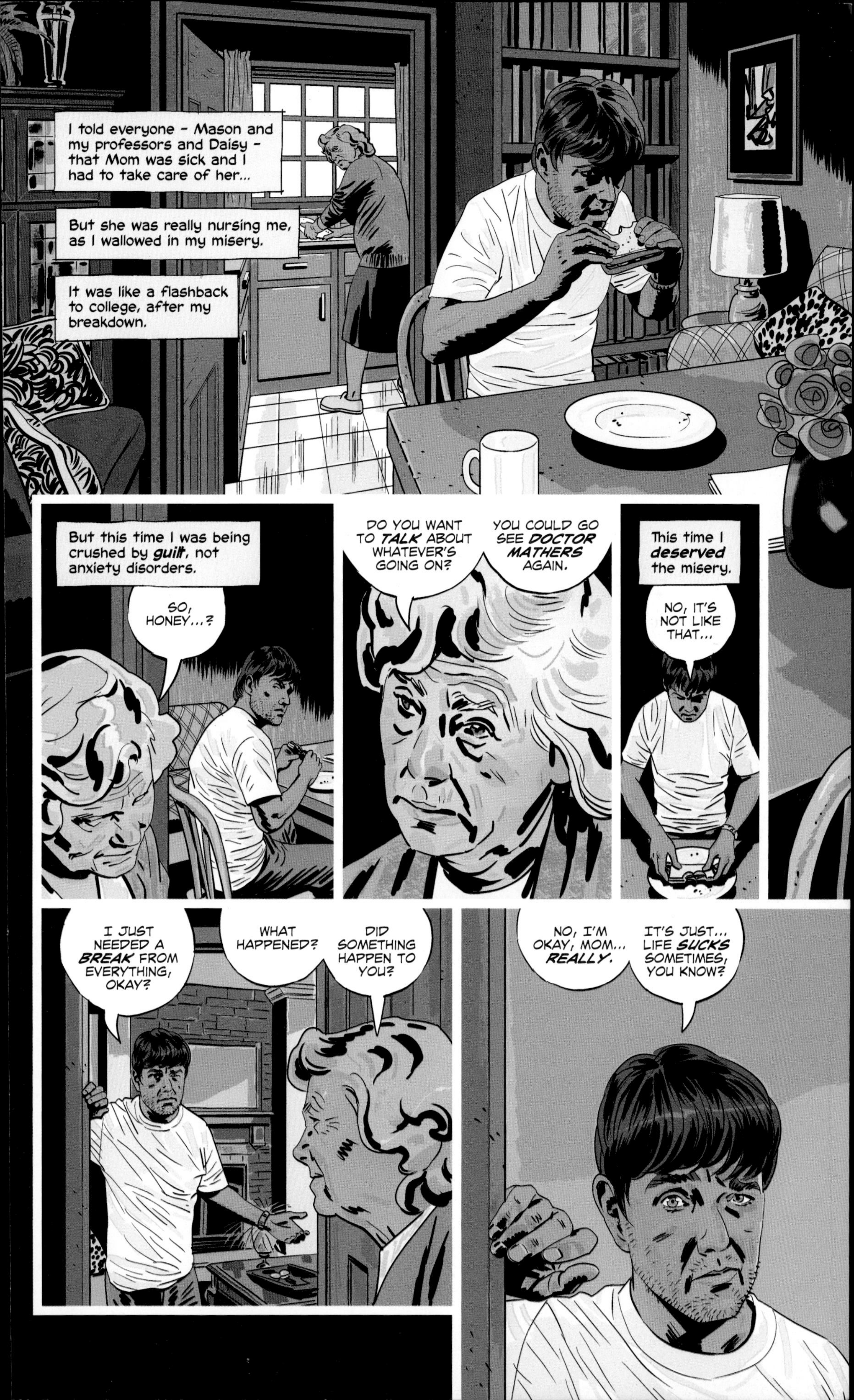
I told everyone - Mason and my professors and Daisy - that Mom was sick and I had to take care of her...
But she was really nursing me, as I wallowed in my misery.
It was like a flashback to college, after my breakdown.
But this time I was being crushed by guilt, not anxiety disorders.
SO, HONEY...?
DO YOU WANT TO TALK ABOUT WHATEVER'S GOING ON?
YOU COULD GO SEE DOCTOR MATHERS AGAIN.
This time I deserved the misery.
NO, IT'S NOT LIKE THAT...
I JUST NEEDED A BREAK FROM EVERYTHING, OKAY?
WHAT HAPPENED?
DID SOMETHING HAPPEN TO YOU?
NO, I'M OKAY, MOM... REALLY.
IT'S JUST... LIFE SUCKS SOMETIMES, YOU KNOW?

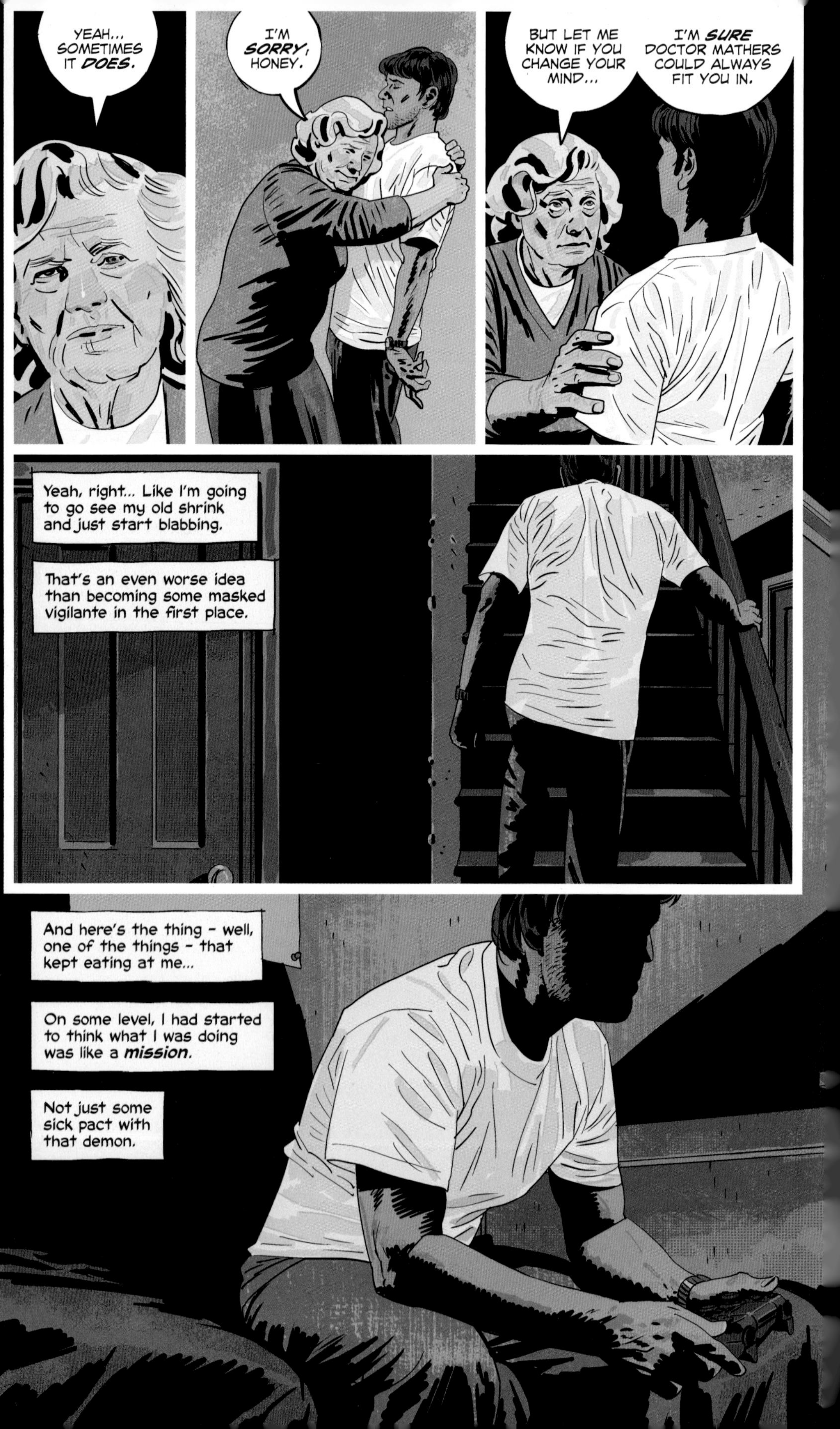
YEAH... SOMETIMES IT DOES.
I'M SORRY, HONEY.
BUT LET ME KNOW IF YOU CHANGE YOUR MIND...
I'M SURE DOCTOR MATHERS COULD ALWAYS FIT YOU IN.
Yeah, right... Like I'm going to go see my old shrink and just start blabbing.
That's an even worse idea than becoming some masked vigilante in the first place.
And here's the thing - well, one of the things - that kept eating at me...
On some level, I had started to think what I was doing was like a mission.
Not just some sick pact with that demon.

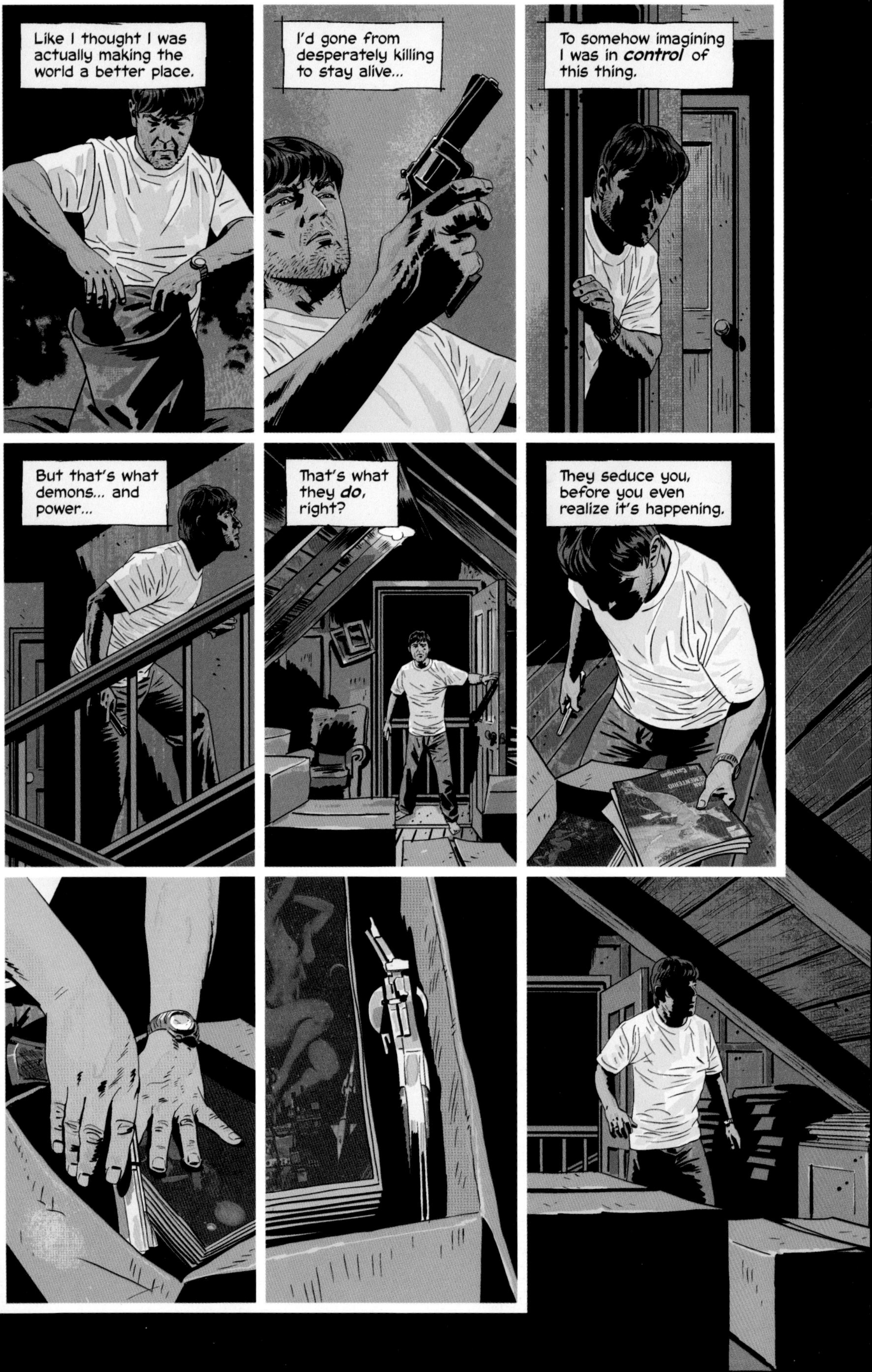
Like I thought I was actually making the world a better place.
I'd gone from desperately killing to stay alive...
To somehow imagining I was in *control* of this thing.
But that's what demons... and power...
That's what they *do*, right?
They seduce you, before you even realize it's happening.

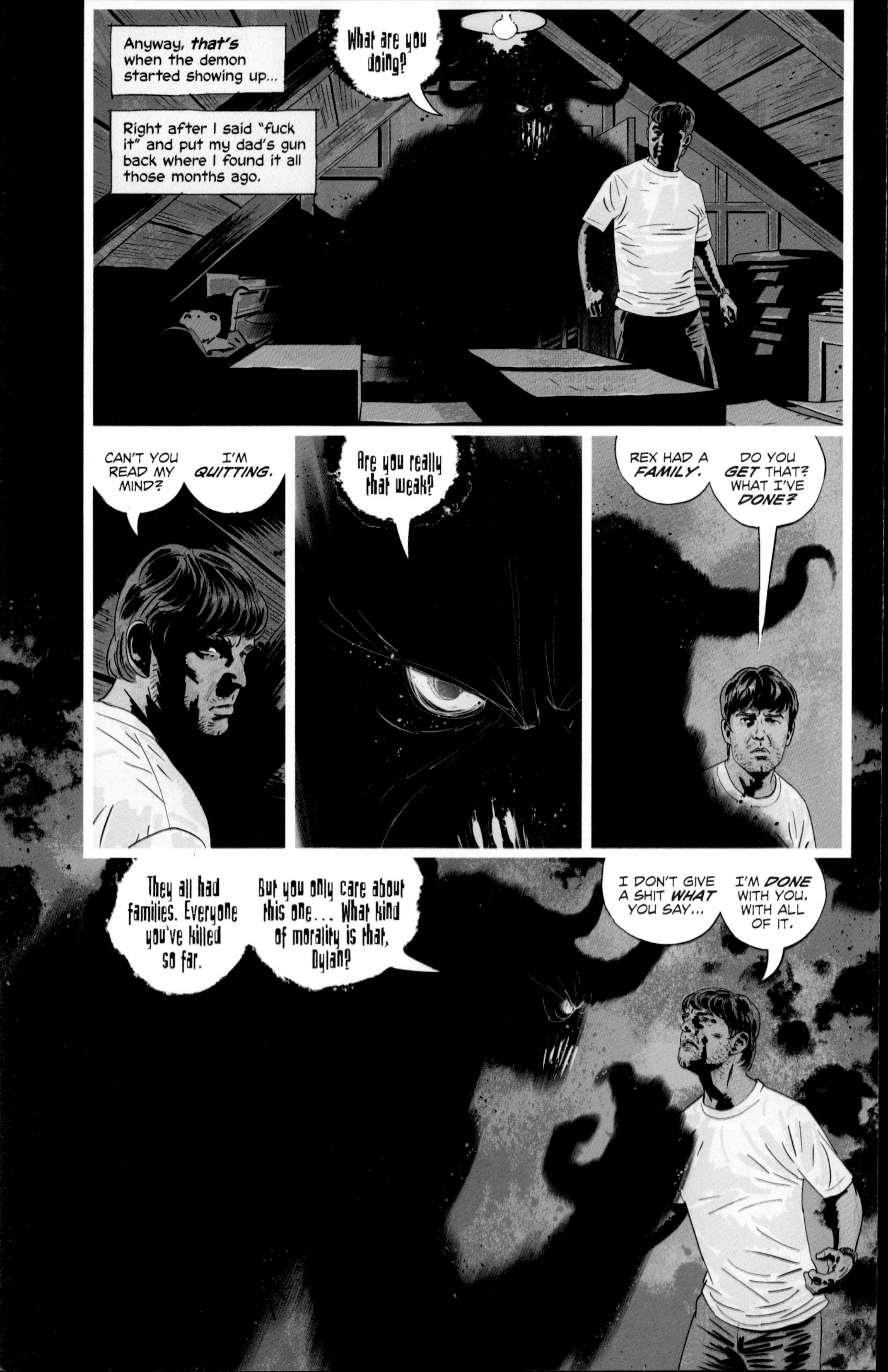
Anyway, *that's* when the demon started showing up...
What are you doing?
Right after I said "fuck it" and put my dad's gun back where I found it all those months ago.
CAN'T YOU READ MY MIND?
I'M *QUITTING.*
Are you really that weak?
REX HAD A *FAMILY.*
DO YOU *GET* THAT? WHAT I'VE *DONE?*
They all had families. Everyone you've killed so far.
But you only care about this one... What kind of morality is that, Dylan?
I DON'T GIVE A SHIT *WHAT* YOU SAY...
I'M *DONE* WITH YOU. WITH ALL OF IT.

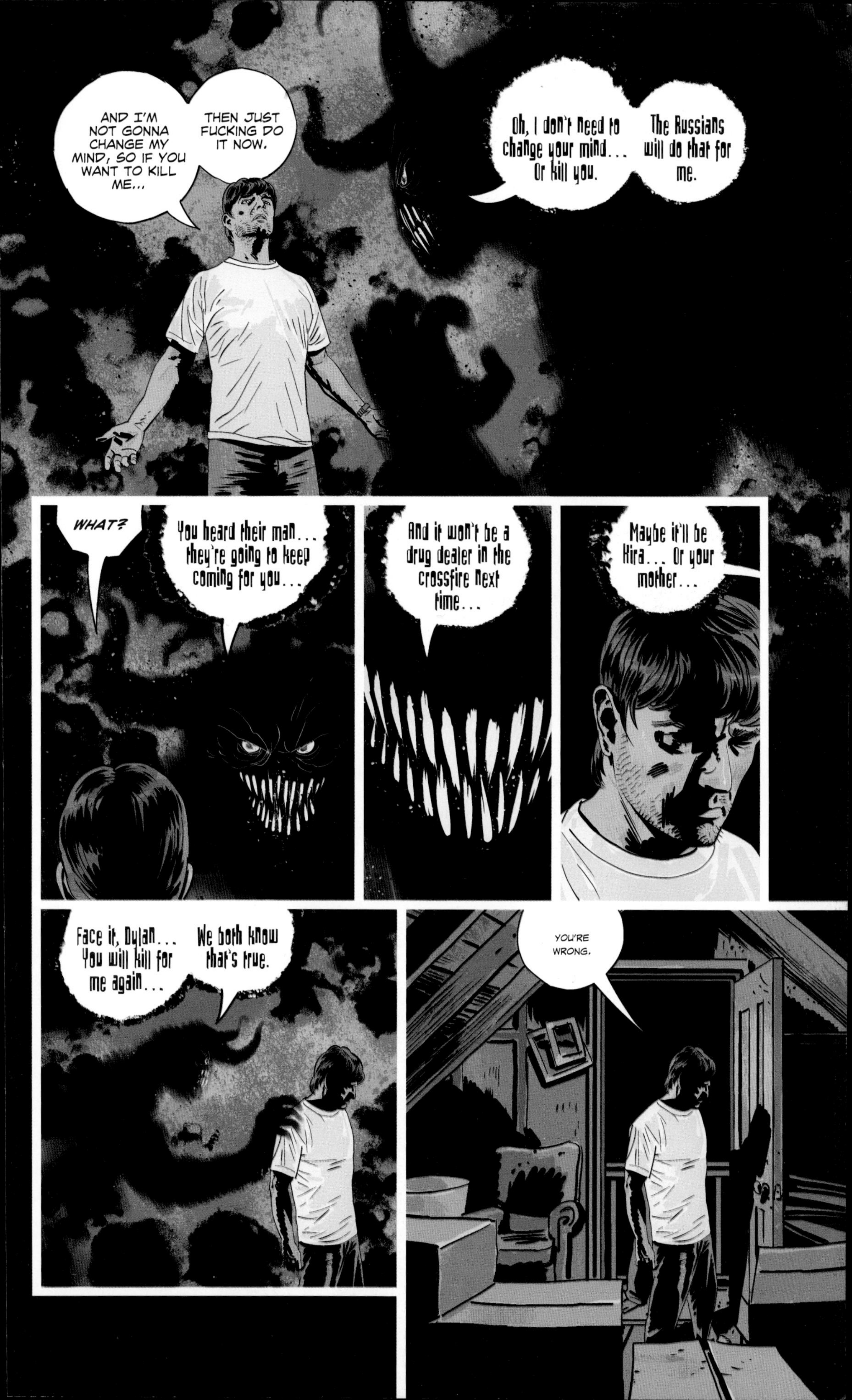
AND I'M NOT GONNA CHANGE MY MIND, SO IF YOU WANT TO KILL ME...
THEN JUST FUCKING DO IT NOW.
Oh, I don't need to change your mind... Or kill you.
The Russians will do that for me.
WHAT?
You heard their man... they're going to keep coming for you...
And it won't be a drug dealer in the crossfire next time...
Maybe it'll be Kira... Or your mother...
Face it, Dylan... You will kill for me again...
We both know that's true.
YOU'RE WRONG.

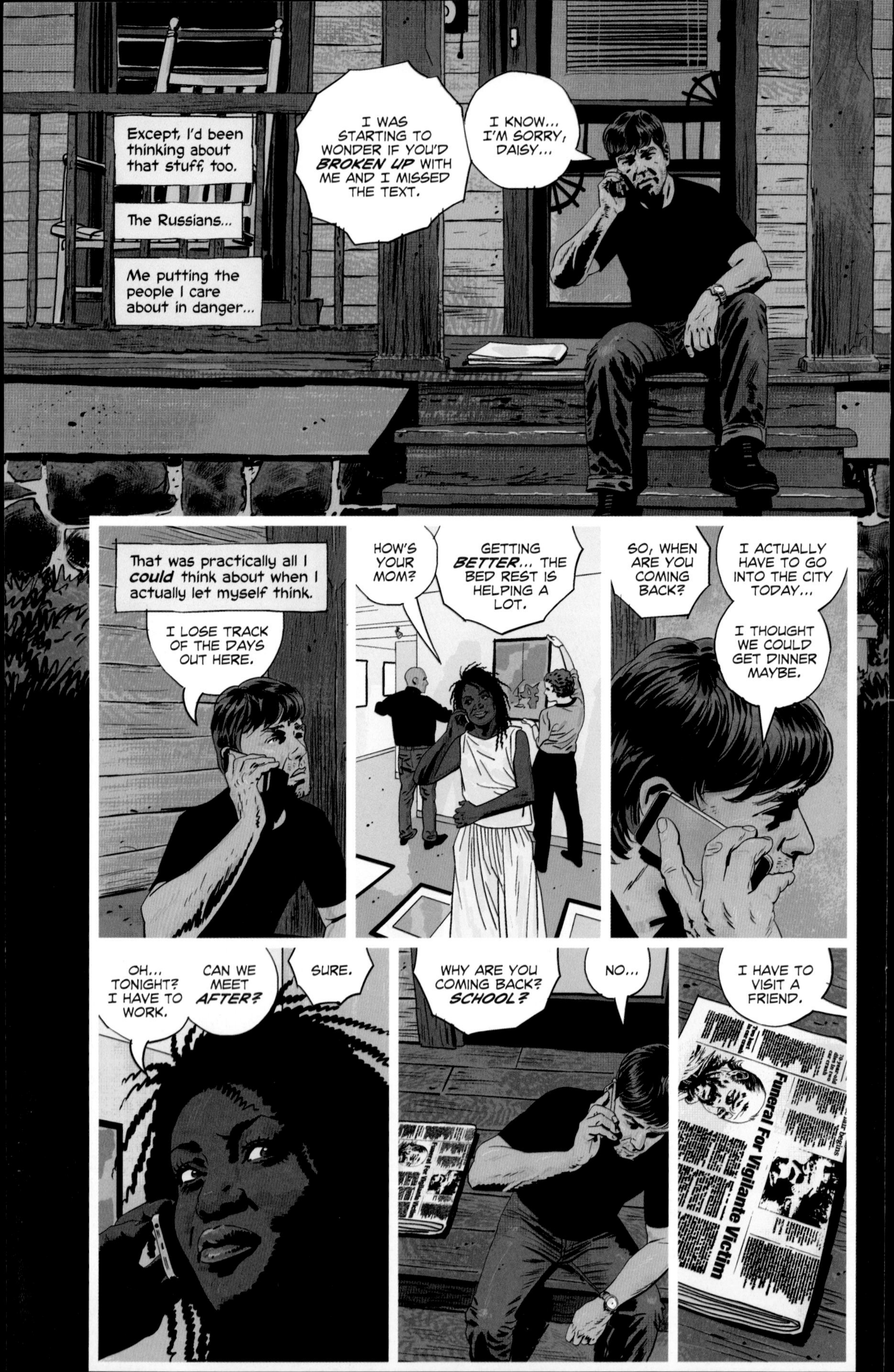

Except, I'd been thinking about that stuff, too.
The Russians...
Me putting the people I care about in danger...
I WAS STARTING TO WONDER IF YOU'D BROKEN UP WITH ME AND I MISSED THE TEXT.
I KNOW... I'M SORRY, DAISY...
That was practically all I could think about when I actually let myself think.
I LOSE TRACK OF THE DAYS OUT HERE.
HOW'S YOUR MOM?
GETTING BETTER... THE BED REST IS HELPING A LOT.
SO, WHEN ARE YOU COMING BACK?
I ACTUALLY HAVE TO GO INTO THE CITY TODAY...
I THOUGHT WE COULD GET DINNER MAYBE.
OH... TONIGHT? I HAVE TO WORK.
CAN WE MEET AFTER?
SURE.
WHY ARE YOU COMING BACK? SCHOOL?
NO...
I HAVE TO VISIT A FRIEND.
Funeral For Vigilante Victim

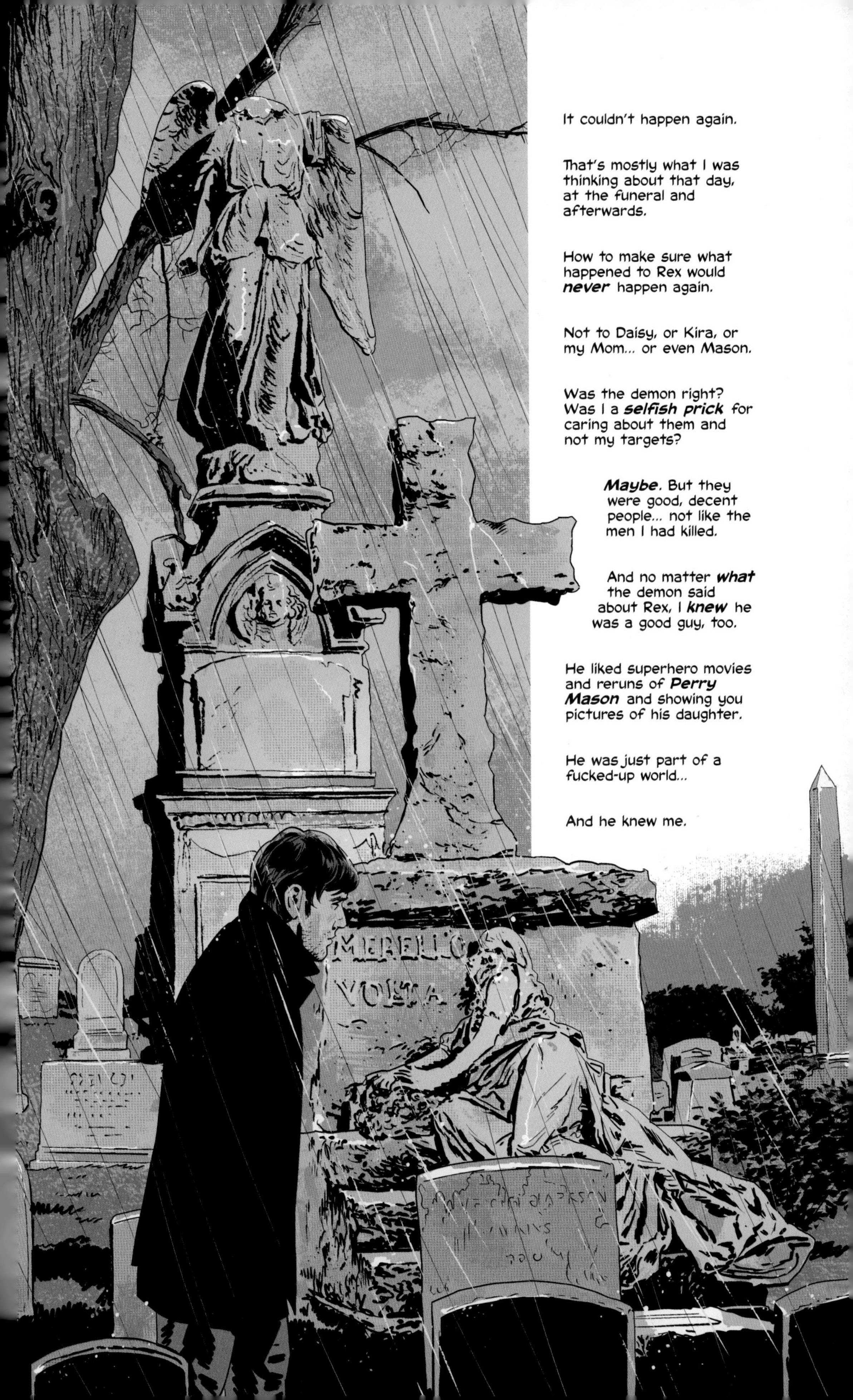
It couldn't happen again.
That's mostly what I was thinking about that day, at the funeral and afterwards.
How to make sure what happened to Rex would ***never*** happen again.
Not to Daisy, or Kira, or my Mom... or even Mason.
Was the demon right? Was I a ***selfish prick*** for caring about them and not my targets?
Maybe. But they were good, decent people... not like the men I had killed.
And no matter ***what*** the demon said about Rex, I ***knew*** he was a good guy, too.
He liked superhero movies and reruns of ***Perry Mason*** and showing you pictures of his daughter.
He was just part of a fucked-up world...
And he knew me.

So what was my plan? How was I going to make sure no one else got hurt because of me?

I had a few ideas.

First, I'd break up with Daisy... Then I'd tell Mason to get another roommate and pack up my stuff.

Then I'd disappear... Find some cheap motel somewhere.

Wait for the demon to come take his payment.

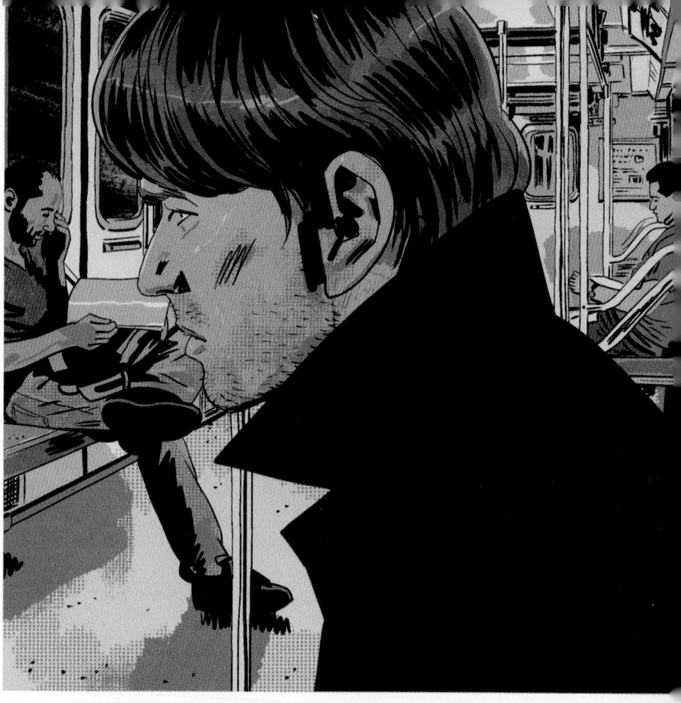

But that didn't really solve the Russian problem, did it?

What if the demon killed me and they never found out about it?

What if they still came and tortured Kira or my mom, thinking I was still out there somewhere?

I needed to lure them away somehow.

Maybe I could write a letter to the press, like the Zodiac Killer did.

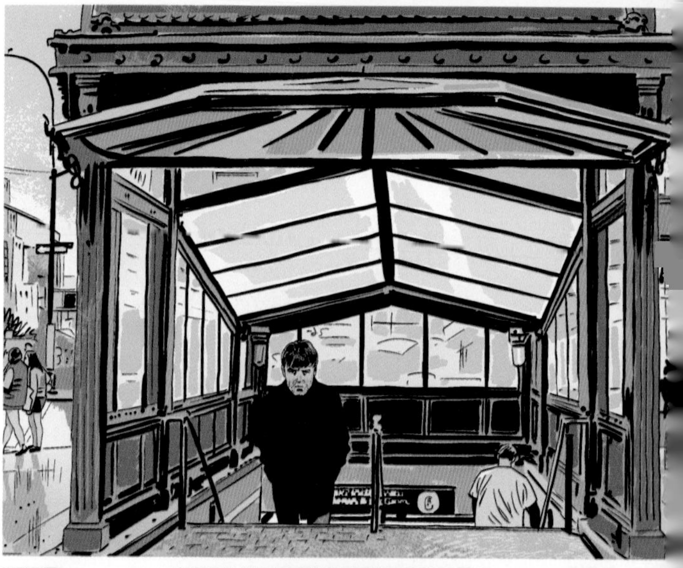

Yeah, that's right.

I'm supposed to be the sympathetic lead in this story and I just compared myself to the Zodiac Killer.

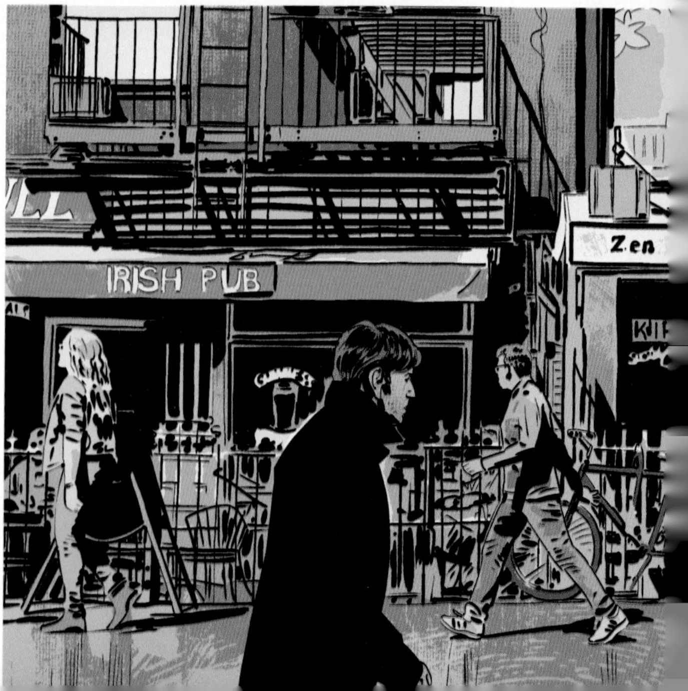
IRISH PUB
Zen

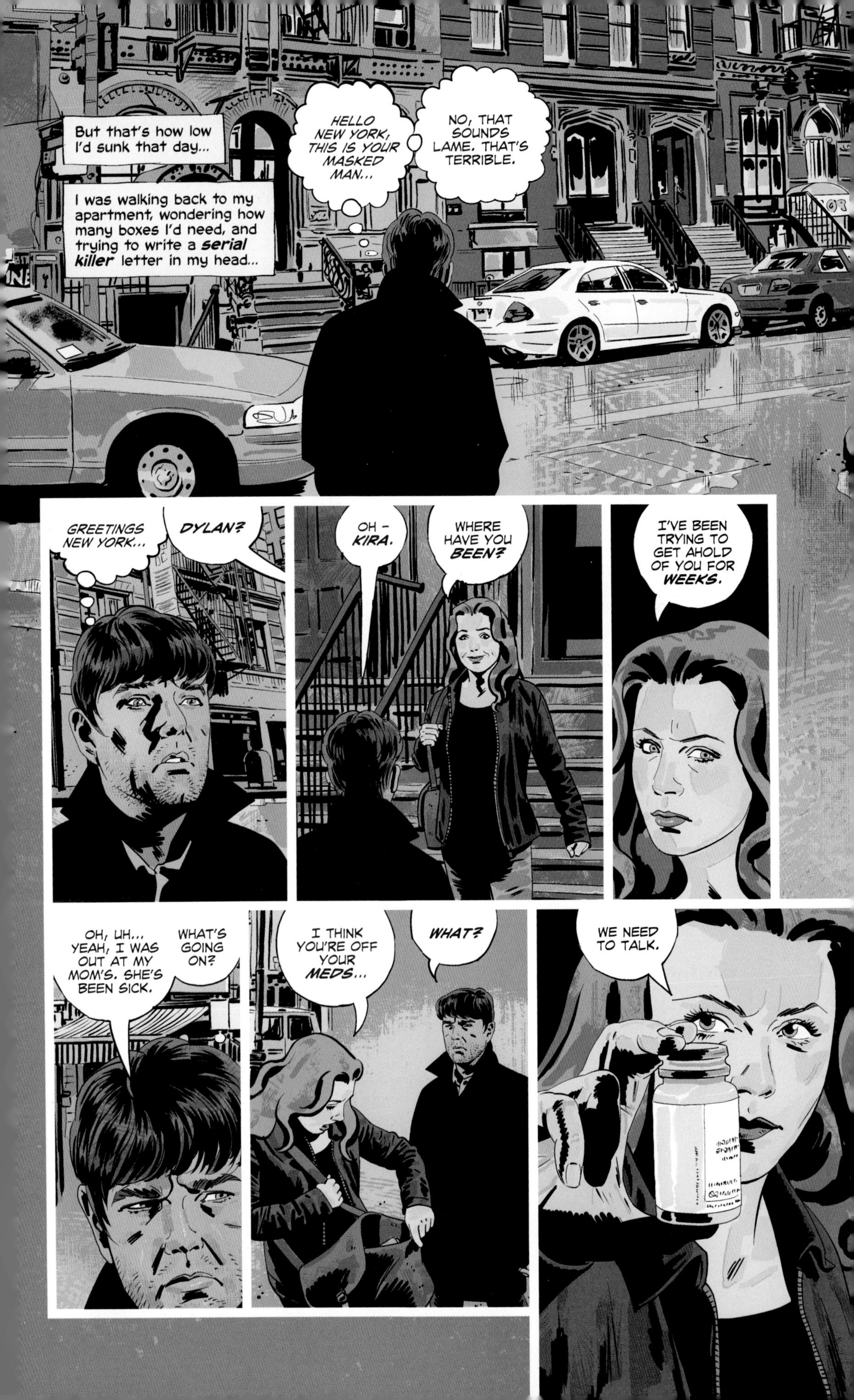
But that's how low I'd sunk that day...
I was walking back to my apartment, wondering how many boxes I'd need, and trying to write a serial killer letter in my head...
HELLO NEW YORK, THIS IS YOUR MASKED MAN...
NO, THAT SOUNDS LAME. THAT'S TERRIBLE.
GREETINGS NEW YORK...
DYLAN?
OH - KIRA.
WHERE HAVE YOU BEEN?
I'VE BEEN TRYING TO GET AHOLD OF YOU FOR WEEKS.
OH, UH... YEAH, I WAS OUT AT MY MOM'S. SHE'S BEEN SICK.
WHAT'S GOING ON?
I THINK YOU'RE OFF YOUR MEDS...
WHAT?
WE NEED TO TALK.

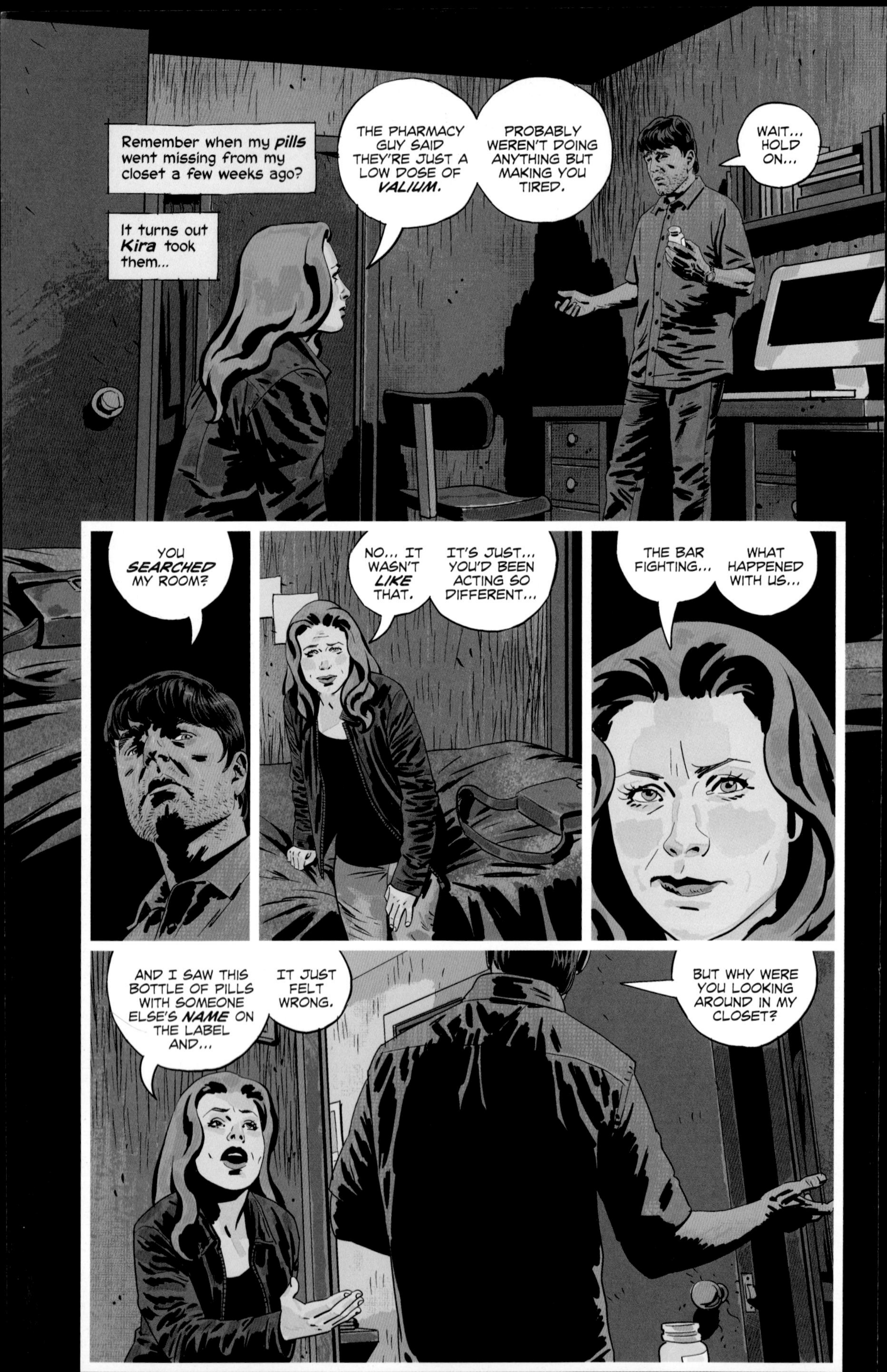
Remember when my pills went missing from my closet a few weeks ago?
It turns out Kira took them...
THE PHARMACY GUY SAID THEY'RE JUST A LOW DOSE OF VALIUM.
PROBABLY WEREN'T DOING ANYTHING BUT MAKING YOU TIRED.
WAIT... HOLD ON...
YOU SEARCHED MY ROOM?
NO... IT WASN'T LIKE THAT.
IT'S JUST... YOU'D BEEN ACTING SO DIFFERENT...
THE BAR FIGHTING...
WHAT HAPPENED WITH US...
AND I SAW THIS BOTTLE OF PILLS WITH SOMEONE ELSE'S NAME ON THE LABEL AND...
IT JUST FELT WRONG.
BUT WHY WERE YOU LOOKING AROUND IN MY CLOSET?

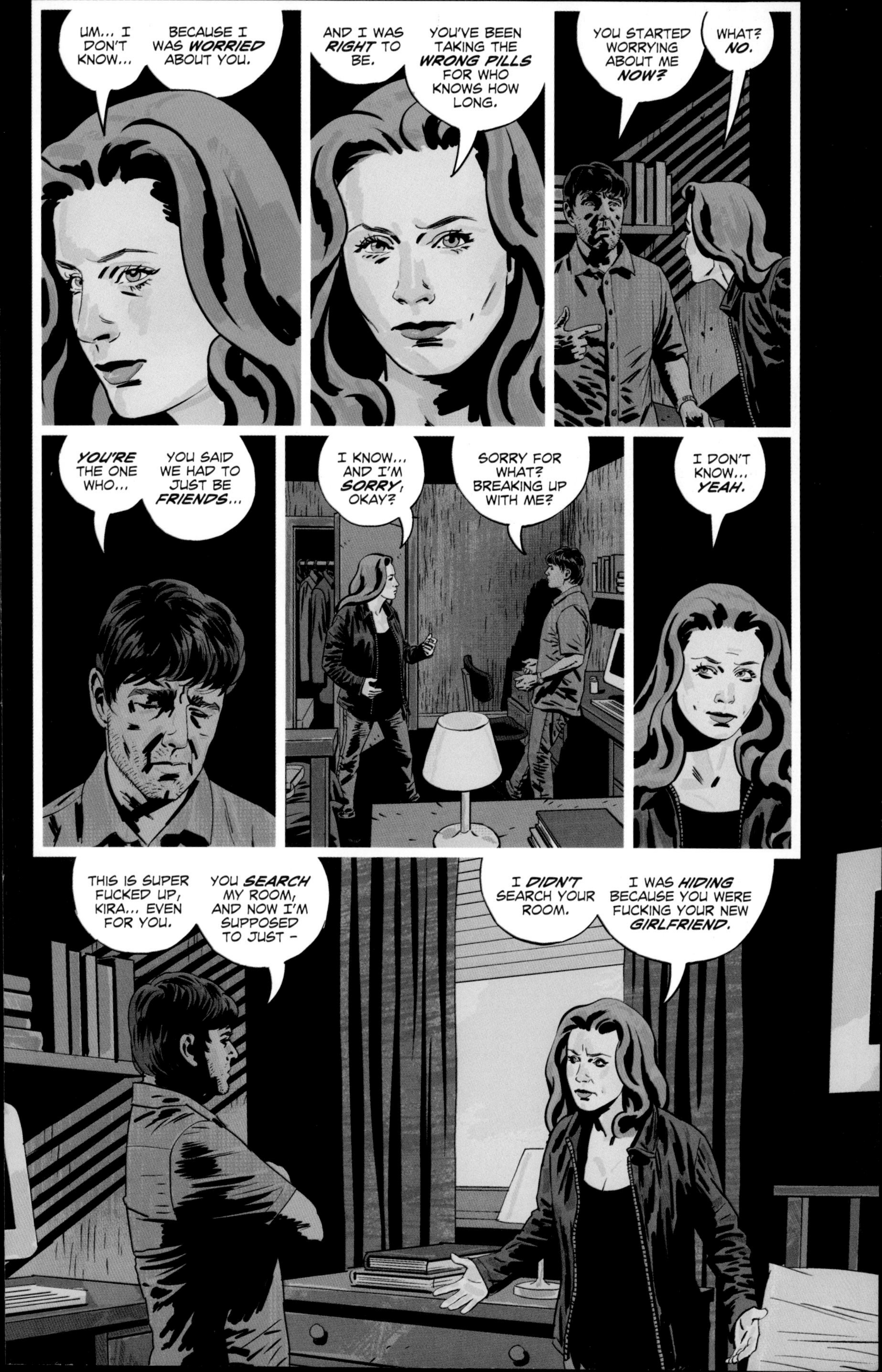
UM... I DON'T KNOW...
BECAUSE I WAS WORRIED ABOUT YOU.
AND I WAS RIGHT TO BE.
YOU'VE BEEN TAKING THE WRONG PILLS FOR WHO KNOWS HOW LONG.
YOU STARTED WORRYING ABOUT ME NOW?
WHAT? NO.
YOU'RE THE ONE WHO...
YOU SAID WE HAD TO JUST BE FRIENDS...
I KNOW... AND I'M SORRY, OKAY?
SORRY FOR WHAT? BREAKING UP WITH ME?
I DON'T KNOW... YEAH.
THIS IS SUPER FUCKED UP, KIRA... EVEN FOR YOU.
YOU SEARCH MY ROOM, AND NOW I'M SUPPOSED TO JUST –
I DIDN'T SEARCH YOUR ROOM.
I WAS HIDING BECAUSE YOU WERE FUCKING YOUR NEW GIRLFRIEND.

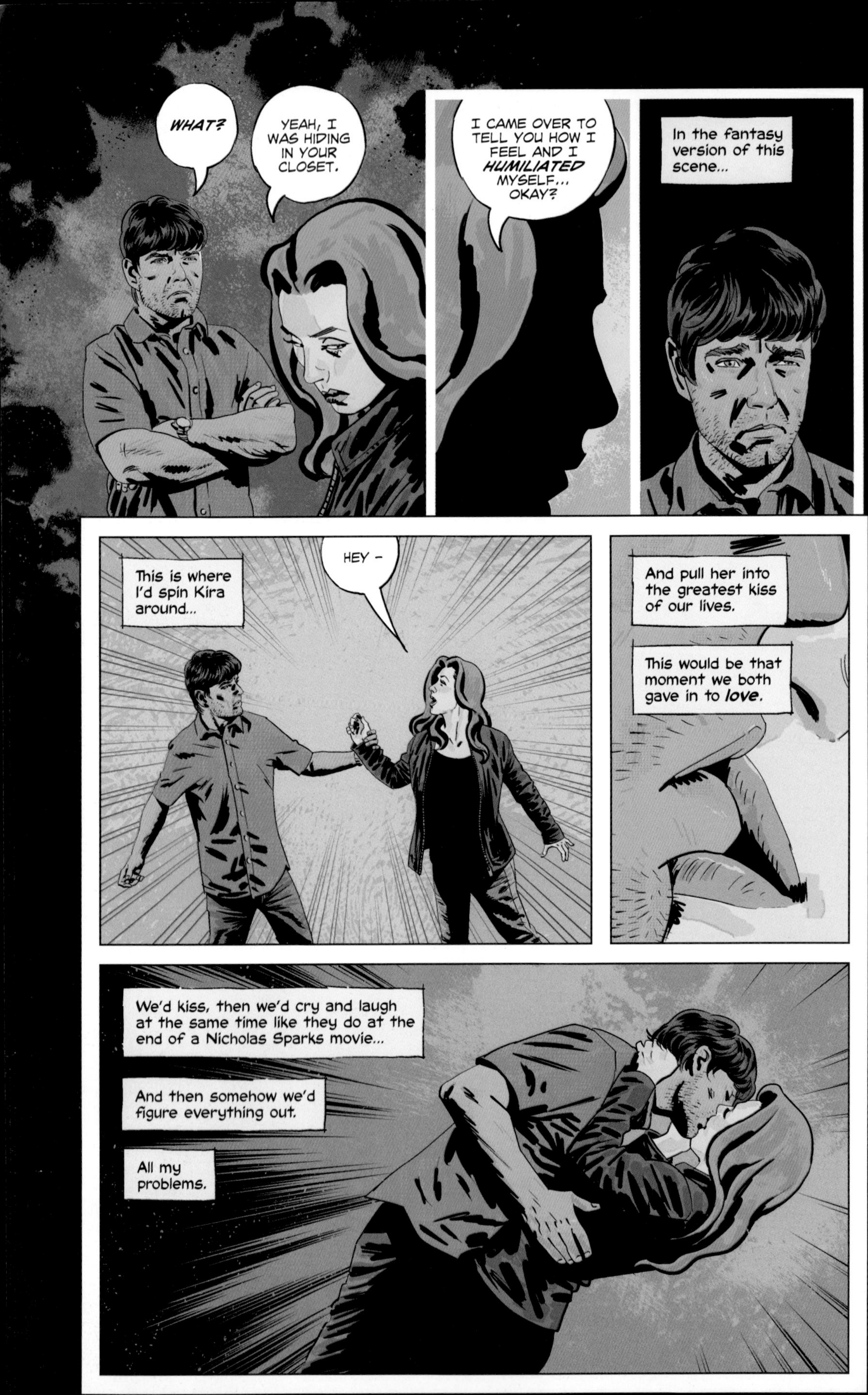
WHAT?
YEAH, I WAS HIDING IN YOUR CLOSET.
I CAME OVER TO TELL YOU HOW I FEEL AND I HUMILIATED MYSELF... OKAY?
In the fantasy version of this scene...
This is where I'd spin Kira around...
HEY -
And pull her into the greatest kiss of our lives.
This would be that moment we both gave in to love.
We'd kiss, then we'd cry and laugh at the same time like they do at the end of a Nicholas Sparks movie...
And then somehow we'd figure everything out.
All my problems.

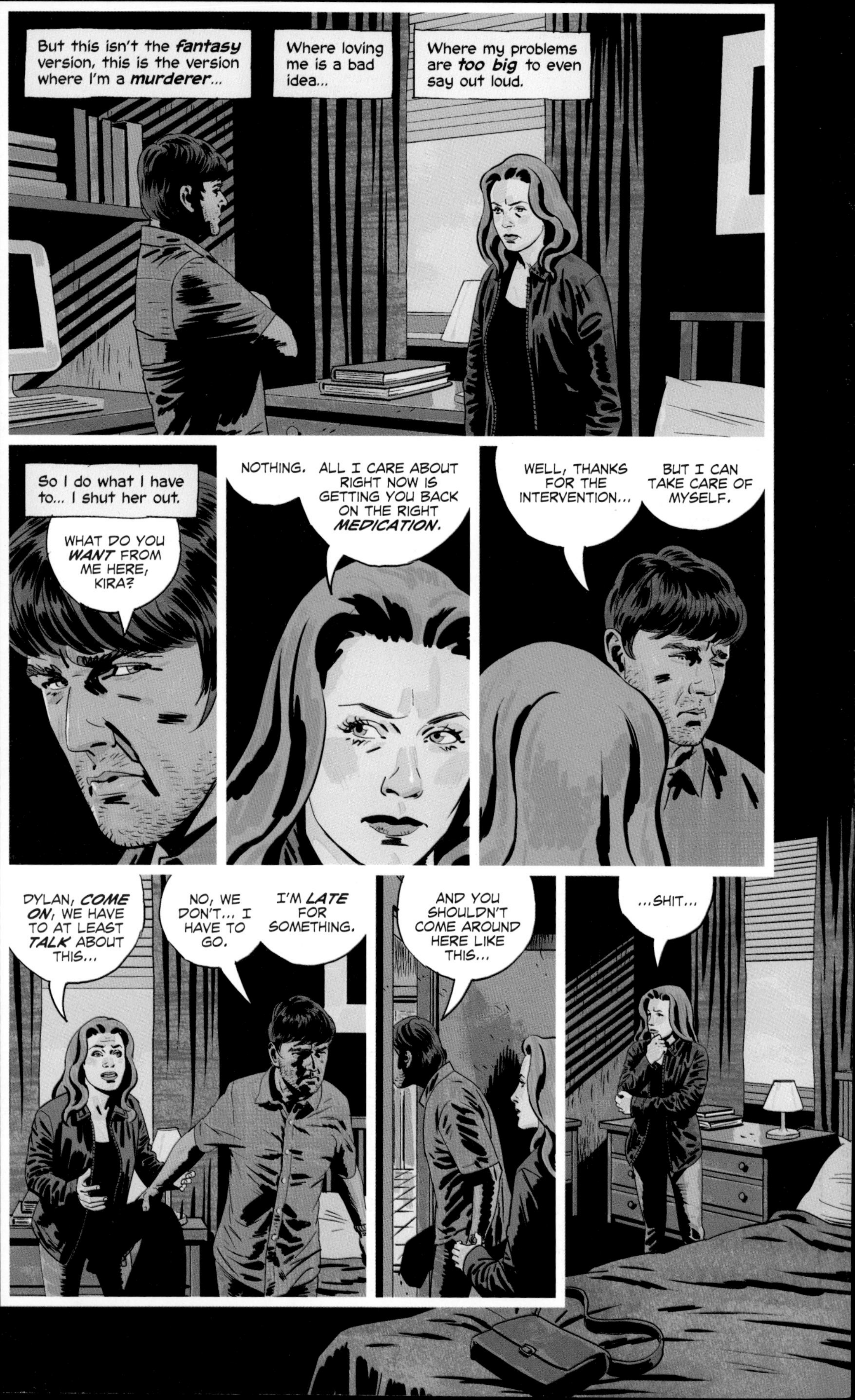

But this isn't the ***fantasy*** version, this is the version where I'm a ***murderer***...
Where loving me is a bad idea...
Where my problems are ***too big*** to even say out loud.
So I do what I have to... I shut her out.
WHAT DO YOU ***WANT*** FROM ME HERE, KIRA?
NOTHING.
ALL I CARE ABOUT RIGHT NOW IS GETTING YOU BACK ON THE RIGHT ***MEDICATION***.
WELL, THANKS FOR THE INTERVENTION...
BUT I CAN TAKE CARE OF MYSELF.
DYLAN, ***COME ON***, WE HAVE TO AT LEAST ***TALK*** ABOUT THIS...
NO, WE DON'T... I HAVE TO GO.
I'M ***LATE*** FOR SOMETHING.
AND YOU SHOULDN'T COME AROUND HERE LIKE THIS...
...SHIT...

Here's the thing – I hadn't actually thought about my meds since Rex had died.

So when I stormed out that night, I was mostly fucked up about the other stuff Kira had said.

I mean, she'd basically admitted she was still in love with me.

I'm trying to run away and here she is, making me feel like there's a hole ripped out of my chest.

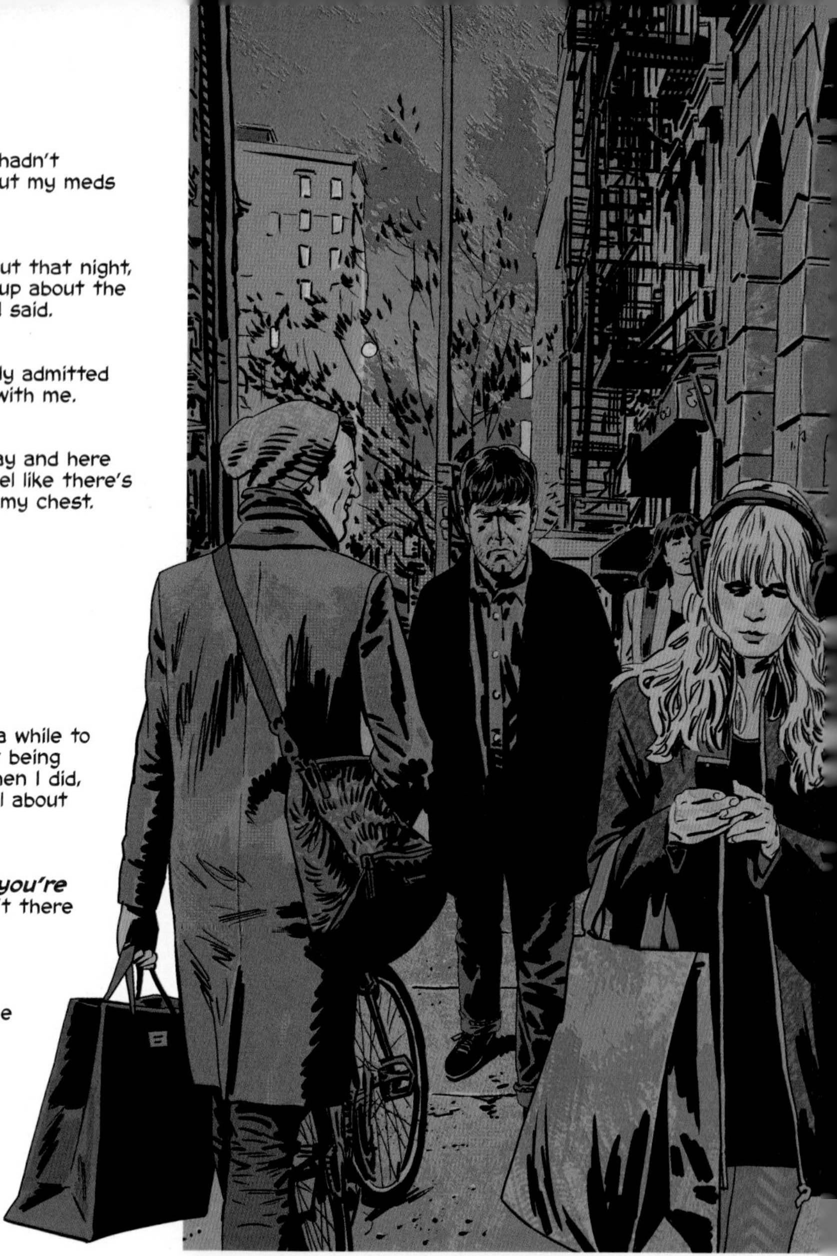

So yeah, it took me a while to start worrying about being off my meds, and when I did, I was mostly in denial about it.

I mean, I know what ***you're*** thinking... but I wasn't there yet.

What had Kira really proven? That one time Rex gave me the wrong pills?

It could have just been a mistake.

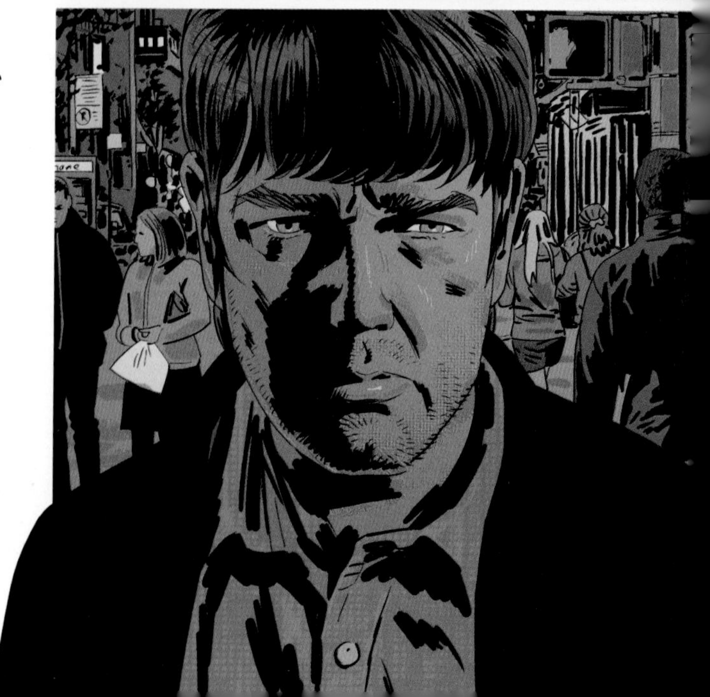

And even if it was more than that, I'd gone off my meds before and all that happened was I couldn't get out of bed because everything felt pointless.

I didn't start seeing demons and run around killing people because I was hearing voices...

I mean, that would be a horror show, right?

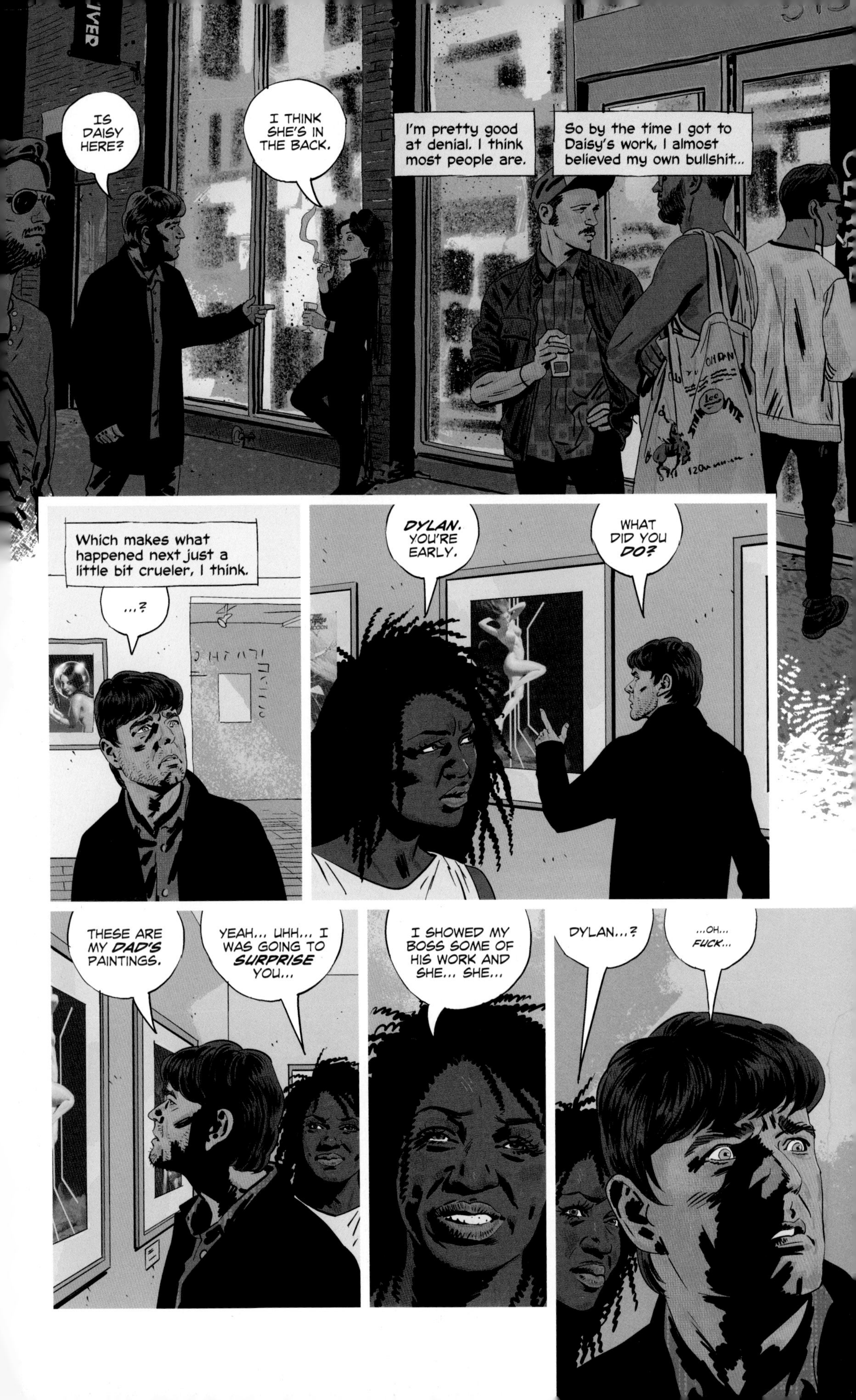
IS DAISY HERE?
I THINK SHE'S IN THE BACK.
I'm pretty good at denial. I think most people are.
So by the time I got to Daisy's work, I almost believed my own bullshit...
Which makes what happened next just a little bit crueler, I think.
...?
DYLAN. YOU'RE EARLY.
WHAT DID YOU DO?
THESE ARE MY DAD'S PAINTINGS.
YEAH... UHH... I WAS GOING TO SURPRISE YOU...
I SHOWED MY BOSS SOME OF HIS WORK AND SHE... SHE...
DYLAN...?
...OH... FUCK...

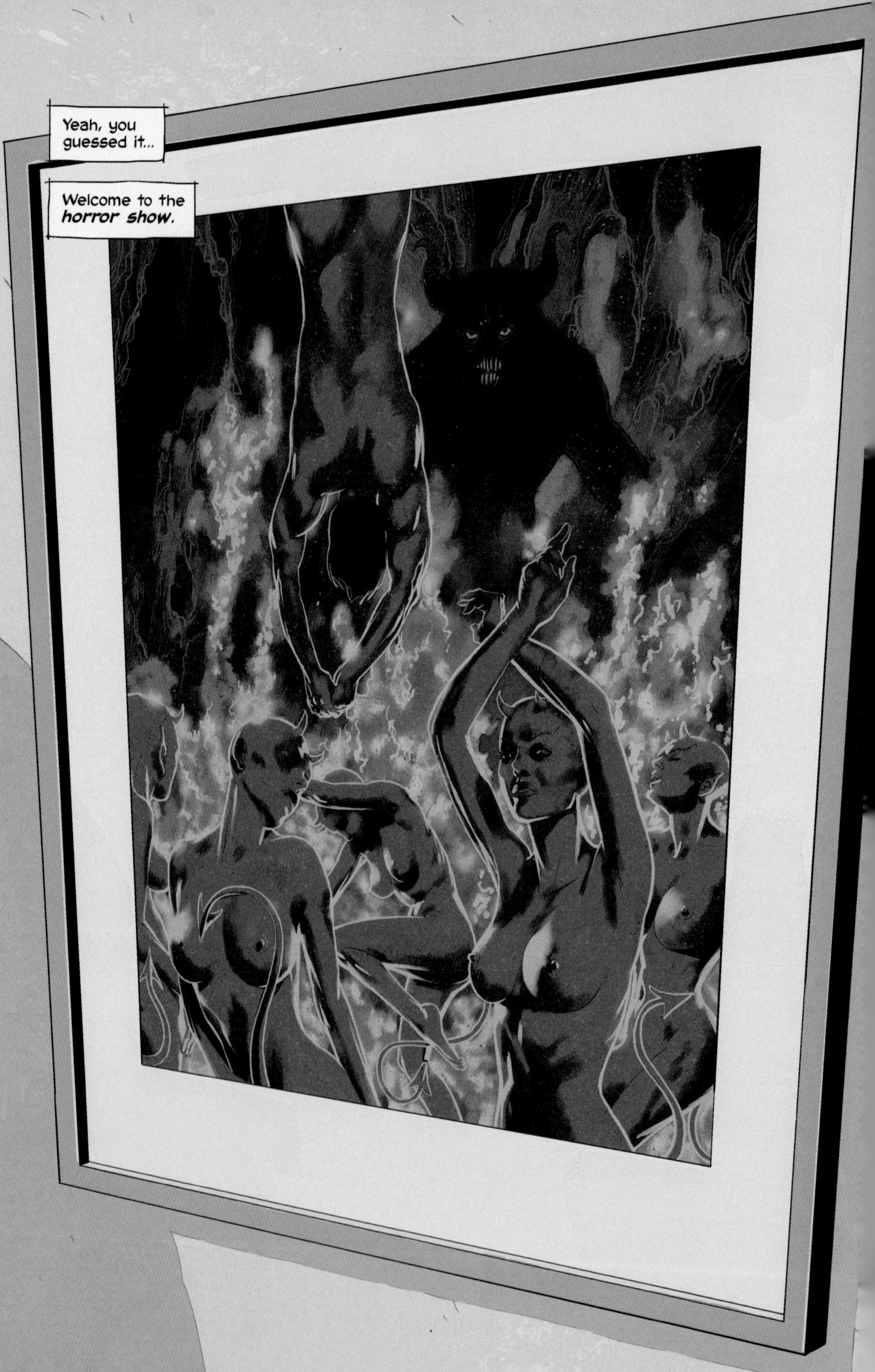
Yeah, you guessed it...
Welcome to the *horror show.*

TO BE CONTINUED

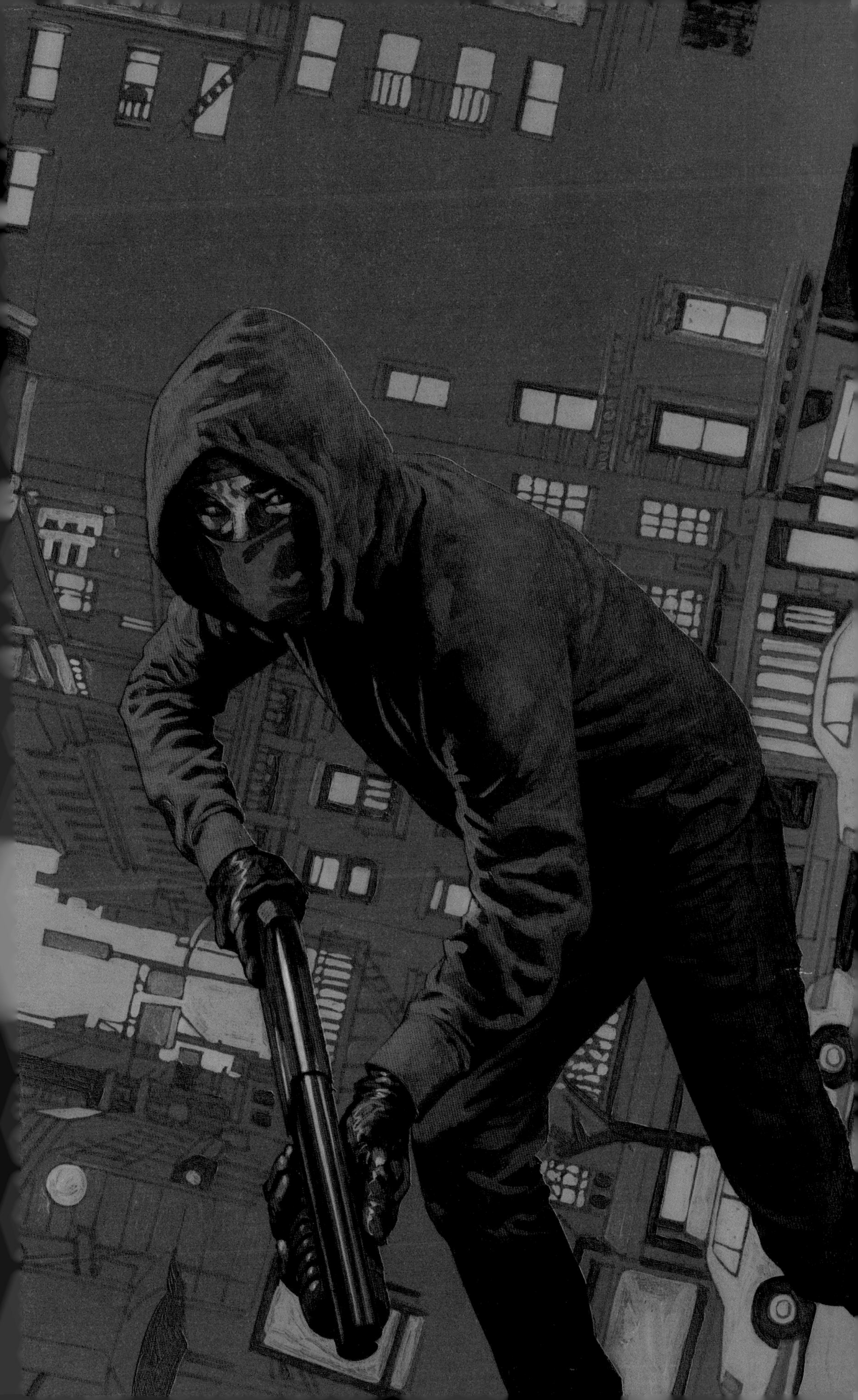

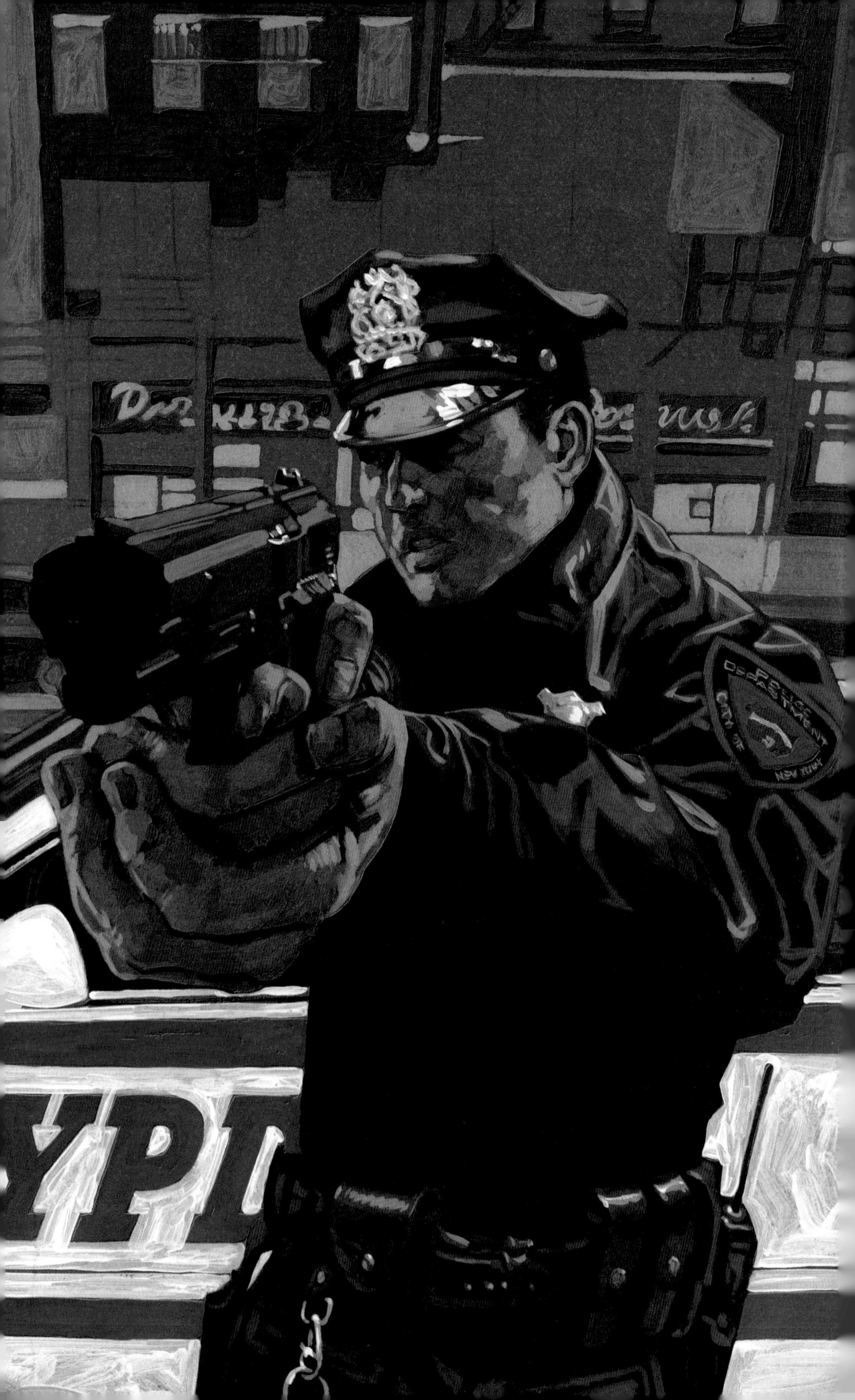

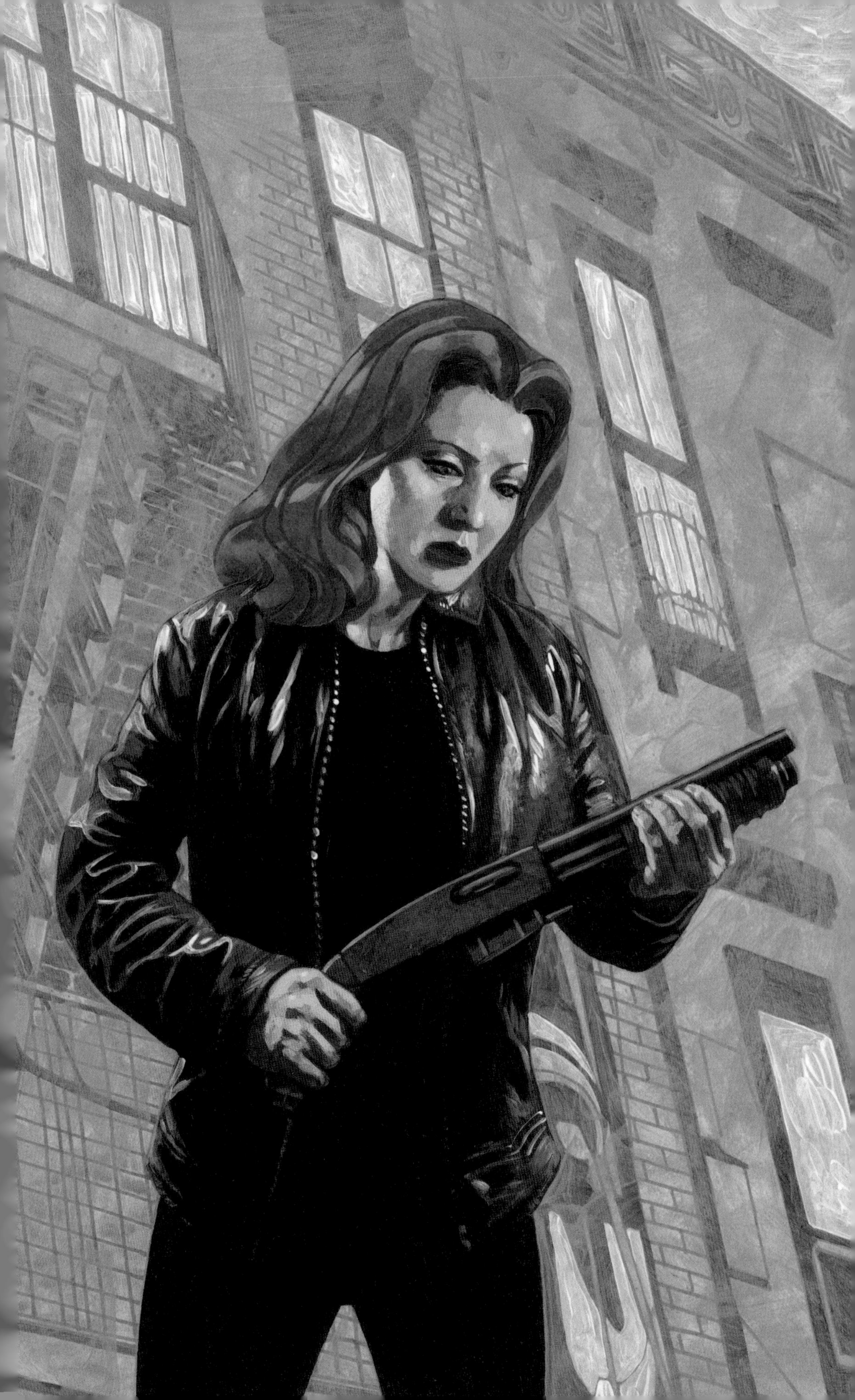

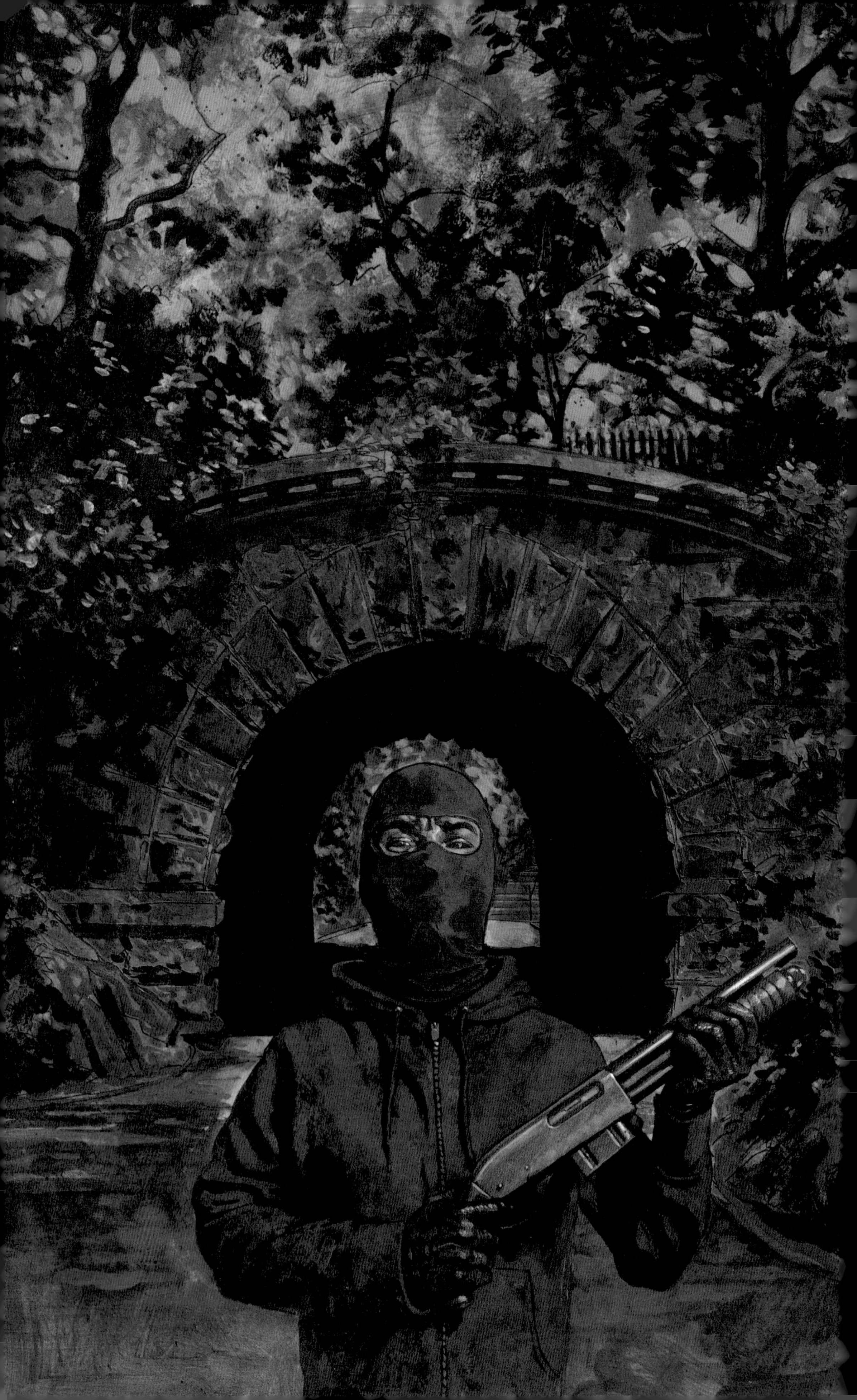

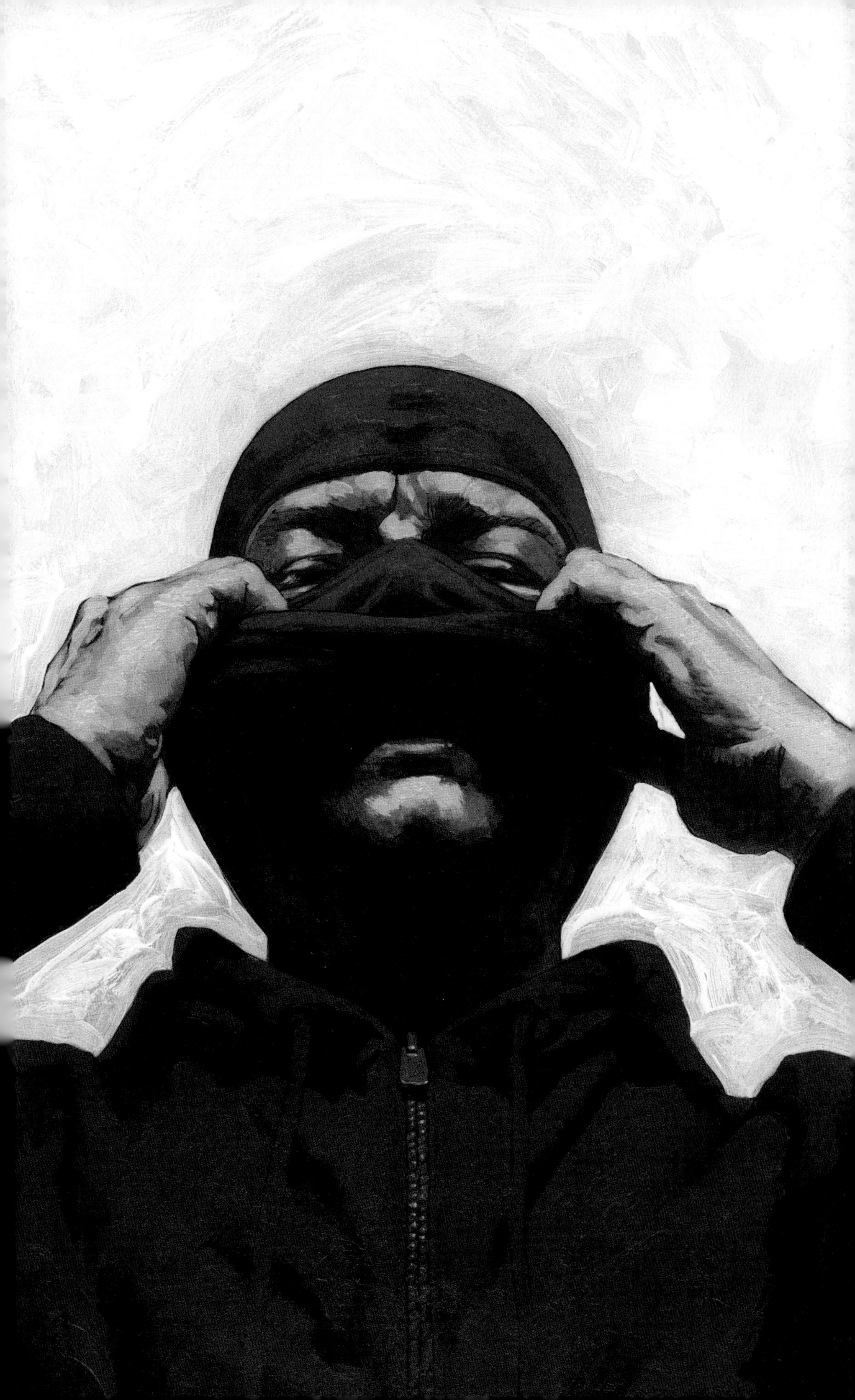

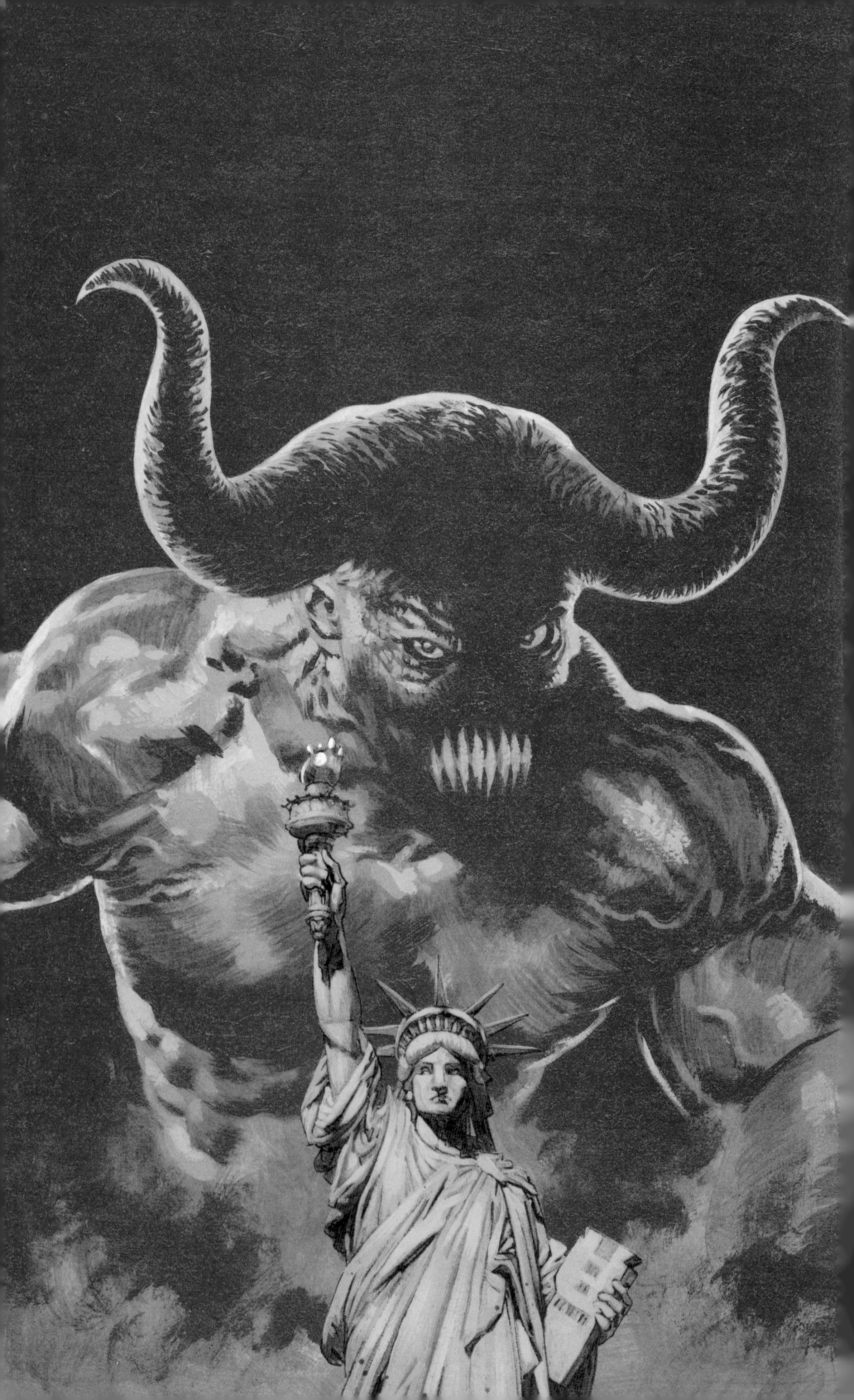

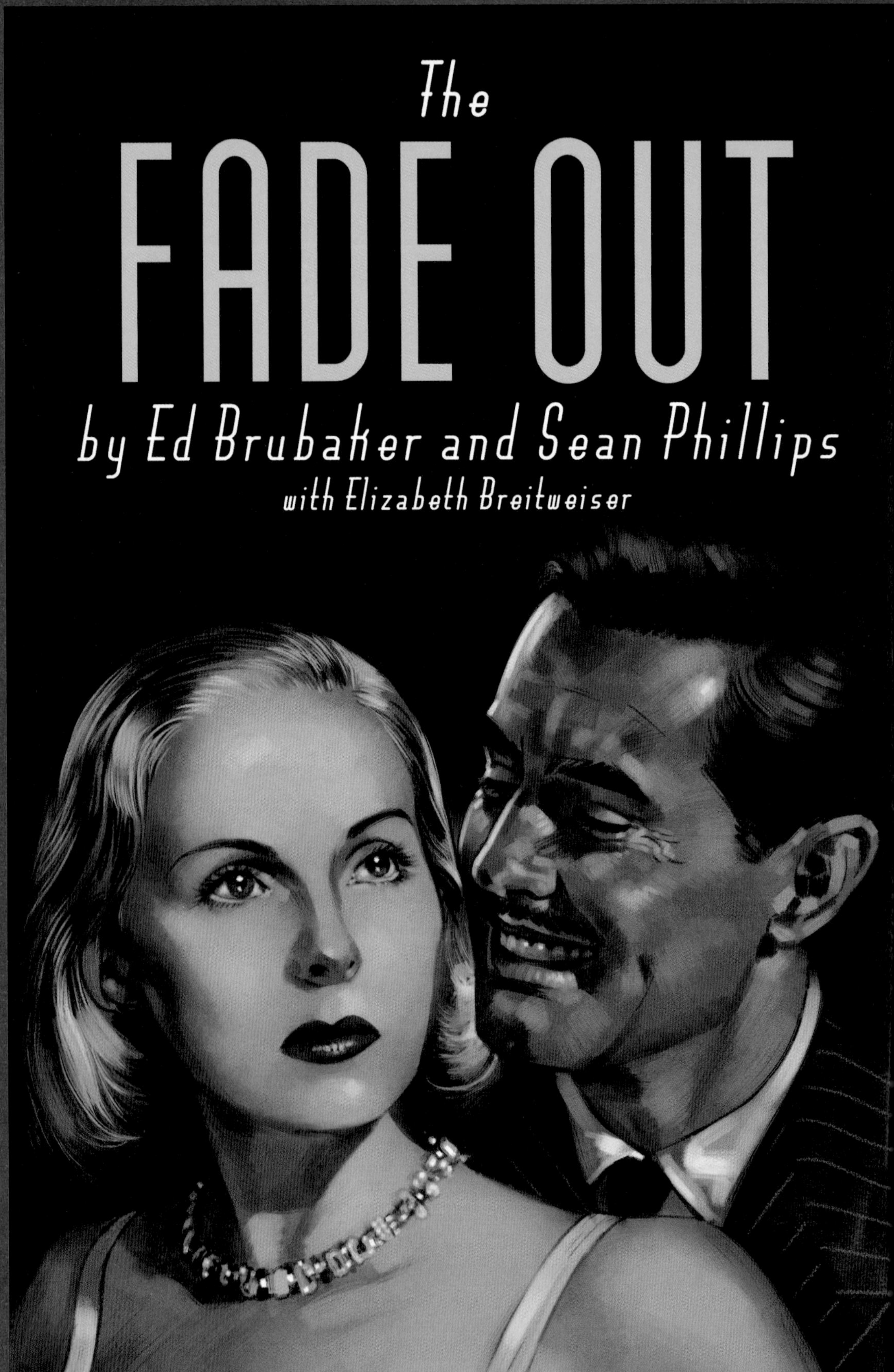
The
FADE OUT
by Ed Brubaker and Sean Phillips
with Elizabeth Breitweiser

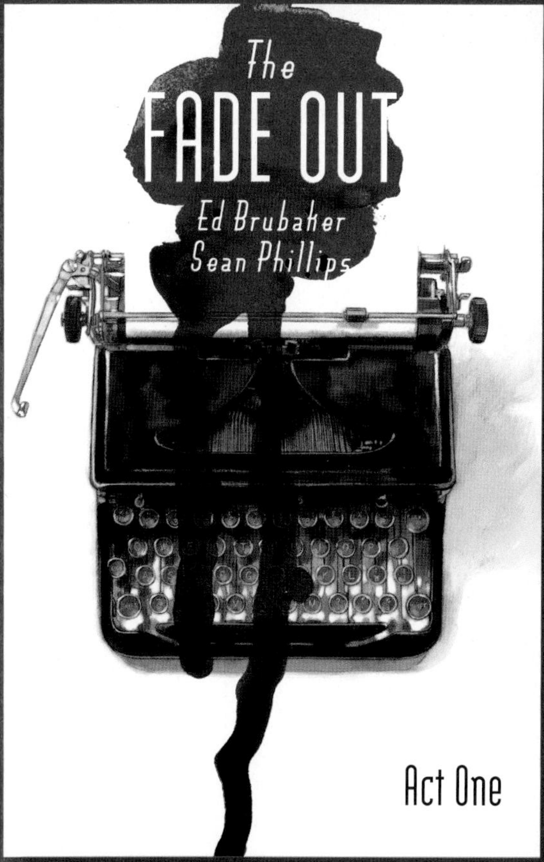
The
FADE OUT
Ed Brubaker
Sean Phillips
Act One

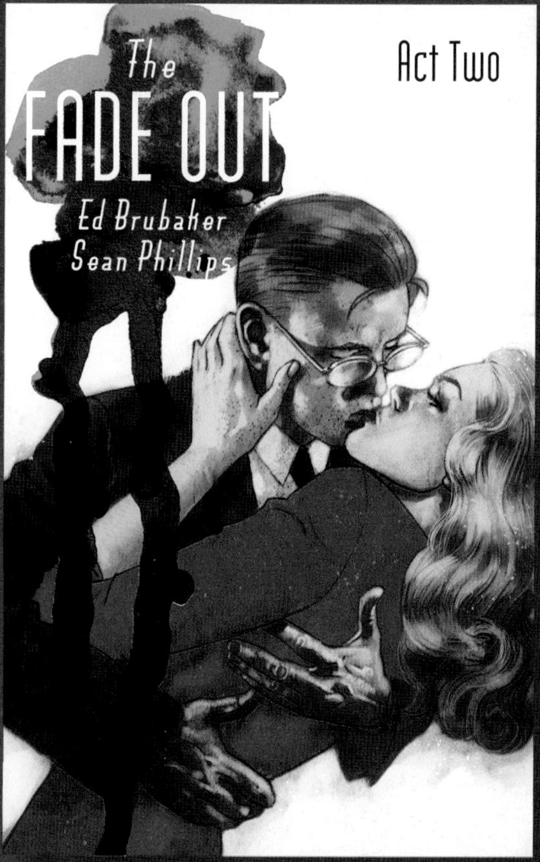
The
FADE OUT
Act Two
Ed Brubaker
Sean Phillips

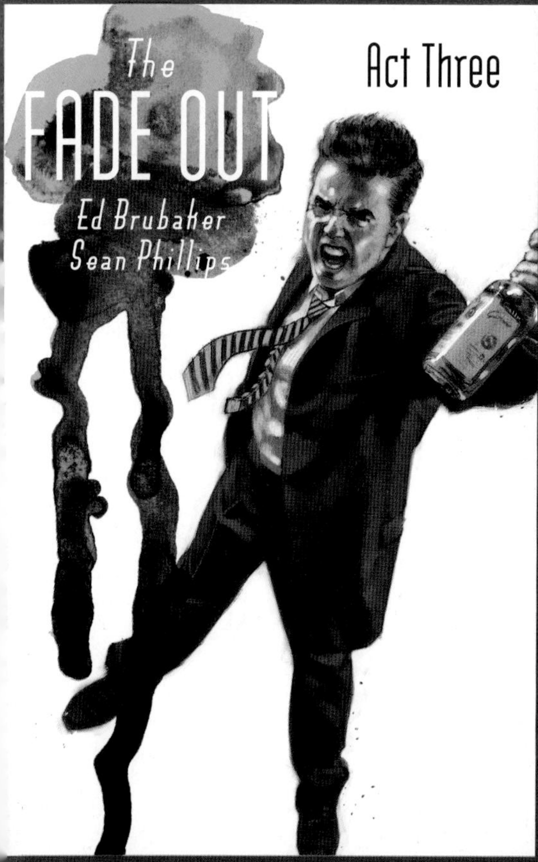
The
FADE OUT
Act Three
Ed Brubaker
Sean Phillips

*"One of comics dream teams delivers their best story yet in **THE FADE OUT**, an old Hollywood murder mystery draped against HUAC and the Red Scare."*

- New York Magazine

Ed Brubaker
Sean Phillips

CRIMINAL
Coward

Ed Brubaker
Sean Phillips

CRIMINAL
Lawless

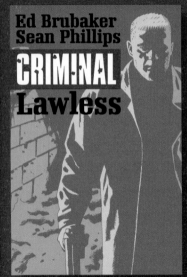

Ed Brubaker
Sean Phillips

CRIMINAL
The Dead
and the
Dying

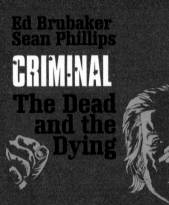

Ed Brubaker
Sean Phillips

CRIMINAL
Bad
Night

Ed Brubaker
Sean Phillips

CRIMINAL
The
Sinners

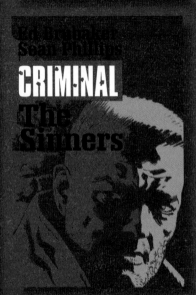

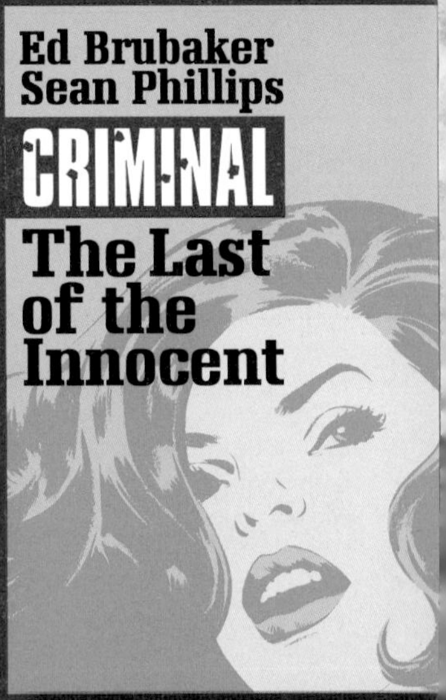

Ed Brubaker
Sean Phillips

CRIMINAL
The Last
of the
Innocent

Ed Brubaker
Sean Phillips

CRIMINAL
Wrong
Time,
Wrong
Place

"CRIMINAL is equal parts John Woo's THE KILLER Stanley Kubrick's THE KILLING, and Francis Ford Coppola's THE GODFATHER."

- Playboy Magazine

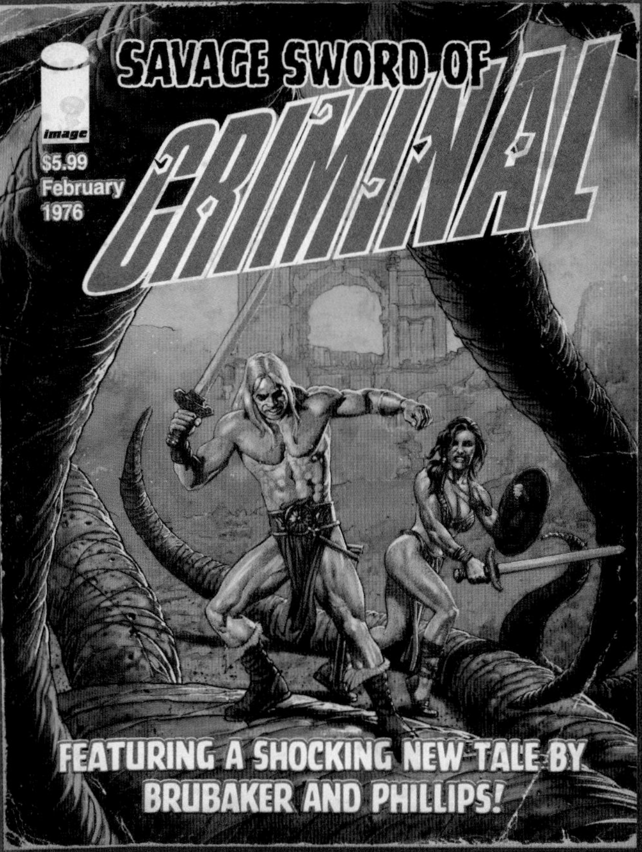
SAVAGE SWORD OF
CRIMINAL
Image
$5.99
February
1976
FEATURING A SHOCKING NEW TALE BY
BRUBAKER AND PHILLIPS!

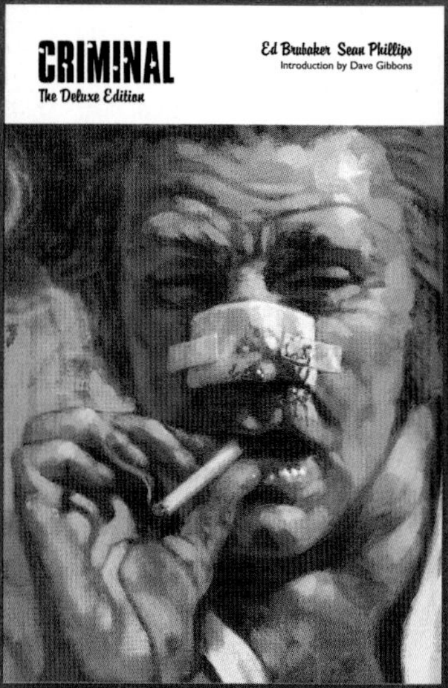
CRIMINAL
The Deluxe Edition
Ed Brubaker Sean Phillips
Introduction by Dave Gibbons

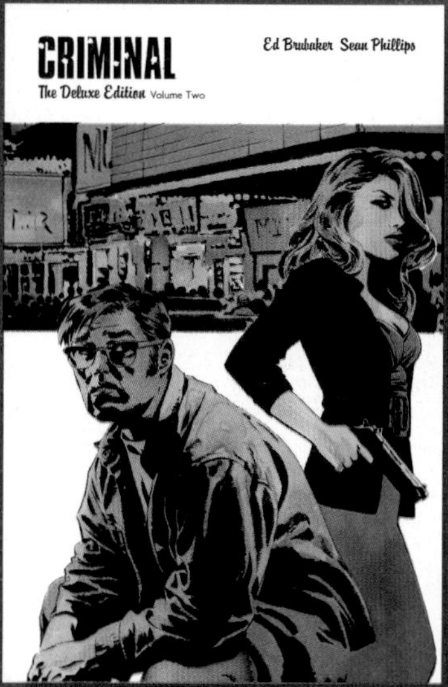
CRIMINAL
The Deluxe Edition Volume Two
Ed Brubaker Sean Phillips

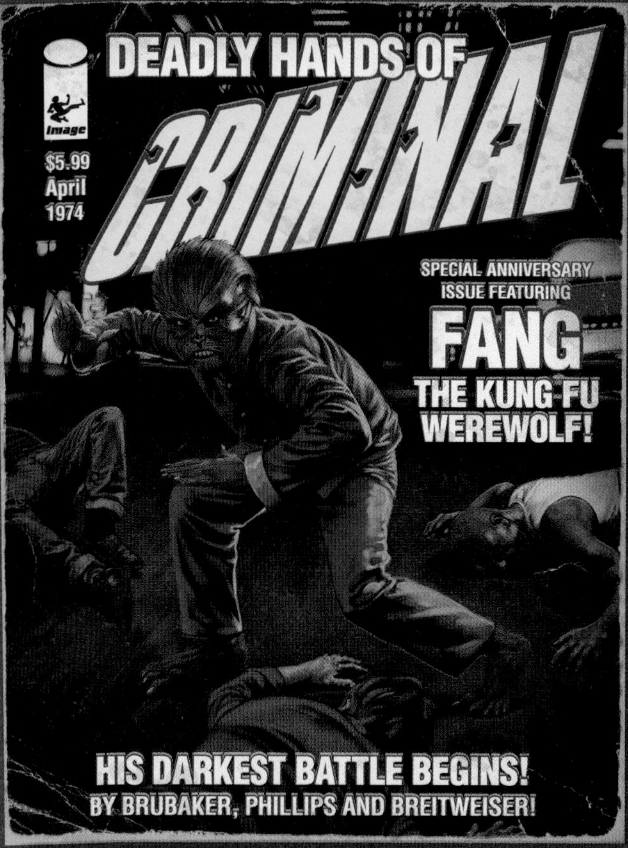
DEADLY HANDS OF
CRIMINAL
Image
$5.99
April
1974
SPECIAL ANNIVERSARY
ISSUE FEATURING
FANG
THE KUNG-FU
WEREWOLF!
HIS DARKEST BATTLE BEGINS!
BY BRUBAKER, PHILLIPS AND BREITWEISER!

Multiple Eisner Award-Winning Series

ED BRUBAKER SEAN PHILLIPS

FATALE

BOOK ONE
DEATH CHASES ME

ED BRUBAKER SEAN PHILLIPS

FATALE

BOOK TWO
THE DEVIL'S BUSINESS

ED BRUBAKER SEAN PHILLIPS

FATALE

BOOK THREE
WEST OF HELL

ED BRUBAKER SEAN PHILLIPS

FATALE

BOOK FOUR
PRAY FOR RAIN

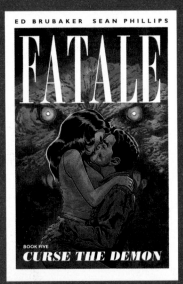

ED BRUBAKER SEAN PHILLIPS

FATALE

BOOK FIVE
CURSE THE DEMON

ED BRUBAKER SEAN PHILLIPS

FATALE

THE DELUXE EDITION VOLUME ONE

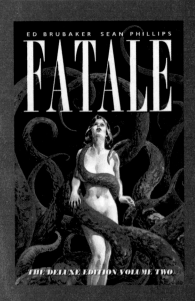

ED BRUBAKER SEAN PHILLIPS

FATALE

THE DELUXE EDITION VOLUME TWO

"Immortality may be a double-edged sword, but it's one the intoxicating Jo wields with a boundless grace in this addictive page-turner."
- Publishers Weekly

sleeper

"**SLEEPER** *is a perfect noir story that just happens to star people who can do fantastic things.*"
- **io9**

"**SCENE OF THE CRIME** is *one of the very few books in the entire world to make me growl 'Ugh, I should have thought of this!'*"
- **Brian Michael Bendis**

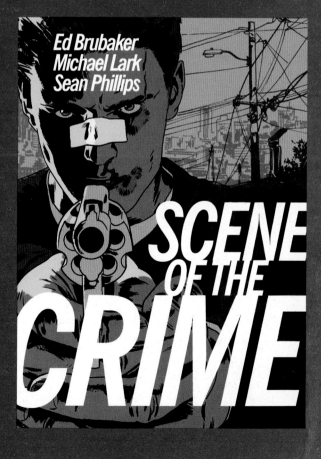

Ed Brubaker
Michael Lark
Sean Phillips

SCENE OF THE CRIME

Clifton Park-Halfmoon Library

0000605144096